The

JOHN
LENNON

AFFAIR

Forge Books by Robert S. Levinson

NEIL GULLIVER AND STEVIE MARRINER NOVELS

The Elvis and Marilyn Affair
The James Dean Affair
The John Lennon Affair

A
Tom Doherty
Associates Book
New York

The JOHN LENNON AFFAIR

A
Neil Gulliver
and
Stevie Marriner
Novel

Robert S. Levinson

THE JOHN LENNON AFFAIR

Copyright © 2001 by Robert S. Levinson

This book is printed on acid-free paper.

A Forge Book
Published by Tom Doherty Associates, LLC
175 Fifth Avenue
New York, NY 10010

www.tor.com

Forge® is a registered trademark of Tom Doherty Associates, LLC.

Library of Congress Cataloging-in-Publication Data

Levinson, Robert S.
    The John Lennon affair: a Neil Gulliver and Stevie Marriner novel/Robert S. Levinson.—1st ed.
        p.   cm.
    "A Tom Doherty Associates book."
    ISBN 0-312-87902-4 (alk. paper)
    1. Lennon, John, 1940–1980—Assassination—Fiction. 2. Los Angeles (Calif.)—Fiction. 3. Music festivals—Fiction. 4. Rock musicians—Fiction. 5. Journalists—Fiction. I. Title.

PS3562.E9218 J6   2001
813'.54—dc21   2001023892

First Edition: August 2001

Printed in the United States of America

0 9 8 7 6 5 4 3 2 1

ANOTHER ONE FOR SANDRA
The Music and Lyrics of My Life

and for

ERIN AND DANIEL
with Love

On this earth there is one
thing that's terrible. It's that
everyone has his reasons.

JEAN RENOIR
The Rules of the Game

A Special Note of Appreciation

Throughout his lifetime, A. K. Fowler, at one time the acclaimed crime reporter of the Los Angeles *Daily*, made it a practice to keep meticulous notes, intending at a future date to weave his journals and files into an autobiography that would include revelations about people of prominence and importance he encountered during the past fifty or more years.

Upon learning I planned to write about a series of events involving the late John Lennon, Mr. Fowler, prior to his leaving on a soul-searching mission to India, graciously offered me access to one of these journals. The journal contained information only he was privy to and, before now, had shared with no one.

I have made significant use of these data, condensing them at times and at other times expanding on them to bring a greater clarity to critical moments in the unfolding story, in many instances enlarging on details and dialogue he set down, doing so in my own

style, but never at the expense of the truth as observed by Mr.
Fowler.

For the record, I note here that any and all errors in fact or
judgment relating to his written recollections are wholly uninten-
tional and solely the responsibility of the undersigned.

Furthermore, toward acknowledging my debt of gratitude to
my good and generous friend, I have pledged a percentage of any
profits that may derive from this work to the Order of the Spiritual
Brothers of the Rhyming Heart, to help in advancing the good
deeds carried out under the direction of its founder and guiding
force, Brother Kalman.

Thank you, Augie, and God bless.

—Neil Gulliver

I

1980

1

SLUG LINE: IMAGINE

By Neil Gulliver

On December 8, 1980, the night John Lennon was shot dead outside his home on Central Park West in New York, I was eighteen years old and working for the *Twin Counties Sentinel* as the number two guy in the newspaper's one-man news bureau in Sunrise City, a sleepy desert town of barely twelve thousand that straddled the old 60-70-99 freeway two hours east of Los Angeles.

I'd gone out there to get some hands-on experience in the summer break between my freshman and sophomore years at UCLA and would have been back on campus by early September, except Charlie Stemple, the bureau chief, was still missing and Easy Ryder, the *Sentinel*'s managing editor, had sweet-talked me into sticking around until Charlie returned.

It was costing me the fall semester, but I figured I owed him.

It was Easy who originally got me to Sunrise, offering me a chance to intern after I won first place honors in the news feature category of the annual Los Angeles Press Club Awards for a series of pieces about the death of Elvis that ran in *Rolling Stone*. I had beaten out a bunch of topflight news guys, old pros who weren't too happy seeing a sixteen-year-old kid sweep off with the kind of glitzy, gold-plated trophy they give bowling league champions and a two-hundred-dollar gift certificate from McDonalds, and that struck some chord with him.

Easy tracked me into the men's room of the Grand Ballroom of the Beverly Hilton Hotel and, from the next urinal, told me, "I see something about you not many boys your age have," in a sonorous voice as slick as an oil spill. "No question, you have the makings of a real comer."

For a moment or two I thought Easy might be a perv in a sleek tux and a fastidious mustache like Adolphe Menjou, the old movie actor, but before I could tell him to beat it, he flashed a business card at my anxious glance and identified himself.

"If you ever think seriously about becoming a reporter, get me on the blower and let's see what we can work out," he said, spitting out the words like he was running a sentence ahead of deadline.

I took the card, slipped it into a pocket, thanked him, and forgot about it until a few weeks before graduating high school, when I phoned wondering if there might be something at the *Sentinel* for me through the summer, before I planned to start UCLA.

He didn't wonder why I wasn't trying closer to home and I didn't feel any need to tell him the best the *Times* had to offer was copy boy on the overnight shift—a job my teenage ego said was beneath the proven talent of a Press Club first place award winner—and the *Daily* invited me downtown for an interview, but never called back.

"I can let you intern with Charlie Stemple over at our Midway bureau," Easy said, his voice racing for the finish line. "The hours stink to high heaven and the pay sucks like a hooker with no lips, but Charlie's one of the best if he's not testing the grape and you can learn a lot sticking close to his shins. It works out, maybe I'll have something better for you next year, like a shot at general assignment here at the main plant in Mountainside. How's that sound, son?"

"When do I start?"

"I like a man who knows his mind. Tomorrow too soon?"

"I have to pack, let people know where I'll be—"

"Day after then."

"Find a place to stay—"

"On what we're paying you?" Easy laughed like my salary was the punch line to a joke. "Tell you what—I'll fix it up for you to shack with Charlie."

"You're sure Mr. Stemple won't mind?"

"Charlie? Charlie loves company. Besides, what better way for you boys to get to know one another?"

Two days later, Charlie was waiting when my Greyhound pulled into the Sunrise City station. I recognized him from Easy's description even before I stepped from the stairs to a blacktop driveway that sent up slender wisps of smoke and crackled beneath my feet, like it was getting ready to melt under the oppressively dry summer heat.

He was a small, compact man, no taller than five-five or five-six, with a stepped-on face full of cherry red speed bumps and pit stops, set off by a broken nose that seemed to be glued in the wrong place between a set of unhappy, olive-sized black eyes. Salt-and-pepper hair in a stand-up butch cut that went out of style thirty years ago, when Charlie must have been in his twenties. Wrinkled crimson and yellow Scotch-plaid slacks and a short-sleeved, sweat-stained blue dress shirt open at the neck and dripping from the midday sun.

"You must be Neil Gulliver," he said, a safe guess, as I was the only passenger off the bus, besides a young mother in pigtails, whose infant twins had cried the entire trip in from Los Angeles. His voice carried the baggage of a million drinks.

He leaned in for a closer look, like he was inspecting the steaks in a butcher's showcase, and I smelled the booze on his breath at once. The smell also permeated the beads of sweat that formed inside the ridges of his massive convex forehead, raced down his face, and splashed onto his neck.

Who Charlie Stemple saw was an insecure kid confident in his talents, but still too young and inexperienced to be certain about much more than that. A kid who was already smart enough to know that not knowing and being able to recognize and admit to such ignorance, to know that asking questions and not being afraid of sounding dumb was the key to learning; listening a main ingredient in the art of digging for a story; uncovering and assembling a jumble of facts that put the truth over here, the rest over there, the skill that made for a real newspaper reporter, not one who took everything at face value, put more questions than answers into tomorrow's history today, and read collecting a weekly paycheck as proof of superior performance.

I can't remember when I wanted to be anything but a newspaperman.

A jazz pianist I thought for a while, after my brother the jazz know-it-all introduced me to the magic of his own prime passion. I took lessons on the family upright, same as he did, for a year or so, fancying myself another Bill Evans but never getting good enough to graduate past the junior-high orchestra.

Oh, an actor, maybe, but that notion passed anytime I looked up at the big screen and saw some movie star like a Newman or Redford, a Warren Beatty, and tried to put myself in their company. Based on my looks, acting wasn't going to work for me. Talent, either, anytime I saw Brando, Pacino, Hoffman, DeNiro.

I was not that tough on the eyes, exactly, but not the heart-throb type; not good-looking the way my brothers were, but definitely not a candidate for the bell tower of Notre Dame, either.

I had already reached a height verging on six feet and I was packing about a hundred sixty-five pounds on a broad-shouldered, skinny-hipless frame that wouldn't fill out for another five or six years, when I took up health-nut stuff, regular workouts at the gym, and a daily jog.

The high school annual shows a face highlighted by a smile that the girls said reminded them of Steve McQueen's smirk and my buddies said looked like I had a wad of taffy stuck inside my right cheek. Bright hazel eyes that even in a photo gave the impression of constant movement. A mass of neatly trimmed brown hair that waved across a wide brow but years later would begin receding like an ocean tide with a bad memory. A small scar above my right eye that was half-hidden under my eyebrow, the result of an argument with a neighborhood kid when I was about seven. I had a stronger point of view over who'd won the coin toss, but Don Cannon won the argument and the quarter by whacking me with one of his roller skates and running away. I ran after him, caught up, and we fought. He had half a head and half a ton on me, and I lost the coin toss then and there. I didn't mind losing as much as I'd have regretted not going after him.

It goes back to something I was taught by my father, who had lost a leg in the war and always said he was ready to lose the other one if it ever came to that.

He said, more than once, "Don't be afraid to fight for what you believe in, even if other people say you're wrong. Listen to your own voice and trust yourself to do the right thing."

My true talent turned out to be writing, not acting or playing jazz piano.

It stemmed from a love for reading. From the time I could, the library became a second home to me, especially to check out and devour the biographies of famous people that transported me into worlds I might not otherwise ever experience. The desire to become a newspaper reporter, I suppose, traces back to the same time, when I first read, *Look, look, look. See, see, see.*

The words were parent to the need.

I needed to know who was telling Jane to look.

I needed to know where she was meant to look.

I needed to know who or what she would see.

I had to know.

See Dick run.

I had to know who Dick was. Why he was running. Where he was running to.

Or from.

Was it Don Cannon?

That would tell me a lot about Dick.

And I chased after them, Dick and Jane.

I've been chasing after them ever since.

Charlie Stemple said, "So, you're the latest little dickhead being rammed down my throat by Ryder." Looked me in the eye like any answer I gave him would be a lie. "He said you won some prize or other. I never won a damn anything my whole life."

Charlie Stemple.

Another bully.

"It shows," I said.

My answer pushed him away a few steps. He aimed his chin at me and reduced his eyes to slits.

"Was that your idea of an insult?"

"An observation."

"An insult! Nobody ever teach you to have respect for your elders, sonny boy?"

"I was taught respect is something you have to earn."

He thought about it, decided, "You work hard enough at it, you will. Earn my respect, I mean."

"How do you know I'll even want your respect?"

A smile circled his face. "Bet you a dollar," he said.

He swiped my suitcase from me, wheeled and headed off, calling back over his shoulder, "The bummed-over Impala in the red. C'mon and I'll give you the Grade A guided tour of this Toonerville."

By nightfall, we'd fallen into a workable relationship and, by September, when it was time to head back to LA, I'd come to respect Charlie Stemple as much as anyone I had ever met.

I told him so in the minutes before boarding the bus, while I fished a buck out of my billfold and handed it over.

"What's this for?" he said.

I reminded him of our bet.

"Oh. Yeah." He crumpled the buck and stuffed it into a pocket.

"I want it, Charlie, your respect. Have I earned it?"

He shifted his bloodshot eyes off me and onto a wad of pink bubblegum stuck to the blacktop. "Too early for me to say, buster. You can try me again next year."

Charlie's way of telling me I was welcome back.

At least, that said something.

I spent my freshman year making a reputation for myself on the *Daily Bruin* staff, using tricks Charlie had taught me to break stories that scandalized the campus. The story that cost three varsity starters their eligibility, scholarships, and source of cocaine and poppers also made me a pariah, and I was thankful when I could pack my suitcase and escape back to Sunrise City.

Charlie was waiting for me at the Greyhound depot, at about the same spot where I'd caught my last glimpse of him out the window before the bus driver eased around the corner heading for the freeway. He looked like he had slept in his clothes. Smelled like it, too.

It was hard to believe nine months had passed, and I said so. Charlie shrugged. "Time only matters to people who don't know what to do with it," he said. Coughed his throat clear behind the inside of an elbow.

I was used to him saying things like that.

"What do you mean, Charlie?"

"If you don't know, you don't know," he said.

Things like that, too.

Another reason I'd been anxious to return to Sunrise.

Charlie was a private person who, drunk or sober, hoarded the significance of his thoughts and emotions in a way that made me listen more carefully, think longer and harder, hear truthful sounds beneath the surface of a story that could be missed by someone just pulling out facts by their roots.

There were still lessons to be learned.

"Easy tells me he offered you a shot working out of the city room this year, home base, and you turned him down like a pancake."

"Better pay, too, but money isn't everything."

"Try that one on a man with a wife, some brats, no job, and no prospects. Besides, Easy hates rejection. He'll get you for it, you better believe, one way or another."

"I told Easy thanks, but Charlie Stemple still owes me an answer and I need to be here to collect."

I challenged Charlie with my gaze.

A smile flickered briefly at the corners of his large, flaking lips. He winced and finger-patted the thick bandage taped to his left cheek. A swollen puff of blue skin peeked out at the top, just under his squinting eye.

"Fighting again, Charlie?"

"Life's a bitch, and so is she," he said.

"Anyone I know?"

"Mother Nature."

I was used to Charlie taking off and disappearing, but only for a day or two at a time, not the verging-on-a-month since he said, "Be right back, Neil," and with a backhanded wave over his shoulder passed through the double doors and down the wooden veranda stairs onto Central. I watched him out the plate glass window that gave me a panoramic view of Sunrise City's main intersection as he headed up the street, strutting smartly like a soldier, and made a keen right turn into the Wyatt Earp Bar and Grill, surprising me, since he'd been boycotting the Earp since early July, after an order of oysters almost put Charlie on display at Weaver's Mortuary.

That was a Tuesday afternoon in August.

On Friday morning, I picked up the phone and reported him missing to Easy Ryder.

Easy thought about it a minute, then in a voice that always sounded to me like he was gargling and speaking at the same time, asked, "Charlie start drinking again? That would explain it."

"No, sir, not at all since about two weeks after I got back here two months ago. Only coffee. By the gallon."

It was true. I wasn't protecting Charlie.

He still typed with two fingers, but no longer kept a bottle of cheap vodka in a desk drawer, pulling at it every half hour like it contained life's secret, swallowing deeply with his head tossed back, like he was Bix Beiderbecke free flying on a cornet solo. Instead, it was a carafe of instant on a hot plate on top of the filing cabinet, which he drank black, believing any other way would dilute the caffeine and destroy any therapeutic benefits.

He also had quit smoking, he claimed, although I often smelled burning tobacco leaking out from under the john door at the office and in the one-bedroom apartment we shared in a six-unit garden court on the poor side of town, across the rutted dirt road separating Sunrise City from the sprawling San Gorgonio Indian Reservation.

He could have been sneaking the booze, too, of course, but it would have been as easy to detect as the cigarettes. I wasn't drinking enough to matter, just a beer or two with dinner, but Charlie kept nagging me to quit, like I was the one with the problem. He never seemed troubled by my smoking habit, which was up to two packs a day. Lucky Strike, same as my mother and father.

Easy said, "He on to something? He say anything to you like that, maybe? About him being on to something? Could be he's chasing down some lead, and we both know how secretive Charlie can be when he wants, which is most of the time.

"Drinkers have that way about them," he said knowingly. "Exdrinkers the worst. Especially ex-drinkers with ex-wives and don't ask me how I know. When Charlie shows, one of you call and let me know. Meanwhile, keep at it, son. Don't let the beat go sour."

Call it intuition. I wasn't as certain as he was about Charlie, and trapped him with his name before he could hang up the phone.

"Mr. Ryder! . . . Maybe it would be better for you to send out another reporter, Mr. Ryder, seeing as how I'm due back at UCLA pretty soon?"

Silence.

"Mr. Ryder?"

"None to spare, son. Besides, you know the Midway beat better than anybody, next to Charlie. I know you don't want to let him down while he's putting together his story. Don't want to let me down, either, certainly not after everything I've done for you?"

Payback time.

"Son, I can not even begin to imagine you leaving me in the lurch that way. Would you?"

"Of course, not, Mr. Ryder, but—"

"Tell you what. Minute I finish here, I'm calling over to the university, mucky-mucks I know, they owe me big, and arranging for you to get unit credit for any extra time you spend here. Whatever else you lose, you're a hundred watter, Neil Gulliver, and you'll make it up in no time once Charlie gets back. Any day now. You'll see."

Only, suddenly it was December.

I had written off the entire semester.

Charlie still was missing.

And, some miserable bastard had just shot and killed John Lennon.

Of course I remember where I was when I heard the news, oh boy:

The Fox Midway Theatre.

An hour and twenty-seven minutes into the main feature, *Raging Bull*, the theater's manager, Hal Gibbons, found me in my favorite seat, left side section on the aisle, halfway up from the screen.

He bent over and whispered in my ear to follow him back to the lobby. DeNiro as Jake La Motta was about to commit more mayhem in the ring, and it wasn't the moment I'd have picked for popcorn or peeing, but I had heard an urgency in his request that was unusual for someone of Hal's normally quiet demeanor.

We passed through the burgundy door curtains and out to the empty concession stand, where Hal paused momentarily to say, "The news just came over the radio. John Lennon's been shot and it doesn't sound too good for him. Come on."

He led me past the concession stand to his small office between the rest rooms and the main entrance, a space hardly big enough for his desk and chair. Boxes of old records were piled on top of a row of file cabinets that took up half the room. Old movie posters and lobby cards, most of them faded from years of exposure, were taped haphazardly to the walls. The radio was on a corner of Hal's desk, next to an ornately framed photo of his two pet poodles, Joan and Olivia.

He had it tuned to the local station, KMID, built years ago to fulfill a congressman's election campaign promise. I recognized the voice of Ray Claxton, the overnight jock, who had trouble controlling his voice as he read and reread copy from the AP news wire, stumbling over words whenever he tried to ad-lib, repeating like some mantra, "Damn. Oh, damn. Damn, damn, damn."

"... shooting occurred about eleven P.M. outside the Dakota, the luxurious Upper West Side cooperative apartment building across from Central Park where he lived with his wife, Yoko, and son, Sean. Police said Lennon was hit by three, possibly four bullets. The former Beatle, forty, was rushed by police to St. Luke's-Roosevelt Hospital Center, where he died shortly after his arrival. Police have Lennon's alleged assailant in custody, they said, and ..."

I cleared a spot on the edge of Hal's desk and listened in a state of aggravated silence, too stunned, too deep into grieving to acknowledge Hal with more than a quiet finger to my lips when he said gently, "I knew you'd want to know, how big a Lennon fan you are."

A fan?

He was one of my few heroes, Lennon.

I hurt from the news.

My temples at war.

Eyes wet with grief.

Belly burning with pain and rage.

"... crowd outside the hospital and congregating on the street in front of the Dakota, fans drawn there by some need to be close. Hundreds growing into thousands in a candlelit vigil. Murmurs of disbelief mixed in with makeshift signs of farewell. Floral bouquets being placed on the wickets of the Dakota's iron gate. Portable tape decks toted by middle-aged people, playing old Beatles songs. Tears. Lots of tears. The police, many officers as mournful as the people they've been sent in to control, letting the crowd control itself, one of them telling an army of TV and radio news reporters, 'We're giving peace a chance.' "

Ray Claxton interrupted himself again.

"Damn. Oh, damn. Damn, damn, damn."

I turned to Hal and said, "I have to be there, Hal. I have to go to New York."

When the switchboard put me through to his home, Easy Ryder was less understanding than Hal had been.

He knew it was a page one murder, but he'd grown up on the big bands and his tastes still ran more to Glenn Miller and Benny Goodman, Harry James and Tommy Dorsey, than rock and roll, more Streisand and Manilow than Blondie and Bowie, although he had appreciation for Bruce Springsteen, who, he once explained to me, put enough truth in his story-songs to have become a newspaperman, if he chose.

Lennon was another celebrity death to Easy, that's all.

He feigned no sense of Lennon's impact on my generation and the couple generations that came before me.

He said, "You need to get something out of your system, do a think piece for the op-ed page, how's that?"

"Not good enough, Mr. Ryder. I have to be there. I have to go say good-bye to John. It's something that's hard for me to explain to—"

"Hard? *Impossible* might be a better word for it, son." I could hear his mind turning over the situation. Finally, his voice as strong as a hangman's rope, he said, "I can't spare you, so that's that."

"I'm leaving after this call, Mr. Ryder. I'm booked on the red-eye out of LAX and should just make it."

He was quiet again, then philosophical.

"Gulliver, I sensed you were turning into trouble when you passed on my invitation to work out of the plant. I felt it in my gut again when Charlie went off. Any reporter worth his salt wouldn't need to be told what loyalty's all about."

"I'll only be gone a day or two."

"What is it with you, like you make these decisions?"

"No, sir, but—"

"You care more about some commie-talking, dope-smoking, anti-American guitar player than you do about the *Sentinel*, well, it doesn't play so well with me, mister. You leave and you're finished here. Not just here, either, I ever get wind you're looking to catch on with another newspaper."

"I'm sorry you feel that way, sir," I said, but he had already hung up.

I caught my American flight with ten minutes to spare.

By the time it touched down at Kennedy International, I had myself convinced Easy would feel differently once I got back to Sunrise City, after he'd had time to cool down.

After all, as Easy had said, only Charlie Stemple knew the Midway beat better than me.

It didn't work out quite that way.

2

Whenever Stevie thought back to the night John Lennon was murdered, it always began with a memory of her mother's voice tickling her ear.

"Stevie? Stevie, honey, wake up, honey."

Not easy for a tired eleven-year old to do, even for her mama, and she tried to push her away like a bad dream, only Mama was insistent.

"Stevie? C'mon, Stevie, honey."

"Mama, please . . . Tired."

"No, really. You haven't been asleep that long anyway," her mother said, and kissed her softly on her forehead. "We got to go someplace, baby doll. Come on now, rise and shine and I have to get you dressed up."

"Unh unh," Stevie mumbled. She turned over on her side, facing away from Mama, and scrunched the pillow up over her head, but the next thing she knew she was on her feet being helped out of her jammies, almost a rag doll as Mama guided her one foot at a time back into the jeans and sweater she had taken off what seemed like only minutes ago. Years later she'd learn it had been hardly an hour before that they were in the coffee shop with Mama's friends, Mama as usual doing most of the gabbing while little Stevie drowsed on the green Formica tabletop, using her arms as a headrest.

"Why is this?" she asked as Mama helped her on with her sneakers. "Where we going now, Mama? What?"

"Don't ask so many questions yet," her mother replied. "Straighten out your toes so I can get your—C'mon. That's it. Good girl. Now, the other foot."

Mama was on her knees, Stevie size, and Stevie saw a look in her eyes she usually saw for days at a time after another one of her uncles had stopped coming around. That couldn't be it now. It had been a long time since Uncle Moe stopped visiting, and no one else from the family had come around. She was sorry, too, because she liked Uncle Moe.

Uncle Moe treated her like she was a person, not like the ones who'd growl and make faces at her, and he brought her candy or some toy whenever he came over, and called her "Stephanie," saying it was a beautiful name for a beautiful child.

Mama's big blue eyes were blighted by tears, some of them puddled on both sides of her nose, ready to fall down onto her cheeks the way some already had, cutting roads in her makeup.

"What is it, Mama, what's wrong?"

The way Mama looked at her was so awful, Stevie felt like she was getting ready to cry herself.

"I think the heavy sweater will be enough," her mother said, rising, signaling Stevie to follow her into the front room of their third floor walk-up on Tenth Avenue and Forty-fifth Street, above Frio's Deli, that smelled so much from years of damp wood and dead pests inside the walls, Stevie sometimes had trouble distinguishing the odors from any of the freshly baked breads and pastries in Mr. Frio's case or the hot pastramis and hot corned beefs hanging on the wall behind Mr. Frio's counter.

That's all there was to the apartment, the front room and the bedroom, along with a kitchen that hardly had room for a fridge, a hot plate and a toaster oven, laid out like a railroad car, one room after the next. A bathroom too tiny for a bathtub, so Stevie had

had to pretend to like showers in the seven months since they'd moved in.

At least, this place was better than their last place, the place in Rockaway, Queens, only a room in the basement of a house a block from the ocean, where she had to go out in the freezing cold of winter to get to the bathroom. But that was all they could afford, Mama said, and then because it was off-season, not the summertime, when the room would be renting to people on vacation for hundreds of dollars a week.

Later, Mama said they got out just in time, before it would have cost them, but someone Mama knew from her acting class knew someone with a band that was going to Europe as the opening act for somebody named—Mama said she couldn't remember—but a big rock-and-roll star, so this guy with a band needed to sublet his place, the place above Mr. Frio's, until he got back, Mama said.

"You know how lucky we are?" Stevie always recalled her Mama saying on the day they moved in. "We would of been out on the street otherwise, so you and me, we should count our blessings. And furnished in the bargain."

"I hate the furniture, Mama. It's old and cruddy."

"Baby doll, it's a palace, a palace, compared to some of the places you don't remember. And we're in the city, so we don't have to shlep back and forth on the subway for my classes and it'll be easier for your mama to find herself a job, believe me."

"I believe you, Mama," Stevie said, and she meant it, too.

In the front room, her mother piled Stevie's shoulder-length blonde hair on top of her head and adjusted her ski cap with the silly silver and blue pompom until it covered her head almost to her eyebrows, then did the same with her blonde hair under an identical ski cap.

"Twinsies," Mama said, the way she always did.

In fact, they'd often been confused for sisters.

Mama was hardly older than she was, only twenty-six going on twenty-seven, and they had the same kind of face and color hair, although her eyes were greener than Mama's and she had more freckles.

"You think you're going to be warm enough, honey? I don't know if maybe you should take your coat. Mittens?"

"Fine like this, Mama, I ain't going, not until you tell me where."

"How many times I got to keep telling you not to say *ain't*? How you ever going to be a movie star saying *ain't*? Movie stars don't say *ain't*."

"My daddy said *ain't* all the time."

"Your daddy he *ain't* here no more," Mama said, "and he was no movie star besides, was he?" She forced a smile. "You don't have to answer that, so stop with the face already."

Fresh tears welled in her mother's eyes.

Stevie regretted at once having mentioned Daddy.

She was sure that's why Mama was crying again.

Her mother picked up a packet of tissues from the mail table by the front door. She took one and stuffed the packet into a pocket of her windbreaker, turned her head away from Stevie, and dabbed at her eyes.

Before Stevie could say she was sorry for making Mama cry, Mama turned back to face her.

She brought a hand onto Stevie's cheek and said, "Not what you're thinking, why I'm crying," like she was able to read Stevie's mind.

"Why then, Mama?"

"For what happened where we're going, honey. You hear us talking sometimes at the coffee place about a great old-time band called the Beatles and how one of them's a person named John Lennon?"

"Yes."

"We no sooner got back upstairs and you were in bed that the telephone rang and it was Ralph Burns calling to say I should turn on the radio, because John Lennon got shot at his house, a place not far from us called the Dakota, and how Ralph and some of our other friends were going on over there to see, so we should go on over and join them."

Mama's voice began to falter.

"I said to Ralph I couldn't leave my little girl, who was asleep already, but then I turned on the radio, low so it shouldn't wake you, and it was all over the news and it sounded a whole lot worse than John Lennon just being shot, and I wouldn't feel right about not being there."

John Lennon didn't mean anything to Stevie then.

He was a name she barely remembered, someone Mama and her friends would talk about once in a while, the way they talked about a lot of actors and musicians.

"You go on without me then, it'll be all right," she told Mama.

Mama shook her head. "I'm so tired, Mama. I can take care of myself, so you go on."

"I know you can, baby doll, but something else." Mama crouched in front of her and they locked eyes. "I think this is a night for the history book, honey, so I don't want you to not be there. I don't want you to miss it and say after you're all grown up how you wish you could of been there."

Mama retreated into the kitchen and found whatever she was looking for in the food cabinet, stuck it in a pocket of her windbreaker, and was back in a minute. She pushed Stevie out the door in front of her, reminding her, "Don't you talk to no strangers, remember."

The only stranger Stevie saw on the way down was curled up in a corner off the second floor landing, one of the bums who prowled around Tenth Street at night looking for a warm sleeping place in the ice-cold corridors of the walk-ups that didn't have front door locks or buzzer systems. None of them ever tried anything funny with Stevie, though. She knew this was because she never looked at them or answered them, and she was always ready to run fast, like Mama said, if they seemed like they wanted to start trouble.

When they got to the subway, Mama waited until she was sure no one was looking before she had Stevie inch under the turnstile, then paid herself in. The wait for the local was less than five minutes and ten minutes later they got off at the Seventy-second Street station, part of an anxious crowd, everyone looking as sad as Mama as they headed up to ground level in double and triple-time, footsteps and conversations bouncing incoherently off the station walls.

The Dakota was overhead, at the corner of West Seventy-second and Central Park West and, as the cool breeze charged against Stevie's face, Mama gripped her hand tightly and weaved with silent determination in and out of a growing multitude that already numbered hundreds strong.

The people were massed behind a police barricade of saw-horses that blocked the sidewalks on both sides of the ornate iron gate guarding the tall arched entrance to the Dakota and moved up and down Central Park West. Across on the park side, too, where the crowd already was fifteen or twenty deep and growing by the minute.

Cars approaching from the north slowed to glimpse the scene. Not every driver knew what was happening here and a lot of them came to a complete halt, rolling down windows and calling questions to one of the officers directing the traffic, who would lean over into the window and say a few words before withdrawing and gesturing the driver forward.

The size of the crowd reminded Stevie of the night Mama took her to Times Square for New Year's, only that time the people wore smiles and made noises as bright as the Broadway lights that Mama was always swearing would some day include their names.

Here the people also came in every size and shape but, instead of happy smiles and frivolity, tonight she saw only a mask of grief on everyone's face. She only felt the gloom that comes on rainy days.

"We're almost there, honey," Mama called down to her over a kind of noise Stevie wasn't used to hearing on the street.

The noise drifted overhead like one of those sad songs on the Frank Sinatra tape Mama would play whenever she felt truly lonely and depressed, but always making sure to tell Stevie it would be much worse if she didn't have a daughter with her to put the blue back in the sky.

Mama stopped momentarily and grabbed up Stevie in her arms, turned sideways, and used her shoulder as a battering ram while calling forcefully, "I got a sick child here! Let me through! Sick child! Let me through!"

A minute or two later, they had managed to reach the sawhorse abutting the north side of the Dakota, steps away from the gated entrance. The stone wall was thick with the accumulated dust and grime of decades and scarred in places where wire brushes had scrubbed hard removing graffiti, not always successfully. Stevie could make out many of the ugly words and images, including words Mama forbid her to say. A lot worse than *ain't*.

It seemed to her that all the policemen in New York City were here right now at the Dakota building.

Out on the driveway entrance, police in uniforms and others with badges fixed to their jacket pockets talked in hushed tones among themselves, frequently breaking away to disappear through the archway. All wore intense looks on their faces as they went about their business, sometimes illuminated for an instant in a flash of light from a camera somewhere.

Mama put her down on the sidewalk. The sawhorse was almost eye-level and Stevie had to stretch to see over it. Mama drew a hand around her back, locked onto her arm, and drew her closer, instructing her the way her teacher always did whenever she assigned homework, "I want you should see and remember everything here, honey. Remember all you're gonna see and hear tonight. Okay, honey? You hear me, baby doll?"

"Yes, Mama."

The first thing she remembered hearing after that was someone declaring, "It's confirmed. He's dead. John's dead, for sure. It's coming over the radio."

The words began playing over and over again, charging through the crowd like electricity and spoken by different voices in different combinations.

Mutters of disbelief were almost as rampant.

The man standing next to Stevie pounded on the police barrier with both his fists, like it was some kind of drum, a look of outrage rising on his face.

All over, she saw candles being lit.

Mama pulled two from her windbreaker pocket, lit them with her Zippo, and gave one to Stevie, who recognized the candles as leftovers from her birthday, probably what Mama had gone into the kitchen to get.

People began singing a song Stevie didn't recognize.

The size of the chorus grew quickly, on both sides of Central Park West.

People with wet eyes and long faces were cutting across the street, dodging traffic, to place flowers on the pickets of the iron gate and along the foundation walls of the Dakota.

Ignored by police, who seemed to understand their need.

Crudely hand-printed signs on cardboard appearing.

Saying good-bye to John.

Simple messages of peace and love.

Some messages angry, telling people to end killing by banning guns.

Hot-white television lights illuminating the darkness.

Reporters standing in front of cameras, their backs to the building, speaking solemn-faced into microphones.

Cameras aimed suddenly at Stevie and her mother, then to the people who were crowding shoulder to shoulder across the drive.

She looked up at Mama.

Mama was crying again.

Stevie started crying, too, although she still wasn't entirely sure why or who this John Lennon was, except for what Mama said before they left home, how John Lennon was one of the Beatles band and this might be a night for the history book.

FROM AUGIE FOWLER'S JOURNAL
December 5, 1980

I had spent the morning in federal court watching one of my favorite bad lawyers, Joe Conn, spring another one of his nasty clients
from custody on the kind of technicality they don't teach in law
school, and now was waiting for him over a shot of cheap vodka
at Marty Ging's Hole in the Wall, an out-of-the-way windowless
bar between the courthouse and Chinatown, where people who
don't want to be seen—or don't want to be seen with certain people—go to become invisible.

Conn walked in about fifteen minutes after me, a black shadow
against the open door fronting a sun-drenched Spring Street, twist-
ing his face left and right trying to find me in the dim light. He
spotted my hand twirling above my head and duplicated the twirl.
Weaved a path across the room to my booth against the back wall,

where we were least likely to be noticed or disturbed; why I'd picked it.

His suit pants made a screeching noise sliding across from me on the fractured red naugahyde, sounding a lot like chalk on a blackboard. He noticed me studying him and said, "Handmade cashmere and silk. Brioni. Set me back over three grand, including the tax."

"What's that in your hourly, Joey?"

"About three minutes," he said, a sharp, high-pitched giggle cutting into the sonorous monotone that came with a built-in buzz saw. "As long as it took me to recite statues and precedents giving Judge Mikey no choice but to dismiss the indictment against my client, Mr. Lodger . . . Admit it, I was pretty damn great in there this morning, especially for a kid not yet ten years out of law school."

"Why you invited me here, for a review?"

He put a look on his muffin face that meant, "You should know better than that." A double gin martini on the rocks with two olives and a cherry was sitting on Conn's side of the table. "This mine?" he said.

"Yeah."

"How nice of you to remember."

"Your drink is easy. It's you I'd like to forget."

"You don't really mean that, do you, Augie?" He locked onto my eyes. Giggled again. "You do mean it." He raised his glass and toasted, "Cheers. May you already be in Heaven an hour before the devil knows you're dead, however that goes."

"Cheers." I finished my vodka in a swallow and moved the beer chaser in front of me. "Now, what's it all about, Joey? Why did you want me in court? Why here?"

He looked around the room, studying the three or four other early-bird booze hounds like a prison guard counting lockdown.

"Anybody suspicious follow you in?"

"Just you, Joey."

"Score one giant yuk for the newspaper reporter," Conn said. He put down his glass and drew a vertical line in the air between us. "Answer me on this, Augie. Did my client Mr. Lodger appear to you like someone you'd ever want to cross?"

"Only if I had a death wish."

"*Exactamente*. What I wanted you to see first, so you'd understand that me paying you back today on past favors due is as gigantico as my Aunt Sophia's ass. Big, big, big. We wipe our tushies clean with this one, my man."

"I'll decide after I hear."

"Of course. But, telling you what you're going to hear, I first need you to promise never to reveal the source. That happened, I'd be joining Jimmy Hoffa in Michigan, Tennessee, Illinois, New Mexico, Utah, Nevada, and New Jersey."

He made the sign of the cross.

His hand had started to tremble.

"Trading on something that dangerous isn't like you, Joey."

"No, but this is something that goes way beyond that kind of consideration." He arched his eyebrows, and bobbed his head.

I hand-gestured for more.

"You promise me, Augie?"

"You've got my word."

Conn blew a sigh out the corner of his mouth.

Checked the room against a sudden blast of air from the doorway opening and closing. An elderly couple in Salvation Army uniforms headed for the bar and mumbled something at Ed the bartender. Ed stepped away, returned moments later with a bottle of brandy and two snifters.

Lowering his voice, Conn said, "They're getting ready to whack Reagan."

"The Salvation Army?"

"Dammit all to hell, Augie! This is serious business!" The Salvation Army couple and the other early birds turned in our direction. Conn brought down his voice level again. "Nothing funny in this. Nothing funny about anyone planning to assassinate the president-elect."

His expression dared me to make another joke.

I studied his face for the lie, couldn't find it. Only ripples of relief, as if telling me had freed his system of a virus.

Whatever my reservations about Joe Conn, he wasn't the kind to play me for a fool. Conn had always played straight with me, from the time I saved his license by making a few calls that got his bust for possession permanently lost.

He'd paid me back over the years with leads I turned into front page exclusives for my paper, *The Daily*, adding oak leaf clusters to my deserved reputation as the town's top crime reporter. And, once in a while, he'd call asking for a helping hand with one of life's losers not worth the cost of sending back to the joint.

"Why bring this to me, Joe? Why didn't you go straight to the Feds?"

Conn tilted back his head and drained his glass. The two olives went next, then the cherry, before he said, "I told you." He slashed his throat with a finger. "Besides, the Feds would be faster laughing me off than you tried to do just now, admit it."

"Guilty . . . You want another one of those?"

"One's my limit before five, but you go ahead."

"Five's my limit before one," I said.

I caught Ed's attention and pantomimed my order.

Conn and I waited in silence until Ed had brought two fresh slugs of vodka and my beer chasers and retreated back behind the bar and a conversation he'd been having with the Salvation Army couple and a regular I recognized from Mayor Bradley's office.

I downed one in a hurry and followed it with half a beer, unable to remember the last time this kind of jingle-jangle coursed through my system.

"Besides, Augie, I remember you once telling me how you know him, Reagan, so I figured you could take this right to the top. Hurry up and get the action going."

Knew him, yeah, I thought.

I knew Ronnie.

Past tense.

A couple lifetimes ago, his and mine.

We did some running around town together.

The Dutchman, when he was a star on the Warner Bros. lot.

Me, while I still believed I might make something of myself in show business.

Before I found out my true gift was for putting words on paper. Before Dutch found out all he had to do to become governor of California was show enough voters the real life Mr. Nice Guy he took home every day after acting the part on a movie set.

Over the years since, we'd bumped into each other every so often, and Dutch always greeted me with his golden smile, squeezed my hand like it was a trowel handle, and remembered my name introducing me to Nancy, who wasn't ever as certain.

What a memory that guy has.

A big part of the magic that wins votes.

Dutch might even have gotten mine once or twice, except I've never registered to vote. Down the road, I only want to be accountable for mistakes I make on my own.

Conn's voice pulled me from my thoughts.

Conn was saying, "The impression I got when I overheard Lodger on the phone is that they're looking to do him pretty soon. Reagan. Maybe even before he's sworn in next month."

"Who are *they*, Joey? Aaron Lodger and who else?"

I watched him debating with himself how to answer my question.

Finally, "*They* are Aaron Lodger and I don't know who else."

"Tell me true, Joey." He raised his right hand, ready to be sworn. "Okay, then, tell me what you do know. All of it."

"First, maybe I will have one more," he said.

I called the Dutchman from home.

His office got back to me in less than an hour, some third- or fourth-tier kid in the press office, who knew my name and spoke in somber tones, with the kind of imagined authority that inexperience breeds.

I hate that in a kid. I hate that in anybody.

"The governor's in transit, so maybe I can help you, Mr. Fowler?"

"It's something I can only discuss with him. He knows me. Does he know I called?"

"I field all calls from the media when he's in transit, Mr. Fowler."

"And I'm sure you do a swell job, Tom." He'd identified himself as Tom, "This is Tom from the governor's office" his full name. I always make it a point to throw back names like bones to a pooch, because applying identity and recognition loosens an honest man's tongue the same way greed unlocks a dishonest man's character. "When he un-transits, where will he be?"

"Excuse me?"

"If Governor Reagan is on his way to the ranch, I can call him up there, Tom. I have the number in my Rolodex."

Spoken with too much authority for the kid to ignore.

In fact, I'd tried the ranch waiting for the callback.

The machine answered without ID, only instructions and a clicking sound after pickup that meant the Secret Service was monitoring Dutch's calls.

I didn't have to leave my name and number, aware that the automatic trace would have me pinned before I hung up, but I made a point of doing so. An anonymous call was more likely to bring agents with questions to my doorstep, and I wasn't ready for them yet.

Working a big story, the less said to the least number of people protects the exclusive. That was as important to me right now as protecting the Dutchman. Call it reporter's scurvy. It is what it is, and I am what I am.

Mentioning the ranch, I was hoping the kid would spill something to prove to me how wired he was to his boss's ass.

He did.

"Only if Governor Reagan's ranch is on the East Coast," he said smugly.

"Oh, great. I wasn't sure he'd left already, Tom. My own flight has been delayed, and I wanted him to know that. He might want to reschedule our breakfast meeting, push it an hour later tomorrow, switch things around, work someone else into the schedule."

A beat, then, "Hold on, please, Mr. Fowler."

I knew by his tone the kid didn't believe me, but he wasn't about to challenge me, either. He'd need a year or two more of seasoning before he'd be ready to risk making mistakes and possible trouble for himself.

I heard papers being shuffled, then, "I can't find a breakfast with you on Governor Reagan's calendar."

"Strange, but maybe not, Tom. A last-minute thing, his idea last time we spoke, when it turned out we'd both be in New York at the same time. Presidential Suite at the Pierre. Six-thirty. You mind checking again?"

"Tomorrow Governor Reagan will be in Washington," the kid said, clearly delighted at having trapped me in a lie.

"Oh, right, the Watergate," I said, trying to stretch the bluff. "Now that I look at my calendar, I see we're set for breakfast on Sunday, not Saturday. The Watergate. Six-thirty. His suite."

He hesitated before answering.

"Please hold again while I check, Mr. Fowler," he said.

I could tell the kid wasn't buying anymore.

"My other line's going, Tom. I'll get back to you."

"This'll only take a minute."

"Okay, I'm going to put you on hold," I said, and hung up on him.

———

My next call was to Paul Chitlik, who runs the *Daily*'s Washington bureau. He had one foot out the door and was not happy about delaying his weekend, especially after I said I couldn't explain how I knew Reagan was due in Washington or why I was flying there tonight and had to know where Reagan would be staying.

"You know I can't stand anyone poaching stories on my turf, not even you, you old drunk, as much as I love you," Chitlik said.

"Who you calling old, you Scotty Reston wannabe?"

"Like there's someone else on the line with us I could be talking to?"

"It could be," I said. "You understand that, Paul? It could be."

He thought about it through a hum. Paul always hummed when his mind was turning. It used to drive the guys on the beat at Parker Center crazy.

"Augie, you saying my line's tapped?"

"More likely mine."

"Who's mad at you now?"

"Before I called you, there's a good chance I got some minds aroused trying to contact Reagan at his ranch, at his office. The less you know right now, the less likely you'll have any suits with shiny badges dropping by to borrow a cup of sugar."

"Will I want to know more?"

"If it turns out there's more to know."

"The story happens, you cut me and the bureau in?"

"The first break is mine alone. We share everything after that."

"You clear this with the main office?"

"So big, I'm not even clearing my throat."

Paul hummed a little.

"A minute." He put me on hold and I heard half a record by the Temptations before he returned. "We have nothing that says the actor is due in, Augie. *Nada*."

"Not according to his office."

"What I'm holding here in my left hand and reading via my new pair of half-moon glasses is from his office."

Paul's response made me wonder if I'd misread "This is Tom from the governor's office." Did the kid get wise to me sooner than I'd figured? If so, he could have rigged in the Feds before I disconnected us and they could be sharing the conversation.

I listened hard for any sound, line interference, that might answer the question.

All I heard was Paul's humming.

It stopped and he said, "When do you get here?"

"Booking the flight is next. I'm going to try for as early as possible."

"Okay, listen. You keep my home number?"

"Of course."

"Call me at the house when you land. I'll have done some calling around by then and should have something to tell you."

December 7, 1980

I never got to Washington.

The direct flights were booked solid and I wound up on an American 747 to New York, with a connection from Kennedy to National after an hour's layover. The weather on the East Coast was mild for December, so I packed light, barely more than the clothes on my back, a bomber jacket, a muffler, and the Russki-style silk-lined fur hat Reg Mowry gave everyone a year or two ago to publicize some new Fox movie starring my old friend Larry Olivier and Gregory Peck, *The Boys from Brazil*, I'm sure it was.

My credit card was waltzing the limit, as usual, so I asked the desk for a five-hundred-dollar advance and got it with no questions asked. Me being as broke as an old maid's hope was old news downtown.

Wimpy Angleman, the copy boy I've had my eye on and was touting for a shot on the court beat, brought it to my place and I had him drop me off at LAX, instructing, "Nobody knows I'm out of town, understand?"

Wimpy knew better than to ask me why.

"Call if you need somebody to pick you up when you get back," he said, giving me that kind of worshipful grin I've grown used to getting from kids who see their own futures in my byline.

I gave Wimpy a thumbs-up sign and headed for the check-in counter, where a clerk ran my name into his computer and in a flash put some truth behind his plastic smile.

"Fowler, A. K., correct?" Hardly bothering to check me against the stats on my driver license, he lowered his voice and said, "American Airlines is pleased to upgrade you from coach to first class, Mr. Fowler."

The announcement came as a surprise, not that I haven't been upgraded dozens of times. A call to an airline's public relations department takes care of that. It's against *Daily* policy to solicit perks, but some rules need to be ignored, especially those that would deny an intrepid, award-winning reporter wider seats, a better meal, and free champagne and cocktails.

"When I called ahead, they said first class was booked solid," I said.

The clerk's finger danced across and down the passenger manifest. He shrugged. Turned his palms to the ceiling.

"Your lucky day, Mr. Fowler. The request to upgrade you came in about five minutes after we had two cancellations."

That didn't sound right.

Except for Paul Chitlik and Wimpy, no one knew I was traveling. Paul didn't know my flight and would not have made that kind of call even if he did, too much a company man. Wimpy wouldn't have had enough time to make the call.

I asked the clerk, "Who put in the request?"

"Not a clue, Mr. Fowler. A flag by your name is all." He punched out my boarding pass and handed it over. I had the first window seat on the right side of the 747, facing the partition wall. "Have a wonderful flight and thank you for flying American."

Less than an hour later, as the 747's doors were being shut and I examined the azure sky while waiting for a refill on my champagne cocktail, someone plopped down in the aisle seat next to me and said in a familiar male voice I couldn't immediately place, "As I live and breathe, Augie Fowler. What a pleasant surprise!"

I turned from the window and, in a glance, knew who the voice belonged to and what the upgrade was about.

"Small world, too," Martin Halliwell said. "Us winding up seatmates like this. How long's it been, Augie?"

"Five years ago, in seventy-five. Twenty-two September. Frisco. And you don't look surprised enough to be surprised finding me here, Marty."

"Damn, you got some memory. It was the day that Feebie informant-turned-kook-brain Sara Jane Moore stepped out of the crowd and fired a pistol at President Ford. How long was it after Charlie Manson's munchkin, Squeaky Fromme, tried to do the trick on the president in Sacramento, fifteen days?"

"Seventeen days. Five September. Two lucky breaks for the Secret Service in the same month, not to mention Ford."

"Maybe more than luck, Augie. Maybe the Service knew something and that's why we were able to act so fast and so efficiently."

"I'll drink to that," I said. The stewardess had just brought my refill and a choice of champagne or orange juice for Marty. He pointed to the juice, and that told me he was on duty. Marty had come close to holding his after-hours own with me on a tour of San Francisco's saloons after the Moore incident. "I'll drink to it, but I won't necessarily believe it."

He laughed and raised his juice to toast me. We clanked glasses and he emptied his in a swallow, then sat quietly in a contemplative stupor, hands gripping the armrests, fingers turning snow white until we were airborne. His flight fright was surprising, for all the miles he had to have logged with the Secret Service over the years, protecting presidents of the United States.

Marty, a Treasury Department agent since Romulus met Remus, had been assigned to the White House detail in a general housecleaning that followed Nixon's resignation.

He hadn't changed much in appearance in the years since San Francisco, except for a forehead that I remembered being about three inches lower under a mop of neatly trimmed hair the color of weak tea. I put him in his late thirties, a six-footer who carried his height in his legs and looked like he worked out daily, his grass-roots-handsome, oval-shaped face sporting a chronic tan that had turned his skin to fractured leather.

He was wearing a navy blue rack suit that gave him the look of someone in middle management, a bank branch manager or insurance agent. Thick lenses in a plain silver-colored wire frame enlarged his brown-flecked green eyes to the size of quarters and added to the impression.

"It's business taking y'all to New York, Augie?" Marty said, resuming our conversation.

His voice had a gentle innocence and carried traces of his southern upbringing, in Tennessee, he had once told me. Nashville. Sounding then and now like no one else I'd ever met who was from Nashville. Right now sounding like someone steeped in Kentucky bluegrass.

Long ago I'd written off his slip-and-slide accent as part of some game he played, part of some trickery in some Secret Service Agent's Oh-So-Secret Handbook, up there with fake IDs, phony passports, fright wigs, and putty noses.

"You tell me, Marty."

"Say what?"

"I said, *You tell me*. Tell me why we're both sitting first class waiting for a stewardess to bring us the hors d'oeuvres tray. My case, an upgrade I shouldn't have. And you also where you don't belong, unless the Service has a new rule about travel that no longer says fly lowest fare when the ticket is coming out of the department budget."

41

"No clue, though New York wouldn't be the first time I'd know you to stray off your beat. Sacramento, after we took Fromme down, that was the first. Then, San Francisco ahead of Sara Moore's bad aim. I wondered about it at the time, you kin remember that?"

"I also remember what a truly bad actor you can be, like now."

He tried faking a look of ignorance.

"Enough with the game, Marty, okay? What's it about? Both of us know it's not coincidence. I'm here because of you and you're here because of me, right?"

Marty lowered his chin to his chest and laughed into his lap. "Same ol' Augie. I should have remembered y'all are not one to go by face value."

"Not when the voice says one thing and the face shows another, Marty. Spill it." I saw he wasn't ready yet, so I sped things up. "New York is a change of equipment on my way to Washington. I'm hoping to catch up there with an old friend of mine." His mouth worked into an easy smile. "But, of course, you know that already."

"The president-elect," he said matter-of-factly.

"The Dutchman, yeah."

"Y'all going to shoot the breeze with your old friend or planning to just shoot, Augie?"

"What the hell's that supposed to mean?"

"What does it sound like?"

4

FROM AUGIE FOWLER'S JOURNAL

Martin Halliwell waited until the dinner service had concluded, when the lights were dimmed and almost everyone settled down to nap or watch the in-flight movie, before he leaned over and, keeping his voice just audible enough over the drone of the engines as the 747 cruised at thirty-four thousand feet, said, "Listen Augie, I know y'all too well to believe for one minute you're party to this business being hatched by the bad guys, but my bosses are real hemorrhoids and not taking my word for it."

Until now Marty had resisted conversation, explaining apologetically that he didn't want to unnecessarily risk someone overhearing what he had to discuss with me, the same reason he'd personally arranged for us to have these seats facing a partition, for the added privacy they afforded. From the way he had dug into his prime rib, like it was from the last cow on Earth, I suspected the time out was really to appease his appetite.

I tossed back another pop of Johnnie Walker Black Label and followed with a drag from the complimentary Upmann Toro I'd selected from the cigar tray, blew a long stream of used smoke away from him, and said, "What business? Your word for what? Spell it out, Marty."

He took the last bite of his second peach cobbler à la mode and washed it down with coffee, and I could see he was struggling to find exactly the right words.

"History, Augie. Y'all were there when Fromme messed up with Ford. Y'all were there when Moore missed with Ford. Out of the way for a reporter who covers crime, the cops, the courts, in Los Angeles."

"History, Marty. I got on the plane to Sacramento after Squeaky blew it, not before. I'd worked the Manson killings, the trial, extracted some exclusive quotes from that little kook and her brain-damaged friends when they were parked on the courthouse steps showing off the swastikas they'd carved onto their faces. Went on to win the Press Club 8-Ball Award for my coverage. Who better than me to go after more of the same from Squeaky?

"More history. I stayed with the story after that, and the story was Ford. Our president still goes out among them after an attempt on his life. Why I was in San Francisco for Sara Jane Moore and her rush to immortality. All your bosses had to do was call my brass or check out the *Daily* files. My series was front page again, and it bought me another 8-Ball Award for my collection."

"Reagan?"

"I told you, Dutch and I are old friends. I'm angling for an exclusive interview before he's sworn in."

"More history," he said. He pushed nearer to me, his mouth close enough to sink his tongue into my ear if he wanted to, and somehow made a whisper of his whisper. "The Service received information several weeks ago indicating there are a bunch of nasty people out there who don't like your old friend Dutch as much as you do. Who are serious about—"

He moved his left arm across his chest and fired a finger gun at me.

"There's always some loony out to get the president, Marty. You owe your own job to a bullet in McKinley that got the Secret Service into the protection business with the White House detail."

"In 1901 and a lot more than the White House over the years since."

"Information from who? Drop a name."

Marty used two fingers and a thumb to show me his lips were sealed. "Reliable," he said, "so we checked it out, and y'all will never guess what? The trail led us to Los Angeles and a man named—"

Marty stopped and looked at me like he expected me to fill in the blank.

I let him see I wasn't going to be helpful.

Marty said, "Aaron Lodger. The name mean something to you, Augie?"

I did a Buster Keaton deadpan. "Should it?"

Marty helped me out. "Lodger is a two-bit hood angling to be a half dollar, a made man with connections Back East. They call him 'Lodger the Dodger' because he's never caught a felony conviction or done hard time. We're running a tail on him and it takes us into a federal courtroom last Friday. Surprise! There you are, too, an interested spectator."

I gave a look like I was trying to focus my memory.

"Oh, that Aaron Lodger."

"My people hear about it and wonder, A. K. Fowler, can this possibly be that reporter friend of Martin Halliwell, who was there for Squeaky Fromme and Sara Jane Moore when they tried to ambush President Ford and is now sharing air with someone we're convinced wants to take out President-elect Reagan? I say I am absolutely positive Augie Fowler would have a logical reason for being in that courtroom."

"His lawyer invited me," I said. "Joe Conn. We've done some business in the past. He wanted to impress me with how he's learned to work the system, even for a worm like Aaron Lodger."

"What else?"

"Nothing else."

"You're sure."

"As certain as a bitch in heat."

Marty laughed and patted my forearm before wondering, "Afterward, when Joe Conn met with y'all at the Hole in the Wall, was it also to celebrate his triumph?"

He cocked an eyebrow, shifted away from me.

Reached for his coffee and took a sip.

Made a face.

Put the fine bone china cup back on the utility tray.

"You know that much, Marty, you know the rest."

"Not. Only that you got all hot and bothered enough to call up the Reagan office looking for him, the *Daily* office in D.C. to ask for help tracking him down. Somebody who did not know Augie Fowler might be led to think he was following orders from Aaron Lodger passed along to him by his attorney Joe Conn, for Augie Fowler to do what he had to do to locate President-elect Reagan."

"And now I'm supposed to be heading back East to be in on the kill, that it?"

"Maybe put yourself in line to win another one of your 8-Ball Awards?"

"You believe that, Marty?"

"Y'all said it, Augie, not me."

I finished off the Black Label in a swallow.

The 747 hit an air pocket and bounced hard enough to throw Marty's coffee cup into the aisle. His hands clamped onto the armrests and his eyes froze inward. His breathing became labored. He stayed like that until the plane leveled out and the captain came onto the intercom to tell us what we already knew.

The break gave me time to think and, after the captain had strolled past—a security blanket for poor fliers like Marty to grab onto—and the stews had cleaned up the aisles and restored hand baggage and other personal belongings to overheads that had popped open, I'd decided something.

Where there was margin for doubt with only Joe Conn's word about an assassination attempt on the Dutchman, it was voided when Martin Halliwell showed up here.

Any business about me being in on the plot was a ploy, Marty trying to fake me out, the Service stitching together bits and pieces of history to give me a scare, pull out of me what Marty knew I wouldn't give up voluntarily, a source or an exclusive.

I waited until the color had returned to Marty's face before I said, "Your guys are right, kiddo. I was on my way to knock off the Dutchman." His eyes widened and a look of surprise passed across them. "More than just an eyewitness to history and, yes, an 8-Ball Award and, better than that, a Pulitzer."

A flash of amusement crept onto his face and, just as quickly, fled into a sour façade.

"Y'all are playing with my head, Augie."

"Isn't that what you've been doing with me?"

He leaned forward, planted his elbows on the armrests, and held his face with his palms shielding his nose and his thumbs supporting his chin; his head barely moving left and right.

Quietly, his voice flat and unyielding, he said, "I have people waiting for us at Kennedy. We'll need to take you into town, get your formal statement."

It wasn't what I expected to hear.

My pulse started to race.

"Marty, I was kidding."

"I'm not, Augie."

"Am I under arrest?"

"Let's call it protective custody. Does that work for y'all?"

"Another Black Label would work better," I said, and pressed the signal button for a stewardess.

December 8, 1980

I woke up today not sure at first where I was at, only that I was stretched out on my back in my long johns on top of a bed watching what looked like a ceiling pretend to be a merry-go-round. It was not a new sight for my sore eyes.

I'd been on this adventure thousands of times before.

As usual, I had no idea how I'd arrived.

The last I remembered was being cut off by the stews, both of them, who insisted I'd already had one Black Label too many, and arguing with them to no avail. That also was not a new adventure for me. My head hurt, like someone was drilling for oil between my ears. My entire body ached and, with my eyes closed, I could almost see as well as feel the bones disintegrating inside me.

I managed to roll over and into a sitting position. A look around informed me it definitely wasn't the 747. Hotel room. Small, but neat. Comfortably furnished. I picked up a notepad from the night table and moved it back and forth to get a reading focus and learned I was at the Essex House on Central Park South.

Less than a minute later, I was in the bathroom, on my knees with my head sunk in the toilet bowl, throwing up like it was an Olympic event and this was for the gold medal.

Also not a new adventure.

I used the rim of the bowl to hoist myself onto my feet and traveled carefully on unsteady legs, using the walls and surfaces for support, back into the bedroom and over to the mini-fridge. I helped myself to a can of tomato juice and a couple miniature bottles of vodka, then crossed over to the desk and fixed myself some hair of the dog in a water glass. The dog was hairy, but not hairy enough, so I went back over to the fridge and treated myself to the last two Smirnoffs.

I moved back to the bed and propped the pillows against the headboard, then eased into a half-sitting position with my Bloody Mary. I felt the normalcy returning to my life as I glanced at the electric clock on the table. It said it was five minutes after eleven. By my woozy calculation, allowing for travel time in from JFK as well as flying time, I'd been asleep for about four and a half hours.

I picked up the phone and pressed zero. The operator came on after three or four rings and I asked to be connected to Martin Halliwell's room.

"One moment, please," she said and put me on hold. A moment or two, she was back on the line wondering, "Is Mr. Hollowall also a guest in the hotel?"

"Halliwell," I corrected, and spelled it for her.

"One moment, please."

When she came back this time, it was to tell me, "We show no Halliwell registered. Would he maybe be registered under some other name maybe?"

"Maybe," I agreed, and thanked her before hanging up, thinking, *This is not as curious as it seems. The Service has a field office in New York, so he might keep a pad of his own here or be staying with a friend.*

I had another thought and hit zero again. This time it took a dozen rings before the same operator answered. I knew it was her because of her broad New York baritone, only this time there were breaks and stutters in her voice, as if I'd caught her crying. I was also aware of a radio or TV playing in the background, but too soft for me to make out more than a certain urgency in the voices.

"This is Mr. Fowler again. Do you have any messages for me from Mr. Halliwell?"

She struggled to steady her breathing. "I'll check." A moment later, "No, sir."

"From anyone for me?"

Another moment.

"No, sir," and at once the operator began bawling into the phone, like she was uncontrollably disappointed for me over the absence of messages.

"What am I missing?" I said.

Through hysterical sobbing she said, "He's been shot and probably killed. It's just coming over the radio now. Just now. Just now. Just now."

"Who?" I said, instantly frozen in panic at the notion that Aaron Lodger and his mysterious *they* had killed Dutch Reagan.

"John Lennon," she blurted out.

I let the name register.

"The Beatles' John Lennon?"

"Yes, yes, yes! Can you believe? Can you believe it? Can you believe it?"

I couldn't respond past a desperate *No*.

I hung up on her, grabbed the remote control off the table, clicked on the TV set, and found CNN.

John and Yoko were apparently returning home from a recording session tonight. They were entering the Dakota when they were assaulted by a lone assailant. John was hit by five or six bullets. He was raced in a police squad car to St. Luke's–Roosevelt Hospital. First reports suggest he may have been dead on arrival.

John.

As well as I once knew the Dutchman, I'd known John Lennon better and more recently.

How long ago? Five years? Six?

While John was in LA, during what came to be known as his "Lost Weekend," although it lasted eighteen months, with me around for most of it.

Me and John and Harry Nilsson.

Keith Moon of The Who sometimes.

Sometimes Bobby Keyes. Randy Dexter. Jerry Roach.

Sometimes Alice Cooper.

Sometimes Ringo.

The news had sobered me.

I knew I couldn't be in New York, this close to John, and not try to be closer.

Not for a story, although I confess that thought was also in my mind.

I had to be there for a friend.

For John.

5

So, here I was, Neil Gulliver, an eighteen-year-old, newly unemployed reporter and grieving John Winston Lennon fan, in New York, where John's murder was the story *du jour*, today's heartbeat, in a city that had treated him with more celebrity than respect from the time he'd settled here with Yoko in September of '71, first in a deluxe suite at the St. Regis Hotel, later in a classic brownstone on Bank Street in Greenwich Village.

By December of that year, to most adults, John was some one-time rock star who'd become an outspoken and ultimately feared rabble-rousing political activist and a major nemesis of the government.

Not to people who'd grown up with the Beatles, though, and not to people like me, who'd come to the Beatles later and found in them a link to the future that, once the group broke up, Lennon alone continued to manifest in the present.

John's death was news because the death of a celebrity is always news and because he'd emerged after five years of self-imposed seclusion to reclaim his position on top of the music world with *Double Fantasy*, an album that included "(Just Like) Starting Over," a single that was hitting Number One on all the best-seller charts.

"(Just Like) Starting Over."

Not a prophetic title, but not Lennon's fault, either, I thought while devouring the newspaper accounts on a smoke-filled taxi ride to the Chelsea Hotel that, with tip to the turbaned hack with, fittingly, a hacking cough, ate into a third of my pocket money.

The blame allegedly belonged to Mark David Chapman, a twenty-five-year-old drifter who'd made no attempt to flee after he gunned down Lennon with a .38 caliber Charter Arms revolver. He dropped the weapon and waited for police to get there, but hung on to a well-thumbed copy of J. D. Salinger's *The Catcher in the Rye*.

Salinger, who had spent more years as a recluse than as a writer, was in his sixties now, living a private life out of the limelight, decades removed from his native New York.

I wondered how safe Salinger would have been from Mark David Chapman's .38 caliber Charter Arms revolver if he had been as public about his privacy as John Lennon?

Would Salinger have been Chapman's first choice?

Was he Chapman's first choice?

Only John Lennon was more convenient, more accessible, a 7-Eleven to Salinger's *La Grenouille* or some other pricey five-star restaurant they were always writing up in the *New York Times*?

And I got to thinking how it was a question I'd like to put to Mark David Chapman one day—

If another reporter didn't get to him with it first.

Lennon instead of Salinger, Mr. Chapman?

Or—

A new thought, as valid as the other:

Both of them, Mr. Chapman?

Lennon first, because he was so available.

Afterward, Salinger.

Find Salinger.

Assassinate Salinger.

For you, would that be "A Perfect Day for Bananafish," Mr. Chapman?

Bring your own *Double Fantasy* to life, Mr. Chapman?
You bastard.

The Chelsea on West Twenty-third between Seventh and Eighth was the only hotel in New York I knew by name and reputation. It was the place where rock stars on the rise and on the decline could create trouble and be ignored by the management, unlike the legendary "Riot House" on the Sunset Strip in LA, where the management was less tolerant and routinely called the cops whenever some bona fide rock star or a rolling clone tossed a TV set or the remains of room service, including the cart, onto the boulevard from his eight-hundred-dollar-a-day suite.

The bohemian landmark showed all of its seventy-five years and then some. There was something imposing about its street parade of balconied windows, something intimidating about the history I smelled inside, like Dylan tucked in a corner of his room writing "Sad-Eyed Lady of the Lowlands."

I had to knock on the counter to get the attention of the desk clerk, who was following the news about John on a small-screen black-and-white TV on the shelf underneath the open-faced room-key cabinet.

He wheeled around on his stool with an expression that showed he was not happy about being disturbed. I put him in his early to mid-thirties, with penetrating black eyes he'd accented with a thick coat of mascara on his eyelashes and a slash under his lower lids. A tumbleweed of hair dyed black vying for attention with collagen-impregnated lips painted a rich shade of green. Clearly, no one had told him Halloween was last month.

I apologized for the interruption, and that seemed to satisfy him, but not his need to spray me with the kind of once-over that advertised its intention. A twice-over kind of once-over like he was looking for a place on me to plant a few bills and had just the place in mind. He gave me an immense smile of confirmation that showed off a mouthful of misshapen teeth and unredeemable decay.

I let him see I wasn't interested, but he flexed his muscles and did some shoulder exercises in case he hadn't read me right. Let me see what I was missing under his too-tight Freddie Mercury T-shirt that seemed ready to burst at the seams.

"I'm Neil Gulliver," I said. "Called you last night from LA and reserved a room?"

He shrugged his biceps and ducked under the counter, came up in a few seconds with a red-covered registry book that he laid on the front counter. Flipped open to a page marked with a pencil on a string.

His fingers, a garden of dirty, bitten nails, trailed downward until—

"Yeah. Here. Gulliver. Two nights, right?" His voice sounded more like a squeal, with a strong English inflection. "And only you for the bedsprings?"

"Maybe three. It depends. A single, yes."

"A bloody shame," he said, and made a clucking sound.

He took the pencil and wrote down something in the registry book before returning it beneath the counter, then moved a registration card in front of me. I took the pen he offered and began filling out the card.

"How you plan on squaring, Neil Gulliver what called us last night from Los Angeles?"

"Sorry?"

"Cash or plastic? You ain't known to the establishment, so the policy is no personal checks. Especially since you're also traveling light." He indicated my backpack and gym bag. "Too easy to disappear, a popular trick hereabouts on more'n one occasion, I might say, so no offense."

"No problem. None taken." I pulled out my billfold from a hip pocket, found the Visa card the *Sentinel* had issued to me, and passed it across the counter.

I knew I shouldn't be using it, given I'd been fired by Easy Ryder and was no longer on the *Sentinel* payroll, but I was owed a last check by the paper and told myself I'd watch it, make sure I didn't spend more than I was owed.

The clerk adjusted his tone again and wondered, "What band you with, mate?"

Making small talk while we did the paperwork.

I shook my head.

"I'm a writer."

He made a face that said that was less than he'd hoped for, but acceptable.

"Judging by your look, so much the clean-cut and proper lad, I'll guess middle-of-the-road. I'd wager you figure to become the next big pop sensation, right?"

"Not that kind of writer. Not a songwriter. A reporter, I meant. For a newspaper back in LA."

"Oh."

He was about to lose interest in me, until I pointed at the TV and said, "He's the reason I'm in New York."

He sat upright and studied me with renewed interest.

"Terrible about himself," the clerk said.

"Terrible," I agreed.

"Put my hands on the bloody bugger what done him, I'd give him a what-for to put him outside Heaven for eternity and a day . . . You can quote me, you're doing a write-up."

"No, I didn't come to work. To pay my last respects."

His eyes took a curious turn.

"You saying you knew him? You knew John Lennon?"

"Not as well as he knew us," I said.

He had to think about that, but quickly began nodding an emphatic Yes.

"So say we all, mate," he said. "So say we all."

"He said that twice, you hear him?" The question came from behind me. "You said that twice, Nigey."

"Say it a million times more before I'm through," the clerk called past my left shoulder.

I glanced that way and found a bear of a man looking back. Six feet and then some, dressed in a khaki fatigue jacket and pants, hands stuffed in his pockets, speckled gray and white buskers cap parked at a jaunty angle on a full head of blond hair, Ray-Bans hiding his eyes, and a scruffy blond beard otherwise disguising a puffy face.

He cupped a hand behind an ear.

"What's that you said, Nigey?"

"Said I'd say it a million times before I'm through."

The bear aimed an accusatory finger.

"You said that twice," he announced gleefully, then to me, "He said that twice."

"I heard him," I said, pivoting around for a better look at him.

"What's that?"

"I heard him."

Pointing the finger at me now.

"You said that twice."

And he raised his chin and hooted at the ceiling like he'd just invented humor.

Nigey said, "You have to forgive Harry. He was a true mate of the guv. That's his way of mourning."

"Afternoon and night, too," Harry said, duplicating the voice of Groucho Marx. "I knew John was dying to get back to woik, but he got carried away this time."

His mouth was open, as if he planned to say more, but instead of words, a gasping sigh worked its way up and out of his throat, and his cheeks dropped out of his half-moon smile.

"Fuck," he said after a moment and patted himself down searching for the cigarette pack he found in a pouch pocket of the fatigue jacket. He replaced the pack and placed the cigarette in his left palm, then slapped the inside of his left arm.

The cigarette flew between his lips.

He removed it for study, held it out like both he and the cigarette were waiting for applause, and with a modest nod parked it in a corner of his mouth.

He said, "Anybody got a light?"

Without pausing to think, I answered, "The people at General Electric."

I could feel his eyes dissecting me from behind his shades before he began nodding energetically and let the smile back. He plucked the cigarette from his mouth and stashed it behind an ear.

"Good one," Harry said. "You remind me of me."

"Is that a compliment?"

"Not necessarily," he said, cackling once more. "In fact, it's a line from the movie *True Grit*. And the book. John Wayne. The Duke as Rooster Cogburn. He won an Oscar, pretty impressive seeing as how Oscar Levant never won a John Wayne."

He repeated, "You remind me of me," sounding like the Duke and walking like him as he ambled forward, extending his right hand.

I took it and said, "Neil Gulliver."

"Harry Nilsson," he said.

I looked up at him.

"*That* Harry Nilsson?"

He surveyed the lobby.

It was old and run down, the walls stained by time and the smoke of a thousand joints.

Framed concert posters hanging askew.

A smattering of framed photos of musicians, lots of faces familiar to me from *Rolling Stone*, some of the photos autographed.

"I don't see anyone else around," Harry said, except for her, and she's far more likely to be Brigitte Nielsen than Harry Nilsson."

His voice was guttural, showing years of abuse, and I would

have bet no longer able to produce the lyric falsetto of his earliest albums.

He waved at the girl hanging back several feet from us by a lobby armchair that may have been previously owned by Good Will Industries.

She looked fifteen or sixteen years old and spaced out, dead eyes and a face full of puss pimples, some picked clean and scabbed over. Close-cropped bottle red hair styled in a Mixmaster. A black summer coat too big for her that reached the tops of her cowboy boots, the leather peeling and broken in some places.

"No, I don't think she's Brigitte Nielsen, either. Or Brigitte Bardot, for that matter. For any matter. Not that it matters."

The girl held up a blue Bic lighter for Harry to see.

He excused himself and stepped over to her, moved the cigarette from his ear to his mouth, and let her light it.

Dug into his pocket for a roll of bills and peeled off what looked from here to be two twenties.

They exchanged words and then he was back, telling me, "She wanted to know what she had to do for it and I told her she had to go home."

"Doesn't look like she's leaving."

"They never do," Harry said, forlornly, almost like he was reliving a bad memory, until he shrugged his shoulders, took a deep drag and let the smoke escape from a corner of his mouth.

"Careful what else you say," Nigey called over. "The bloke's a reporter in from Los Angeles, because of John."

"John's dead," Harry said, "and to think that for all these years everyone thought it was Paul."

"Not to do a story," I said.

"Oh?" Harry eased his Ray-Bans an inch down on his nose and peered over them. "You just flew in from Los Angeles and boy are your arms tired, but not for a story?"

Sounding like Groucho again.

"Needed to come here to pay my respects," I said. "Had to be."

"Let it be," Harry said.

Released more smoke.

Pushed the sunglasses back up the bridge of his nose.

"I'm heading over to the Dakota," he said. "We can go together."

I charged up to my room and stayed only long enough to dump my gear and check it out in a blink. By the time I got back downstairs and out onto the street, Harry was settled in the back of the black stretch limo waiting curbside with the motor running. The driver took a last greedy swipe from his half-finished butt, tossed it into the gutter trash, and shut the door after me.

He slid in behind the wheel and decided in the mother of all New York accents, "I think we're gonna be best off heading straight up Tenth, becomes New Amsterdam, then on over to Seventy-fourth or Seventy-sixth, then across and down to the place, Harry. From what dispatch keeps putting out dere, dere is enough people up and down the park awreddy to start a small army."

"Aye, aye, captain, whatever it takes for you to get us right in front of the entrance."

"A-course," he said, gunned the motor, and eased away from the curb and into the flow of traffic. Another moment and the privacy partition rose; the glass tinted deep gray like all the other windows except the windshield.

Harry hoisted the bottle of Guinness he was working on and invited me to try one, or something harder, indicating the rack on top of the glistening mahogany service cabinet installed between the jump seats. Crystal liquor decanters and glassware. Assorted mixers and beers. An elegant silver bowl filled with a variety of snack packs. Cashews. Peanuts. Pretzels. M&Ms. Wrigley's Juicy Fruit gum.

Except for my occasional beers with Charlie Stemple, or Hal Gibbons after a movie, I'd never been much of a drinker. Besides, it wasn't yet ten in the morning.

"Thanks, Harry. Maybe later?"

"It may already be later than you think," he said. He brought his wristwatch closer to his eyes. "No, still time to be later. For some of us."

He finished the Guinness and pulled a bottle of Bass from the rack. Popped a fresh Camel from the pack and lit up, indifferent to the Camel burning in the ashtray. Found the bottle opener and snapped off the cap, poured the amber-colored contents into a brandy snifter, then opened another bottle of Guinness and added that.

"A favorite drink of John's and mine, half and half, half the ale and half the Guinness. The Bass sinks to the bottom, the Guinness swims on top. A few of these, you're ready to swim the English Channel, unless you know how."

Harry set his cigarette in the ashtray, next to the other burning Camel, and offered me the snifter.

I shook my head.

"You sure?"

"Sure."

"What?"

"Sure."

"You said that twice," he said, and chugalugged enough for both of us.

I pushed myself into a corner of the soft leather seat, between the backrest and door panel, and let my eyes wander to the TV monitor built into the cabinet.

The new CNN channel with Lennon coverage.

The Dakota and Central Park.

The sound was too low to make out, but no words were necessary.

The pictures told the stories.

Already growing into the thousands:

A gigantic audience of regret, but—

Not a mob.

Orderly.

Intense with a sense of purpose.

I could feel it radiating from the screen.

Harry toasted the TV.

"To you, John. For you. Forever."

He dipped into a pocket.

This time came up with a handful of pills and capsules. Didn't bother to look before washing them down with another swallow.

Toasted the TV again, silently, then turned and stared out the window.

His speech had been taking on a blurred edge and now I thought I'd seen why. Because of more than the beer and the ale.

Harry Nilsson's penchant for drugs, pills, and booze was well known to anybody who knew anything about the rock-and-roll scene, assuming one believed the rumors one of my older brothers swore by during the years he was guiding me by the hand into sharing his obsession, while another older brother was advocating all things jazz.

A dozen years ago, about a year after release of Nilsson's *Pandemonium Shadow Show* album, the Beatles were holding a press conference in New York and a reporter asked them to name their favorite American artist.

Lennon shouted, "Nilsson!"

Next, they were asked to name their favorite American group. McCartney declared, "Nilsson!"

Until then, Nilsson was virtually unknown outside the music industry, but this gave him an instant international celebrity and sent my brother rushing to Tower Records for his copy of *Pandemonium Shadow Show*, which he wore out and had to replace.

In the intervening years, Harry had given acts like Three Dog Night hit songs, had turned the songs of others into hits of his own, won a Grammy, and began spinning his own legend as a reclusive figure who did not do television and would not tour.

He only made records.

Hung out with others getting high in the hierarchy of rock music.

And did enough of the bad stuff to spin out of control while his career, as it had for others wigging out in the drug culture, spiraled downward, leaving by this year the legend, royalty checks, and some album reissues aimed at a new generation of rock fans trying to catch up.

On the strength of his music alone, I'd become a fan, and I was in awe of him now, not quite believing I was in Harry Nilsson's presence, sitting here right next to him, wishing there were some way to let my brother know.

Without turning from the window, Harry said, "You're a better man than I am, Gunga Din."

Reporters have to ask questions, from habit and out of a disease called *Need to Know*. We're the basic busybodies of recorded history. No way I could prevent myself from letting Harry's declaration pass unnoticed.

"Why's that, Harry?"

"Exactly, so I'll tell you. You're a better man than I am, Gunga Din."

"You said that twice, Harry."

He swung his head around and leaned in close, his face only a few inches from mine, stale breath escaping from his downcast mouth. Dismissed my response with a wave, and took a heavy drag from both his Camels at once.

Coughed out smoke signals.

"You come all the way from Los Angeles to say good-bye to John," he said. "I've been in for days, at the Chelsea, looking to build up the nerve to ring up John. Only I don't. Next thing . . ."

He shifted again to look out the window. "Too late. Too late to say hello and too late to say good-bye . . ."

He started humming, improvising a tune, and when he was satisfied, he laid in lyrics: *"Too late to say hello and too late to say good-bye, oooh ahhh a whadda wee wah, so I ain't sayin' nothin' until after you die."*

His tenor barely on tune.

He scatted a little before quitting, turned and looked at me like it was an audition.

Need to Know.

"If John's your friend, and I know he is, why would you have to build up the nerve to give him a call?"

He backed off and went back to looking out the window, at what I saw as a typical New York day. Breakneck traffic on the sidewalk, people in a hurry to make it here so they can make it anywhere, and a bumper-to-bumper parking lot on the street.

Weather that lets you make up your mind how to dress. Natives wearing fewer layers of clothing than tourists, or—putting it another way—if you've seen a Woody Allen movie, you've seen New York, with only the jazz score missing.

He said, finally, "Because I knew I wasn't welcome."

Then abruptly changed the subject.

"How's your room?"

I didn't press. Charlie Stemple had taught me patience. There'd be a time to draw Harry back.

"Affordable. Looks okay, why?"

"A lot of newcomers Nigey put there said they felt the ghosts." I waited him out. "Nigey gave you Sid Vicious' old room, where Sid's old lady, Nancy, was stabbed to death in the bathroom."

Harry started singing, *"Sid so Vicious, Sid so Vicious, Nancy so dead and . . . Nancy so dead and . . ."*

And couldn't catch a rhyme.

I knew the story.

How two years ago, in October of '78, the mainlining ex-bass player of the disbanded Sex Pistols was accused of his girlfriend Nancy Spungen's murder.

He couldn't remember what happened, because they were mindless in heroin hell at the time, but he confessed anyway and, ten days later, out on bail, tried to commit suicide by slashing himself with a razor, screaming, "I want to die. I want to join Nancy! I didn't keep my part of the bargain."

The attempt failed, but Vicious was more successful at catching up with her on February One of '79, after he scored some garbage heroin, shot up, and floated into OD Land.

He was twenty-one. She not even that.

Harry sang, *"Nancy so dead, Nancy so dead, and no more of her spungen off-a life."*

Gave a thumbs up above his shoulder and filled the back of the limo with more smoke.

I said, "I was in and out, not long enough to check for ghosts. Besides, I don't believe in ghosts."

"Later, if you find some hint of her blood maybe still there, brown and stale on the floorboards, maybe in a crack somewhere?"

Singing again, to the same tune: *"Some hint of her blood maybe still there . . . Brown and stale in a crack somewhere—*

"Crack doesn't really do it," Harry said.

I said, "Nice play on words, though."

A pause. "Yeah, right," almost surprised, like he hadn't thought of it. "I'll have to work on it."

Harry turned around and faced me again.

"Everyone else Nigey's played the trick on, after they found out, turned turd green and demanded a different room."

"I may be young, Harry, but I've already seen a lot of death. Plenty of blood."

"Yeah, right, you're a reporter. Where so in LA? The *Times?* The *Daily?"*

"No, not yet, anyway. Riverside County? A place called Sunrise City. Running the news bureau there for the *Twin Counties Sentinel.*"

He said, "The Midway area." Saw my surprise, chuckled, and began freshening his Bass and Guinness. "Cruised through there many a time, past Sunset City, then Sunrise, then that old Indian reservation—"

"The San Gorgonio tribe."

"That one. You know where Colton is?"

"About an hour west on the 60."

He toasted me and raised his chin and the snifter in perfect synch.

Swiped at his mustache and mouth with two fingers and dried them off on his jacket.

"San Bernardino County. Lived there around four years in the fifties. My mother waited tables at a diner by the railroad tracks. We lived in a trailer on the parking lot. Sometimes, it felt like we were living on the tracks.

"We'd go to Palm Springs sometimes, my mother and me,

when the bucks were there, to see someone like Sinatra, or Jerry Lewis without Dean Martin, at the old Chi Chi Club, where the stars partied when they weren't hanging out at the Racquet Club, the in place owned by Charlie Farrell from *My Little Margie* and Randolph Scott and some others.

"This was around the time Francis was fighting to find his voice again and, believe it, I spent some ignorant years thinking Lewis was the better singer. I was only thirteen or fourteen years old, so chalk it up to juvenile stupidity. A misdemeanor."

Just then the privacy partition lowered halfway and the driver called back at us, "Getting close to Seventy-second, Harry. Looks like maybe I could make the turn there over to the Dakota, and—"

"No!"

Harry suddenly uptight. Pills and booze kicking in?

A mood swing I read in that one-word command as Harry having second thoughts about going to the Dakota.

The driver said, "Stick with the plan then. I'll do it from Seventy-fourth."

"No. Just keep driving uptown until I say otherwise, Dom."

Definitely something bothering Harry. His body now as tight as the way he'd issued the order. His head launching left and right. Coughing Camel smoke. Sucking in enough of a fresh drag to swallow the whole damn cigarette.

"Okay, Harry. You're the man."

I wasn't buying it.

I called out, "Hold it, Dom. Stop here."

A screech of brakes. The blare of a horn immediately behind the limo. Out the back window, a nasty-faced white-haired woman in a BMW shaking a raised fist at us. Rising from her fist, the universal symbol of bad driving habits.

"I said drive, Dom," Harry said.

I sensed that whatever nerve Harry thought he needed to go to the Dakota and had achieved had now failed him.

For whatever his reasons, he didn't want to go there.

Not now.

Not later.

"Not until I get out," I said, louder than Harry. I opened the door and began my move. "Thanks for the ride, Harry. I appreciate it. Nice meeting you."

Harry patted after his pack of Camels.

"What's your bloody hurry, Neil? Don't get so uptight with me. We're going there. We'll get there."

〉
〈

Trying to sound like he meant it.

Me, too polite to say, *Yeah, but when?*

Imagining the look behind Harry's shades that might be accompanying his pleading.

"Thank you, but I didn't come here, fly three thousand miles, to sightsee New York. I'll walk over to the Dakota, maybe catch you later."

I got out and heard the automatic door locks click as I moved around the front of the limo and past a blue Toyota with a bashed-in fender getting ready to make a left turn onto Seventy-second.

I wasn't the only one heading toward Central Park.

The street was crowded with foot traffic moving in that direction. Some people carrying flowers, some signs; some plugged into cassette players.

"Neil!"

I turned around.

Harry had rolled down his window, had his head jutting halfway out, and was waving for my attention.

"Told you you're a better man than I am, Gunga Din," he hollered over the traffic noise.

He pulled back out of sight.

The light changed to green.

I watched the limo crawl forward, wondering what it was Harry was afraid of. He said he'd been in town for days, but didn't have the nerve to contact John before the shooting.

Why?

Too late to say hello and too late to say good-bye.

My mind started playing the Nilsson tune that went with Harry's impromptu lyric.

Why, Harry?

I'd hardly stepped into the crowd when someone grabbed at my shoulder and spun me around.

It was Harry.

"Okay, come on. We'll go together."

A smile he had to work on.

His shoulders sagging like a French or German soldier struggling to escape defeat in a snowbound Russian winter, but the desperation had disappeared from his voice. Another mood swing.

He locked onto my shirt and began tugging me toward the limo.

I didn't resist.

I felt for Harry and what he must be going through, for whatever the reason.

The limo was blocking the intersection to a symphony of belligerent noises, two cops on horseback maneuvering toward it through the gridlock.

Harry pushed me through the door and ducked in behind me, signaled Dom to start moving again, and called through the open partition, "Change of plans again, Dom. Make that turn at Seventy-fourth. The Dakota or bust."

6

The Dakota is a New York City landmark built in 1884, when the area around West Seventy-second contained mostly shacks and vacant lots. The architect, Henry J. Hardenbergh, went for an elegance he boasted would one day transform the neighborhood. People scoffed at his vision, suggesting the building was located so far out of the way it might as well be in the Dakotas.

The ridicule fathered the name.

Hardenbergh's eight-story folly stretched about half a football field high, around a central courtyard he invested with a mind-dazzling array of interior and exterior turrets, towers, gables, pyramids, peaks, finials, wrought-iron and stone balconies, columns of bay windows rising to the roof, and other gaudy ornaments of the time.

Nowadays the Dakota defined New York more than any of the duplicative, characterless high-rises that surround and encase its history, coveted real estate that had become the prestigious home to many of the ultrarich and celebrated, like Leonard Bernstein and Lauren Bacall and Roberta Flack and—

John and Yoko.

They'd moved into the Dakota in early 1973, during the period they were being assailed by the government because of their political activism, frequently alongside radicals like Abbie Hoffman and Jerry Rubin. J. Edgar Hoover's FBI was on their case and senators like Strom Thurmond were calling for the Lennons to be deported.

Since then, I remembered from a "Random Notes" piece in *Rolling Stone*, they'd added to their holdings in the Dakota, buying up apartments as they became available in the co-op, Yoko applying her sharp business acumen and John's royalties to her understanding of real estate values in Manhattan.

Cruising down Central Park West at a solid no miles per hour gave me the opportunity to admire the Dakota as much as the solidarity of the thousands of Lennon fans who, like me, had to be here to feel the sting of John's mortality; mourn at close range. I lowered my window for a better look at the crowd blanketing Central Park.

Sights and sounds and signs and floral tributes whose impact was far greater for their actuality than any scenes pouring from the TV screen.

Caught by the light at Seventy-second, Dom hopped out and charged over to one of the uniformed cops commanding the intersection. Words flew as fast as their hand gestures, and a few moments later Dom was back behind the wheel following a path the cop opened for him. Sawhorses were moved, putting us in line to exit in front of the Dakota.

Dom was out in an instant, running around the limo to open the door for us.

Harry emerged first and started for the gated entrance with me trailing behind him, but we had traveled only a few feet before a cop sporting a mustache too old for his face stepped forward from some inner recess.

He blocked our way, wondering quietly, "Can I help you gentlemen?"

"Here to visit Yoko," Harry said.

"Will she know you?" the cop said, his glassy blue eyes roaming from me to the limo and back to Harry.

"Harry Nilsson. This is my friend, Neil. She won't know him, but she'll know me."

The cop's expression responded to the name.

"Fan of yours, Mr. Nilsson," he said. "Let me see what I can do. Shouldn't take more'n a minute or two."

He took a few steps backward, then turned and hurried through the gate.

While we waited, Harry nodded discreet acknowledgments at some of the people rimming the entrance, who recognized him and called out his name.

"John Forever!" a guy in a leather jacket and hair to his shoulders shouted at him from a front row spot behind the barricade, pumping up and down a cardboard sign saying the same thing in bold red letters.

Harry gave him a thumbs up. Locked his arms across his chest and rocked from one foot to the other. Stared at the pavement until the cop returned looking uncomfortable.

"Afraid we can't let you up, Mr. Nilsson."

Harry noticeably winced. "Yoko said that?"

"Not her, no. Some guy what answered the intercom. He takes all the calls. He said to tell you they got too many people there now, so it wouldn't be a good time, you know?"

"I don't know."

The cop said, "Ringo just beat you here by ten or maybe fifteen minutes. Him and his wife. They're up there now with Mrs. Lennon."

Like that might matter, make a difference to him.

Harry drew further into himself.

I had the sense he was getting ready to explode.

His body was trembling, his hands shaking as he worked a cigarette from the pack to his mouth and, unable to locate his lighter, stepped over to the barricade to accept a light from a stunning green-eyed, freckle-faced blonde in her mid-to-late twenties.

Harry told her thanks and finger-snapped the silver and blue cotton ball dangling from her ski cap, did it again to the ball on the cap of the young look-alike standing by her side, who I figured might be her kid sister and looked half out on her feet, like she had been standing there all night.

He did a crude about-face and rejoined the cop and me, nervously inhaling.

Firing bolts of smoke at the sky, just now losing its morning cloud cover to the emerging midday sun, but not yet so warm that overcoats were coming off.

I saw the wheels of his mind spinning as he tried to decide his next move and I felt myself tensing up, fearful Harry was sufficiently loaded to try a run at the entrance gate or, worse, say something ugly.

Possibly take a poke at the cop.

Both.

Instead, he snapped at me, "I told you this was not a good idea."

He bombed the ground with his cigarette and killed it under a heel before disappearing inside the limo.

I looked around and thought about staying. After all, that's why I was here in New York, at the Dakota, to honor John Lennon, not to keep Harry Nilsson company.

Instead, I thanked the cop and joined Harry, driven by some form of emotional confusion, telling myself there would be plenty of time to be here later.

He sat indifferently with his hands locked on his lap. His head was traveling left and right on a private mission of disbelief.

Barely taking note of my presence, without looking at me, he said, "Exactly what I told you." He could have been talking to himself. He instructed Dom, "Split. Out of here."

I said, "Harry, you didn't tell me anything. What you meant before, when you talked about having to build up the nerve? Was that it? You knew you wouldn't be welcome here?"

Dom said, "Back again to O'Neal's Baloon, captain?"

Harry chose to answer Dom instead of me.

"Closer," he said. "Patrick's other place."

And sank into himself.

About ten minutes later, Dom had engineered through the traffic and was holding open the door for us by the curb in front of the Ginger Man on West Sixty-seventh, where we were surprised about an hour and a half later by another reporter from Los Angeles, one who had a history with Harry Nilsson.

With me, too, although I wasn't so sure I wanted him to remember that.

His name was A. K. Fowler.

His friends called him "Augie."

"Expected I'd find you here," Augie Fowler said as he slid into the booth next to me, facing Harry across the oak plank table in a far corner of the bar that gave a measure of privacy against the bustling lunchtime crowd that seemed to consist of Lincoln Center types after a fast, cheap meal and business execs trying not to spill their midday pick-me-ups on their Countess Mara ties.

"Didn't have to think twice. You leopards never change your spots," he said, at the same time waving his arm high to get a waiter's attention. "Either here or the Baloon."

Harry stopped studying the contents of his glass and shaded his forehead to get a better look at the new arrival. Taking off his Ray-Bans didn't seem to be an option.

He was working on his third Brandy Alexander and I was on my third Diet Coke, another difference being that he was only drinking, but I had managed to wolf down a beef French dip, fries, and a side of coleslaw. I hadn't eaten since the flight and was starved.

"Or your drinks," Augie Fowler said, taking note of the table. Then me. "All the years I've known Harry, his poison of choice has been the Brandy Alexander. It permits Harry to get into trial and tribulation on an accelerated schedule."

Harry decided, "Screw you, Kalman."

Went back to studying his glass.

"Well, he's still enough of our world to recognize me. He calls me by my middle name. Kalman. Too easy for him to call me Augie, like everyone else I know. I'm Fowler. Augie Fowler. Who are you?"

He plucked a cold fry from my plate without asking and popped it into his mouth.

I didn't want to answer him.

I had recognized him on sight, but found myself hoping his memory wasn't as good as mine.

Augie Fowler was A. K. Fowler of the *Daily*, one of the re-porters my *Rolling Stone* pieces about the death of Elvis had beaten for the LA Press Club 8-Ball Award.

I still had a vivid image of him that night, a strut that was almost a Kelly dance as he table-hopped before the ceremonies, soliciting congratulations like his victory was preordained for his emotionally charged series about serial killers and the families of their victims.

More vivid was my memory of what happened afterward.

I was halfway between the stage and my table, clutching the trophy, not yet believing I'd really, actually won, when he leaped up from his table like someone had screamed *Fire!*, blocked my path, and growled, "You're a lucky punk kid, you know that?"

I thought he was going to slug me.

His fists were balled and his rigid arms hung tight against his body.

"A bad imitation of good journalism. A mental Munchkin trying to pass for the great Menken."

He was of average height and build, me about half a head taller, at least thirty years younger, and in better physical condition, but I sensed in Fowler the reckless power that anger creates, in much the same way a head-on crash will multiply speed beyond miles per hour.

My adrenal glands, already overworked, shifted into overdrive.

I took two steps backward and Fowler moved two steps forward.

I smelled whiskey on his breath.

It helped explain the network of red veins growing in the whites of Fowler's angry coal black eyes, and the tiny cherry blossoms decorating his cheeks like spider webs.

The spoilage was on an otherwise strong face dominated by a broken nose and a jaw slightly off-kilter that also may have taken a punch or two over the years. A full head of shaggy rich brown hair going to gray.

Not the neatest dresser, but presentable.

Without thinking, I said, "And you're not a good loser, Mr. Fowler."

"I don't have to be," he said. "Beginner's luck is all you had going for you, you nursery school newspaperman."

"Then I'm glad I was a beginner."

"It won't happen again."

"Don't count on it."

We'd been joined by two people from his table, both of whom were trying to gentle him back while sending me signals of apology. It was clear this wasn't the first time they had been in this kind of situation with A. K. Fowler.

He turned to go, then pulled free of them, and pushing himself back at my face, said, "You have a smart mouth, kid. I won't forget you."

"Me, neither, Mr. Fowler. One other thing?"

He waited defiantly.

I don't know what compelled me to do it, but I tossed the 8-Ball Award to him. On reflex, his hands went for it. He almost bobbled the catch before pulling the trophy into his chest like a wide receiver.

"It means that much to you, it's yours; I want you to have it," I said.

That was the only time I saw Augie Fowler before now, only now he was sober.

He said, "What's it, young man, Coke got your tongue? Somebody says *Hello* and you're stumped for an answer?"

I was saved by the waiter, who invited orders like he was auditioning to take over for Jim Dale in *Barnum*.

Fowler ordered a Brandy Alexander.

"Same as my friend there," he advised the waiter. "In fact, make it a double, pal. Give Mr. Harry another of the same, and I think the young man here is ready for his next Coca-Cola." He said the name like he was W. C. Fields.

Coh-ca–Coh-la

Harry looked up from his glass cooing, "Coh-ca–Coh-la."

His W. C. Fields was better.

I told the waiter, "Coffee, instead, please."

Fowler said, "Ah, upgrading your caffeine intake, are you, Mr. Neil Gulliver?"

Injecting my name casually.

Suppressing a smile.

Latching his eyes onto mine to monitor my reaction.

I let him see my surprise and braced myself for what might be coming next.

"Still have a smart mouth, kid?"

He remembered me, all right.

I wasn't going to be intimidated.

"Still have my 8-Ball Award, Mr. Fowler?"

"Yeah, still a smart mouth. Like Harry here."

"I represent that!" Harry said with mock indignation.

Fowler said, "I keep it on the shelf along with all my other awards. By the way, don't think I ever thanked you for the gift. Thank you, and no hard feelings."

He swung his arm around and we shook hands.

"Bygones be bygones," he said.

"Bygones be bygones."

I felt instant relief, but I'd heard a twist to his tone that told me he was not entirely the forgiving sort. Nothing showed on his face and, I didn't know why, but I found that worrisome as well.

Maybe because I was figuring someone of the forgiving nature Augie Fowler was putting forward now would not have kept my 8-Ball Award. Would not be calling it a *gift*. The award would not be on his awards shelf, but on mine, where it rightfully belonged—

If I had an awards shelf.

The waiter returned with the double Brandy Alexanders and my coffee and, after he'd cleared away the empties and disappeared, Harry said, "He's a reporter like you, Kalman."

"You're a beat behind, Mr. Harry."

"I'm lucky, maybe in a million years like Mr. Fowler," I said.

Fowler showed he liked that.

"Call me Augie," he said.

Harry said, "Kalman, you know about John?"

"Make that two beats," Augie said. "I was just at the Dakota and heard from Ringo—"

He stopped and gave me a fish-eyed look I understood.

I said, "I came here on my own hook to pay my respects to Mr. Lennon, Mr. Fowler, not to work the story."

"Kiddo, like cops and cocksuckers, a reporter's never off-duty."

"Being here's cost me my job."

"Cheap at twice the price," Augie said. He eased back against the naugahyde and searched my face for a trick. He must have been satisfied by what he saw. "I was just at the Dakota and heard from Ringo you had been around and rejected like a rotten apple, Mr. Harry, so I told them what I had to tell them and then came looking for you. Figured you needed a friend. Knew if you weren't here you'd be over at O'Neal's Baloon."

For my benefit: "Close doesn't only count in horseshoes where our Harry's libation is concerned."

He raised his glass.

"To John!" he said exuberantly.

Took a hefty test of the Brandy Alexander.

Rinsed his mouth with it.

Swallowed and ran his tongue around his lips.

"The gulp that keeps on giving," he announced.

"To John," I said.

I raised my cup and put it to my lips.

The coffee was steaming hot and seared my upper lip.

Harry rolled his glass inside his palms and said, "You had to tell them something, so that's why you got up there?"

"Not the only reason, and not only today. I was there last night."

Harry said, "How come you get to go up?"

"Same old reason, amigo. You're the one they blame for John's lost weekend, not me."

Looking at me: "Did Mr. Harry tell you about that yet?"

I shook my head.

Augie dismissed the subject with a wave.

"Too long to go into now, but it put a wall up between Harry and them as indestructible as the one running through Berlin."

Harry, growing edgier than I'd seen him all morning, said, "What was so important you had to tell them?"

He pushed deeper into the pocket between the paneled, poster-lined wall and the high-rise back of the booth, and used silence to defy Augie not to answer him.

Augie pursed his lips and pushed out a hard draft of air.

"What it was like out there last night in Central Park. The hospital. When the *gendarmes* booked that prick who shot him, Chapman. Mark David Chapman. This morning, sitting out the autopsy on John. In another—"

Augie checked his watch.

"Christ, right on top of it. Chapman's scheduled to be arraigned at the courthouse at three and I said I'd be back with an eyeball account. It's become my role, like those old Paramount newsreels, *The Eyes and Ears of the World* . . . I hate to split, but I promised, and you know how that is. You come with me, Mr. Harry, how's that? Let's close out the tab, and you piggyback along."

Augie caught our waiter's eye and scrawled in the air.

Took a hard swallow from his Brandy Alexander, then another. Emptied the glass.

Harry stopped playing finger piano on the table.

"Not in the mood for a murderer, Kalman. You go ahead without me. Take the limo. Out front somewhere. Tell Dom I said it was okay and to come back for me whenever he drops you off at the courthouse, the Dakota, wherever you say."

Stewing his words now.

"You're sure, *amigo*?"

"As certain as a Dylan lyric."

"Nothing wrong with a Nilsson lyric, either, kiddo."

"Don't try to make me feel good, Kalman, just when I'm getting the bad feeling to where I want it."

I said, "I'd like to go with you to the courthouse."

Augie looked at me like I had just committed a crime of my own, equal in his eyes to Mark David Chapman's. He was about to say something when the waiter arrived and pushed the blue faux-leather bill holder at him.

"Here you are, sir."

Augie gave him a sour look and investigated the holder, wondering, "You give him your card, Harry?"

Harry had to think about it.

"Probably."

The waiter shook his head.

Rolled his hands in the air like that would help him decide how to answer.

Said, "Seems Mr. Nilsson's maxed it out for now, you know what I mean?"

Augie grunted and turned to me.

"You have a credit card that works?"

I nodded and immediately wished I hadn't.

"Mr. Gulliver will take care of it."

"I don't think, I—"

"Thinking gets us into wars," Augie declared. "Give the man your card and, you, sir, keep the tab open for Mr. Harry here until we get back from the courthouse."

He emphasized the *we*.

He was trading off the courthouse for my credit card.

"That work for you, kiddo?"

"Works for me," Harry said first.

The limo was parked half a block down, Dom reading the *Post* and listening to an all-talk station heavy with someone lamenting John's death.

Augie explained the situation to him.

Opened the passenger door for himself, and was about to duck inside when he stopped abruptly, slapped himself on the forehead, and cursed himself for a faulty memory.

"More holes than a Vegas whorehouse," he said, pulling a folded sheet of paper from an inside jacket pocket. "Meant for Harry to see this. A public announcement Yoko wrote this morning. Asks everyone to participate in a silent vigil and pray for John's soul. You mind running back and laying it on him?"

I could hardly say *No*.

Less than two minutes later, when I got back onto the street, the limo was gone.

A. K. Fowler with it.

I should have been angry, fluid with rage, but instead I found myself laughing loud enough to reach the sun, at how dumb I had been to not even suspect Augie's generosity as professional treachery.

Recognized I may have come here to mourn John, but—

Reporters, like cops, are never off-duty.

Augie understood that.

I should have.

"Owe you one, Mr. Fowler," I said. "Next one's on me."

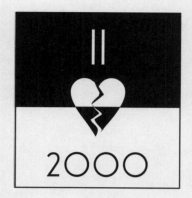

2000

7

oney, you know somebody named Martin Halliwell?"

"Who?"

"That seems to answer my question," Stevie said. "He's left half a dozen messages on the machine. Keeps saying how it's important he speaks to Neil Gulliver soon as possible. Here's his number; two-one-three area code."

"Somewhere downtown." I took the slip of paper from her and stashed it in my shirt pocket. "What's for dinner?"

"I thought maybe Le Dome? Shouldn't you call him first, and then we can discuss dinner? He made it sound like it was an emergency."

"Whoever the guy is, it's his emergency, not mine. How about someplace closer? Victor's? I'm too famished to drive clear across town."

"I don't feel like deli tonight."

"You don't look like deli," I said, and made a *badda boom* rim-shot noise. "We haven't tried that new place yet, the one over on Hillhurst. How's that sound? Any interest?"

"Across from the Derby, that one? The one you were so up in arms against when I suggested it last week? That one? The Los Feliz?"

"You didn't suggest it. Billy Blythe suggested it. Just because he plays a chef on *Bedrooms and Board Rooms* doesn't make him one."

"Billy has made some wonderful recommendations before."

"You mean like the time he suggested a weekend in Ojai for the two of you? Or did you forget to tell me the invite also included yours truly?"

"Honey, why do you have it in your head that every guy I meet wants to do me?"

"Probably because every guy does. You didn't become the Sex Queen of the Soaps because they want your recipe for ice cubes. Besides, that was before the PR lady called trying to talk me into doing a column. Dinner for two, including wine, and the sky's the limit . . . They have Cristal. I asked. We can order a bottle and celebrate our divorce."

"Big deal," Stevie said. "I've been celebrating it for the last seven years going on eight."

"You realize we're bickering again. Anyone walked in on us right now, they'd think we were still married."

"Anyone walked in right now, they'd be dead before they got through the front door and here to the den."

The *anyone* she meant was a mass murderer we'd exposed not that long ago, whom we'd come to think of as "our James Dean," the movie icon who'd moved into the mythology of show business, not the latter-day singer of country sausage fame.

Our murderous James Dean managed to get away, was still on the loose, and had made it clear Stevie and I were on his list. High up.

I'd been bunking with her ever since behind the gates of her modest, fourteen-room, million-buck bungalow in the lush Oaks of Griffith Park, part of the Los Feliz area east of Hollywood that became ultratrendy upon an influx of hot celebrities in the nineties, like Madonna, Matt Damon, Brad Pitt, and Leonardo DeCaprio.

I was there at Stevie's request.

She asked before I could make the suggestion.

Scared?

Damn right.

Both of us.

We weren't going to bed with guns beneath our pillows so we could wake up the next morning and find the gun fairy had come calling and exchanged them for shiny quarters.

Also, because I love the lady still and preferred that to sleepless nights at my own place across town in Westwood, wondering if she was safe.

We'd since beefed up her security systems and friends of mine with LAPD, at their insistence, were running off-duty cruises by the estate on a twenty-four-seven schedule.

We also had an armed bodyguard in bedroom number five, across the hall from Stevie and next to mine, where all the electronic gear was installed. TV monitors. Sound detectors. Other stuff I didn't understand, as sophisticated as a Cole Porter song, that the installation crew said could monitor a feather floating in the breeze; an ant's sneeze.

The bodyguard's name was Armando Soledad.

At least that was the name on his passport.

He was a Corsican who'd done some special work for the Israelis over the years, who had come highly recommended in a call I made to friends with friends who had friends and no questions asked.

I figured him for late twenties. Five-eight or nine. A solid, well-proportioned body under a Bermuda tan. Close-set green eyes always traveling on an unlined face that made him look more like a spirited public school teacher or librarian than a hired gun. His angelic appearance hardly disrupted by a head he kept clean shaven and the tiny gold earring dangling from his left lobe.

Armando's primary job was to keep Stevie in his sight, and he performed it like a ghost. He was a quiet, almost invisible presence whose conversation, when he bothered to speak, was of the *Yes* and *No* variety. Most of the time he answered with a tight smile for *Yes*, a looser frown for *No*.

"Everything okay, Armando?"

Smile.

"Stevie and I are both home today, Armando, so maybe you'd like to take the day off?"

Frown.

Lately, Stevie was home most of the time.

She was on a self-imposed hiatus from her soap, while the agents and lawyers battled over the terms of a new deal that would give her less screen time for more money and the freedom to accept some of the movie roles she'd had to pass on last year because of scheduling conflicts.

The one that hurt her the most losing was a remake of *Of Human Bondage*, the W. Somerset Maugham classic that made a major movie star of Bette Davis.

She had been offered the part after it was reportedly rejected by Jodie Foster, Julia Roberts, Meg Ryan, Gwyneth Paltrow, Winona Ryder, Charlize Theron, Cameron Diaz, Cate Blanchett, Natalie Portman, Angelina Jolie, Annette Bening, Sarah Jessica Parker, Sarah Michelle Gellar, Sandra Bullock, Drew Barrymore, Jennifer Lopez, Jennifer Aniston, Jennifer Love Hewitt, Catherine Zeta-Jones, Calista Flockhart, Mira Sorvino, Minnie Driver, Sharon Stone, Salma Hayek, Heather Graham, Ashley Judd, Christina Ricci, and Trudy Squaile.

Some others.

Okay, not that many names.

My bummer of a joke.

Only enough names to squash somebody with less self-worth than Stevie had and had proved herself deserving of since becoming a major soap star, but no less a real person.

The big problem, according to Army Archerd's column in *Daily Variety*, wasn't the producer's desire to remake it as a musical so much as a sex switch that had Chris Rock in the Bette Davis role and his costar, rumored to be Oscar winner Dame Judi Dench, essaying the Leslie Howard role.

Stevie, however, was game for anything that might lift her out of *Bedrooms and Board Rooms* after seven years and put her on the big screen; shrugged at this as well as being so low on the list that the copy of the script the producer sent her was more dog-eared than Lassie.

She explained with the calm logic I'd watched her grow into over the past fourteen years, "Honey, if it were about ego, I'd have died years ago. It's really about the work and showing whoever matters in this town that Stephanie Marriner has talent beyond playing a bimbo with boobs for brains. Why those acting classes. The singing and dancing lessons. Still after all this time. It's about recognizing opportunity when it comes along and being ready to grab the brass ring."

No cop-out.

Stevie meant it.

To know her said as much.

Her mother, Juliet, said even more to me when she first found me sniffing around her sixteen-year-old and gave me an evil eye on spec.

"My kid's a minor, you aware of that?"

"Yes, but only since she stopped lying to me about her age."

"She gets that from me," Juliet said. "A woman's age is sacred, like the color of her unmentionables. Mine are black if you want to know."

"Not really."

"They're also the untouchables—until I really get to know someone."

"Are you propositioning me, Mrs.—?"

"Who you take me for, that darling Annie Bancroft in *The Graduate?* I'm putting you on notice, Dustin, is all. I already got more boyfriends than I can handle. Been so ever since Stevie's daddy did his disappearing act on us. I and Stevie, we're ham and eggs. Sure, she can be wild, like any kid, and I can't control her sometimes. She's a free spirit like her old lady, smart like her old lady. But she's still got a lot to learn about life, about men. Anyone think he's gonna come around and play hit-and-run with my kid, he's got another think coming."

"Not what this is about, Mrs.—"

"Juliet to you, Romeo."

"I saw her, got one look at her, and—"

"Got a look at that angel puss, that body to die for, and you said to yourself, *Gotta get me a piece of that pie.*"

"Juliet, shame on you for saying that."

"Tell me otherwise, whatever you said your name was."

Juliet stood in the middle of her living room with her long legs spread apart, her hands on her hips, a look on her face that said she was ready to take on the whole world, if necessary, in defense of her daughter.

"Neil Gulliver. Maybe that's what I saw at first—"

"Ah! A grain of truth." Holding her hands up to the heavens.

"But that's not all I saw. I see that all the time in this town."

"Yeah. I'm listening."

"I saw more to her, sensed more to her. It was almost like we were communicating the minute our eyes connected."

"Where do they sell your line of bullshit? At the local feed and grain I suppose . . . So, tell me something else, Neil Gulliver, what else was there connected between you and my Stevie?"

Stevie said, "Nothing, Mama. I told you."

I don't know how long she'd been standing and listening by the bedroom door. Juliet had exiled her a minute after I arrived, for a private heart-to-heart, she explained.

"Who invited you back, baby doll?" Pointing her out of the room. Stevie shook her head, threw an anxious glance at me that said, *Mama's testing you.*

I said, "Juliet, what do I have to do to prove myself to you?"

She didn't hesitate with her answer.

"Go away and don't come back. I and my daughter, we got plans and they don't include you. She's gonna be a big star, Neil Gulliver, as sure as I'm working my ass off to get her to her dream. Two jobs, no waiting. The lessons she needs in how to act, sing, dance. Modeling school, so she'll know how to carry herself around like another Grace Kelly, with style and dignity. Maybe, someday, latch onto some prince the way Rita Hayworth did, if that's what she wants, not some Prince Charming who collects a weekly paycheck because he knows how to play with words."

"I want to help you. I want to help her. Not the prince part, but everything else—and more."

"Neil really does. I believe him, Mama. Neil isn't like some of the others."

"Baby doll, they're all like some of the others."

It wasn't long after that, Stevie and I eloped to Las Vegas.

Her idea, headstrong then as now, a girl-woman intent on taking control of her own destiny, and—

Her dream became our dream.

With Juliet's blessing.

Don't ask.

Now, because of our James Dean, I was staying home with Stevie most of the time.

Just in case.

And, because I had the need.

Call it obsession.

That's what my shrink kept calling it.

I have this love for Stevie that didn't go away just because she did.

The divorce was her idea, and lately I'd been thinking the little nightmare we currently were living through might show her we could try marriage again, only better this time around.

Sometimes I got the feeling from her, the way she said something, an expression, a hand on my cheek for no apparent reason, that Stevie might be nourishing the same idea.

Only not often enough.

Only enough to turn my wishful thinking into an art form.

Staying home didn't interfere with my ability to knock out eight hundred words for my "On the Go" columns that run in the *Daily* seven days a week.

The subject matter rarely requires me to stray from the phone or the computer, although today was different.

I'd driven out to Marina del Rey to tour a company that sells herbal products made with curiously named ingredients: echinacea, saw palmetto, bovine bolostrum, ginkgo biloba.

One of them was supposed to be good for your memory, I forget which.

Bovine bolostrum struck me as a name better suited to a World Wrestling Federation nasty—

Ladies and gentlemen, stepping through the ropes, here he is, the killer cow of the ring: Bovine Bolostrum!

And the ginkgo biloba—

I just liked the name when I spotted it in the company press kit. It sounded like something by Kurt Weil from *The Beggars Opera.*

Careful of that shark, Mackie!

You know what they say about pearly teeth!

"The Ginkgo Biloba Song."

I hummed it on the drive home that took three times as long as it might have if the CHP hadn't blocked entrances to the 405's northbound lanes to accommodate their pursuit of a driver in a late-model Plymouth who ran a red light in West Covina two hours earlier and had been running from them ever since; was inventing new words to the melody passing my Jag through my ex's guarded gates with a wave to the cameras and the invisible eyes of Armando Soledad.

Palermo is a cheap spaghetti joint on Vermont between Los Feliz and Hollywood Boulevards, a mile and a half east of Stevie's place, where people are always spilling out onto the street, waiting for their tables over complimentary wine drawn from cartons and served in plastic cups.

A combination of locals and customers of the multiplex down the street, whose old-fashioned marquee overhanging the street was advertising the newest Tom Hanks, Al Pacino, and Denzel Washington movies.

And, whenever we've gone to Palermo for dinner, lots of cops. Lots.

Their squad cars parked conspicuously out front and on the side street.

Inside, blue uniforms with weapons holstered at their hips scattered at tables around the main dining area, maybe one or two more at tables in the annex on the other side of the half wall.

Our underpaid, underappreciated guardians of the law enjoying an economical Code 7.

Probably why Stevie and I were going there so often lately.

More for the safety that's not on the menu than for the basket of hot bread soaked in garlic and the half order of "Sicilia" antipasto we always split before our main courses arrive.

And, too, a brief relief from the constant presence of Armando, who reluctantly remained behind to keep watch over the house.

"It's okay, Armando, plenty of police there to protect us."

Frown.

"This way we don't have to worry coming home, because you're here."

Frown.

"Something we can bring back for you? Maybe some nice scampi? The linguini with clams?"

Frown.

There's no pleasing some people.

With Armando, maybe because of some lingering blood feud between the Corsicans and their Sicilian neighbors across the Tyrrhenian Sea.

I'd asked him once.

Frown.

Stevie and I aren't usually excessively nervous about the Dean thing, not at the same time, anyway, but tonight was different, for a reason neither of us could figure, so we blamed it on the full moon that trailed us on the drive over in her Jeep Cherokee.

She had on one of her "privacy disguises," a shapeless black silk dress that hid her famous profile, under a full-length charcoal cashmere coat with a notched collar, cinched at the waist.

Long blonde hair swept under a floppy-brimmed cream-colored hat that rested on top of her oversized Holly Golightly shades.

White sweat socks and democratic tennis shoes on her feet.

A Bloomingdale's tote bag dangling from her shoulder.

I was dressed for inconspicuousness in my gray jogging outfit, Lakers team jacket and cap, Air Jordans, and shades a third the size of Stevie's.

The *Daily* had my face plastered in bus bench display cases around town, additions to the "Stay 'On the Go' with Gulliver" poster boards that dressed the sides of a couple hundred busses, but I never expected anyone to know me for the retouched photo that removed about fifteen of my almost thirty-nine years, the small eyebrow scar above my right eye, and most of the character wrinkles, cracks, and crevices I had worked hard to achieve.

The retouch artist, of his own volition, had airbrushed in enough light-brown implants to eliminate the widow's peak growing out of my receding hairline.

Okay, so maybe he acted off the hint or two I dropped.

Where's it written that Stevie can have all the vanity?

Not in my column.

The parking attendant in the lot behind Palermo greeted us by name. So did Tony, one of the owners. I'd called ahead and he was waiting for us at the rear entrance, a slightly built man in his mid-forties with thick curly brown hair, a fulsome brown mustache, and conversation as cheerful as his smile while he led the way to a wall booth by the small bar at the back. The one I always requested. It gave us a good view of customers coming and going.

Four cops nearby, relaxing over their pasta and pizza, engaged in the monotone happy-buzz of off-duty conversation. Close enough to react efficiently to a sudden call for help, giving Stevie and me a special sense of safety and comfort.

It lasted until about midway into our meal.

That's when Martin Halliwell showed up.

Stevie was picking at her *melanzane alla parmigiana*, I had just about cleared my platter of *lasagne alla bolognese*, and neither of us were giving too much notice to the booths and tables emptying of diners we supposed were hurrying off to the movies with a seven-thirty starting time.

She was analyzing her status with *Bedrooms and Board Rooms*, weighing career options if a new deal could not be worked out, and making it sound like leaving the soap was something she'd enjoy.

Her tone called for agreement, not discussion.

"Seven years, long enough. Don't you think so, honey?"

"Not for our marriage. Me, I was always fixated on the 'until death do us part' part."

I take these openings where I find them.

They're like a drug with me.

Stevie wrinkled her brow, briefly inched her head left and right, like a toy winding down.

"The marriage died, we parted," she said firmly, and returned to the subject. "It's not just about playing the same old role year in and year out. It's the constant in-fighting, locking horns with people out to do me in. Like sweet what's-her-name."

"Karen Walls."

"That one, the virgin whore."

Karen Walls had started playing between the bed sheets with one of the *Bedrooms and Board Rooms* producers and two of the writers shortly after joining the cast last year, as a means of stealing screen time away from Stevie and to her own character. Walls' ploy had worked and was instrumental in Stevie's decision to go on hiatus after she found out.

"You'll feel better after they settle on the terms of your new deal," I said.

"Better, yes, but not differently. How do you think you would feel doing the same thing year after year?"

"This may come as a surprise to you, but that's what I do. The same thing. Year after year. Like maybe two or three other people I can think of—if you'll give me a minute."

"You're talking down to me again, honey. Please don't."

"Sorry. You're right, and I apologize."

She reached across the table and patted the back of my hand. Fingers long and elegant. Her manicured nails painted white on white, as perfect as a Beverly Hills lawn.

"It doesn't sound like I'm running away, does it? I've come up against people like what's-her-name at least a half dozen times before and where are they now? Whatever happened to them?"

"Isn't Lindsay Carmichael costarring with Bruce Willis in something? *The Ninth Sense? Tenth Sense a Dance?*"

A half shrug.

Oblivious to the pun I'd try to remember for a column.

"I liked Lindsay," she said. "A real hard worker with real talent I could admire and respect, even the one year she won her best daytime actress Emmy out from under me."

"I seem to recall she was in the running the two years you won."

"We were always friends, Lindsay and me. Still. Built like a stick, so they let her act. All I get to do is flap my boobs at every Tom, Dick and Horny who comes around."

"So, do we record that as one Emmy per boob?"

"Hah. Hah. Hah."

"The big movies happened for her, they'll happen for you, babe."

Stevie glanced up from playing with her fork in the *melanzane* and reached across to pat my hand again. Gave a little smile that didn't last.

"Shit happens, honey, not big movies. Never, unless I get off the damn show and work to make it happen for myself, instead of leaving it to others."

"And what if it doesn't happen?"

Stevie pulled her mouth and squinted her eyes into one of her "You've got to be kidding" looks. Put down her fork. Planted her palms on the table.

"Honey, to quote a favorite saying of my dear mother, 'The crime is never in losing. The crime is in not trying.' "

She trapped my gaze with hers.

Held it.

Her green eyes catching some reflected light from the bar and turned a glistening emerald.

Intense as they studied mine and seemed to beg for the vote of confidence she knew was always there for her, but—

Sometimes you have to hear it, too.

Before I could say anything—

A cough.

A throat being cleared.

A man's voice, loud enough for us and no one else:

"Ms. Marriner? Mr. Gulliver?"

I looked up.

He was hovering over our booth.

For moments or minutes? No way of knowing.

A toothsome smile for each of us.

"And Mr. Colt," Stevie said, inclining her head at the table, where her right hand rested on the edge with her .32 aimed approximately at his chest. "As loaded as anyone over on those barstools."

An understanding nod.

"Really unnecessary, Ms. Marriner."

His tone reassuring.

The barest traces of a southern accent.

Fingers locked below his ample belt line.

Nonthreatening.

He was somewhere in his late fifties, and the years showed on a face that might have been considered handsome before it fell. Bald, except for a narrow monk's fringe of artificial dirt-brown hair. Eyebrows half as wide as the fringe, dyed the same shade. Green eyes behind prescription lenses in narrow-rimmed metal frames. Milk-white, mottled skin, liver freckles as well as signs he might have suffered skin cancer from too many years of exposure to the sun. A long-legged six-footer, looking a few inches shorter, because of a spine bending with age that craned his neck forward and put a slight hump on his slope-shouldered back. Wearing a suit off the rack for someone at least a size smaller. A blue single-breasted pinstripe. The jacket tight under the arms and no shot at getting buttoned.

"I'm one of the good guys. Halliwell's my name. Martin Halliwell. Treasury Department. Let me dip into my pocket, I can show you some ID."

"A move before I say so and I'll show you something not even Viagra'll ever make good again for you," Stevie said.

Halliwell shifted his eyes to me. They glittered with gigantic good humor through lenses thick enough to read the fine print on a sweepstakes application.

"Ms. Marriner means it, doesn't she, Mr. Gulliver."

"Taught her myself how to use it. I didn't know you were packing, babe."

"In my coat. Better safe than sorry."

"Every time?"

"All the time."

I pulled out my weapon of choice, the Beretta 92f I'd stashed under my Lakers jacket before leaving home, cinched inside my jogging pants in the small of my back.

"Better safe than sorry," I said.

"You might of told me," Stevie said.

"Sure. Like you told me?"

"Every time?"

"Every time."

Halliwell guffawed.

"You don't mind my asking, was it like this when y'all were married?"

"Worse."

Stevie said it louder than me.

A middle-aged gay couple heading for the back door, the way blocked by Halliwell, spotted our guns, gasped, twisted, and fled toward the front of the restaurant, past a table of cops, neither bothering to reclaim the doggie bag dropped en route by the older of the pair.

Halliwell said, "Seems strange that you'all'd both be armed and her so ready to kill a stranger means you no harm, being so involved and all with the John Lennon Imagine That! music festival that's raising money to fight the gun lobby."

I said, "How'd you know? It hasn't been announced yet."

His luxuriant eyebrows climbed up into his forehead and brought out furrows deep enough to seed.

"I know a lot of things, Mr. Gulliver. Why don't you let me show you that ID, and then maybe I could sit down, join you, and we can talk like civilized folk? I can share some news with y'all that y'all might not cotton to."

8

Sure y'all don't mind?"

Stevie shook her head, pushed the plate closer to him, and gestured Halliwell to continue. He'd already dipped my fork into her *melanzane alla parmigiana* and rescued another generous chunk of the sautéed eggplant dripping in a light, garlic-laced red sauce.

Plop. Into his mouth.

The T-Man's head traveled in a circle while his wilted facial muscles and his wattle danced along to the languorous rhythm of his noisy chewing. Eyes shuttered to anything that might intrude on his pleasure.

He rinsed his palate with a swallow of domestic Chablis from the bottle he had insisted on ordering, repaying us, he said, for our kindness in letting him intrude on our dinner. Ran a napkin across his mouth and scraped at the corners for good measure. Patted his stomach and expelled a throaty moan of delight.

"Damn, that was fine," Halliwell said. Appeared ready to go for another forkful, but changed his mind and placed the utensil on the lip of the plate.

"I thank you again, Ms. Marriner. Had a late meal with the boys since coming off the flight from D.C., but I allus like try'n a new restaurant I get the opportunity. This place for certain going on the A-list. And got a barrel load of old-world charm. I like that, too."

He made a sweeping gesture that took in the walls, all decorated with painted murals meant to conjure up memories of Palermo, especially the largest, a panoramic illustration of simple cliffside dwellings overlooking the sea.

Halliwell turned his smile from Stevie across the table to me, then back again.

Stevie answered him in kind, but I could tell she had grown impatient with him, by the way her jaw muscles flared under the bite of her molars.

Halliwell's credentials checked out.

He was an agent with the Treasury Department.

But that's all we'd learned since stashing our guns and letting him squeeze into the booth next to me.

He was yet to explain why he'd been phoning and leaving messages all day.

How he knew where to find us.

What it had to do with the Imagine That! rock festival I helped create in John Lennon's memory almost twenty years ago.

Anything else.

Halliwell was more disposed to small talk, like he was measuring us for some *Big Secret*.

Maybe that's the reason I didn't trust him.

Granted, nothing rational about my reaction, coming so soon and on no evidence.

Call it gut instinct. Just that, but—

My gut has always served me well.

Stevie seemed to be sending the same signal at me, to go with her shin kicks under the table, her eyes demanding, *Get this show on the road*.

I said, "So what's this all about, Mr. Halliwell?"

"You sure you won't try the wine? Tasty and too big a bottle for me alone. They grow fine grapes up in the Napa Valley, and even some of your Hollywood folk got wineries going, like Francis

Ford Coppola. You know, *The Godfather?* Even the Smothers Brothers. Remember them from television? Regular rabble rousers they also were in their day. Antigovernment as all get out."

I remembered the Smothers Brothers for another reason, but Halliwell wasn't about to co-opt me into a game of show business trivia.

"How did you know we were here?"

He must have sensed from the edge in my voice that it was time.

"Putting it bluntly, Mr. Gulliver? I had a man watching over Ms. Marriner's abode since sometime midday. Y'all steal a peek at that single table closest the cash register. That is him by his lonesome, slopping up the spaghetti."

He turned his meaty palms upward.

Stevie narrowed her eyes and made a seething noise.

Halliwell pretended not to have noticed.

He studied me for a reaction.

I swallowed my irritation and gave him a false smile.

"Discourteous but no choice, sir, after I got no calls back from my messages and me needing this chat with y'all. Went on over to your place first, it being down the street from the Federal Building over to Westwood. The Heathcliffe? Security fella at the front desk was reluctant until he saw my badge. Most people this country know to respect a badge."

"Respect, or *react* to one?"

"Respect, I choose to think, Mr. Gulliver. No law, no order. A badge, it makes the point quicker'n sweeter'n any politician's speechifying."

"Okay, already," Stevie said.

She sailed a hand into space and almost clipped one of the two uniforms heading in from the parking lot.

He stopped, displayed a glimmer of recognition, like he wanted to make conversation, maybe ask for an autograph, but continued on after judging the look on Halliwell's face.

"I'm counting to ten," Stevie told Halliwell, "and I'm going to start with eight."

Halliwell nodded and held her off like a traffic cop.

He reached for his wineglass, settled back against the booth cushion, toasted us before taking a liberal taste, and said casually, "Mr. Gulliver, Ms. Marriner, I'm here because of our mutual friend, Mr. August Kalman Fowler?"

"Augie?" I shook my head. "Augie Fowler's not around to send you to me, to us, or to anyone, Mr. Halliwell."

"Exactly," he said.

August Kalman Fowler had become Brother Kalman, founder and spiritual leader of the Order of the Spiritual Brothers of the Rhyming Heart in the years since we met. Before that he was the only newspaperman who had measured up and beyond my first great teacher, Charlie Stemple, twenty years ago at the Midway bureau of the *Twin Counties Sentinel*.

Augie could not have sent Martin Halliwell to see me because right now he was sitting alone in a cave somewhere in India. Emulating the Hindu mystics. As they do, trusting villagers to bring him sustenance while he worked out some mystery of life. Maybe more than one.

No intention of returning until then, Augie said, or—

Until the death sentence hanging over our heads since the James Dean business was resolved—

I said.

Not just Stevie and I had been targeted by the killer.

Augie was high on his list, too.

Higher than us.

Got there even before us.

"You are dead wrong," Augie said, spitting the words at me, the day he announced his plans and I told him what I thought. He said, "Here I am, in my sanctuary on the hill. Surrounded twenty-four hours a day by as faithful a flock as any man could pray God deliver, but something is missing. I have felt it almost from the onset, since I first assembled a following as certain as me there's room in this world for the quietude essential to a meaningful existence."

"A cult by any name . . ."

Augie arched an eyebrow. "I'll pretend you didn't say that, my pretentious journalistic genius."

"Don't they have to give up their worldly possessions to make the grade here?"

"Only to enter, kiddo. Making the grade, as you put it so eloquently, calls for spending however long it takes to reach, keep, and carry on at the level of elevated grace you often show me is well beyond your childish understanding."

"If they miss the elevator, do they get any of it back, their worldly possessions?"

"I don't know why I even bother with you," he said, his grated potato voice dismissing me.

"Tell me one other thing then—If Wimpy Angleman hadn't been killed in that explosion . . . Would you still be working the crime beat down at Parker Center, instead of gazing out the picture window at your godly view of Griffith Park?"

Augie's eyes glazed over and he turned away from me.

I'd struck the exposed nerve that seemed like it never was going to heal and wished I could take it back.

"One of the answers I'll be looking for after I arrive in India," he said at last, his voice breaking.

"That was really crappy of me, Augie, injecting Wimpy Angleman like that. I'm sorry."

He pivoted on the heels of his handmade sandals, adjusted his sable-colored cassock, adjusted the similarly colored patch guarding his missing eye, and threw open his arms to me.

"Forgotten, amigo," he said. "I can forgive you easier than you forgive yourself." After a moment, a wistful smile. "Easier than I can forgive myself . . . Maybe India will change that. We'll see. Time will tell . . ."

I had not heard from Augie in the weeks since he left and was missing him almost as much as I missed the marriage that my job and an obsession with losing race horses helped ruin seven years ago.

The nuisance of his obsessive, generally cantankerous phone calls throughout the day, every day, correcting the faults of the world.

I missed it.

Our ritual weekly lunches, when Augie could put a face on his outbursts.

Missed.

We bickered frequently—the old warrior protecting his need to be acknowledged the best, his abiding student always pursuing approval from the master—in a battle of words that substituted humor and sarcasm for malice. Most of the time.

Missed.

Stevie viewed Augie as my father figure, the way I had once served in that role for her, not the first and far from the last man she hoped could fill a gaping hole in her heart that I was convinced defied repair.

I told that to Stevie early in our marriage, and many times afterward. Each time we traded torrents of words that turned mean and cruel and invariably resulted in one of us bolting from the house.

Never for too long.

Stevie and I needed each other too much for too long.

Just long enough to recharge our indefinable bond.

Those times led me to hours of introspection, brought me to wondering when I had become prone to fighting hardest with the ones I loved most, when I had become so cynical in my general outlook.

A protective shield, Stevie said.

Against what? I asked her.

She never had the same answer twice, and neither did I.

Maybe Augie had the right idea.

A cave.

Maybe the answer was waiting somewhere in a cave.

"Brother Saul over to Augie's place said Augie was gone to India for the duration, something about searching for his soul," Martin Halliwell said, his voice hauling me away from my thoughts and back to the table. "Know how reporters like digging out dirt, but if that ain't the damnedest thing. Him living in a cave."

"Searching for reality."

"Beg pardon?"

I said, "Augie is searching for reality."

Halliwell patted my shoulder sympathetically.

"Putting *Augie* and *reality* in the same sentence is like looking for pork chops on the menu at a kosher delicatessen. Makes sense only until y'all know better."

"Mysticism is about transforming your consciousness by getting a clear vision of reality."

"In the mountains up around New Delhi?"

"Wherever you can find it."

"Me, I'm far more inclined to start closer to home, Mr. Gulliver. Like say, Sunrise City?"

"Why would you and Augie ever be talking about Sunrise City and me?" I remembered. "The Imagine That! festival. Is that how you knew I was going to be involved? Augie?"

"Bingo! Months ago, before he went off to become Herman the hermit without bothering to call first, we got the whole history from him. How the both of you and Harry Nilsson came up with the idea for the festival after John Lennon's tragic death and how you were already talking about being on board when the twentieth anniversary came around in December. Back where it began, in Sunrise City. Augie said y'all would be perfect to help the department with what we need."

"Being?"

"An inside man. Someone the concert promoters will have no reason not to trust, especially since they already have a commitment of sorts from you. We'd like you to monitor their activities. Search out certain things the department expects you'll be able to uncover for us."

"Like what?"

Halliwell considered his answer.

"Nothing they would want uncovered. The task comes with a degree of danger, given the nature of the criminal element the department is dealing with here, but be assured we would have our eyes on you at all times."

"Why didn't Augie tell me any of this?"

"The timing was off. First, we had to get some things in place, in motion. By then, Augie had gone off to get his cave. If y'all are bothered by what you've heard so far, would rather not, I won't take no offense no how. There's allus a Plan B."

Curiosity finally got the best of Stevie, who had been sitting quietly, studying us like a spectator in the tennis stands.

She said, "Plan B?"

Halliwell said, "We send you instead, Ms. Marriner."

I said, "How you fixed for Plan C?"

Halliwell laughed like he meant it.

"One of those, too, Mr. Gulliver, although Augie was certain you would want to help us once you understood the extreme seriousness of the matter."

"It'll take more than I know so far."

He turned and stared at me full in the face.

"To tell you more would require strict confidentiality on your part. Augie said you were a person to be trusted, to the same degree I've always trusted Augie. He said if I ask you to give me your word, that'll be good enough. That so, Mr. Gulliver? That good enough?"

"Augie told you that?"

The sagging edges of his mouth climbing as high as he could make them.

"Almost his exact words: *Tell my amigo to give you his word,*

Marty. You have his word, it's as good as your having my word."
Turning to Stevie: "Augie said I'd be comfortable applying the same
condition for you, Ms. Marriner."

She gave me a long, sober look and pursed her lips to keep
from forming the smile I saw trying to escape, shifted her Holly
Golightlys down from her forehead and pushed them tight against
the bridge of her nose. Settled her hand over her mouth to smother
a sharp grunt.

I understood why.

A long time ago I had shared with her one of the first rules
Augie drummed into me after we began working together:

You *give* your word, but you *keep* a promise.

Giving your word is only as meaningful as you choose to make it.

What I didn't understand was why Augie had been so specific
with Halliwell. He could just as easily have told the T-Man to get
my promise. Did he have reservations about Halliwell, same as I
did? Had he planted a message for future delivery?

"My word on Plan A, Plan B, Plan C, or on all of the above?"
Stevie said, swallowing her words a few times in a struggle to sound
serious.

Halliwell said, "Y'all do seem to share the same sense of humor."

"She got it from me as part of the community property settle-
ment."

"Don't flatter yourself, honey." To Halliwell: "I give you my
word."

"Mr. Gulliver?"

"On one condition: There's the kind of story here you suggest,
I get to run with it first. My exclusive."

"You news people are all the same, aren't you? Always looking
to make headlines."

"Not always. Most of the time we're happy just to make a
deadline. Do we have a deal?"

Halliwell acted like he was thinking about it.

"Done deal. Signed, sealed and delivered, sir."

Gaveled his fist on the table, almost tipping his wine glass.

A little too easy?

A little too fast?

"Then you have my word," I said. "I'll listen to what you have
to say and tell you what I think. But we're still considering Plan
A, Mr. Halliwell. Only Plan A."

"I understand, and seeing as how we'll likely be doing business, all right with y'all if I dispense with my inbred Southern manners and call you Neil? You, too, Ms. Marriner? Stevie? And y'all please call me Marty."

A little too down home to go with too much y'all-ing?

An accent that couldn't make up its mind what part of the South it was from? At times too much magnolias and mint juleps, at other times not enough.

I'd no sooner pegged Halliwell as being from one of the Carolinas than his cadence and inflections took a left turn west to Georgia, I think. Sometimes somewhere else. Alabama? Mississippi? I was no expert about regional accents; neither was he. Or maybe he meant to be this obvious? Clarity in the name of confusion?

"Sure," Stevie said. "So, whaddaya wanna do, Marty?"

He did a quick survey of the room.

"Maybe go someplace where we'll have privacy?"

The minute Halliwell said the name Aaron Lodger, I knew the situation was as rife with risk as Stevie and I had been forewarned. "Aaron the Baron"—how he was known to the crime beat crew for two decades before I got there—was supposedly retired from the mob he once ruled. Nobody who knew the mugg behind the manicure that was Aaron Lodger or about organized crime in LA believed it for a minute.

He enjoyed power too much to give it up.

Aaron the Baron had come up through the ranks, starting in the fifties, the days of Mickey Cohen, Joe, Frank and Al, the Sica brothers; Louis Tom and Tom Dragna, Dominic Licata, Jimmy "The Weasel" Fratianno; hoods bearing equally colorful nicknames, like "Ruffy" Goldberg, "Happy" Meltzer, "Scarface Louie" Lieberman, "Gummy" Cuda, "Stumpy" Zevon, "Horse Face" Pete Licavoli. John Stomponato, Jr., the glamour-puss killed by Lana Turner's daughter, Cheryl, under less than glamorous circumstances.

He was a transplanted New Yorker, whose parents traded the Lower East Side of Manhattan for the lower east side of Los Angeles: Boyle Heights, a Jewish ghetto before the Jews began moving west toward Beverly Hills, making room for the Hispanics, who migrated in from Mexico and made the Heights their own.

His father, Jacob Luegerwirtz, was a baker who made a comfortable living after he borrowed the money necessary to start Boyle

Heights Bagel Company, "Where Even the Hole in the Middle is Kosher." Before that, Aaron's mother, Malvina, helped support the family, which included an older brother who died in the Second World War and three younger sisters, working in a fabric button factory downtown, a forty-minute bus ride twice a day for seven years. Later, she stayed home and tended roses in the backyard of their craftsman bungalow home on Cornwell Street, below Soto.

A three-sport letterman at Roosevelt High, Lodger quit school in his senior year and neither his police jacket nor the *Daily* files cover the years before he emerged seemingly from nowhere as one of Cohen's inner circle, a seven-member group known collectively as the "Seven Dwarfs."

He kept his profile as low as his reputation. The only file photo was taken in '61, when he spent some time in the county jail on an aggravated assault charge, his first and only encounter with the law that went beyond a dismissal of charges.

A Sunset Strip nightclub owner had landed in Cedars of Lebanon with busted kneecaps, a ruptured spleen, and a face that only a plastic surgeon could love.

Scuttlebutt of the time had it that Lodger volunteered to take the fall for Cohen, who decided to teach the nitery owner a lesson after he refused to introduce the gangster to a post–Academy Awards group of celebrants that included Burt Lancaster, Elizabeth Taylor, Greer Garson, Claire Cavanaugh, and Sir Laurence Olivier.

About a year later, the nitery owner disappeared.

Foul play suspected.

His wife shouting Aaron Lodger's name at anyone who'd listen. A sidebar to the main story by Augie Fowler quoted him as saying, "The man disappeared, maybe he's a magician."

It was the last time, so far as anyone knew, that Aaron the Baron spoke to anyone from the media.

Halliwell observed my reaction closely after speaking the name and couldn't miss the question mark that formed on my face even before I asked, "What does Aaron Lodger have to do with the Imagine That! festival?"

We were sitting in Stevie's den on facing leather sofas across a huge mahogany and etched glass coffee table stacked high with old issues of the tabloids, soap opera magazines, *Vanity Fair, Cosmopolitan, Talk, Vogue, Bazaar, W, Premiere, New York, The New*

Yorker, Daily Variety, Hollywood Reporter, People, Entertainment Weekly, and piles of pawed-over movie scripts she constantly received from marginal and wanna-be producer graduates of the Roger Corman University of Shlock. (The one atop the pile had a scribbled message on its cover from her *Bedrooms and Board Rooms* nemesis Karen Walls: "You gotta be kidding!!!! Try S. Marriner.")

Halliwell tinkered with the dials on a black metal box about the size of a matchbox he'd placed on the table within moments of our settling down, explaining, "Know you have the place wired for sight and sound. This little ol' gizmo sends out a high frequency sound that stops the most sophisticated electronic eavesdropping."

Satisfied, he put it back down, careful to line it up parallel with a similar metal box, only gray and maybe an inch taller and wider, that he had not bothered to explain to us.

"*Imagine That!* is Aaron Lodger's show," he said.

"The call I got was from Rick Savage. Richie didn't say anything about Lodger being involved."

"Would you?" Shrugging. "If you were the mayor of Palm Springs, would you want to be connected in any way to Aaron the Baron, especially if you had your eyes on a seat in the United States Senate?"

"Richie Savage? I once had a thing with Richie Savage," Stevie said, rejoining us from the kitchen. She was carrying a sterling silver platter loaded down with a sterling silver coffee pot and service for three. She cleared a space on the table, set it down, plopped down next to me, and said, "Help yourself, guys. The maid act ends here. Richie Savage, huh? You didn't bother to tell me that's who had called you about the festival, Mr. Gulliver."

"I guess I forgot."

"Yeah, right." She poked a finger into my cheek. "Tell me, does your tongue catch fire immediately or does it take a few seconds?" To Halliwell: "There should be a statute of limitations on jealousy."

Halliwell said, "I remember reading something about it in *People* magazine."

"Cover. I got it somewhere. That was a year after I cut myself free from my bud the stud here. Richie, too. Or so I thought. Didn't know about the little missus and the moppets he kept hidden back home in Arkansas. Not until I read about them in *People.* Remember the headline on the cover, honey?"

I did, but shook my head *No* anyway.

" 'Stevie the Sex Queen Savaged.' I was devastated, but it

turned into a real career boost. I got my first movie-of-the-week offer right after that, that awful flick with Barry Roman. Now, there was a letch if ever there was one."

"Can we put your sex life on hold until later?"

"Marty looks like he doesn't mind. You mind, Marty?"

"Careful, Marty. She's into older men."

"Rude, Neil Gulliver. Horribly, dreadfully rude of you to say something like that to an almost complete stranger." She leaped up and seemed to fly across the table, sat down next to Halliwell and asked him, "You ever been jealous like that, Marty?"

Halliwell finished stirring the four lumps of sugar he had dropped into his cup, took a taste and, satisfied, told her, "Every time my wife looks at another man or a man looks at Melanie. Going on twenty-some years now."

She cooed, "How sweet. How romantic."

I said, "How come for him it's sweet and romantic, but for me it's possessiveness?"

"Because Marty and his wife are still married—going on twenty-some years—and we're still divorced."

Halliwell seemed amused.

"In defense of Neil, I'll confess that going on twenty-some years, when Melanie and I get us to bickering, we sound just like y'all. Just like newlyweds. Stevie, y'all certain that divorce of yours ever got finalized?"

Her face displayed a million emotions in the fraction of a second silence that clogged the air.

Stevie rose in slow motion, threw back her shoulders, and marched to the piano stool, calling to Halliwell as she sat down, "None of your business."

"No offense, Stevie." To me: "I'm sorry if I upset the lady."

"I'm not," I said, with a flick of the wrist, and moved us back to the subject. "So, Lodger's involved. How, why, and what else? Wipe Out Weapons International won't be getting a full count on the proceeds from the festival, something like that? Is that enough to bring on the T-men?"

"More than that, Neil. The Treasury Department believes the Lennon tribute has been revived after ten years as a way for Aaron Lodger to launder dirty money coming into the U.S. from Cuba, South America, Las Vegas. Other places where he's got his tentacles out. Possibly old funny money that's been out of circulation.

"We believe Rick Savage figures big in the scheme and plans

to use his payoff to move up from being a dirty mayor to being a dirty senator.

"We're certain whatever is being schemed also involves operators of the gambling casino on the San Gorgonio Indian Reservation."

He paused to try his coffee. Studied the cup, looking as if he had a canary in there as well as the four lumps of sugar.

I said, "There's something else, right?"

"Correct. Someone else. Another reason the department believes you're the man best qualified to get inside for us. We are convinced Aaron Lodger and Rick Savage's link to the San Gorgonios was Michael Wilder."

"Who?"

"Michael Wilder, the husband of your former fiancée."

"His what?"

Stevie had stopped pretending she wasn't listening and wheeled around on the piano stool.

Eyes brimming with irritation.

Staring at me like a mortician measuring a corpse for a coffin.

"Oh, my," said Halliwell, locking his hands in his lap, staring at the ceiling and rolling his eyes. "If I just gave away a secret about your—about Leigh Wilder—I am terribly, terribly sorry."

I didn't believe him for a minute. Not his apology and not—

What else?

What else was phony about this guy?

What was it Augie also must have felt about the T-man, that led Augie to have Halliwell ask for my word?

I made a promise to myself to find out.

9

FROM AUGIE FOWLER'S JOURNAL
December 9, 1980

By the time Dom had slipped the limo through the last crack in the late afternoon traffic quagmire and got us to the Criminal Court Building at Foley Square, John's killer, Mark David Chapman, had come and gone.

Wufffft. Like that.

In and out again after his arraignment on a murder one, on his lawyer's advice standing mute.

Back to Bellevue Hospital, where the cops had taken him for a psychiatric examination in the first hours of morning, after one-stopping at the Twentieth Precinct headquarters on Eighty-second Street to get Chapman's signed statement.

It was already all over the news, that the little turd had confessed to shooting John, telling the cops, "I can't believe I could do that."

It would have been nicer if he'd told that to the judge and waived trial, been sentenced immediately, and led off to the black beyond.

Instant bye-bye.

Saving taxpayer dollars.

That's the Augie Fowler Common Sense Theory of Justice.

Keeps Death Row from staying cluttered with convicted killers surviving year after year on legal appeals and loopholes.

And, yes, maybe swift justice sucks in an innocent man once in a while, but getting it right nine times out of ten is a great average in any man's league.

With Chapman, no doubt he's one of the nine.

Yoko and everybody back at the Dakota was expecting an eyeball account from me, but who figured a New York judge to run his courtroom like one of Mussolini's railroads?

Wufffft. Over and out.

Judge Martin Rettinger sends Chapman back to Bellevue under maximum security conditions and orders continuation of a round-the-clock suicide watch.

"Not allowing no visitors over there," the bailiff told me before he was dragged away to face the TV cameras massed in the corridor outside the courtroom doors, making it sound like the order had come down as a papal decree.

I heard it as a challenge.

Charging back to the limo, I could already smell the exclusive, see the headline set in old woodblock typeface:

EXCLUSIVE! LENNON KILLER CHAPMAN TELLS ALL TO DAILY'S A. K. FOWLER

Give the local news jockeys a little lesson in how to make the front page LA style.

Dom was double-parked outside the courthouse, leaning out the driver window and furiously dragging on a cigarette, charging the air with a lot of blue smoke while a horse cop, poised to cite him, studied his light-blue cardboard license for traffic violations.

I hurried over, hauling out my wallet on the run, and flashed my LA County Sheriff's badge at the cop, too fast for him to see it was the playground version Pete Pitchess' office routinely handed out like peanuts to news types and select VIPs. Nothing like an NYPD shield, but enough glitter to give the cop pause.

In the same move, I patted his horsie on the shoulder and eased the license from his fingers.

Made as if I were checking it out.

"Yeah, you're the one they said they'd send for me," I told Dom. Handed Dom his license.

Said to the cop: "He's the one they said to look for. Posh wheels, huh? The DA got me playing messenger boy from that dickhead Chapman's plea just now on over to Bellevue, where we're tossing the creepola again."

Doing my first New York accent since Cagney got me two lines in *Love Me or Leave Me*, the MGM movie from '55, where he played Moe "The Gimp" Snyder to Doris Day's Ruth Etting.

"The one killed Lennon?" the cop asked, at once beyond any interest in ticketing Dom and, like me, not letting due process get in front of his personal verdict.

"Couldn't get Chapman to admit it to the judge, but you seen the papers, the TV, you know our guys over at the two-oh got signed paper from him'll hold up any court of law."

"Fuck him!" the cop said, stashing his citation book. "My missus, she was up on a crying jag all night. She was a big Beatles fan. Especially him. Was one of the screamers in the audience when they did Ed Sullivan."

He saluted me with two fingers to the brim of his cap, and trotted off down the street.

I jumped into the limo and called at Dom through the partition, "Bellevue, like the end of the world is already snapping at your ass."

As he edged into the flow of traffic, I glanced out my window and did a double-take at the sight of a familiar face heading down the courthouse steps:

Martin Halliwell.

I hurriedly lowered the tinted glass for a better look, thought about hopping out and confronting him, but I was too late.

Marty had disappeared inside the pedestrian madhouse as easily as he had lost himself after our flight landed at JFK and a pair of hulking blurs greeted him warmly as he steered me from the arrival tunnel into the terminal.

"Mr. Fowler appears to have had a wee bit too much to drink on the plane, gentlemen, and he needs a helping hand," I now remembered Marty saying, just before the hulks took me by the elbows and armpits and navigated me away to—

Where?
Not the Essex House.
Somewhere else first.

Bellevue Hospital is at First Avenue and Twenty-seventh Street.

I could have gotten there faster on the subway or by borrowing Mister Ed from the cop.

I had Dom drive past the news crews clustered outside the entrance and stop a block away, thanked him, and said to go on back to Harry Nilsson at the Ginger Man—have one on me—and doubled back on foot to the hospital.

Found the entrance to Emergency.

Flashing my sheriff's badge got me past security and a smile and some smooth talking to Mark David Chapman's floor, the jailhouse section of the psychiatric ward, its walls as antiseptic as the powerful dose of disinfectant rising from the worn linoleum.

Now I had to get buzzed through the thick security door adjacent to the guards' station on the other side of a thick glass and wire mesh security window.

The guard behind the desk, a small woman in her sixties with kind eyes and skin brighter than her immaculate uniform, answered me with a doubtful look when I identified myself as Chapman's uncle, and told her, "Been in the air all night. I flew in from Honolulu and came straight on over."

"His brother said nothing about no uncle," she said.

"His brother?"

"Been in with him the last fifteen, twenty minutes." Eyeing me suspiciously. "Wudda thought you'd fly together, him also just here from Hawaii and being family and all."

Good luck, I thought.

Timing is everything.

Not only am I this close to an exclusive with Chapman, get inside the room and I get his brother as well.

I turned up my palms.

"No, me alone," I said, quickly improvising. "All of this happened so fast, no time to do anything but hurry to the airport, loving our Mark as we do. A terrible tragedy, this. Horrible. Just horrible. Makes no sense. No sense at all, Officer Geyer."

Lifting the name from the ID pin above her shield.

Personalizing the conversation for a friendlier effect.

About to learn it was a mistake.

She inched up and strained her neck, her eyes searching me for something. "Where's your visitor's permit?"

Her tone strictly business; a hint of suspicion.

I felt around my jacket pocket, both lapels. "Had it a minute ago. You think maybe it fell off in the elevator?"

"Can't help you without a badge."

Too close to quit now.

"I wasn't planning on staying long anyway, Officer Geyer. A minute or two, only long enough to let our Markie know I was also here. Let Markie see more'n his brother are standing by his side. His uncle, too. I'm the one who named him, you know that? After my blessed father, Markie's late, dear grandfather."

She didn't seem convinced.

Averted my gaze.

Reached for the phone.

"You got a family, Officer Geyer?"

She pressed a series of numbers on the dial plate.

"Lord pray a tragedy like this never happens to you or any of your loved ones, Officer Geyer. But it ever does—" I shifted my eyes upward, as if searching for heaven past the dust-encrusted ceiling, and turned into my pal Lancaster in *Elmer Gantry*. "Lord pray your kinfolk come together as mine have, Officer Geyer, come together as one . . . in the darkest hours before the dawn."

She studied me from the corners of her glossy eyes and said into the phone, "Campbell? Geyer up at the front desk? I have Mr. Chapman's uncle out here to see him?"

She covered the mouthpiece with her hand and explained, "Tight security, death watch and all, so your nephew can't have but one visitor at a time." After another moment: "Him and his brother were just finishing, the officer says. He'll be bringing him out in a minute. Then you can go in and have your quick hello."

I smiled, clasped my hands at my chest, and gave her an appreciative nod, but—

My mind was already working on the new problem.

I hadn't thought about Chapman's brother being anywhere but in the room with him, where I could sell him a fast bill of goods.

Less chance of that out here.

He'd ID me for the stranger I was, and—

Good-bye, Augie.

Good-bye, interview.

"Officer Geyer, is there a men's room I could use? A little bladder problem and something I must have eaten on the plane. It's urgent."

She smiled knowingly.

Pulled from somewhere a key attached by link chain to the handle of a tennis paddle that could have come from my old high school, and slid it through the transfer slot in the glass security panel.

"Behind you, by the elevator, a left turn end of the corridor, and the third door on the right."

"Thank you."

I half walked, half ran down the hall and hid out in a stall, hoping nothing would be said to Chapman's brother and he'd go away wondering whatever happened to whichever uncle.

Assuming, of course, Chapman's father had a brother.

A weak plan, leaving too much to dumb luck, but it was the best I could come up with on short notice, and—

The hydraulic door closer screamed for oil as someone entered the men's room and a voice wondered in a delicious New Yorkese baritone, "Mista Chapman, you in heah?"

Quickly, I propped my legs above the baseline of the stall door.

Heard shuffling on the tile.

"Hello? Anyone?"

Held my breath.

Eternity dawdled by.

A grunt.

More shuffling.

More squeaks as the men's room door opened and closed, and—

I let out enough air to fill the Goodyear blimp.

Gave it another five minutes.

Not long enough.

As I emerged, a uniformed cop and a compact, smartly attired man in his late twenties who I assumed was Chapman's brother were standing by the elevator, about ten feet away.

Their backs were to me, but they swung around like the door noise was a dance cue.

"Mista Chapman?" the cop said.

The same voice I'd heard in the men's room.

My eyes grazed him and held on Chapman's brother while I considered a thousand possible responses. I was the black sheep of the family, the brother his father refused to speak to or mention since I broke Mom's heart by joining the army?

That one? Why not?

"Yes, officer."

My "nephew" narrowed his eyes into questioning slits, creating deep ridges between his neatly trimmed eyebrows, and started toward me, as if aiming for a closer look at this imposter uncle.

Here it was.

I braced myself for the moment of truth.

"I'm Detective Breckenridge," he said, extending his right hand. "Officer Campbell went looking for you in the head. You din't hear?"

A tight grip, like he had no plans to let go.

"I guess not. My stomach was burning like a five-alarm fire," I said, trying to mask my sense of relief with a sickly sort of smile.

It appeared I still had a crack at getting to Chapman.

"Lotta that goin' 'round," Breckenridge said in a voice that sounded borrowed from an old episode of *Dragnet*. "Gotta be careful whatchu eat nowadays."

"Both my kids are down," the uniform said. "Wit' dem, I think a cold or the flu, from all this lousy weather we been havin' lately."

Breckenridge released my hand and said, "The bad news is you won't be able to spend no time with your nephew right now, Mr. Chapman. The meds they fed him kicked in, and he's out to the world for the duration, the doc said. But you can come back later, you want. Maybe after dinner hour, when his bro said he'd be back. No problem-o with that on our end."

I said, "His brother's gone?"

More relief. Trying to sound casual about it.

"You just missed him. By five. Said he was late for an appernt-ment, but to tell you, you want, you can hook up with him after that at his hotel. The Chelsea. He said you'd know the place."

"Famous rock-and-roll joint," the uniform volunteered. "Your nephew, he said they give him the same room where that crazy mutt Sid Vicious killed his girlfriend. Wouldn't catch me staying in there on a bet."

I heard that and my pulse began racing.

Brother, hell!

It was Gulliver.

That Hildy Johnson hopeful had beaten me to Chapman.

Said he had flown to here to pay his respects, been shit-canned by his half-assed rag, and I bought his bag of bullshit. All along he was yanking my chain and working the Lennon story, the son of a—

I started laughing, loud, louder, the sound ricocheting off the walls and down the hallways like water gushing from a busted main. By their expressions, I was certain the two cops thought I belonged on the far side of the door leading into the psycho ward.

Gulliver could wait.

I braved a subway ride uptown to the Dakota and tracked along the curbside traffic lane, easier than trying to crack the people packaged like sardines on both sides of the front entrance. New faces, and some I remembered from earlier, who had endured the cold night and made a feast of their grief.

Still intact on the park side of Central Park West, an immense mourner's convention.

A uniform who recognized me told some others I was okay and directed me through the archway to the courtyard, where I waited outside the small security office while he radioed upstairs on his two-way.

I felt my eyes misting at the sight of bloodstains in the yard and past the yellow crime tape blocking the office doorway. Snapped them shut, tight, drank up a barrel of air and held it in my lungs until I was sure my emotions would not run amuck again, as they had after I got here last night.

According to the eyewitness report of Jay Hastings, the doorman on duty, a bearded, bearish-sized man in his late twenties, he had been startled by what sounded like a series of gunshots.

A moment or two later, John stumbled into the office, dropped to his knees, and fell forward onto his face after crying out, "I'm shot!"

Hastings dashed from his desk to John, saw a cavernous wound in John's chest.

Blood pouring from John's mouth.

A distraught Yoko had entered right behind John. She settled by his side, cradled his head, while Hastings took off the jacket of his blue uniform and draped it over John.

John was barely semiconscious.

He tried speaking, but only gurgled and vomited.

Hastings called for cops. Then, brave beyond common sense, he dashed from the security office looking for the gunman. He found Chapman standing in front of the Dakota, like a man waiting for a bus. Calm. Reading a copy of *The Catcher in the Rye*.

Hastings shouted at him, "Do you know what you just did?!"

Chapman answered quietly, "I just shot John Lennon."

Behind them, the sound of tenants wondering what the noise was, alarm and dismay mounting as the details moved from person to person, rumors turned into truth, and—

Yoko screaming hysterically.

FROM AUGIE FOWLER'S JOURNAL

The last time I saw John alive was two years ago.

I had come to New York tracking a serial killer who had a penchant for dead comedians and was preparing to add Chick Rainbow to his list sometime during a Friars Club "roast" in Chick's honor.

John was going through a bad time and, I'd been told by Harry Nilsson, had strayed from his bedroom only twice since January, first for a vacation in the Caribbean and later for a trip to Japan, where he reportedly chose to stay locked in his hotel room the entire time.

Instead of dialing the Dakota switchboard, I called on the private line. After a ring and a half, someone picked up and answered with a whistle.

John's way of identifying himself.

Strangers who somehow managed to get the number usually were confused enough to hang up.

His friends knew better.

I said, "Can this possibly be the asshole goes around Los Angeles wearing a Kotex on his head?"

Immediately, John exploded with delight and, laughing uproariously, demanded, "This can only be the bloody bugger himself. A cement mixer for a voice and guaranteed to scare the wee ones, day or night."

We went back and forth like that for a minute or two.

He asked after Harry and another mutual friend, Stanley Dorfman, the renowned BBC-TV director who'd done shows with all the great rock-and-rollers, frequently at their begging request, and in recent years was working in Hollywood; then, wanted to know what brought me to New York, insisting on all the gory details when I told him.

"No laughing matter that," John said, his own laughter suddenly punctuated by a hacking cough.

I started to lecture him about one Gauloise too many, and he cut me off with a reminder about my own preference for Montecristo cigars.

I shook my head at the phone. "Two a day. Three, maybe. Can't picture ever seeing you without a cancer stick perched between your pretty Liverpudlian lips."

"Safety in numbers, mate. Besides, yours is contraband. Cuban contraband. Cuban, for Christ's sake, Kalman. The FBI ever gets wind they'll straightaway snap on the cuffs, march you off to foogin' jail." A beat. "Maybe, I should call and work a deal. Get them onto you and off me own foogin' bloody arse."

The Feebies had been on John's case since '71, when he arrived in New York for a visit and promptly hooked up with targeted "Chicago Seven" activists like Jerry Rubin, Rennie Davis, and Bobby Seale on causes unpopular with the Nixon administration, right wing extremists, and even the Ku Klux Klan.

Working tightly with the Department of Immigration, the FBI was determined to get John tossed out of the country as an undesirable alien.

The battle carried on for five years and produced more than twenty-six pounds of sealed files before Federal Judge Ira Fieldsteel granted him a green card for resident status and the right to apply for full citizenship in 1981.

The Feebies never stopped smarting from the defeat.

I'd heard as recent as this summer from a Washington source I considered as reliable as a Rolls-Royce that they were still dogging his steps.

At once, I got on the phone to let John know.

He already knew.

"Go down the bloody foogin' basement sometime and see who's bloody foogin' picking through me garbage. Know what they find, Kalman?" A beat. "Bloody foogin' garbage."

John was a Chick Rainbow fan, but he declined to join me at the dinner, sounding almost apologetic and remarking prophetically, "You got a serial killer running loose, last thing I want to do is bloody put myself in the bloody way a bloody foogin' bullet."

Softening and sounding as sweet as his best love song, he said, "Besides, your killer's picked a date happens to be Sean's third birthday. We've plans to celebrate royally with the little rascal, over to Tavern on the Green."

John told me to hold on and I heard a snatch of muffled conversation before he suggested, "You free in the morning?"

"Free as a bird."

"Familiar imagery that. Fly on over here then, but not so early you'll wake the living dead."

We agreed on ten o'clock.

The next morning, maybe fifteen minutes early, my taxi pulled up to the Dakota and I headed for the security office past eight or ten fans who congregated by the entrance arch hoping to catch sight of John. They were always there, rain or shine, this morning their headgear pulled down and jacket collars raised, hands in their pockets, grabbing some warmth against a bone-chilling cold that had sneaked down overnight from the northeast. They all had cameras or autograph books, albums by the Beatles and John and Yoko, that they hoped to have him sign.

Who'd have believed then that, two years later, one of them would be John's assassin, Mark David Chapman.

By all accounts, a man matching Chapman's description had been noticed hanging around the Dakota over the weekend and again around five o'clock on the afternoon of December 8.

John and Yoko emerged at that time and walked briskly to their limo, parked today at the curb instead of inside the Dakota courtyard.

Chapman quickly approached them. Pushed a copy of the new, career-reviving *Double Fantasy* album into John's hands.

John signed the cover, "John Lennon, 1980," as another fan, Paul Goresh, a photographer, ran over and captured the moment with his camera.

"Is that all you want?" John inquired.

Chapman, awestruck, responded, "Thanks, John."

He watched John and Yoko duck into the limo and drive off to a recording session at the Record Plant, then turned to Goresh and asked in a voice thundering with excitement, "Did I have my hat on or off? I wanted to have it off? Boy, they'll never believe this back in Hawaii."

Chapman and Goresh hung out at the Dakota until around eight o'clock, when Goresh grew tired of waiting for the Lennons to return.

Chapman tried unsuccessfully to talk him into staying, asking, "What if you never see him again? What if something happens to him?"

He was alone when John and Yoko returned to the Dakota around eleven o'clock. The limo parked at the curb, although the security gates were wide open. John and Yoko eased out and headed for the entrance, Yoko walking ahead of John, who was carrying tapes of the song they'd been working on, "Walking on Thin Ice."

As they pass him in the archway, he calls out softly, "Mr. Lennon?"

John turns and stares myopically into the dark recess.

Chapman is standing about five feet away, in a combat stance, gripping in both hands the .38 caliber Charter Arms Special revolver with a two-inch barrel he had purchased in Honolulu two months earlier.

He opens fire and gets off five shots before John can say anything, striking John in the head and shoulders.

John staggers away.

Chapman eases up and releases his hold on the .38. It bounces onto the ground.

He makes no effort to flee.

A young girl, drawn to the scene by the sound of the gunshots, goes up to Chapman and nervously inquires, "What happened?"

Chapman tells her, "I'd go away if I were you."

The guard verified I was expected and escorted me to the elevator, held open the doors, and shared the ride up.

Someone I didn't know was waiting for me at the door, one of the young recruits who were always coming and going, eager to be in John and Yoko's presence for however long the job might last.

I padded after him, through the hallway decorated with photographs cataloging moments in the life and times of the Lennons to the immense kitchen, painted since my last visit, stocked as usual with containers of spices and grains, teas and coffees, the radio tuned to a rock station blasting out the latest hits, the end of "You're the One That I Want" by John Travolta and Olivia Newton-John feeding into—the small world of coincidence—"With a Little Luck" by Paul McCartney and his current band, Wings.

A pot of water was boiling on the stove, and there was evidence of what John called "dead fish," sushi and sushimi delivered fresh daily by a Japanese restaurant on Columbus Avenue. I assumed this would be our meal and looked around for a place to settle down, but before I could a different assistant materialized and led me to Yoko's outer office.

The apartment was buzzing with activity, more than I'd seen on previous visits over the last two or three years, a lot of fresh faces filling up the desks, carrying on in all directions, on the phone or searching through drawers at the wall of files. The phones ringing incessantly to a rhythm of their own, under a driving layer of Motown that fed the room from the revved-up stereo system.

John materialized from somewhere stifling a yawn behind his fist, taking in all the activity with mild interest, and decided, "No good for us here, mate." He pointed at the door leading to Yoko's office. "Besides, don't feel like sharing you."

He excused himself and was back in a moment wearing a light winter, military-style coat over his casual outfit of cowboy shirt and jeans and an incongruous pair of sneakers, to which John had added a black, broad-brimmed Stetson.

He motioned for me to follow him.

A minute later, we were moving down a flight of stairs that creaked under our weight, ducking under beams before we reached a door that led into the Dakota basement.

He seemed to travel on radar as we dodged around rusty water dripping from overhead pipes to a door on the far side of the building.

It opened onto Seventy-second Street.

This was his escape route.

John checked in both directions to make sure the coast was clear of fans, then traded his regular eyeglasses for a dark pair of lenses in the same type of simple round frames, and we headed off for his favorite coffee shop, La Fortuna, a block and a half away on Columbus Avenue.

Our reunion lasted about two hours after we settled at a table in the rear and he listened politely to two or three of the regulars who came over to say "Hello" and a sentence or two of small talk, something they could take back home or to the office.

Bragging rights.

"You know who I had coffee with again this morning?"

Forgetting to mention it wasn't at the same table.

I had never seen John less than polite, no matter where or under what circumstances he was bombarded by this kind of unceasing fan adoration.

I asked him about it once, and he told me, "Like with the autographs and the pictures, it's easier to do than not to do."

This morning's conversation stayed generally light and casual. I gave him more fill-in on our friends in LA, and he had reports on people we knew in New York and England. He wanted to hear again about the serial killer tracking Chick Rainbow and remarked off-handedly, "Well, a far cry from the music business, where too many of the famous people we could name spend their time doing the dirty deed to ourselves."

He made a finger gun and used his thumb as the trigger.

"Gulp! You're a goner."

Fired it again.

"Snort! You're a dead man!"

Shook his head.

"Tell you, Kalman, and take it from one who knows: Fame carries a penalty as well as a burden. Being a celebrity is not all it's cut up to be."

"Who would know better than you, John?"

He didn't have to think about it.

"Paul!" he said, loud enough for everyone in the shop to hear. "Paul thinks he knows everything better'n me, and he always has."

He sent a wry laugh across the table and made a face that seemed to say, "What a naughty boy I'm being," but I sensed the truth of the comment in a rivalry that had come to rank with the best of them.

I said, "I hear Paul has a new hit single with Wings," just making conversation, but I had thoughtlessly struck a nerve.

John's face soured. He rolled his eyes at the ceiling, growling, "Wings? With us Paul only flew the bloody foogin' coop."

"So, when are you going back into the studio, give us your own Number One?"

His spine grew five inches, and he gave me a cockeyed look. Lit up a fresh Gauloise, spit out the smoke.

"No bloody chance. Yoko and me, we do our other things now. Yoko minds the store and does fine at it. She launches our own personal charity soon, the Spirit Foundation. Me, I also have my work cut out for me. I read. I watch the telly. I smoke. I sleep. Sometimes, just for a change, I sleep, I smoke, I watch the telly, I read."

John let me see he wanted off the subject.

He signaled our waitress for another cappuccino and a second Napoleon for himself, a coffee refill for me.

When she delivered the order, as he had with the first Napoleon, he painstakingly dug out the sweet golden cream from the center of the cake and licked it off his knife in slow motion.

"Better than Oreos," he said more than once, urging me to try one for myself, but my latest diet had limited me to fruit and cottage cheese and enough coffee to float what was left of the Royal Navy; black or with a sugar substitute, no cream.

"Means more for me," John said gleefully, carving into the Napoleon. He shut his eyes and ran his tongue along the knife, once more savoring the taste of the cream like it was God's repayment for a good deed.

I had that image of John in my mind, that dear man with his knife mining the pastry for the treat inside, on my way to the Dakota last night, earlier today, and again now, as a red-eyed assistant with bad skin and a pony tail down to his waist guided me to Yoko's office and reminded me I'd have to remove my shoes before entering.

"I know," I said, working off one and then the other.

He said, "She's gone, but she'll be back soon, she said to tell you," his voice verging on emotional breakdown. "She said to tell you to make yourself comfortable. Can I get you anything?"

I shook my head and passed into the room.

"She say where she was going?"

"Unh unh."

"Ringo? Mr. Geffen? Mr. Rosenblatt? Mr. Mintz? Mr. Seaman? Any of them around?"

"Not that I know . . . Buzz me on the phone there, if you change your mind about liking to have something," he said, and closed the door behind me.

I wandered the room, enjoying the comforting feel of the plush white carpeting under my stockinged feet, wishing the ceiling, painted in blues and whites, could erase the black cloud hanging over the apartment.

The Dakota.

New York.

The world.

I studied the variety of rare Egyptian artifacts Yoko collected and housed in cases made of cut-glass, then moved on to a portrait of John and Sean hanging at one end of the office. Both with shoulder-length hair. Painted early last summer in the Bahamas.

Below the painting: a piano.

I strained to hear some of the songs that were tested out here, but they only played at a distance, in my mind.

I headed toward the plush white couch and matching arm chair that formed an L on two sides of a glass coffee table encased in black iron, a snake of gold adorning the crossbar below the glass. I chose a corner of the couch. The cushions collapsed under my weight with a sigh of acceptance.

On the table was a copy of the public announcement Yoko had written for release to the media this morning. I picked it up, put on my specs, and read it again:

"There is no funeral for John. Later in the week we will set the time for a silent vigil to pray for his soul. We invite you to participate from wherever you are at the time. We thank you for the many flowers sent to John. But in the future, instead of flowers, please consider sending donations in his name to the Spirit Foundation Inc., which is John's personal charitable foundation. He would have appreciated it very much. John loved and prayed for the human race. Please pray the same for him. Yoko & Sean."

Reading it was a mistake.

I needed a drink, fast, and—

Somewhere I could be alone with my misery over the friend I'd lost last night.

I fled the room and, half-hopping up the hallway as I put back on one shoe, then the other, I found the kid with the ponytail in the kitchen, meditating over a Perrier.

"Tell Yoko I was here. Tell her I'll be back," I said, and two or three minutes later was racing down Central Park West, south on my way to the Essex House.

They had a good bar there and I was a guest on someone else's tab.

I was desperate for a Brandy Alexander, the only drink I deemed proper for quenching the emotions coursing through my mind and body, and so intent on my need I was unaware of the car rolling alongside me until it honked.

And honked.

And honked.

And I realized I was the target of the noise.

It was a Chrysler four-door, dirty black and bearing a history of street attacks, a dent here, key marks there, a smashed-in front fender on the passenger side.

A license holder that identified it as a Budget rental.

I stopped and so did the Chrysler.

The back door swung open and I recognized the man who was beckoning me.

"Need a lift?" Martin Halliwell called, and before I could answer, "Climb on in, Augie. We got us a lot to talk about, you'n me."

11

Neil told Stevie, "I am going on record. Again. You are here in Sunrise City and getting involved in this damn thing against my better judgment."

She looked across him and manufactured a yawn.

"I mean it, Stevie. I wish you'd listen."

"If wishes were diamonds—"

"I wish you'd pack your bags and go back home. Take Armando with you."

"Honey, you can mean it all you want, from now until cows can talk and squirrels can sing, but understand your vote didn't count. I'm here because I want to be here and because of how essential I am to getting at the truth for the government."

"Truth and the government!" His snort carried across the hotel room and landed on her face. "I hear it worked like that in the time of George Washington. If you'd been paying attention, you'd have realized how clever Halliwell was being. He roped you in first only to make sure he could get my cooperation."

"Maybe that makes him smarter than the both of us?"

Neil drilled her with a hard look.

" 'Cunning' would have been my word. 'Calculating' is another good one."

"How about 'devious,' honey? Also a good word."

If Neil saw the humor in her remark, he wasn't sharing it with her.

"Admit it, you jumped in for the chance to see Richie Savage again. Why's that? Visions of becoming Mrs. United States Senator down the road, the way Elizabeth Taylor did? Assuming, of course, Richie doesn't turn out to be as dirty as Halliwell thinks he is."

"Of course. Especially if he's still married. We both know how hard it is for Stephanie Marriner to find a single guy, right?"

"Finding them is easy for you. Keeping them around is the hard part, babe."

"You always look positively mean when you say things like that." He swung his face away from her. "How does the old song go, honey? 'You only hurt the ones you love'? If that's so, stop it, please. Once and for all, stop loving me. Okay?"

His face turned back to her, and Stevie saw she was the one inflicting punishment now.

He undid the arms that had been wrapped tightly across his chest and threw a dismissive hand at her.

Bellowed, "Do what you want!"

Pushed his shoulders back and stalked past her without so much as a glance, pulling the door shut so hard it tilted the watercolor of a desert landscape at dawn hanging above a small writing table filled with tourist literature about the city and the historic Sunrise Hotel.

A moment later, the door opened a crack and a slice of Neil's face appeared, only long enough for him to demand, "Remember to turn the dead bolt after you throw the chain."

Stevie allowed herself a minute to rein in her pulse.

"What is it with him?" she thought as she wheeled into a sitting position on the edge of the narrow bed, the inner springs squeaking as her bare feet settled on the threadbare rug, its geometric Indian designs invisible in the pathways worn by time. "Neil, honey, what is it with you?" she asked the door.

She had not meant to come down so hard on him, but they

had been arguing constantly like this since even before they piled their bags into her Jeep Grand Cherokee and caught the Golden State southeast onto the San Bernardino Freeway.

She was tired after almost two hours of driving, having refused his offer to take the wheel, not willing to give him command of any situation in the ongoing tug-of-war that over the last seven years had become so much a part of their life together apart.

It was almost as if he viewed the trip as new community property to be divided, thirty-two-and-a-half miles an hour for Neil, thirty-two-and-a-half miles an hour for her. He'd even suggested a compromise: Armando drive the Jeep instead of trailing behind them in his own, a late-model Wrangler.

Even Armando shook his head at that one.

Sometimes she loved Neil more than she ever did, maybe as much as when they were married. That much she could admit to herself, never to him, of course. When she shattered him with her declaration of independence seven years ago, she'd hoped Neil would understand he was responsible—deserved a lot of the credit—for turning the young, untamed, fitfully educated girl he spied in a crowd into the woman she became, still headstrong, but far smarter and savvier than she might have been without his firm hand to guide her.

She knew she owed him a lot, but not her life.

Her life was hers, to do with as she pleased.

Right now, it pleased her to be in Sunrise City.

It pleased her to be in Sunrise City with him.

Neil.

For him.

The minute Halliwell explained the situation, she knew she wasn't going to let Neil face that kind of danger alone.

Explain that to Neil?

How?

When she couldn't explain it to herself, except—

They were not married anymore, but they were still a team, a team of well-matched misfits.

Quickly, Stevie scanned the room, as if someone might be eavesdropping on her thoughts.

Stevie moved from the bed to the old-fashioned dresser, settled on the frayed pink stool cushion, and reviewed her face in the mirror. Pushed loose strands of hair back over her ears. Used her fingers to smooth out the wrinkles under her eyes that had been brought on by far too many sleepless nights caused by a revenge-bent murderer who could show up anytime, and a negotiation with the producers of *Bedrooms and Board Rooms*—a different breed of killer—Stevie felt was a disaster waiting to happen.

"I did not come because of Rick Savage and for sure not because of this old *amore* of Neil's, this Leigh Wilder," she told the mirror, knowing she wasn't being entirely truthful.

Damn.

Lying to a mirror.

Stevie drew her lips tight until she saw the quotation marks that formed at the corners of her mouth.

Made them disappear with a pucker.

"Okay, Stevie, maybe a little because of that. But only a little. Happy now? It's out in the open now, but don't ask me why I even should care about that. Ancient history. Leigh Wilder was gone from Neil's life long before he even saw me, right? Right. Same as he was out of my life when Richie and I—Oh, you know. Right? Wrong."

She fled the mirror, unhappy how the conversation with herself was going.

Sold herself on the idea of washing away the drive and her irritation with a languid bath and moved into the rinky-dink bathroom. It was not quite the size of her shoe closet, with an antique tub on cast iron legs standing free in the middle of the room, encircled by a plastic shower curtain with a floral motif yellowed by years of exposure, hanging on brass rings from an oval metal track on the faded, paint-chipped ceiling.

She turned on the twin faucets and adjusted the flow to an acceptable temperature, shut off the drain, and added two capfuls of the bubble bath oil recommended by Cossette, her masseuse, a blend of aromatherapy, mandarin, chamomile, aloe vera, rosewater, and vitamin E named "Overtired and Cranky."

" 'Overtired and Cranky,' just the ticket," Stevie was telling herself when the phone rang.

She dashed after it, expecting it to be Neil, calling from his room to back into an apology, maybe suggest a late lunch, or—

"Stevie?"

Not Neil.

Her smile evaporated.

"Who is this?"

"You don't recognize my voice?"

"Do you recognize the sound of a phone hanging up?"

Stevie replaced the receiver, not in the mood for games or fans or other strangers or—

The phone rang.

She snatched it up and barked, "Maybe you didn't get the message, mister, when I—"

"See if this clue works," he said, and began singing.

No hesitation: "Richie Savage!"

He laughed and said, "Is that your final answer?"

"Richie, what a real surprise. What a—Wait! How did you know I was here?"

"Where else but Sunrise City's oldest and finest hotel, 'A Window on Main Street, Where the Edge of the Desert Meets the Dawn of the Day.' Isn't that what it says in all of the brochures?"

"Where the Really Old Meets the Really Older would be more like it," she said, and they shared a laugh. "Really, Richie. How?"

"I was just talking to Neil. He let it drop, and Rick Savage was never one to miss an opportunity, especially not with a beautiful woman. How about I send my car for you and we have an early dinner, catch up on old times?"

She didn't answer him at once.

Thinking it through.

Finally, "What will your wife say?"

"What she's been saying for years: Where's my alimony check, you son of a bitch!?" An edge to his laugh.

"Oh. I'm sorry. I didn't know."

She did know, of course.

"What'd you think? You'd cornered the market on exes? I told Neil he and I, we'd get together tomorrow night to talk about Imagine That! But, my heart couldn't take that long a wait to see you, knowing you're only a half hour away. Okay, then. I send the car? Say forty-five minutes?"

Not the way it was supposed to happen.

She gave herself answer time, like she had to weigh her decision.

"Give it an hour," Stevie said.

She emptied the tub in favor of a fast shower, checked the outfits she'd brought for something suitable for meeting an old boyfriend—deciding on an Ungaro black jersey blouse over loose-fitting heather gray donegal tweed pants, a black deerskin jacket, and thick-soled black calfskin loafers—and spent the rest of the hour slaving over her hair and makeup at the dresser mirror.

On her way out of the room, she thought about knocking on

Neil's door and letting him know where she was going, but decided against it. It would only lead to another round of ugly confrontation.

Instead, when she got to the lobby she scribbled an explanatory note and had the clerk put it in Armando's room slot. It instructed him to keep an eye on Neil and not worry about her. Thanks to Mayor Savage, she would have the entire Palm Springs police force for protection.

The car was waiting for her directly outside the hotel entrance, motor purring, a neatly groomed driver in a suit, tie, and wraparound shades waiting to help her into the back seat.

She answered his salute with one of her own and said, "Why don't I ride up front with you?"

Stevie became aware of the car tailing them about the time the Lincoln Continental passed the towering neon sign that directed motorists to an off-ramp that led straight to the gambling casino on the San Gorgonio Reservation.

A cream-colored, late model Lexus.

At first she thought it must be her imagination, but the Lexus was too tenacious about staying two or three car lengths behind, shifting lanes when the Lincoln did and more than once risking a sideswipe or a rear-ender in the crowded rush hour traffic on the 10.

Richie's driver, Frank, was a black man in his mid-to-late forties with a pencil mustache and skin the color of fine ebony, who had been orating since they left the hotel about the various accomplishments of his boss.

Grinning like they were his own personal victories.

Assuring her the mayor would be making a fine United States senator one day soon.

Stevie waited for Frank to make the long throaty hum he used as a break between Richie's triumphs on behalf of Palm Springs and said, "Check it out, Frank. That Lexus over on our right. Two back. I think it's been following us the last couple of miles."

Frank's head tilted up to the rearview and held there.

A shallow grunt instead of a hum.

He decelerated, seemed to study the lanes like a long jumper girding for his next run, speeded up enough to angle into the fast lane.

The Lexus managed the same maneuver, only now was four cars behind them.

Frank crossed the double-double lines into the commuter lane, where there were fewer cars, earning lots of honks and shaking fists that grew fingers.

The Lexus followed suit, inviting its own symphony of angry hand signals, and was now directly behind them.

Frank took the Lincoln past 70 mph, then 80 mph.

The Lexus kept pace.

"No question. Following us," Frank said. "But you watch now. Only a couple minutes more."

"Meaning?"

"The freeway is my friend," he said, leaving Stevie to ponder what that meant.

"See there?" Frank said after another minute, pointing with his chin to the overhead destination sign. "Half a mile from where I want us to be."

"Right now I'd say we're in the wrong lane and blocked off from it by too much traffic," Stevie said, not sure what made her more jittery, the Lexus or Frank's driving.

He said, "Yes, but knowing a little geometry helps in a tight squeeze," and—

Cranked the wheel hard to the right and floored the gas pedal.

The Lincoln bolted across the lanes.

Brakes screamed as motorists bent helplessly to Frank's determination.

Stevie let loose a yowl as a Texaco twin-tanker hit its brakes and fish-tailed, blocking the commuter lane, and—

The Lexus stopped short of ripping into the tanker.

Whereupon, a pickup truck bashed into the back end of the Lexus, showering the lanes with its cargo of fruits and vegetables while pushing the Lexus over a lane and into the path of an oncoming minivan.

Frank charged down the exit lane and maneuvered onto a surface street that paralleled the 10, all the while howling exuberantly, "Nobody is following us now, Miss Marriner. The freeway is my friend!"

He picked up the 10 again at an entrance two miles down the one-way street, by this time back to raving about Richie Savage's results as a mayor and why that alone qualified him to be California's next senator.

Stevie watched the silent desert whiz by while waiting for her stomach to unbend and her pulse rate to return from Uranus. She studied the undulating shadow shows a retiring sun was painting onto the San Jacinto range that filled the horizon line to the south.

Let Frank know she was listening to him by making an occasional noise, nodding, or smiling, but—

In fact, her mind was working a puzzle.

Why hadn't he asked her why she thought they were being followed?

Why didn't he seem surprised or bothered at the concept of someone following the Lincoln?

Why had he seemed to make almost a game out of escaping their pursuers and laughingly indifferent to the demolition derby he'd created on the freeway?

Stevie knew Frank wasn't the one for her to ask.

Richie Savage was.

The Sunrise Hotel sits on the northwest corner of First and Delivery, the city's main intersection, and catercorner from where the *Twin Counties Sentinel* offices were until two years after I was hired away by the *Los Angeles Daily*. Real estate developers posing as visionaries, with their familiar disregard for history, tore down the old Barnaby mansion, a three-story marvel of Victorian era design that once was the heart of local society, and replaced it with a strip mall.

The car rental agency was next door.

Everything small and cheap was already spoken for, and I wound up cruising onto the freeway in a two year-old Lexus showing the wear and tear of heavy feet on the brakes, on my way to the San Gorgonio Indian Reservation.

I was going to check out the site of the Imagine That! festival, then explore the gambling casino. It beat sitting in the room and continuing to feed my foul mood.

I needed the rental because Stevie had the keys to the Jeep and I wasn't about to go knocking after them. My mood was still too foul to sue for no-fault peace, and right now I didn't need Armando's company either.

Just the thought of being alone for a few hours brought relief.

I hadn't traveled more than a mile when a black Lincoln whizzed by me and I saw Stevie in the front passenger seat.

Clear enough to know it wasn't my imagination.

I took off after her.

And shortly became the CHP's newest freeway statistic.

" 'Fess up now, Mr. Gulliver," Leigh Wilder demanded playfully. "What was a nice boy like you doing at a place like that, besides hogging the freeway lanes in his rented Lexus and failing his driving test?"

I answered her smile instead of the question and said, "More to the point, Mrs. Wilder—How did you know to come running, that it was me you'd find there?"

"Police calls, Mr. Gulliver. After leaving us for Big Time Journalism, did you forget some of the basics we Small Town Editors utilize, like keeping the newsroom tuned in to the police radio frequencies?"

"And a freeway salad of cherries, apples, lettuce, and tomatoes is still big enough news at the *Sunrise Gazette* to get someone to the scene?"

"Absolutely, trusty camera in hand, once I heard them running your name and driver's license," Leigh said. " 'Local Boy Makes Goo.' I think that'll be the kicker on the caption for my shot of you studying all those crates of demolished tomatoes. We'll run it page one in this week's shopper, so you'll also be the big story in the *Sunset Gazette*."

"The shot of the truck driver, Gary Gargantua himself, all eight hundred pounds being wrestled away from my throat by the CHP guys would be a better choice."

"Still the teacher, are you, Mr. Gulliver?"

"An old habit dies hard, Mrs. Wilder."

"Like an old flame, Mr. Gulliver?"

A hungry look in her eyes, or—

My imagination?

"Like you driving us here to this place on automatic pilot, Mrs. Wilder?"

She tickled out a wry laugh from the side of her mouth and wondered, "Who said people who forget their history are bound to repeat it?"

"Your father, I think."

More rippling laughter, like notes on a musical scale.

"Father knew best," she said.

She raised her wineglass and toasted, "To Daddy, and to old friendships, Mr. Gulliver. Ever young. Ever bright. Never out of style."

Her eyes handcuffed mine with a forlorn look that said she meant it as more than a toast.

We were at the Chez Europa, Sunrise City's most popular restaurant for years before I joined Charlie Stemple in the Sentinel bureau; still so twenty years later, judging by the Happy Hour crowd already spilling over from the bar into the lavishly appointed dining hall that looked like it had been lifted from one of provincial France's more elegant chateaus and brought over intact to this restored ranch house on the easternmost outskirts of Sunrise, about a hundred yards shy of the city limits sign.

Without waiting to be seated, on a shared glance and a nod of agreement, we'd headed straight for our old mahogany-lined booth and the privacy its thick partitions guaranteed. The wood glistened under a thickly applied coat of forest-scented polish. The soft cushion seats had a crisp freshness and an old familiarity to them as we settled as always next to one another against the back wall and mated our thighs, but—

Only for an instant.

I flinched and felt sweat rising on my forehead and the back of my neck as I slid away from Leigh with some excuse about wanting to sit where I could better see and enjoy how well the years had treated her, how she was more beautiful than ever.

She let me see she didn't believe me for a moment, but otherwise accepted the shift without comment.

There had been electricity in her thigh.

The connection felt good—an unexpected sexual charge—but not right.

Not here.

Not now.

It was here in this booth that I proposed to Leigh and, two years later, where I broke off our engagement with the rueful truth that was as hard for me to speak as for Leigh to hear:

"Yes, Leigh-Leigh, there is someone else."

The expression in her eyes that day, as she slipped off her finger the diamond engagement ring I'd bought at Lawton Fine Jewelers for a discounted two hundred dollars, dropped it in my wineglass, and fled, went from girlish adoration and a "That's nothing to joke about" comment to disbelief to denial to recognition of the truth in what I was saying; to an ocean of tears; to throwing up on her medium-rare prime rib; to contained rage in the final words she threw at me:

"I. Have. To. Go. Now."

She escaped before I could explain to her about Stevie Marriner, the "someone else" I'd met a week earlier. Stevie, who did
not know she was a "someone else" or that she and not Leigh Maxwell—the woman who happened to be my fiancée—was about to
become Mrs. Neil Gulliver.

Leigh Maxwell.

That was her name when I met her, this scrawny little kid
playing reporter at the local paper owned by her father, Ben, a
gregarious refugee from Hitler's Europe whose *Sunrise Gazette* and
Sunset Gazette were published three times a week and were competition to the *Sentinel* mainly in Ben's mind.

Ben never liked Charlie Stemple; he was on record with that
from the day we met, never sharing the reason with me, but I
suspect it was because of Charlie's habit of insulting Ben Maxwell
and his journalistic ethics every chance he got, usually to the
delight of whatever Charlie's audience was at the time.

Ben was not a popular figure in Sunrise.

He was generally arrogant, dogmatic in his demands of adver-
tisers, especially those who spent less with him than he believed
proper, and city officials, whom he instructed constantly in the
merits of giving the "local" newspaper a story before giving it to
anyone else, meaning, of course, the *Twin Counties Sentinel*, and
barely tolerant of anyone whose intellect didn't meet his arbitrarily
high standards, meaning just about everyone.

Ben didn't flaunt his IQ, but never let you forget you could
see the top of Mount Everest from it.

For whatever reason, Ben Maxwell took an instant liking to me,
maybe because I was not intimidated by him the way he thought
an eighteen-year-old kid—or anybody—should be.

It didn't happen at once, only after I had beaten him on stories
Ben didn't know were there to be reported—

Until he read them in the *Sentinel* under my byline.

Nothing particularly big or significant, but steady.

Like a city council decision to pave a remote road on the Sunrise "Bench," a fertile agricultural area above the city abounding in
apricot, peach, plum, pear, prune, cherry, and almond orchards that
kept the farmers here after hordes of disappointed gold miners and
the work crews building the Southern Pacific Railroad and the Col-
orado River–Los Angeles Aqueduct moved on.

After the first ten or twelve times it happened, Ben tried hiring
me away.

"College can wait a lot longer," he decided for me. "I can give you the same kind of education with a desk next to mine. The Ben Maxwell College of Practical Knowledge. Don't get any better than that."

When I thanked him and declined, he decided, "Because of that no-goodnick Stemple, that's why? You think you can be better off at his doorstep?"

"No way, Mr. Maxwell."

"Okay, so we got that out of the way. The right answer there, at least. Well, you come to dinner at my house next week and we'll review again. You're never going to change your mind on an empty belly."

For the rest of my time in Sunrise, the weekly dinners at Ben and Sadie Maxwell's became ritual, and—

That's where I first met Leigh.

"Not a kosher name, Leigh," Sadie Maxwell confessed the night we were introduced. "Leah, really. Supposedly after my great-aunt, who died in the camps, but also for Vivien Leigh the movie actress. You seen *Gone with the Wind*? I loved that movie. I seen it a dozen times already, and not enough."

As if on cue, Leigh raised the back of a hand to her forehead and pitched in with an overdramatic, "I'll think about it tomorrow."

She was sixteen then, in 1980, two years younger than me. The same age Stevie was five years later, when I saw her for the first time and fell magically in love with her.

Anyone who's ever opened a fan magazine or watched the Emmys and the Golden Globes knows Stevie is how Hepburn was described by Tracy in *Woman of the Year*: "Cherce." I'd been struck by what the French call a *coup de foudre*, a bolt of lightning.

This is no reflection on Leigh.

Leigh was wondrous in her own way.

A lean and lanky stunner with a mind as sharp and agile as her father's. A baby-faced shrimp who shot up to an inch shy of six feet, matching me eye to eye, in the year before we got officially engaged. The classic middle-European face, heavily lidded hazel eyes complemented by raven tresses and sensuous Angelina Jolie lips that begged to be kissed.

Leigh was spectacular in the sack. Eager to learn and not the least shy about experimenting, like it was part of her commitment to Woman's Lib, sexual equality, whatever it was called in her current crusade, an educational wanderlust that had Ben Maxwell's full endorsement from the time Leigh was old enough to start hanging around the *Sunrise Gazette* office and learning the business.

She was an only child, and there was no question about the two *Gazettes* being hers to inherit, own, and run one day. The day came about two years after I broke our engagement, when Ben suffered a fatal heart attack during a heated city council meeting.

He'd been orating in his fractured English cadence at the visitor's mike, delineating mistakes and blunders made by council members since the last meeting, one mistake after the next, tackling one member at a time, his tightly clenched fist hammering the air on almost every word.

Funny thing about Ben's accent?

It was a put-on.

I asked him about it after I got to know him well.

"Why you should wonder?" Ben wondered.

"Because your news stories are so clean and spare and always composed in pitch-perfect English. Or is it that you don't write all the stories, the way you say, and you have a gremlin in the back shop writing them for you?"

Ben raised his arms in surrender.

"*Boychick*, I'll tell you. It's already bad enough being a Jew in a town like Sunrise—any small town—where everyone is a bigot, only he don't necessarily know it. So, how much hurt does it do making them happy by showing them, yeah, the *shtarker* might run an okay newspaper, but you ever hear him talk? That makes them better than me, and they don't mind so much having to give advertising dollars to that damn Jew. I take the money and laugh all the way to the synagogue."

Looking back, I'd say it was my affection for Sadie and Ben Maxwell that drew me too close too often to Leigh.

I included her in the family package and our engagement sprang from that, along with subtle encouragement from Ben.

I was still young enough to confuse "love" with "being in love."

Certainly, so was Leigh.

Maybe Ben thought he could get me onto his staff this way, endow Leigh with a personal life as easily as he was giving her the business.

Or, is this a cop-out fifteen years later?

Neil Gulliver still harboring a sense of guilt over any pain he'd inflicted on Leigh?

I didn't see her again until I came back to Sunrise for Ben's sparsely attended funeral.

If Ben held any resentment over my jilting his beloved daughter, he'd never shown it. He had stayed my friend. We communicated through the occasional letter, sometimes by a phone call, after I left for LA and the *Daily*.

Ben always asking, "How goes, *boychick*? Remember I got a warm desk waiting for you at the *Gazette*, you ever want."

Never mentioning her.

Leigh spent the entire service ignoring me, but seemed to make a show of the man standing beside her, who could not have been more attentive to a grieving daughter. I was glad he was there. Leigh clearly needed support.

He was a head taller than Leigh, big-boned, husky, and handsome in a Jack Armstrong, All-American Man, sort of way. Early-to-mid forties. Ears that stuck out like Clark Gable's did. Even a Gable mustache. Deeply set eyes that roamed the chapel and the gravesite like a lighthouse beacon when they weren't set on Leigh.

I didn't know who he was at the time, and it didn't really matter until Martin Halliwell pulled out photos of the guy during our last briefing session and said he was Leigh's late husband, Michael Wilder, a key player in the criminal fraud I'd be helping the feds expose, and—

The reason I would soon be lying to Leigh.

12

Frank traded the 10 for the 111, the old narrow stretch of state highway that fed into Palm Springs' main drag, Palm Canyon Drive, explaining to Stevie, "Traffic won't be so bad now, or the winds either. Sometimes it gets so bad here that every loose pebble, stone, and rock comes flying in your face before you know it and gets your windshield more pits than a cherry orchard. The rest of the car, fenders, and doors, they can fare as bad or a whole lot worse you pick the wrong day, like you've been through a war."

The sun was behind them now, and he lifted his visor, then reached across and turned up hers. Cranked up the air another notch and remarked about the dancing ribbons of dry heat rising from a parched desert floor not yet through baking from temperatures that had swelled past a hundred and five by mid-morning.

Frank said, "Like I told you about the freeways, Miss Marriner? The winds are also my friend."

Spoken almost confidentially, but also like he wanted to share a treasured family recipe with her.

"How's that, Frank?" Stevie said, happy to have Frank talking about something besides what a great senator Richie would make when he was elected, *when* not *if*, as if Frank had already counted the ballots in a race a good two years off.

And that assumed Richie would be able to first wangle his party's nomination.

Frank began humming, worked his jaw like he was trying to crack a piece of hard candy. Stevie sensed he was having second thoughts about taking the subject further, until—

"No harm," Frank said, as if reassuring himself. "Like this, Miss Marriner. People what can afford pretty toys like to keep them looking pretty. And, because they got loads of the old moola and no interest in parting with more than they got to, they're always on the lookout for a bargain. Where I come in, especially if it's cash flow crunch time and my own lettuce patch can use some replanting, which is most of the time.

"I got well-heeled friends of mine from the years when I was working Vegas and they have friends, and there are the okay types I get to know through being around Richie . . . Mayor Savage. The word is out there in a lot of the right quarters about this little sideline I got going for me.

"So, I happen to hear about a beautiful specimen of a Rolls-Royce or a Bentley, a drop-dead gorgeous Mercedes or BMW, a high-end trophy like that with a ding or two on the hood, a fender maybe got keyed, but they don't want to pay retail for fixing? Maybe, a car that's seen better days and needs a face-lift. Understand?" He winked and gave it sound bite. "So, on a day where I've checked with the weatherman, I take their fine vehicle for a little spin on the old 111. Not my fault up comes nasty winds what play the devil with their windshield, the body, make a real mess.

"Next thing you know, that fine vehicle in an auto body shop getting itself fixed up as good as new, the wind damage and anything there before, usually a fresh paint job, that's desirable, all paid for by the insurance company carrying the policy, except for the deductible, and what's that? A hundred dollars? Two? Birdseed compared with what the owner might of needed to shell out all by his lonesome making the car good as new on his American Express Platinum-Plus card. And—" Another wink "—he's got no reason to be mad at me for accidentally driving into a wind tunnel, considering he gets back a car that looks better than brand new."

"And out of gratitude he pays you—"

"Not one red cent."

Frank's head veered left and right.

"Oh, every once in a while someone might slip me a C-note, just to Big Man it, but I like it better having them think I'm doing them a favor, because down the line I might have to call on them for one. Odds are that the favors pay off higher, you know?"

Stevie was confused.

"Favors I understand, Frank, but did I miss hearing the part where your little sideline helps you with the cash flow problem you mentioned?"

He tapped the side of his head with a forefinger.

"Where I make my bread, Miss Marriner, is at the body and fender shops."

"You have a deal with them. A finder's fee?"

His head twitching left and right again.

Subdued laughter.

"Smarter than that, Miss Marriner. I own them, the body and fender shops that bid on the jobs. I make sure estimates are in line and there's never a reason for my competition or the insurance company to complain."

"If somebody did complain?"

"Hasn't happened so far, but if it did I'd either have to straighten out the party or, that didn't do it, call in a favor, you know what I mean?"

Stevie wondered to herself if Frank had meant to make his reply sound as ominous as she'd heard it.

"Does Mayor Savage know about your little sideline?"

"Not in a million, Miss Marriner, and I'm counting on you not to blow the whistle with him. Anyone."

"Why even tell me in the first place?"

"Because it does the ego good to brag once in a while, and because you asked." His head bobbed up and down. "I read you as someone I could trust to keep my little secret, so no big deal."

"And if I don't?"

He said grimly, "I suppose I'd have to use up another favor."

An involuntary shudder passed through Stevie's body.

It didn't go unnoticed by Frank, who began to laugh.

"Kidding, just kidding," he said. He let the laugh play out, then told her, "Listen, I can read people the way some people read a book. You been reading better than okay in my book from the time you waltzed out of your hotel."

"Because I'm an old friend of Richie Savage?"

"Because you asked to sit up front with me. You didn't have to do that. Stars I've met or know, VIPs and big shots, they never ask, like it's some kind of downgrade or demerit to be anywhere but in the back. Whatever else you might be, you're real people, Miss Marriner. An up-front person. That's how I knew it was okay to tell you. Right?"

What was she supposed to say? She preferred it up front because the air conditioning was always better there, in her experience in any make car except a stretch. She didn't have to put Frank down by confessing as much. Besides, she knew a lot of people who would sooner die than be caught sitting up front with the hired help; status snobs she had no tolerance for.

Stevie said, "I like you, too, Frank."

The truth.

He had startled her with that business about a favor, but she was a good enough judge of character to be certain there was a pussy cat living inside the panther.

Frank beamed at her, showing off two rows of perfectly formed snow white teeth. "Your car, you ever need, you let me know," he said, at the same time making a soft left off Palm Canyon Drive onto Indian Canyon Drive.

Stevie had visited Palm Springs often enough over the years to know they were heading for what the locals called the "Movie Colony" neighborhood, where the homes were like slices of Beverly Hills, homes away from home, built in the twenties and thirties and after the second world war, when the Springs was the weekend retreat of choice for stars who preferred the desert to a Malibu beach getaway.

"Shame we got slowed down," Frank said. "More time and we could have done a little tour, hit a few highlights. You ever see Francis Albert's grave? No? Put it on your list for sometime. Cemetery's over on Ramon Road. A simple gravestone with his name and the dates. Calls him a beloved husband and father, which he was, you know? Then, from one of his songs, it says, 'The best is yet to come.' " Frank began humming the melody, de-dum-dum-dumming the lyrics. "Inspirational, don't you think so? Only one chairman, one Sinatra.

"Was a time he lived up around here, from '47 to '57. Including the Ava years. Not far. Was 1148 Alejo Road. He called the place Twin Palms. They rent it out a lot of the time, but not to live. For fashion shoots, photo layouts. A pool shaped like a grand piano. You hear of Dinah Shore? She was one of his neighbors. Singer. Big time. Even had her own TV talk show. Burt Reynolds her boyfriend while he still had his own hair."

Frank eased up on the gas pedal.

"Coming up on it now, Miss Marriner. The Palm Springs Yacht and Polo Club. Meeting the mayor couldn't get out of or he would have gone and gotten you himself. Said for you to go right in while I'm parking."

Stevie wasn't dumb enough to deny it.

Certainly not to herself.

The old vibe was there again—

From the moment Richie spotted her and sprang up from his table in the center of the recessed dining room, raced forward with the speed and super-charged energy of a scared gazelle, took the carpeted steps two at a time, and scooped her into his arms.

Even before Richie kissed her hard, then softer as his tongue found hers, stayed on her lips a million years before he pulled back with a breathless sigh and, trapping her with a wicked smile, wondered, "Ever kiss a mayor before?"

She pretended to think about it.

"Before what?" she said, batting her eyes at him.

"Still so sassy cute," he said, and kissed the tip of her nose. "Come on, Blondie, I want you to meet someone."

Richie gripped Stevie by an elbow and led her down the steps. Except for the man sitting at his table over a glass of milk and the remains of a toasted bagel, the dining room was empty.

As if reading her thoughts, Richie said, "Place isn't open for another hour. Except for weekends, dinner service only this time of year, so I use it for my private meetings that are really private."

"Fifteen years ago, that would have been your bedroom."

"Yeah," he agreed. "Ain't aging hell?"

"Prettier in person," Richie's company said. He was on his feet, pressing his fingers on the table to hold himself erect. He was mid-to-late seventies, a trim body that seemed to be a size too small for a blue silk pinstripe too elegant to have come off the rack; a tiny fresh red rose growing out the lapel; a multihued silk tie over a subdued yellow silk shirt, the collar sitting below an Adam's apple the size of a plum that rose and fell when he spoke, his voice as sweet and reassuring as a mother's embrace; not tall, five-five or five-six; outsized hands a six-footer would envy, decorated in a random pattern of blue veins and liver spots. "Come and sit here next to me, the one on the left, where my hearing's better."

He was used to giving orders.

She heard it in his tone, saw the warning inside a warm smile that probably fooled most people.

A man to be careful around.

She took the seat he'd indicated while Richie slipped into the one on his other side and wondered, "Coffee? Still plenty in the pot there."

"No, thank you."

"Good for you," the man said. "Corrodes your insides. I learned that when I was a kid growing up, and why I stayed a milk man all my life right till now." He picked up the milk glass. *"L'chaim,"* he said, and finished what was left of his milk. "Why I'll live to be a hundred years old, which, of course, isn't saying very much anymore."

"The shape you're in, you'd make it to a hundred even if all you drank was your regular glass of wine with dinner, Mr. L."

"Wine is good for the blood flow. Coffee? It's good for nothing, except to rot your guts out, while all the caffeine turns you into a jumping bean. I sometimes tell some friends of mine from Colombia, 'Coffee and cocaine, don't you people down there have anything healthy you could ever export?' "

He laughed at his joke.

Richie laughed to keep him company, then told Stevie, "Mr. L, when he heard you were meeting me for dinner—"

As far as he got before Mr. L banged a fist on the table. His eyes disappeared inside his forehead and his cheeks.

"I can tell her myself, Richie. I need a mouthpiece, I got a lawyer already I spend enough on year in and year out on business, even if he wasn't my sister Bertha's husband."

Richie laughed like that also was a joke, but she saw he knew better. Knew he had been put down, put in his place, and she wondered how he would have reacted with anyone else who showed off in front of her, exactly what this Mr. L had done. Let her see who mattered most here, the mayor of Palm Springs or him.

She knew who her money was riding on.

Especially if Mr. L was who she thought he was.

If he was Aaron Lodger, "Aaron the Baron," Stevie would have to be on her toes every minute, extremely careful about everything she said and how she said it.

"Lodger's nobody's fool," Marty Halliwell had cautioned Neil and her during the briefings. "Don't go looking for him and bring down trouble on yourself. Stay with the plan. Find out what the department has to know through Leigh Wilder and Richie Savage. Aaron Lodger? Too dangerous for you."

Dangerous?

This shrinking old man?

Innocently, "Richie, you haven't really introduced us yet . . ." Extending her hand. "Do you have a real name, Mr. L? It has to be more than Mr. L."

He kept his hands clasped on the table and considered the question for a moment.

"Not to any of my friends," he said, adding pleasantly and irrevocably, "Be my friend, Stephanie Marriner—and I'll be yours."

"But you know my name."

"Yes."

His eyes drifted to the top of the staircase.

Frank was there, arms folded across his chest, watchful inside his Ray-Bans.

He smiled and returned Mr. L's wave.

Stevie said, "Do I at least get to know what kind of business your brother-in-law takes care of for you?"

Like a little girl negotiating for a cookie.

He studied her face. "Are you always this nosey?"

"Only with friends."

Her answer put a trace of legitimacy into his smile.

"My business? A little bit of this, a little bit of that."

"You're Tevye in *Fiddler on the Roof*?"

Mr. L couldn't contain his laughter. He gave Stevie a thumbs up, then reached over and devoured her hands in his. "A good one. You have a marvelous sense of humor . . . I knew I was going to like you. When Richie said you were coming for dinner, I said I got to stay and wait. She and I have things to talk about."

"We do?"

Trying not to show her concern.

He raised his hand like he was taking an oath.

"Your show. My favorite. *Bedrooms and Board Rooms*. Like a religion to me. Hooked. Haven't missed an hour in years. I go away sometimes, it's all on cassettes waiting for me when I get back."

Stevie sneaked out a sigh of relief.

"All because of you, young lady."

"Thank you."

"And don't think I haven't been missing you lately."

"Just a little hiatus. Some time away."

"That Dean business I heard something about?"

"Part of it."

"Problems with the show and you? Something else I heard about."

"Nothing that can't be worked out," she said, sounding optimistic for his benefit. The negotiations were a private matter, nothing she was inclined to share. No useful purpose served by telling him how badly she thought they were going.

Mr. L locked onto her, looking for something beyond her answer, elbow propped on the table, his forefinger and thumb rubbing the nub of his aquiline nose, running back and forth across the raised scar, thick, pink, more than an inch long, that sat like a mustache above his almost nonexistent upper lip.

She read the doubt on his face.

"Okay, then," he said. "You can think about letting me know, if the problems get any bigger, and maybe I can help. I know people. Just ask Richie here. Richie?"

Richie nodded agreement.

"Let her hear the words, Mayor Savage."

Emphasizing the word *mayor* to make some point.

"Mr. L knows people."

"And the people I know know people, so there's never a problem too big that I wouldn't want to try and do something for a friend. You try and remember and, you need me, Richie knows how to get ahold of me. Day or night. Right, Richie? I said, 'Right, Richie?' "

"Right, Mr. L."

Stevie said, "Thank you."

Mr. L lowered his head and leaned toward her. "Now, I got two things I want from you."

There it was. She should have known. Mr. L wasn't one to ask for favors. Instead, he offered them, then collected his payback in advance.

"One, an autographed photo. For my den back home, to go with other people I admire who I've met. Got a spot all picked out between Tommy Lasorda and Bill Clinton. Place of honor."

"Thank you. I'll take care of it the minute I get back to LA."

"You won't have to trouble. I already got the picture I like and I'll give it to Frank when he drops me off home, to bring back here to you for signing. Richie, it's still okay for Frank to drop me off, right?"

"Of course."

He veered toward Richie and patted him on the cheek.

"That's my boy. What a mayor. Nothing he won't do to make a voter happy."

"Not a voter, a friend, Mr. L."

"We'll compromise. A friend who votes."

He laughed at his joke, nodded approvingly when Richie joined in, and turning back to Stevie, Mr. L said, "Now, the other thing I want—an answer to something I been dying to ask you I ever got the chance . . . When you were acting those twins, the good one and the evil one?"

"Candy and Dandy Lyons."

"Those ones. Which one was it that really died in the avalanche? Me and some others I know, we argue over it all the time."

By the time Frank got back from dropping off Mr. L, the Yacht and Polo Club had picked up about a dozen tables worth of early bird diners, a mix of casually dressed middle-aged men with younger women and middle-aged women in outfits too young for them, as were the lifeguard types in khaki shorts and open Hawaiian shirts most seemed to favor. A lot of gold neck chains and earrings. More tattoos than wedding rings. A conversational hum drowned out by the air-conditioning and a sound system playing hits from the seventies and eighties at eardrum-splitting levels.

Stevie and Richie had finished their meals, a steak for him, New York cut, served with a mound of shoestrings and a side of fresh melon chunks, a shrimp and tuna salad for her, oil and vinegar dressing on the side, and moved to the bar, where he ordered a bottle of Dom and, while it was chilling, a fresh carafe of the Napa sauvignon blanc they had had with dinner.

The area was decorated in an ersatz nautical theme, a lot of sailing canvas, sea lanterns, and miniature steering wheels to go with giant photo wall murals of rock-and-roll stars dressed to raise anchor. Bowie, Mick, and Elton. Tommy Boyce. Harry Nilsson pretending to be Popeye the Sailor. El Zeno. The Eagles. Jimmy Buffett. Faces she could no longer give names, rockers who either fell off the horizon line or were sailing the nostalgia circuit, performing old hits for aging audiences with a fondness for yesterday.

"No, Nick Cravat, not David Lee Roth," Richie corrected her about the Gilbert and Sullivan admiral astride a stuffed horse, wielding a polo mallet in one hand and a Fender bass in the other. "I think he's doing the chitlin' circuit as a solo act nowadays. Don't know whatever happened to the other Tie Breakers, except of course Pat Vollare the drummer. OD'd on stage in the middle of his drum solo back in '85, a month or so after they did the last Imagine That! festival. If you gotta go, that's the way, I suppose. Give the fans something to remember you by."

"I remember Pat from Imagine That!, and how he got the crowd roaring 'Patty Whack! Patty Whack!' every time he hit the drum kit. I was sitting on top of someone's shoulders, but already higher than that, and I yanked off my halter and started twirling it like a lasso over my head."

"Catch anyone?"

"You already know the answer to that one. Got caught."

"Neil Gulliver."

"Best thing that ever happened to me up to then. If he hadn't come along when he did . . ." Stevie let the rest of the thought drift. "But that one is you," she said, indicating the photo mural hanging on the other side of the oval bar.

"Yeah. The Zapata mustache, ponytail and all. Twenty years younger and twenty pounds lighter. Okay. Twenty-five pounds. Just coming off my fourth Number One, selling out all the stadiums, and Clive had ripped up my old deal for a better one. It was around that time some of us who made the Springs our private playground got together and bought this old supper club, turned it into the Yacht and Polo Club. We were going for the same kind of exclusivity the olden times movie stars like Ralph Bellamy and Charlie Farrell, the guy from *My Little Margie*, got when they built the Racquet Club up the street. The difference being, of course, they really were in it for the tennis. Yacht and Polo Club, our little joke. Like thumbing our noses at them. Show me a yacht in the middle of the desert. Polo? Think it was Rod who really got pissed when he finally came around and found out there was no polo field. He had actually packed his playing gear, and one of his people was supposed to drive up Rod's horse early the next morning."

"How come you never brought me here?"

"Club rule. The playground had to stay a playground. No birds allowed anyone was serious about. They got in the way of all the easy pickings all over town, the tight body, taut titty secretaries who crowded around all the hotel and motel pools every weekend from Los Angeles. During the week it was mostly groupies from the road, good enough in bed to merit a guest card. And the garbage press never picked up on it. We never had a single paparazzi haunting the entrance while it lasted."

"While it lasted?"

"After a few years, like any game, it stopped being fun and we sold the place to some restaurant people. Some of us got too old for the sport. Some of us had found better ways to invest our money. Some of us . . . Some of us had run out of money and needed the bucks."

"You?"

Richie picked up his wineglass and rolled it between his palms.

Finished what was left and helped himself to a refill from the carafe.

"Me, Blondie? I'd been on top of the world so long, I'd forgotten that what has a beginning also has an end. No idea I'd be over before the decade was. History, except for Vegas and the kinds of venues that have a one beer minimum. I had a habit that was costing me into five figures a week. I was separated from a wife whose own habit put mine to shame, had a boy toy with muscles for brains, and a death wish for me bigger than anything Charles Bronson ever imagined. And, I was being drained, it turns out, by a personal manager and a business manager who I'd trusted and gave power of attorney when the three of us started out together."

"When we were going together? You never said a word."

"It's nothing you run around bragging about, especially not to someone you've fallen in love with."

Stevie covered his mouth with her hand.

"Don't say that, Richie."

He peeled off her fingers.

"It's the truth, Blondie. I fell in love with you, and I think you had real feelings for me. It'd only been a year since you divorced Neil and I sensed you were still not over him, so I didn't rush it. I was clear-headed enough for that, but there were a lot of nights I didn't sleep, thinking, 'I won't let myself drag her down with me.' It almost came as a relief when *People* broke the story and we busted up."

"You should have told me. I would have understood. We could have—"

Richie wagged his hand for her to stop.

"We couldn't have. Your career was on the upswing and I wasn't going to get in the way of that. I had already hung onto you too long. A little longer and the garbage press would have been tarring you with the same brush they were already using on me. I couldn't handle that. Why I quit you clean for all of these years.

"It wasn't so easy after I called Neil about getting involved with another Imagine That! festival. Put you back in my mind strong and solid. Then, today, to find out you were with Neil . . . Too much and too close. I had to see you, Blondie. Had to. In my mind I was already imagining dinner and what might happen with us after dinner . . ."

Richie averted her stare. Searched the room like he was seeking other ghosts from his past. Settled on a photo mural of Jim Dandy, the lead singer of Black Oak Arkansas, riding Silver's twin; naked except for his polo helmet and mallet.

Stevie stayed focused on Richie, found herself unable to turn off the vibes that hadn't quit since she got here, not sure why. She fiddled with the collar of her blouse and ran a hand through her hair, nervously fluffing and pushing strands into place. Of course she was sure why.

His looks.

That was part of it.

A six-foot frame thicker than in '93, but not out of control. As attractive and commanding in a sports coat and tie as he'd been in the mismatched outfits that passed for style when he was one of the ruling kings of rock-and-roll.

A rugged face, browned beyond tan by the desert sun, that still pulled you in by its sheer masculinity.

The same luxurious brown hair, only styled executive tight and gone silver and gray at the temples.

Wide-set brown eyes hiding under lids that drooped as sensuously as those she'd always adored on Robert Mitchum.

A dangerous mouth that curved sensuously at the corners and seemed to say to every girl looking, "I dare you."

More than his granite good looks, though.

Also, the traits she needed in all of her men.

Kindness and understanding.

Wit and intelligence.

Passion and intensity.

Appreciation for what she brought to a relationship.

But there were things about Richie that were new and not to her liking.

Maybe not so new?

Maybe just that she had never seen them before.

Richie turned back to Stevie, although his eyes avoided hers. He picked up a cocktail napkin and began playing with it one-handed, rolling it into a ball.

"Some band, Black Oak," he said. "I opened for them at one point, when I was starting out. A major tour. Getting it was the only way we'd agree to sign with Premiere and Frank Barselona, their agency. Later, when I was the one up there and they were scrambling for dates, when Butch Stone, their manager, called, I didn't hesitate about returning the favor although I had moved to the Morris office by then. I knew I owed them.

"Ganja was that band's god. Big time. They stoked up right before going on, turned the dressing room into a fire hazard. To this day I don't know how they managed to make it to the stage, much less through a show. I ever tell you the time my hotel room was next to Jim Dandy's and—"

"Richie, I want to say something."

"Jim had brought home this groupie after the concert—"

"Richie, listen to me, please."

He winced, like someone expecting to feel a vaccination needle.

"I know, I spoke out of turn before. Should of kept it to myself. Intended to. Finally, couldn't . . . Listen, Blondie, I'm real sorry. I apologize. I'll have Frank get you back to Sunrise. Okay? Give me a few minutes to sign the tab and—"

She pushed out a palm at him.

"Richie, your Mr. L treated you like shit in front of me and you let him get away with it. A side of you I never saw before."

He seemed relieved.

"I thought you were getting ready to tell me to fuck off."

"That can wait. For now, tell me about you and Mr. L."

She had finally managed to lock onto his eyes.

Refused to let go.

"It makes a difference?"

"Big."

After an eternity of silence, Richie took a deep breath and said, "Where would you like me to begin?"

13

When Leigh and I left the Chez Europa, the heap of rags slumped forward and sitting cross-legged on the steps at the base of the portico entrance rose up, directed an upturned palm at me, and demanded money in a harsh, husky, and barely intelligible voice.

It was dark, the quarter moon making tricks in and out of shifting clouds, and the beggar's face was hidden in half shadows, but I knew at once it was Bobby San Gorgonio inside the rags.

Not by just the voice.

Even the smell was familiar, a mixture of caked dirt, sweat, and cheap hooch that stained my nostrils for hours in the old days, working the Sunrise City bureau, after Bobby floated in on a whiskey haze and haunted me until I dug into a pocket for a couple dollar bills and sponsored him to his first shots of the morning.

Instead of a thank-you, he'd spear me with a scornful look and shuffle up First Street to the Wyatt Earp Bar and Grill, down one or two with Charlie Stemple and other early birds getting their hearts started, then head to Germain's Liquor Store for a bottle of Gallo Hearty Burgundy.

Everybody knew Bobby, but his fame didn't rest solely on being the town drunk. (On a strictly territorial basis, he was the San Gorgonio Reservation drunk, not Sunrise's.)

Bobby was the town firebug.

Every summer, when the brush could be counted on to be dry and crisp as corn flakes, a rampant fire exploded on the San Gorgonio range.

A four- or five-alarm blaze, depending on where and how fast it was spotted, how high up the receptive slopes, how accessible to county fire crews navigating the tricky dirt reservation terrain and fat-bellied planes unloading their cargoes of flame-eating chemicals.

Bobby's doing.

Although, except for proximity—Bobby somewhere near the determined point of origin, usually asleep in a fetal position inside a ragged circle of empty wine bottles—no way of proving he was the guilty party.

At best, Bobby was a circumstantial arsonist.

The reason he usually served short time, sentenced for vagrancy or drunk and disorderly after explaining to the judge in words that crossed English with some unintelligible dialect how the mountain fire resulted from a tribal curse dating back more than a hundred and fifty years.

Bobby wasn't an easy man to understand drunk or sober.

He decided on two hundred and four years the one time I was able to wangle some of the story out of him, something Charlie was never able to do.

"Because I give him money to buy booze and you don't," I answered Charlie's complaint the day the story ran on the front page of a *Sentinel* Sunday edition, not just our zone section.

"Christ's sake! Noxious enough I find it in my heart to drink with that dirty damn nigger Indian, I am sure as hell not going to pay for the privilege," Charlie grumbled before heading off to Wyatt Earp's for a wet lunch.

The story Bobby told me dealt with a supreme being he called Pakrakitat.

It was through Pakrakitat's doing that the human race came to exist. He also created the ancestors of the San Gorgonios from demigods and had a white eagle guide them to the land that became their sacred home.

A series of wars took the tribal members one by one, until the only one left was a mighty warrior named Serrano. He sought out and married two sisters from a tribe on the far side of the San Jacintos and from their loins spawned what became the San Gorgonios as they exist today.

In 1876, when Pakrakitat was overseeing Custer's defeat at the Little Big Horn, Henry Pabro was named leader of the San Gorgonios and entitled to be called "captain." Captain Pabro, a direct descendant of Serrano, spread the news about Custer with unbridled joy, earning the wrath of the cavalry unit assigned to "protect" his reservation, although against whom was never quite explained.

A gang of army blues marched him off one night and hanged him, also without explanation, from a willow tree. Left him dancing in the overnight winds for the vultures and crows to feast and bedded down at the base of the willow, in case any tribal members thought to come after him.

Or them.

Next morning, when it was time to cut Captain Pabro down they found the hanging rope still dangled from the heavy limb high overhead, its fat knot as secure as ever, only the noose was missing something vital to its purpose, Captain Pabro's sturdy neck.

Captain Pabro was gone.

Disappeared.

Somehow, right out from under the troops.

Bobby San Gorgonio lowered his voice reverently and told me, "Pakrakitat himself he came for the captain and to this day Captain Pabro sits to the right of Pakrakitat on a throne of gold in the kingdom of the sky."

"And the mountain fires, Mr. San Gorgonio?"

"Pakrakitat. Telling the white man to do right by all the San Gorgonios or suffer the consequences. If not, one day braves led by Serrano and Captain Pabro will bring the fires of hell down from the mountains to scorch the earth beyond fixing."

"Who told you that, sir?

"Some things you don't got to be told. You hear it in your heart and you know it's the truth."

"Mr. San Gorgonio, do you know when that will be, when the fires of hell might be on their way?"

"I am a simple man. I only know to watch for a white eagle. A white eagle will carry the message."

Charlie Stemple snorted and said, "A simple man! Simply a goddamn falling down, face-in-the-dirt drunk is what Bobby is and meant to tell you. Sonny boy, the only eagles you are going to see anywhere around here are on golf courses. Lots of birdies, too, and you shouldn't need one of them to tell you you bought yourself some nigger arsonist's bullshit on a shingle."

Hardly a week went by that Charlie didn't find some way to mention the story, curse Bobby, and make fun of me, but I think deep down it all had to do with me making page one on a story that got by him. Augie Fowler was the same way and, I suppose, so was I, sometimes, before I was promoted to the column, where everything I wrote, one way or another, was an exclusive of my mind.

Leigh, who had learned about Bobby San Gorgonio and the legend years ago, stepped back and waited patiently while I fished out a fiver and handed it over, inquiring, "Remember me, Bobby? Neil Gulliver? Neil Gulliver from the newspaper?"

Bobby twisted his body around to catch some light while he brought the bill to about a half inch from what was left of his nose and verified the denomination.

"You got old . . . Been a long time. You can't do better?"

I pulled another five and gave it to him.

He didn't bother checking it out, just shoved it in a pocket with the other one.

"Better." He yawned a smile, showing a black hole for teeth. "You ain't been around. New people coming and going all the time. Never one friendly like you."

"Don't you remember when I said good-bye to you, Bobby? Told you I was leaving the *Sentinel* to work for a newspaper in Los Angeles?"

Bobby gave me a desperate look, like a contestant who's run out of options on *Who Wants to be a Millionaire*.

Not sure how to answer.

So he didn't.

I said, "Every year, when I read about the fire in the mountain and see the pictures on television, I think of you. I think of you and hope you're well."

He pointed to the traveling sky.

"The white eagle," he said. "Time soon."

"How do you know that, Bobby?"

He shook his head, placed a hand over his heart.

"Soon," Bobby San Gorgonio said, and headed off down the street, chasing after his shadow.

I turned down Leigh's suggestion of a nightcap at her place. The sparkle in her wine-stained eyes was signaling she had more than brandy and conversation in mind for us.

Not what I had in mind.

I might be getting ready to lie to her, deceive her, hurt her, and use her, but—

Not tonight.

Or that way.

The way Martin Halliwell had programmed it for me was bad enough.

She rounded the corner and glided the Seville 2000 to a stop across from the Sunrise Hotel, put the gear in neutral, gunned the motor, and cooed, "Last chance."

"Need my Zs," I answered for the third or fourth time, unbuckling the safety belt and reaching for the door handle. "Tomorrow, I square things with the car rental agency, then we have brunch, then you drive me out to the reservation to take a look at the casino," I said, confirming plans we had made at the Chez Europa.

Earlier in the year, California's voters overwhelmingly passed Proposition 1A, a controversial measure that allowed casinos on Indian land to add Vegas-style slots, blackjack, high-stakes bingo, and off-track betting on horse races to poker and pan games.

Oklahoma crude all over again.

By the most conservative estimate, a single slot could bring a casino two thousand dollars a day, banks of them as much as fifty million dollars a year.

I had Leigh believing I was in Sunrise City to research a piece on what it would ultimately mean for the state's 107 tribes.

Forty of them already operated casinos and were talking expansion. Another fifty had plans for lavish casinos on the drawing board.

I told Leigh I was starting with the San Gorgonios for sentimental reasons, then moving on to the Cahuillas in Palm Springs and Rancho Mirage.

She bought it, allowing, "We get there, I can introduce you to the people running the casino."

"Friends of yours?"

Leigh thought through her answer. "If you mean the way any heavy advertiser is a publisher's friend, you bet."

"How do I know you won't be trying to steal the story out from under me?"

She gave me a bemused look and garnished it with light laughter. "Cookie Monster, what you want to make news in LA is already ancient history out here."

Now, studying me studying her in the Cad, Leigh said, "All right for you, spoilsport, no nightcap, but don't ask me for a rain check."

"Can I have a rain check?"

"Sure."

Shared laughter, a sound that took me back to the kids we once were.

I leaned over to kiss her cheek.

She sensed it coming and had turned her head so that I landed on her lips. Moved her hand to the back of my head to hold it in place. Forced my hand onto her breast, the nipple already long and hard, pushing through the cashmere, digging into my palm. Put her free hand on my thigh, slid it between my legs. Began groping and stroking and got the response she wanted. Started purring.

In a flash we were kids again.

Leigh and I at the Midway Drive-In.

Exercising our hormones.

Until I opened my eyes a little to steal a look at the giant silver screen over her shoulder, and—

Saw Stevie instead.

Emerging from the Lincoln parked in front of the hotel, the door being held open for her by a chauffeur type, and—

Followed out by Rick Savage.

Who says something to the chauffeur type before taking Stevie by the elbow and escorting her inside.

Leigh—

Still purring.

Panting inside my mouth.

I freed myself from her, pushed away, against the door.

Saw the disappointment on her face.

Caught my breath and closed my eyes to common sense.

Said, "That offer of a nightcap still good?"

She still lived in the house where I once had spent so much time, a one-story Craftsman bungalow with the typical shallow pitched roof and overhanging eaves; arroyo stones and brick in the foundation, patio wall and chimney giving an impression the place had simply risen out of the desert floor; about a mile north of the hotel, on Jackrabbit Lane.

The house was clean and orderly, the same way Leigh's mother, Sadie, had always kept it. A place for everything, everything in its place, except at Ben Maxwell's rolltop desk, still a classic study in organizational calamity.

Ben's desk was one of the few pieces of furniture I remembered.

Also, Ben's old easy chair.

The upright piano her mother so cherished.

The family portrait hanging above the fireplace.

Silver-framed photos stretched across the mantle.

The rest of the furnishings were new to me, a mixture of contemporary and classical European that had no business harmonizing, but somehow did.

Stylish.

Tasteful.

Expensive.

The mantle photos were mainly of Leigh, at various ages. They chronicled a darling infant growing past the awkward age and evolving into an astonishingly beautiful woman.

Surprise:

The two photos that included me were still in place.

One taken on her prom night.

The other the day we announced our engagement to Ben and Sadie.

The eight-by-ten I picked up and was examining when Leigh returned to the living room was more recent; new to me.

She was with Michael Wilder.

They were locked in a tight embrace, both holding on for dear life. Smiles sending out enough voltage to light the world.

A step behind Leigh on her left: an Elvis impersonator, in his white, glass-studded jumpsuit and cape, looking like a three on a scale of two hundred.

"Our wedding photo, we eloped to Vegas," she said to my back. "I'm out of brandy. What's your second choice?"

Turning, I saw Leigh holding an empty bottle like Miss Liberty.

Except for her black bra and panties, she had shed her clothing somewhere between the living room and the kitchen.

She was still pretty as a picture.

I couldn't do it.

Did I want to?

Maybe.

If I could have erased the picture of Stevie stepping out of that Lincoln and into the hotel with Rick Savage, it might have been a possibility.

That would have made it something more than a jealous, get-even thing going hump in the night.

And, I might even have pictured the spirit of Leigh's father, Ben, floating around somewhere with a saintly smile on his face, overjoyed to see us back together again, like he'd made it happen.

Oh, Ben.

I don't think so.

Not like this.

It was obvious Leigh still felt some sort of bond with me. I couldn't imagine her throwing herself at a lot of men this way.

She'd never been that kind of—

Girl.

That kind of *girl*.

But what kind of woman had she become?

So far, the evidence was circumstantial.

I averted my eyes as she pressed forward, held out the photo of Leigh and Michael Wilder, and asked, "Do you think your husband would approve, if he were to come home now? Not to mention what Elvis might think."

Faked a laugh.

The question stopped Leigh short of me by five feet.

"I told you: Mike disappeared a year ago January."

"Then he's as likely as not to reappear at any minute. Walk through the door, take one look, and, believe me, he would not be a happy cuckold. It could get messy, you know?"

Hah. Hah. Hah.

Me.

No hah hah hah from her.

"Then why did you even bother to come?" she said.

I wasn't ready to mention Stevie.

I said, "Why did you think to invite me?"

She lay the empty brandy bottle on a Bauhaus-inspired, multi-hued, chrome-and-acrylic end table. Struck a defiant hands-on-hips pose.

"It's a memory test. I remember us being good together. I wanted to see how good my memory is."

"Your memory is perfect, but you'll have to take my word for it."

She understood. Her mood shifted at once.

"I don't want your word, Neil, or you, either, anymore. Get out!"

"Maybe we could sit and talk—"

"Get out!" Screaming the words.

"Things about your father," I said, drawing on Martin Halli-well's script, although I would have preferred saving the lies for tomorrow.

Hoping her curiosity would calm her down and I could leave on a friendlier note. I'd feel lousy leaving her in this near-hysterical state.

"There's a second reason I'm in Sunrise, Leigh-Leigh. It's about Ben and—"

"Are you deaf? Get out, damn you!"

Wide eyes shouting at me as loudly as her mouth.

I turned and started for the front door, giving Leigh a weak smile on the way.

In a single motion as slick and fluent as a Kobe Bryant move inside the paint, she retrieved the empty brandy bottle and flung it at my head.

It missed me by an inch or two and hit the George Grosz lithograph that had always hung by the entrance, one of the great "Ecce Homo" images of moral decay in pre-Nazi Germany that made Grosz public enemy number one to Hitler's minions.

The glass fractured, but the print looked undamaged.

"Grosz, like Horonymous Bosch, Goya, Daumier, he showed the nightmares of life and the hell we make for ourselves on earth," Ben Maxwell once lectured me, trying to stimulate my interest in art.

Could Ben possibly know I was experiencing some of that hell right now?

I'd split from there so fast, I was halfway down the rain-rutted road before I realized I was still holding the framed photo of Leigh, Michael Wilder, and Elvis.

Great.

The perfect excuse for calling her in the morning.

Apologizing.

Suing for forgiveness.

Convincing Leigh that our getting together was still a great idea.

Unless, of course, she'd realized the photo was missing and wanted it back now, this minute, and—

That was her kicking loose gravel about ten or fifteen yards behind me.

I did a fast stop and spin, more Shaq than Kobe, and held up the frame, about to say something to—

An empty street.

A quiet street.

Bordered by eucalyptus trees, remnants of the groves that began disappearing in the late 1800s, giving way to blocks of homes built by settlers who followed the railroad tracks and, where the water was good, bought railroad land for as little as $2.50 an acre.

Poorly lit in the residential area above the business district by the original scattered street lamps installed about the time horseless carriages were becoming the rage.

"Leigh, that you?" Just loud enough to be heard. "You there, Leigh-Leigh?"

A coyote came out from a stretch of eight-foot hedge hiding houses on the west side of the road. Paused to give me a challenging once-over. Went on its way.

I continued down the road, at a faster pace.

Stopped—

Certain I'd heard someone again, only now tracking over the lawns behind the hedges.

"Getting even with me, Leigh-Leigh?"

A rabbit hopped onto the road.

I jogged the rest of the way to the Sunrise Hotel.

The Lincoln was still parked out front.

I hesitated at Stevie's door.

Considered knocking, so Stevie couldn't hide the truth inside a telephone. Threaten to hang there all night unless she let me in. Confront her. Confront Richie Savage. And—

What?

Consenting adults who didn't need my permission.

Even if she was pumping him for more than information, it was none of my business anymore.

I'd only look as foolish as my thoughts.

A hand locked onto my upper arm, startling me.

Armando Soledad.

Taking care of business in the dimly lit hallway.

In his other hand, half-hidden alongside his thigh, a gutting blade about six inches long.

He gave me a nod of recognition, stashed the knife inside his belt, and retreated to his room as quietly and silently as he had arrived.

I turned to cross over to my room, was halted by the sound of Stevie's door opening the length of the safety chain.

"Hold on, sonny boy," she ordered me through the narrow slit, "We need to do some serious talking."

"We're not talking at all, remember?"

"That was then. This is now. Big time serious."

"Your place or mine," I asked, with a trace of sarcasm.

"I'll be over."

I could have guessed as much.

"Give me five to throw something on."

That, too.

"First things first," Stevie said, crossing her legs, adjusting herself into a yoga position in the middle of my bed.

"Always a good way to start."

"Where you been all night?"

I checked my Rolex. "It's not even ten o'clock yet, so saying 'all night' doesn't exactly do it. Besides, none of your business and, while we're at it, where'd you go running off to this afternoon?"

"To meet Richie Savage," she said, surprising me with her forthrightness. "I got him to talk."

"Oh, really, and what did he get you to do?"

"What's that supposed to mean?"

"What does it sound like?"

She threw back the blanket and pulled a pillow to her, hugged it like a favorite doll.

"Strictly business, not that it's any of *your* business, and where did you say you were some of the night?"

"With Leigh Wilder, and more like most of the day."

Smiling like a Cheshire cat. "Couldn't wait, huh?"

"It was her idea."

"You mentioned to Richie I was here, when you set up going to meet with him tomorrow; how he knew to call me." Smugly, like she had unlimited use of Bill Gates' credit cards. "How did your Leigh Wilder know you were around?"

"She didn't."

"A lucky guess? 'Golly gee, I wonder if my old beau is in the neighborhood after fifteen years. I think I'll phone over to the hotel and find out.' Or, probably, you wandered over to the newspaper office, gave her your silly grin, and said, 'Guess who.' "

"What's so silly about my grin?"

"Check out a mirror sometime. On Steve McQueen it was sexy. On you it looks like you're passing gas and trying to hide the fact."

"You never complained about my grin before."

"It's only seven years since we split. I been working up to it."

"Remind me to tell you sometime about your—"

"Don't go there, honey!"

"Aw, gee, and it's one of my favorite places."

"That's hitting below the belt!"

"Yes."

Stevie gave me one of her etched-in-acid looks.

"I didn't come here to be insulted."

"Thrown in at no additional charge," I said. "Count to ten and we can try again."

I cranked myself out of the faded chintz easy chair and crossed to the window, opened the drapes and dust-encrusted Venetians, and looked out at the San Jacs outlined in shades of black against a backdrop of stars dancing to the music of the night.

Below the mountain range, across the railroad tracks, where First Street became Old Plow Road on its way to the climb up and over the San Jacs, to the edges of Riverside County and on into San Diego, there'd once been sprawling farms and horse and cattle ranches, one abutting the next. Some of them were still there, but there also were housing developments and strip malls, other requirements of a city close to bursting at the seams with a growing population.

For the first month after I accepted Easy Ryder's job offer, I lived in a converted storage shed on Doc Horton's horse ranch at Old Plow Road and Horton Lane. It consisted of a parlor, a kitchen, and a bathroom; the living room too compact for a regular bed or a Murphy, so Doc had built one that slid in and out under a cavernous closet.

It had once been the playhouse of Doc's daughter, who was murdered under ugly circumstances Doc and anyone else who knew never wanted to talk about. She'd come home from her after-school job at Ardy's Double-Dip Ice Cream Parlor this particular evening and announced she planned to sleep tonight in the playhouse. She had done it many times before, so nobody said anything beyond reminding the girl the heater was still on the blink, so be sure to cover up with enough blankets. The next morning, when Doc's wife sent a handyman to check, because breakfast was growing cold, she was dead.

Stevie called out, "Nine!"

I turned away from my youth, caught her anticipatory smile, and said, "Ten!"

"Friends again?"

She saw I wasn't going to answer her question. A hurt look flashed across her face before she composed it into an "I don't care" expression.

She got off the bed, tightened and adjusted her robe, and joined me at the window.

I said, "What's so big-time serious it couldn't wait?"

"I've been with Richie today, honey. I got a lot out of him."

I held my tongue.

She palm-massaged my shoulder blades, wrapped an arm around my waist. "An earful. If Richie was telling me the truth, Martin Halliwell may have been feeding us a modest load of crap."

14

Check it out and you'll see it could have been worse. I could have been a drummer. Highest mortality rate in rock and roll. Especially the great ones. I'm talking Keith Moon class here. John Bonham. Papa Dee. I could make you a list. They keep the beat. It's life that gives them problems."

Rick Savage, talking almost nonstop to Stevie at the Palm Springs Yacht and Polo Club. On the drive to Sunrise. Trying to get her to understand.

"The good thing about being the bass player or the lead singer, you can be lousy at both—and believe it, I was—and nobody out there cares, as long as you look great on stage, move great, know how to kick that pelvis into overdrive, and you write songs that got a lyric hook that carries a seismic punch and can get all the little girls screaming and making puddles in their seats. The bigger girls, that's a story you already know, Blondie.

"So, I had it all, I lost it all, screwed by the people I trusted the most. In and out of rehab and the music passed me by. Heavy metal came in and that narrowed my chances of a new record deal. Rap. That mosh pit and rave-up stuff. I was a coked-out dinosaur who'd have trouble getting a gig at the La Brea Tar Pits.

"Well, maybe I got one last shot left, a club in Vegas I hear about from a session player who's also doing time at a twelve-step motel in Santa Monica. He tells me it's where stones go when they stop rolling, a place about half a mile off the strip called Moss. A renovated hole in the wall next to a topless joint; a haven for old superstars who can't let go. Any kind of a name or rep that can put two hundred aging asses in two hundred seats—finger-poppers who think the day the music stopped was when the CD finally shut out the LP—and you can pull down a couple grand a week, he says.

"I don't entirely fit the demographic but I figure any shot is better than no shot at all, so what the hell. I beg enough on the boardwalk to buy a one-way Greyhound to Vegas. My thumb gets me to Moss, where enough people have heard of me for the manager to say, 'We'll try you for a week and go from there. Nine hundred, less rental for the bass, and you take care of any backup you pull together.' Like I have any choice?

"Coming up on the weekend, the week has not been going so good and the club manager is saying things like maybe to break even on what I cost them they should put more water in the hooch. You know what that would have done to my self-esteem, if I had any left. I get past it with some cheap blow I beg off the doorman and by show time I'm sky high sick on shit that was cut with rat poison.

"I'm going on anyway, the manager spits at me through his tongue ring, or I can forget about the rest of what's owed me. The house is full for a change and, not only that, but Sonny Bono is out front, sitting in the VIP booth with someone even more important than him. He drops a name that means nothing to me.

"Sonny I know. I mean, really. From the old days, when he was riding high and then after he washed up on the beach. I was one of the few who always thought the cocky little son of a bitch had genuine talent, and I never made it a secret.

"The difference between Sonny and me and the others: He kept all his money. The royalty checks on his songs arrived regularly, so it didn't matter much if some crapshoot like a restaurant on La Cienega, serving old world dishes like his mama used to make, went under. It gave him more time for his golf and tennis.

"I am not going to embarrass myself in front of Sonny.

"Bad enough he sees I'm playing a rat hole like this.

"I go out there and, sick and all, swallowing my puke, I do the greatest set of my life. Better than Three-Rivers, better than the Cotton Bowl and the Coliseum, on the "Savage World" tour Jann Wenner himself covered for *Rolling Stone*.

"Before the medley of hits I close with, I call out to him, 'Hey, Sonny, what brought you to the Moss?'

"He hollers back, 'I was hoping to find Cher playing here.'

"Gets a big laugh from the audience. Plain to see he loves it, being ten feet tall. I invite him to join me on stage. The guy next to him in the booth gives him a nudge, not that Sonny is hesitating. How it is with a performer, even one who's given it up for politics.

"We bring down the house with 'I Got You, Babe,' me doing the Cher part. Again with 'The Beat Goes On,' this time Sonny does the Cher part.

"After the show, Sonny and his friend find me backstage in my smelly toilet of a dressing room. I congratulate him on scoring big as mayor of Palm Springs and wonder what'll be next? The White House?

"His friend gives me a cunning look and says, 'It's been discussed.'

"Sonny treats the idea like a joke before he suddenly turns serious. He says he wants to know my story. 'What you see and probably everything you've heard,' I tell him.

" 'Places like this will only drag you down the rest of the way to the bottom of the barrel,' Sonny says. 'Come on back with me to Palm Springs. Clean you up, get you on your feet again. I'm declaring for the House of Representatives from my district, and, when I win, I want people around me who I can trust.'

" 'Besides me, you mean,' his friend says.

" 'Of course, what I mean,' Sonny says. 'How about it, Richie?'

"I'm staggered by what I hear. An offer that's nothing to spit out. Unfortunately, I have to puke again and make it to the toilet bowl just in time. I come back and Sonny wants to know, 'Was that a yes or a no, Richie?'

"The next day, we're in Palm Springs and Sonny already has me set up at the Betty Ford Clinic. He says, 'You're on an open ticket, Richie. I don't want you leaving there until there's no chance you'll ever have to go back."

Neil moved away from Stevie by the window and flopped onto the bed, found a comfortable position on his back with his hands locked under his head, and said, "What does any of this have to do with Halliwell?"

"You haven't figured that out yet?"

"You mean guessing the friend with Sonny in Vegas that night was Aaron Lodger? I guessed."

"Exactly!"

"Exactly what?"

Stevie left the window and sat down on the edge of the bed, near enough to Neil to finger-poke him on the cheek.

"That was Aaron Lodger, and what Richie told me about him—"

"The *Reader's Digest* version this time?"

"You can be so impossible when you want . . ."

She swiped at Neil's nose and punched him on the arm a few times.

He grabbed her wrists, provoking a playful wrestle that ended with them stretched out inches apart, side by side and facing one another

"Richie cleaned up a hundred percent and, by the time Sonny got elected to congress and went off to Washington, he was ready to try politics himself. He told Aaron Lodger, who said, 'We'll start you out the same way we started Sonny, as the mayor of Palm Springs.'

"Richie said, 'I don't know that I'm well enough known to get elected.'

"Aaron Lodger says, 'I am.'

"Richie says, 'My old drug habit and everything, it's bound to come out.'

"Lodger says, 'Better than being a reformed drunk in today's world. People love it. We make sure it comes out.'

"Next thing Richie knows, he's elected in a landslide. He doesn't waste time following up on the good work Sonny had been doing, rebuilding Palm Springs' reputation and the property values. He becomes a popular, well-respected mayor.

"Then, in January '98, Sonny is killed in that freak skiing accident in South Lake Tahoe and people are saying Richie should run to fill the vacancy in congress. Richie's game, but Aaron Lodger tells him better he should wait, let Sonny's widow go to Washington, and then he'll win the race for U.S. senator.

"Richie says, 'Not the White House, Mr. L?'

"Aaron Lodger smiles and says, 'It's being discussed. Good things all in their time.'

"I asked Richie, 'What is it exactly Lodger does for a living?' Like I didn't already know.

"Richie says, 'Retired.'

" 'Retired from what?' I ask.

" 'Retired criminal. He has that reputation, although I never saw any sign of it. To me he's a gentleman who's been extremely generous to me. He helped straighten out my life, he got me elected mayor, and maybe he'll help get me to the Senate. Otherwise, he plays a little golf, a little pinochle with old associates, and he dabbles in the market. I suppose that makes Mr. L a harmless old retired criminal dabbler?'

" 'His generosity. At what price?' Richie starts to get a little nervous when I ask him this. 'What is it you have to do for him in return, Mr. Mayor?'

" 'I owe him big, Blondie.'

" 'Not an answer.'

" 'You didn't let me finish. I owe him big, but, in all the years I've known him, Mr. L has asked for something one time and one time only. I wouldn't have said 'no' to him for all the tea in China.' "

Neil signaled her to be still.

"I don't hear anything yet that puts a stain on Martin Halliwell. If anything, it, A, links Richie Savage to Aaron Lodger earlier in the game than Halliwell ever mentioned; B, it suggests Sonny Bono may also have been part of the dirty doings we're here to help expose, like the good citizens we are."

"You haven't heard the rest."

"Go for it."

"Richie says, 'Mr. L calls me over to his place earlier in the year and says he wants me to put on another Imagine That! festival for John Lennon. He says he was a big Lennon fan and remembers how the festival I headlined in '85 was a big money-raiser for Wipe Out Weapons International. He says it's time for people to be reminded that guns kill and maybe it'll help to cut down on the number of innocent people shot on city streets every day, kids marching into their schools and shooting teachers and classmates. Mr. L says don't worry about the funding, just go for the right people and make it happen. Why I called Neil Gulliver and got him on board. Mr. L understood how important he was getting the first festival off the ground.' "

Neil cut her off again.

"Would have happened anyway. Harry Nilsson was the real force. His idea. Augie also gets credit. My contribution was the site. Convincing the San Gorgonios to let us use tribal land. What finally sold them was getting the Eagles to agree to headline . . . So, Aaron Lodger is a late-blooming do-gooder, and Mayor Savage is simply paying him back for favors past, and that's why we can forget what Halliwell said about their using the festival to launder dirty money."

"Honey, not that. When Aaron Lodger talked to Richie about the festival, they weren't alone. There was a third man there—"

"Orson Welles was there?"

"Very funny. Martin Halliwell was there with Lodger and Lodger told Richie it was Halliwell who brought up your name to him."

Stevie felt Neil's body turn to stone, except for his eyes, which took on that distant stare that meant his mind was assessing the news, trying to make sense of it, looking for the slot where it fit. The vein at the side of his neck that popped like a chicken's wishbone whenever this happened was vibrating.

He rolled into a sitting position, stood up, and began pacing the floor, floorboards creaking under the threadbare and sunbleached carpeting every third or fourth step.

"If Richie is still up, I want to talk to him," Neil said, giving her a look that peeled the skin off her face.

"What's that supposed to mean, exactly?"

"Exactly. When I got back here, his Lincoln parked out front? Instead of inviting me into your room when you wanted to tell me what you had to tell me, coming over to mine. Why else?"

The accusatory tone Neil pummeled her with whenever he was at his most jealous.

She got up from the bed; adjusted her robe; tightened the belt.

"I'm going now."

Neil made a move to block her path.

"Don't," she said quietly.

He stepped aside.

Let her pass.

Started to follow her out.

"I said don't."

When the phone rang, I leaped for it, figuring it was Halliwell returning my call from last night. It was Leigh, apologizing for what she called her "naughty girl behavior" and wondering if we were still on for brunch.

I slipped into my jogging suit and headed out for my regular morning run.

The Lincoln was gone.

I went back into the hotel and asked the desk clerk about it.

He detached the Marlboro from the corner of his mouth, blew a series of smoke rings at the wagon wheel chandelier, and shrugged indifferently. No Lincoln when he came on duty a half hour ago, at seven, he said.

I checked the guest parking area behind the hotel.

No Lincoln.

No sign of Stevie's Cherokee.

Armando's Wrangler: missing.

The temperature was already in the seventies.

I cut the jog short after a mile of quiet city streets being over-run by fast-food franchises, their logo signs as high as flagpoles to catch the freeway zippers, and did a one-stop at the car rental place. I had expected some anger over the damage to their Lexus, but the agent was as bright as a newly minted dollar.

"Bet you're glad I convinced you to go the extra two-fifty and you checked the little insurance box," he said, his baritone too heavy for his featherweight frame. "You'd not believe how many folks pass and come to regret it. Ka-boom!" Used his hands to make a circle in the air. "A cheap enough price to pay to be free of all liability. Even as we speak, the Lexus is being made as good as new at our garage in Palm Springs."

"Why not closer to home?" I'd noticed at least a half dozen garages on my run.

"Something the boss worked out with a place down there? Basic economics, he told me. I suppose a lot like signing up for the two-fifty or not signing up. You gonna need some new wheels? A great low-mileage T-bird just got back this A.M."

The desk clerk called to say Ms. Wilder was waiting for me. Ten past noon. An hour and ten minutes late. In the old days, Ben would have scolded Leigh about that and extracted a promise from her to do better next time.

Punctuality was Ben's eleventh commandment.

Sometimes.

Whatever he happened to be lecturing about at any given time became Ben's eleventh commandment.

"Always say please, always say thank you, and always return your phone calls."

Ben was fond of saying that, and each was his eleventh commandment at one time or another. Not that he always said please, always said thank you, or returned all his calls.

Ben made a habit of breaking his eleventh commandment.

Whenever I teased him on the subject, he explained, "I do the best I can with His ten, I can give me latitude on my number eleven."

I threw my all-purpose, military-style, fatigue blazer over my basic traveling outfit, sink-washable polo shirt, and wrinkle-resistant black cargo pants, Lakers cap, and stole a look in the dresser mirror before heading downstairs.

Not bad for thirty-eight going on thirty-nine.

Lots of wear and tear, but I'd worked hard for it and wore it like proof of a life being lived.

Leigh looked better.

Even better than yesterday, when I was struck by how little she'd aged, how much more attractive she'd become since the last time I saw her, Ben's funeral, when not even her mourner's mask stole from her beauty.

Today she was beguiling in a rainbow-patterned, halter-top dress, possibly inspired by a Frank Stella litho, that accentuated her bare broad shoulders and the fact she wasn't wearing a bra. Unfettered earthy brown, silver-streaked hair fell to her shoulders. Loose strands drifted across half her wide forehead and above her right eyebrow, giving Leigh an updated Veronica Lake look.

The same lush, tantalizing lips, but—

Her lidded eyes still owned her face.

If I wasn't careful, they might get to owning me again, feeling the way I did about Stevie recapturing her past with Richie Savage.

No! I shook the notion out of my head as fast as it had arrived. I might think less of Stevie for that, but I didn't want to do anything to make me think less of myself.

Not my style. Never my style.

I'd get over it. I always did.

Leigh moved with a model's grace from the registration desk

to greet me with a squeeze and a sister's kiss on the cheek as I cleared the stairway. Grabbed my hand to lead me outside to her double-parked Seville, apologizing for last night, promising it wouldn't happen again, refusing to let me take half the blame.

No apology, not a word about being more than an hour late, until we got to the Belly Bowl, a truck stop in the Midway area between Sunrise and Sunset, our favorite place for a cheap hamburger and fries after a date. The overhead sign boasted, OPEN 25 HOURS A DAY AND PROUD OF IT, while the sign next to the door said, NO GUNS, NO KNIVES AND NO CREDIT. CASH ONLY OR KEEP ON TRUCKIN'.

"Late-breaking news held me up," Leigh said, explaining more than apologizing. "We have a veterinarian in Sunset who fancies himself a ladies' man. He got arrested this morning on a complaint filed by Jane Gottschalk, our Junior Woman's Club president. Allegedly operated on her instead of Groovy, her pet Yorkie. I was tempted to go with a headline saying 'Doggie Doc Confuses His Bitches.'"

"Your father wouldn't have thought twice about it."

"Only reason I was tempted. You ready for the Twenty-Five-Hour Breakfast Buffet? Great selection, unlimited returns, only five bucks per, and, understand this: No matter how loudly you resist, my treat."

"Resist? I was going to insist."

Her playful smile equaled my own.

We worked our appetites around basic breakfast fare, a cheese and mushroom omelet, a thick wedge of ham baked in a pineapple marinade, pan fries, fresh muffins, a fresh-baked slice of apple pie a la mode, and, because it looked too good to resist, fresh pumpkin pie under a cloud of whipped cream.

Our conversation stayed light and in the long-ago. We were two friends reliving happy memories, skirting subjects that might open old wounds. I hadn't felt this comfortable since the good years with Stevie, making me unhappier about the lies to come, the trick I'd be playing on Leigh.

She gave me the opening when she said, "Cookie Monster, last night you said there was another reason you stopped in Sunrise. Something to do with my dad."

Her expression took on an urgency as I held off rushing into a reply, the way Martin Halliwell had coached me.

"She has to believe it's nothing you want to share and it's hurting

y'all much as you know it's going to hurt her, Neil. Too quick on the draw, it might come across as false."

"I don't mind playing your games with Rick Savage, but with Leigh? There's no other way?"

Halliwell shook his head.

"Y'all can get her talking about Michael Wilder and his connection to the San Gorgonios, that can open a door we can go through; find us all the dirty people whose dirty money Aaron Lodger is moving through the San Gorgonio casino like it's the local laundromat."

"Why would Leigh? I'd expect her to be predisposed to protecting his memory."

"The department feels Neil Gulliver can power through that defense if anyone can, Neil."

"I haven't seen Leigh for years. We didn't part on the best of terms."

"But y'all both loved her daddy and her daddy loved you almost as much as he did her. In some ways, more."

"It's a pretty lousy trick to play on anyone."

"Patriotism doesn't always function on a straight line, Neil."

I answered Leigh hesitantly.

"Something, yes."

She tried for my eyes, but I moved them away in time, landing on a trucker sitting alone two tables away, who was driving his way through a plate of deep-fried chicken and mashed potatoes buried in gravy.

"Something I'm not going to like hearing."

Holding back my answer, then, "No more than I did when the government told me."

"The government?"

My eyes on her now, observing her puzzlement.

"The Treasury Department, Leigh-Leigh. They came to me last week. They knew I'd worked out here and how close I'd been to Ben. They said Ben before his death was tied in for years with the mob element that controls all the gambling on the reservation; helped get the casino okayed by the tribal council; that he was paid off in the hundreds of thousands to ignore the crooked games out front, illegal gambling in the back—"

Leigh thrust a palm at me, defensively, but I didn't stop.

"—A whole catalog of felonies they'd have prosecuted your father for if he'd lived. They wanted to know if I had any awareness of any of this and, maybe, could be of use to them."

"Use to them?" Her voice struggling to make the words.

"They're looking for more than the paperwork they have already."

"Paperwork?" A squeal of incredulity.

"They said. Nothing to show me if I couldn't be helpful to them. Something I might have seen or heard. Something Ben might have told me in confidence. As bait: an exclusive when they moved in to attach the *Gazette* and its assets."

She dropped her head into a hand and picked nervously at her ice cream with the fork, like a sculptor. "Paperwork? Neil, I don't, it can't. I don't understand any of this."

"One of the T-Men let something slip."

"What?"

"Michael Wilder."

"What about him?"

"His name. The suggestion was the paperwork came from Michael Wilder."

No reaction, then, "That bastard. That son of a bitch. That ungrateful—"

Loud enough to draw a few heads.

She killed her pumpkin pie; multiple stab wounds.

I said, "I made Sunrise my stopping point on the way to Palm Springs hoping to see you and put this to you."

"For a story?"

"To this second I don't know, Leigh-Leigh. For a story. For old-times sake, out of respect for the memory of Ben. To warn you what was coming down. Maybe just that."

A shrug to go with this latest in my sequence of lies.

"Do you believe what they told you, these T-Men? That my father could do something like that?"

Challenging me.

"That's why, the confusion in my mind."

"Do you, Neil?"

Giving it a moment, then another.

"No. I can't believe it of Ben. I could never believe something like that about him. But, I'd like to hear it from you."

Slyly, "Your honest answer or the newspaper reporter knowing what to say and how to say it, working the story by not working the story? I remember that trick of yours, using your great memory instead of taking notes, using a recorder. You doing that now? Working the story, Cookie Monster?"

Gently: "You'll have to decide that, Leigh-Leigh."

Verging on tears, she began scolding me with a finger.

"My father who loved you like a son never did anything dishonest in his life. Michael Wilder was a son of a bitch, a bastard, who should only rot in hell for eternity."

Struggling for air, her temperature rising.

She leaned over for her Gucci tote bag and moved like she was getting ready to leave, abruptly changed her mind, and settled back in her seat. Her eyes doing some serious rapid-fire blinking. Manicured nails tapping out a nervous jig on the table surface.

"Sorry to be the messenger, but maybe it's better you know what's coming down, Leigh-Leigh."

"All right, all right, I know you're not the bad guy here," she said, inhaling heavy doses of the Belly Bowl's grease-stained air. "It's just that . . ." Her delicate chin swinging like a metronome.

"Why don't we forget about going out to the reservation today? This doesn't seem like the best time—"

"—for you to chase your story?"

Leigh's anger starting to build again.

"The piece that has nothing, absolutely nothing, to do with your father."

Now I was beginning to get upset. At least, that's how I hoped it sounded to Leigh.

"Drop me off at the rental agency; should do it. They have a nice T-Bird on the lot."

She reached across for my hand and took it in both of hers, squeezing it hard enough to crack a few knuckles.

"No. I called him this morning, Roy Bigelow, who runs the casino. He's expecting us."

"I can handle it by myself."

"No. You want to ask him about Daddy, do it. See what Roy has to say. Afterward, we're going back to my place—"

I looked at her askance.

"Don't worry, you'll be safe. I learned my lesson last night. There's some paperwork of my own that I want to show you." I let her see curiosity. "Then you'll know why Michael Wilder is the biggest rotten son of a bitch bastard who ever walked the planet."

Bingo!

I'd read up on the casino, seen pictures, but Captain Pabro's Gaming Mecca was more than I expected, the way no first-time visitor

is ever quite ready for the make-believe reality of the hotels on the
Vegas strip; like the architect had borrowed his inspiration from
Dances with Wolves.

Set about five hundred yards back and invisible from the freeway, on approach you were looking at a chorus line of six connected, appropriately decorated teepees, each as tall as a phone
pole and about the width of half a football field. Sitting on top of
the middle teepees was a gigantic ceramic bird's nest; no sign of
the bird.

The parking lot stretched across the front and up both sides of
the casino and was about a third full. All makes of cars, everything
from ancient gas-hogs to upscale Cads, BMWs, and even a Rolls or
two safety-parking over a pair of slots. Lots of Toyotas and Hondas.
More motor homes and SUVs.

The parking row closest to the entrance had RESERVED signs
posted at each space. Most of them were filled. Leigh nosed into
one of the empties, between a muddied Land Rover and a sleek
ocean blue XK8 that put to shame my decrepit Jag back home,
more than even a dirty Camry put my Jag to shame.

"Where we want to be," she said, pointing to the teepee on the
extreme right, the main entrance to Captain Pabro's.

Surveillance cameras working in all directions.

Airport-type metal detectors about ten feet inside the lobby;
how the sun-drenched security guards dressed in Tonto and Sitting
Bull outfits guessed I might be packing.

"It's my only protection if you guys decide to attack," I explained.

They didn't get the joke, though Leigh looked amused.

I dug behind my back for the Beretta 92f and handed it over
on their assurance it would be safe with them until we were ready
to leave.

Leigh crossed over to the bank of house phones, and in less
than two minutes we were being greeted by Roy Bigelow, who
shared air kisses with her and said, "Was waiting here to catch you
right away, Leigh, but my need to take a leak finally won out."

I figured him for his early fifties, about five-six or five-seven,
overweight around the two hundred pound mark, a stocky, barrel-
chested build made to look better than it was inside a pricey handmade butterscotch brown silk suit. Cocoa-brown silk shirt open at
the spread collar. Handmade Italian leather on his feet, a diamond
the size of New Hampshire on his left pinky.

A plain, flat face with warm, wide-set Indian Ink eyes; a thick, broad nose with a couple break bumps on the bridge; a thicker pair of lips, the mouth slightly off-center. Just enough of a poolside tan to illuminate two rows of perfectly formed snow white teeth. A shaved head in need of a touch-up around the temples.

In sum, a candidate for *The Sopranos*.

Bigelow reached for my hand and we traded names before he pointed to my Lakers cap.

"That fourth quarter?" he said. "Nothing like it, ever, in the history of the NBA, a Game Seven comeback after being down by fifteen? Fifteen?! I mean, Shaq dumping the two free throws to tie it, then his nine-foot jumper? C'mon."

Making *C'mon* sound like the quintessence of disbelief.

Holding his palm to the ceiling for a buddy slap.

I buddy-slapped him and said, "Don't forget Shaw's tie-breaking three-pointer from twenty-five feet out. Kobe's two free throws after Shaq did his thing; the icing."

"On the cake." Roy Bigelow turned to Leigh and said, "I like your friend Neil a whole lot already, keed. My kind of people."

Yeah, but was he mine?

15

Roy Bigelow looked about as much like an Indian as Jeff Chandler in *Broken Arrow*, but he was a legitimate member of the San Gorgonio tribe, who facetiously described himself as "a Beverly Hills Indian" and delighted in dropping chunks of reservation history while guiding me through Captain Pabro's six teepees. I knew most of it from my days at the *Sentinel*, but I acted like it all was new to me. Roy liked to talk and I wanted to keep him in a talking mode and amiable, for when I could inject my questions about the casino operation.

"See, we gave over one teepee to what was legal when we built the place. One for poker, one for pan, one for low-end bingo, and so on. Every room big enough to adjust and expand when the law let that happen, like just happened in the last election, so we could get into gear in a New York minute and not have to slow down or lose any business."

〉
〈
〉

All the rooms were busy, at a third to half occupancy, but filled with a symphony of shuffling cards, dancing chips, and the urgent, sweaty silence of gamblers waiting for the next card. Bursts of conversation, followed by nasty hoots of "Shut up and deal."

"Great for this time on a weekday," Roy said. "After five, people off work and back on the road, we'll go up to maybe three-quarters; full in bingo there most of the time. Coffee shop, the dining room, also twenty-four hours, only the best food and at reasonable prices, trick we picked up from Vegas, of course. Next time you come around, we should have a gift and souvenir shop like none other. Indian stuff. Big with the kids back home. Kid you not, by the way, about my Beverly Hills thing.

"First, you have to understand that the San Gorgonios in the beginning, for a whole lot of years, were dirt poor, without the proverbial pot to piss in. The land, lousy for farming and not much better for cattle. What money could be made came by leasing out the peat bogs you see all over the place. Peat, peat moss; big business, but not big enough to support an entire tribe.

"A lot of our people left to look for something better than a leaky-roofed shanty, outdoor plumbing, and a lot of lip service from government bureaucrats. Didn't give up on the tribe, only the land, and most would come back whenever they got notice about important issues to be discussed at a tribal council meeting or to pick up their share of the peat lease royalties. They come from the East Coast, all over the country, since the casino. Two families fly in from Toronto.

"My family landed in Beverly Hills, in the real estate market, speculating when real estate was at its peak. Stocks also good to the grandparents. Better to my mom and pop. So, I got to be a rich San Gorgonio and now I'm out here getting even richer and no end in sight."

I tried a question. "You own Captain Pabro's, Roy?"

"This going in your story?"

"It might."

"Tribe," he said. "Every family has a piece, like with the peat operation. I get a bigger taste because of running the place, big, big, but that's all she writes. Enough, you want to know. Greedy, I'm not."

"How'd you get the gig?"

Evasive: "Just lucky, I guess."

I didn't press.

"When we got called and asked if we'd let our land be used again for this Imagine John Lennon thing of yours, we couldn't say yes fast enough. You know from before how the tribe charged a little rent and got to operate the portable potty concession. This time strictly *Be our guest*. Great free publicity for us, worth millions in fresh business."

"And it can never hurt to do a favor for Aaron Lodger, can it?"

"Aaron Lodger?" Trying to translate the question, read where it was heading. Turning his palms to the ceiling. "He comes around every so often. Pan is his game. Nice old guy. Did I mention before about having floor seats at the Staples Center, where I saw the playoffs, Game Seven? Two over from Jack Nicholson and that skinny babe of his from the TV show about lawyers, I think. Guy on the other side of Jack, white beard, funny hats? Lou Adler, I heard. Record mogul who made it monster big with Carole King, Cheech and Chong?"

"Ode Records," I said. "He owned the label. You're from Beverly Hills, you know the Roxy?"

"Club on the Strip, where lots of the superstars played and hung out?"

"Yeah. He owned that, too."

"I could never buy my way in upstairs, the private club over the showroom? You had to be important. I was just some wealthy shnook, not some heavy dude like Warren Beatty. Tony Curtis, I remember him being there one night. Steve McQueen. Of course, the biggest of the big rockers. Me always on the outside looking in."

Sad, like the memory hurt.

I said, "On the Rox."

"That's it, what it was called. On the Rox. What made you ask if I knew the place?"

My memory tumbled back to December of 1980.

My exclusive interview with Mark David Chapman was all Easy Ryder had to hear about to forgive what he now decided was my "youthful indiscretion" in disobeying him and flying to New York to pay my last respects to John Lennon. I fed it to rewrite over the phone and caught the next plane home.

By the time I was back in Sunrise City, the Associated Press had picked up the piece, it had played big around the world, and

enough of Easy's peers had called congratulating him on his fore-
sight in dispatching me to New York that he gave me a little bump
in salary, but cautioned, "Don't ever think it's your pass to go sailing off on your own again."

Chapman at first had been tight-mouthed with me after I lied
and finagled my way into his maximum security roost at Bellevue
Hospital, reciting to me how his lawyer didn't want him talking to
anyone.

"Then why didn't you say something when they said your
brother was here to see you?"

"I wanted to see what my brother looked like," he said, like it
could be a game to break the monotony of time. "How old are
you?"

"Eighteen."

"I'm twenty-five. I remember, I always wanted a brother who
was eighteen. An older brother."

"Did you? What if I were only seventeen?"

"I think so. More fun I bet than being an only child. Are you?"

I shook my head.

"Good for you," he said, and moved from his cot to the kitchen-
style table in the center of the room, dropped into a chair, and
invited me to sit down. Parked clasped hands in front of his mouth.
Wondered, "Are you just now starting out to become a reporter?"

I invested the next ten minutes with my background, at the
same time drawing a mental picture of this overweight, ordinary-
looking, somehow pathetic creature who used murder as his passport to fame.

He liked the parts about Elvis and the *Rolling Stone*, the story
that earned me my Press Club award, interrupting me with questions, wondering if *Stone* would be writing about him.

I told him I was certain there would be a story.

He got the notion I'd be the one writing it.

I didn't bother to correct him.

Chapman launched into his background, rushing through basics, like growing up in Atlanta the son of a retired air force sergeant, working as a YMCA camp counselor, moving to Hawaii,
where he met and married an older woman—

Like none of this would be of interest to the *Stone*.

Talking to me like I was a television camera, he wanted me to
know he'd loved the Beatles, distressed his parents by letting his
hair grow long and learning to play the guitar.

Spoke cheerfully about the radical changes in him that occurred when he was fifteen and started experimenting with psy-
chedelic drugs, any hallucinogen he could find.

How he weathered bad trips, found Jesus, wore a large wooden
cross around his neck, renounced the Beatles, sold his album collection, because—

John Lennon had once said the Beatles were more popular than
Jesus.

The song "Imagine" became one of his pet hates.

He sang it with the lyric, "Imagine John Lennon was dead."

Imagine.

And Chapman's hate for Lennon festered and grew over the
years.

By 1980, it was his prime obsession, brought to a boil by the
October issue of *Esquire*, where Lennon was described as a forty-
year-old businessman worth $150 million.

Chapman thought, "That phony!"

Wrestled for more than a month between good and evil spirits.

On December 5, arrived in New York.

Checked into the Sixty-third Street YMCA, nine blocks south
of the Dakota, then into the Sheraton Center Hotel at Seventh
Avenue and Fifty-second.

Began his vigil at the Dakota the next day, carrying Beatles
cassettes, a copy of Salinger's *The Catcher in the Rye*, and—

The Charter Arms .38-special revolver he had purchased at
J&S Sales, Ltd., in Honolulu.

Two nights later, John lay dying.

"Why, Mark?"

He looked at me like I should know the answer by now.

"Because I shot him."

"Why did you shoot him?"

"Why not?"

"You hated John that much?"

"There was no emotion in my blood. There was no anger. There
was nothing. It was dead silence in my brain. Dead, cold quiet until
he walked up. He looked at me . . ."

Chapman lowered his head and closed his eyes.

"He walked past me and then I heard the voice in my head.

"The voice said, 'Do it! Do it! Do it!'

"I aimed at his back. I pulled the trigger five times. The explo-
sions were deafening. After the first shot, Yoko crouched down and

ran around the corner into the courtyard. Then the gun was empty and John Lennon had disappeared.

"Inside the Dakota, behind the door, some people were yelling. Somebody screamed. The doorman, Jose, was standing in front of me with tears in his eyes. 'Do you know what you've done?' he asked me."

Chapman looked up from the table, his eyes screaming at me for sympathy and understanding.

"Did you, Mark?"

"What do you think?"

"I'd rather hear what you think."

"I know you would. Younger brothers look up to their older brothers."

He wasn't going to tell me.

I asked the question I'd been carrying around with me since the murder.

"Mark, *The Catcher in the Rye*. Did you ever have any thought about killing J. D. Salinger instead of John Lennon, or maybe both of them?"

Mark David Chapman looked across the table at me like I was the crazy one.

On December 14, about an hour after a worldwide ten-minute vigil of silence in John's memory had concluded, my private number at the office rang. I answered it, as usual, with my name:

"Gulliver."

"Who?"

"Gulliver."

"You said that twice."

"Harry!"

"Thanks for the memory." Singing it like Bob Hope. "I wanna tell ya—Listen, you doing anything right now?"

"Why?"

"We need to get together."

"If it's about paying me back the tab you ran up on my credit card, it really isn't necessary, Harry. The paper didn't challenge—"

"Money isn't everything. How does eight-thirty sound?"

"Where are you?"

"Where would you like me to be?"

"If we're getting together? Sunrise City."

"What's your second choice?"

"Sunrise City."

"I heard you the first time."

A lot of good it did me either time.

Nilsson could be as aggressively persuasive as he was charmingly insistent.

At a few minutes after eight, battered by almost three hours in merciless rush-hour freeway traffic and a crawl up Sunset, door security at On the Rox checked off my name on the VIP list and sent me upstairs to join Harry.

He wasn't hard to find in a room about the size of an average cocktail lounge in an upscale restaurant, no larger than the Roxy showroom below, where maybe three-hundred people could lock knees uncomfortably on a crowded night. The room was decked out for privilege and privacy in subdued lighting that obscured the quick snort here and there. It offered a balcony-style view of the rinky-dink Roxy stage for those interested in more than expensive liquor, overpriced ordinary food, and camaraderie among equals.

The Roxy was half full with media and industry types turned out by MCA Records for headliner Olivia Newton-John. Some of the invited celebrities were hanging out upstairs, either circulating or huddled around tables in a way that discouraged table-hoppers.

Many of the faces were familiar to me. Don Henley of the Eagles. Brian May, Queen's keyboard player. Kim Carnes, who was climbing the charts with "Bette Davis Eyes." Alice Cooper showing his grip on an imaginary golf club to Weird Al. Ray Manzarek of the Doors. Eric Burdon. Chuck Negron of Three Dog Night, not too steady on his feet. Timothy Leary, a center of attention.

Nilsson was hanging over a corner table, wineglass in one hand, cigarette in the other, pulling laughter from Van Dyke Parks, Mickey Dolenz, Paul Williams, and Eddie Rabbitt. I tapped him on the arm and he bolted upright, spilling some of his wine to cause a growing red stain on the shoulder of Parks' white linen jacket, who waved it off with a gesture, pried the glass away from Harry, and matched the stain on his other shoulder.

"I thought you were the gendarmes for a minute," Harry said. "Were you?" And before I could answer: "Doesn't count if you were for longer than a minute."

Doing his Groucho thing.

Polite table laughter.

Dolenz, the one-time Monkees drummer, making a rim shot noise on the table surface.

Harry introduced me.

"The one who wrote the interview with that psycho prick murdered John?" Rabbitt said.

"Yes."

"Thumbs up, son. Some of his quotes, enough to put him in the electric chair where he belongs."

Paul Williams, more reflective, said, "John hardly gone and his record at Number One. 'Just Like Starting Over.' The irony in that title."

Shaking his head at the concept as Harry led me away to a lonely table in the rear he had staked out with a pack of Camels, a surplus army-issue trench coat, and a Brandy Alexander in front of three empties.

"Sit there," he said, indicating the location with the best view of the room. "Beats the show going on downstairs." Took a long pull of the Brandy Alexander and signaled for a server.

"Anything my friend wants up to a dime, a refill for me, and a shot of Black Label, water back, for our missing friend," he said. Turning to me, "You're early, he's about to be on time, or late, and Ringo couldn't make it at all, but gave me his proxy. The doctor promises it'll go away, around the same time as the rash."

I ordered a Diet Coke and, after the server left, said, "Who's our missing friend?"

Hardly were the words out of my mouth when I saw Augie Fowler prowling the room and was certain I knew.

A generous greeting here, a two-fisted handshake there, hugs all around, Augie seemed to know most of the people. He said something to Van Dyke Parks, who picked at a wine stain while pointing in our direction.

Augie made a beeline to the table, settled across from Harry, put down the paper bag he'd been carrying in front of him on the table, and ignored me.

Wondered, "Mr. Harry, greetings and salutations. Where oh where is our dear friend Mr. Starkey?"

"Excused absence," Harry said. "I have his proxy, but the doctor says the shot he gave me will take care of that. Ordered you a Black Label."

"For starters, although I would have preferred one of those," he said, pointing to Harry's Brandy Alexander.

The server arrived with our drink order and Harry told her to keep the tab running.

Augie tried a taste.

It switched on the intricate network of blue veins and cherry blossoms on his nose and cheeks.

"Perfect," he decided, and ordered two more; doubles.

Finished the shot, moved aside the water like it was poisoned, and asked Harry, "You tell the cub reporter why he's here?"

"I was waiting for you."

"Go ahead, it was your idea."

Harry dismissed him with a flip of the hand.

"Credit where credit is doo-doo, Kalman. Tell him."

Augie grimaced like he'd swallowed the snake with the snake oil. "I suppose, but first things first . . ."

The server arrived with Augie's doubles.

"Perfect timing, my dear," he said, and immediately knocked one back.

Tongue washed his lips and ran a finger across them.

Lit a Montecristo and blew a line of blue smoke into the tobacco cloud hanging above the room.

Said, "As much as it grieves me to say it, you scored a clean beat with Chapman at Bellevue, kid. How you got to see him, something I might have tried myself if I hadn't been so damn engaged, helping out at the Dakota, ministering to the needs of Mr. Harry, working a few story angles of my own."

Not looking as sincere as he was trying to sound.

"Thank you."

"You know how to take me to the limit and piss me off. I learned as much the night you stole that Press Club award out from under me with some nonsense about Elvis in *Rolling Stone*, you remember?"

"Indelibly."

"Then you had the unmitigated gall to throw the trophy in my face and tell me to keep it."

"Which Mr. Fowler did," I told Harry.

"But your score with that deadly little shit who killed our mate John—the reason I've come to conclude you may have the makings of a first-class reporter in you after all."

"Thank you."

"Still years down the road, of course."

"Of course."

He polished off the second double-shot of Black Label and tried to snatch Harry's Brandy Alexander. Harry was too fast for him.

"Okay, then," Augie said.

He pushed the paper bag at me.

"Go on, kiddo, dig in."

My Press Club trophy was inside the bag.

I verged on getting emotional.

Augie recognized the signs.

He settled back, smiled devilishly, and said, "A small congratulatory gift from yours truly. It means a helluva lot more coming from me than it does coming from any damn Press Club, amigo."

Harry said, "Kalman, if you're finished with your first things first, can we move on to second things second?"

Leigh had begged off the tour, claiming she knew the casino awake and in her dreams, and gone to Roy Bigelow's office, to make some calls, take care of a little deadline business, she said.

She was half-sitting on his desk, showing a lot of leg, the phone to her ear and scribbling in her Day Runner, when we arrived.

She put down the phone and asked, "How'd it go?"

Roy made the okay sign with his thumb and forefinger.

"I was just hearing how it was at On the Rox, the club in LA I've told you about before, where the ball got rolling originally on this Imagine That! festival business, you know that? Back in 'eighty, right after John Lennon bought it?"

"Rolling in what way?"

The office was huge, about the size of the old Forum Club, one of my regular haunts before the Lakers moved to the Staples Center, and decorated like an Indian museum.

Roy paused to give Leigh a playful pat on the cheek before going around her and settling behind his desk with his feet up.

I headed for the couch, where Leigh joined me a moment later.

It seated eight, but Leigh picked a spot close enough to me for me to see her breasts shifting inside her halter top when she gestured, catch a flash of rich brown nipple when she leaned forward to snatch a mint from the crystal candy bowl on the coffee table.

Body language, but no way to swear it was intentional.

"Some singer named Harry Nelson, friend of Lennon. He had the idea to raise money and give it to Wipe Out Weapons International, help escalate the war against handguns," Roy said.

"Nilsson," I corrected him.

Roy nodded. "Do it in Lennon's honor and memory. Some reporter thought the perfect place with enough land to pull off that sort of Woodstock was here on the reservation. He knew Neil and that he was out here, so the two of them got Neil to put it to the tribal council. A few concessions and it sailed good enough to happen again in '85. I missed that meeting or I would have known already. I was in England when Lennon got killed; could tell you where and what I was doing when I got the news, if you wanted to know."

He waited for one of us to ask.

Leigh said, "Did he mention my father?"

Roy said, "I was sitting in a theater in the West End with some exotic dancer I got chummy with the night before, seeing this show, *Evita*, and this actor playing Che, David Essex, I think, who had the big record with 'Rock On'? After the curtain calls he comes forward. All choked up, he breaks the news, saying everybody in the cast knew before the show, but they didn't want to ruin the show for the audience. Me and the dancer went off and got drunk, so bad I couldn't get it up for days."

Leigh said, "Did Neil mention my father?"

"You mean, like Ben was also at On the Rox?"

"No. Like it was my father who convinced the tribe to go along with the idea. He had the friends and the influence Neil didn't, and Neil knew that. So, he came over the house and asked my father to help."

Gave me a scathing look, like I was guilty of rewriting history.

Roy said, "As a matter of fact, yeah."

Leigh's face flushed and fell like a bungee jump.

"Also, how Ben stepped up to the line for the festival again in 'eighty-five, when the council's new captain, Captain Tonio Ajenio, wanted the tribe to play squeeze-o for a bigger cut of the action. A word here, a word there, and Ben got it on track again.

"The town may have had it in for him, keed, but your old man was a hero to the reservation. Always looking out for our interests, standing up for us when the government's back was turned away, which was all the time.

"The bread to build Captain Pabro's after we decided to give gambling a try? You think it came from our peat leases? Was Ben who brought us together with the bankers and yelled and screamed a deal into place, good for them and better for the San Gorgonios.

"I know, if he'd lived, there would of been a third festival in 'ninety and another in 'ninety-five, but there were too many harp players pulling strings in Washington. Because of that senator who got himself offed at the 'eighty-five festival."

"Senator Needman."

"Him. Followed by Sonny Bono not wanting anything that would interfere with his plans for reviving Palm Springs. I bet, if he hadn't gone Tree one–Sonny zero, the festival would be going on inside the Palm Springs taxable city limits, not here again. Sonny, he was quite an operator."

I said, "You'd think Mayor Savage would also want the festival in Palm Springs, not the reservation. Yet, it was Savage who called me and got me involved."

"Except, Rick Savage headlined the festival here, and there was a lot of nostalgia playing with his head, the way I heard it."

I memory-slapped my forehead, checked my Rolex.

"I'm supposed to be meeting with Savage in an hour," I announced. Turning to Leigh, who expected us to be going to her place from here: "It went completely out of my mind when we talked earlier about—"

"No problem," Leigh said.

She almost seemed to welcome the news.

Pointed to her Day Runner.

"A few fires to put out before the edition closes. Use my car. Roy can have someone take me back to the plant, and I'll see you after you get back from Palm Springs. How does that sound?"

I got to City Hall to find I'd missed Rick Savage by a half hour.

"Why he had me stay behind—figuring you for late," his aide, a black man named Frank Gordy, said. "We called out to your hotel, left messages, and nothing back, but the mayor figured you right for tardy, not rude. Instinct like that is what's gonna make him a fine senator for Palm Springs. Swing a right next block."

We were heading for Richie's home, me driving, the aide a warehouse of tourist information and unbridled adulation for his boss; in the small-talk department a definite match for Roy Bigelow. Maybe it has something to do with all the desert heat.

"You like the way a Seville handles?" he asked. "How's it compare to the Lexus you had yesterday?"

That caught me by surprise.

"How do you know I was driving a Lexus?"

A sharp laugh, the kind that identifies the person who has the upper hand.

"Two ways, Mr. Gulliver. Firstly, it's sitting over in one of my body and fenders right now, getting fixed up good as new. My body and fenders, they got the freeway concession with the car rental agency. I saw your name on the paperwork after it got towed in by my towing company."

"Secondly?"

"First, really. Yesterday, when you were trailing after Miss Marriner and me? Couple times got a good look at you in the rearview. Same face you're wearing today."

"That was you driving the Lincoln?"

"Nobody else could make the getaway moves you saw. The freeway is my friend. Anybody knows me can tell you that. A left turn coming up next stop sign."

"Does Miss Marriner know it was me in the Lexus?"

"Might of mentioned it to her. Found it curious, seeing how you came on out together for business with the mayor. I didn't know she was your ex. Until she said so, I thought it might be fans of the mayor, chasing to see if he was inside. Happens all the time. Okay, left here, then three blocks and another left. I'll say so."

"The mayor, also? You told him?"

"Between you and me, he doesn't know about my business, and please don't say nothing. Just Miss Marriner, on her way out from the hotel early this morning."

"While you waited for the mayor to come down."

"Say what?"

"It's okay, Frank. No reason to cover up for the boss. I saw the Lincoln parked outside the hotel last night, saw him go inside with Miss Marriner."

He made a noise like someone enjoying his first swallow of morning coffee. Shook his head. Smiled like he understood the unspoken question inside the question.

"Wait for five minutes, you would of seen him come out, too. Can't get into too much trouble in five minutes, unless you're Superman."

"Longer than five, and the Lincoln was still there. How do you explain that?"

Sharply: "I don't, Mr. Gulliver, leastwise not to you. Okay, a left turn here."

"Did Miss Marriner mention where she was going?"

"Ask her," he said, putting a period to the subject.

188

I waited at the entrance gate with the motor running while Frank got out of the car and waved a high sign. The gate, eight or ten feet tall and as high as the brick wall, also topped with rolls of razor wire, eased back.

The house was a quarter mile up a bricked drive lined on both sides with evenly spaced high-rise palm trees, past perfectly manicured lawns and a putting green; a sprawling two-story early Spanish Colonial Revival, lots of brick and covered patio walkway; a smaller version peeking out behind the main building, a guest house or servants' quarters.

In the background, the mountains turning a molten pink in the afternoon sun, giant cloud banks adrift in a radiant blue sky. Nature's idea of a picture postcard.

Clearly, Richie had done well for himself since coming to this small town and, after all, that's what Palm Springs was, bottom line, a small town. On what I'd seen already, I figured the place as a two- or three-million-dollar chunk of real estate.

We reached a parking area and Frank pointed to a slot not far from the Lincoln, near a freshly waxed Cad, a mint green Beatle, a Chevy pickup grimy with desert mud and dust, and a T-Bird whose license plate holder named the car rental agency I'd used in Sunrise.

Frank, back to being affable, was telling me, "Heard tell how Cary Grant honeymooned here with some heiress he married in the forties—"

"Barbara Hutton."

"Sounds right."

"Department store money, Woolworth's."

We got out of the Seville.

Frank was saying, "Wouldn't know about that; K-Mart generation, but I heard some other names I do. Clara Bow, from the silent movies—"

"The 'It Girl.' "

"Her. She was a guest here. Even Harry Truman, who was the president of the United States dropped the atomic bomb on Japan. Lots. Long time before the mayor moved in and had his share of famous people start staying over."

He rattled off a list. Politicians whose names I knew. Big names from the movies, television, and music, but mostly movers and shakers able to write a big check for a political candidate.

"What we got here in all is almost six thousand square feet of house inside these two walled acres," he said. "Let's see . . ." Counting off on his fingers. "Eight bedrooms. Seven baths. A morning room. A Mexican cantina. A wine cellar. A courtyard that's absolutely not to be believed. A spa. The Olympic pool. A sunken tennis court. Driving up you already saw the putting green—"

And the gunshot shut him up.

Loud, echoing.

Startling both of us.

Coming from the direction of the house.

Frank jammed two hands against my back and pushed.

Sent me sprawling off the walkway.

Ordered, "Stay down!"

I rolled into a sitting position behind a lush hedge, reached behind my back for the Beretta inside my belt.

Frank was running a safety pattern to the house, ready to fire the Glock he'd pulled from somewhere. He slammed his back against the wall, to the left side of the door.

Another shot. And another.

And something came down hard on my head.

16

It had taken Stevie an exasperating three hours to get from Sunrise City to Los Angeles.

She'd left early enough to beat the usual morning rush, except for a freeway meltdown about a mile past the El Monte interchange that shut down lanes in all directions while the CHP, paramedics, coroners' wagons, and tow trucks cleaned up after an oil tanker that exploded and ripped into dozens of passenger cars and a school bus.

Bumper-to-bumper inching past the scene.

Lots of motorists, not just Stevie, too caught up in the sheer awfulness of it all not to look. Lots of them on cell phones.

TV choppers circling overhead in the gray morning sky.

A fleet of ambulances being loaded with victims.

Other victims waiting for treatment, some talking among themselves, others sitting alone, staring mindlessly, trying to understand what had happened.

The less lucky under blankets or being fitted for body bags, some of them small enough for her to guess at the ages of those victims, and—

Stevie cried.

She was emotionally drained by the time she got to the *Bedrooms and Board Rooms* production offices at the Sunset Gower Studios.

She knew herself well enough to know the last thing in the world she needed now was the meeting the producers had foisted on her with their call last night, insisting it was too important to wait. Beyond that, secretive.

No help from her agent or her lawyer; unable to reach either; her calls still unreturned by the time she climbed into the Cherokee and, in the mirror, spotted Armando racing for his Wrangler.

She hadn't told him about the meeting, or left word for Neil, but Armando always seemed to know.

Wouldn't that be something, our James Dean popping up today to try adding her to today's body count?

That kind of a day, Stevie.

She forced a laugh, hoping it would bring some sort of relief. It didn't.

Hang in there, girl, hang in there, she told herself, and swallowed a gasp that immediately slipped back out as a sigh.

She one-stopped at her dressing room to douse her face with water, do a fast patch job on her makeup, run a brush through her hair.

Wrote off her bloodshot eyes as a major disaster area.

Dashed down the hall to the producers' office.

Stopped and took a deep breath.

Pushed open the door without knocking.

Waited a beat before making her star entrance, the Loretta Young thing Mama had made her work on for hours, impressing upon her over and over, "You get to be a star, honey, you got to behave like a star or they take it away from you faster'n they gave it to you."

An omen, that she remembered Mama's admonition now?

And Stevie pictured those little bodies under blankets on the freeway, and—

Behaving like a star didn't mean so much, did it?

Carl Houseman, the exec producer, checking his watch as she checked out the conference table searching for a clue to what the meeting was about. Houseman's exec secretary, Lydia Tatt, in her usual spot to his right; co-exec producer Ralph Bonner on his left; seven producers and associate producers; two suits from the network, Lon Overman, the head of daytime programming, and his new assistant, whom she'd met once, at the last network affiliates meeting, but couldn't put a name to; something like Sawhill or Spillman.

Sawyer? Buzz Sawyer?

An oval of somber faces, no one looking at her past a first blink to be sure it was her, except for Dar Armateaux, the only ally she was certain of, a dialogue writer who got promoted to associate producer in lieu of a raise, because promotions are cheaper over time than payouts to the Writers Guild.

SOP at *Bedrooms and Board Rooms*.

A woebegone expression betrayed the smile Dar had for her.

His head going tick-tock ever so slightly—

A signal to her to prepare for the worst?

The vibes in the room saying the same thing, confirming the premonition about the meeting she'd had since last night and all the way in this morning from Sunrise City.

Not good. Not good at all.

And her agent, her lawyer, where were they?

No callbacks.

She'd have words for them later, after the meeting.

Two.

Beginning with "you're" and ending with "fired."

She didn't need them.

Mama's voice again, ringing in her head, "In the end, whenever it really counts the most, you don't need nobody but yourself, baby. Not me. Not no one."

Years later, after the reality of Neil had sunk in, "He's good for you, yeah, but in the end you'll always be better for yourself."

Even Neil had said as much, more than once, when she would thank him for something new he had brought into her life, her mind, her growth as an intelligent, independent woman.

Stevie helped herself to a seat at the south end of the table, across the length from Houseman, locked her brightest smile in place, and apologized for being late. Mentioned the dead batteries in her cell phone, when she tried to call and let them know.

Determined to tough it out, as usual.

Her own best soldier in time of war.

Thank you, Mama.

Neil.

Houseman cut her off when she started to describe the freeway accident, with the same holier-than-thou abruptness he used on writers when he didn't like their proposal for a new story arc.

"Stevie, I felt we should do this in person," Houseman said. He looked around the table for agreement and got a few nods. "Better than a phone or a certified letter."

She could have gotten up and left then.

That preamble told her everything she had to know about what was coming.

Curiosity pinned her to her seat.

"Fast, I know, not even time for our people to reach your people, so I do appreciate your driving in," Houseman said, not enough of an actor to make it sound sincere. His voice a nasal screech. "Isn't that so, Lon?"

"So," Overman said, finally exposing his face to her. Bloated and bland. Looking old for someone who couldn't be more than thirty. Unclogged his throat and said, "Network's fault, actually. An overzealous publicist, a new chap, got out the story late yesterday without all the necessary sign-offs. We didn't want you hearing it on the news if we could help it, why I asked Carl to ring you up."

Houseman said testily, "That was my idea, Lon."

Overman frowned at the challenge, thought about it.

"Be that as it may," he said, rather than get into a fight over credit. Gave the floor back to Houseman with a gesture.

Houseman smothered a victory grin, checked Lydia Tatt for an approval rating, and turned back to Stevie, looking every inch the Hollywood cliché, especially the gold chains that circled his neck like jets at LAX waiting to be cleared for a landing.

"It's just not working out anymore," he said. Shrugged. Turned his palms to the ceiling. Looked around the table to see who was letting her know they agreed with him.

Even Dar managed a nod.

Stevie chalked it up to self-preservation and didn't take any points away from him. Dar already had risked his job once, sneaking by to explain how Karen Walls was doing her damnedest to steal lines and camera time from her.

She summoned all her willpower to sustain an impassive look and not give an inch.

"What's not working out anymore, Carl?"

"I mean, knowing what you went through, probably still, the Dean business, Nico Mercouri's death, your memory in and out and making it tough to learn lines, you know?"

"All in the past," Stevie said, not entirely the truth, but nothing they had to know. "You still haven't answered my question."

"You're off away on hiatus while your people grind our people for more money and more show time, and no closer now than we were when the negotiations started. But our numbers haven't suffered without you, Stevie, as much as everyone at the network was afraid.

"Dar here has been writing great stuff for Karen Walls, especially, and we're getting lots of mail about her, not to mention how fast her TVQ has been rising. *TV Guide* cover and all coming up. *People* magazine. Right, Lon?"

"The network has been extremely pleased, Carl."

"Isn't that so?" Houseman said to the others.

More nods, some murmurs.

Dar unwilling to answer her inquiring eyes.

Did that mean he was screwing her now, as well as Carl Houseman?

"I mean, not that she's any Sex Queen of the Soaps. I don't know that anyone can ever replace you that way, but—"

"I still have a contract, Carl. Pay or play, remember? With a lot of time still left on the meter."

Houseman's jaw muscles started dancing.

He never liked being challenged.

"That's what the courts are for, Miss Marriner."

Before she could answer him, Lon Overman said softly, "Carl, please . . . Tell Ms. Marriner what you and the network decided."

Exerting his authority.

"You tell her!" Houseman said, giving an order rather than lose face in front of his troops.

Overman took a moment, looked fleetingly at Houseman, like he was looking for the best spot to plant the knife.

"No, Carl. It's your place. Far be it from me to take your place."

Houseman, clearly not ready to escalate the argument, took several deep breaths.

He fished out his cocktail-party smile and said, "We plan all along to honor your contract, so long as you do, too, Stevie. Dar and the boys know to give you a scene here and a scene there once or twice a month. You keep on showing up, you keep on getting paid. The one other thing—remember how we own you exclusively."

"Meaning?"

"What it means. You can't do anything else, TV, movies, stage—squat—without our approval."

"How to kill a career, is that the game, Carl?"

Lon Overman said, "The production company and its co-venture partner, the network, merely honoring your contract, Ms. Marriner." The cobra finally baring his fangs. "Perhaps you have a better idea?"

She gave him a look that told him she didn't have to think about her answer.

She rose, adjusted her outfit, and worked the silence into the moment until she knew she had all their attention.

Gave it another beat.

"Lon, sweetie. Boys . . ."

Broke for a generous stage smile.

"You can take your threats and your contract and shove them up your collective asses."

Saluted, turned, and did a military march out the door without a glance backward.

Smiling now for real.

Satisfied she owned the world again.

The freeway was wide open most of the way, and Stevie got back to Sunrise a little past noon. Neil wasn't in his room. Missed him by a few minutes, the desk clerk said; no idea where to, he said, only that he had gone off with Mrs. Wilder, the lady from the newspaper.

Back in her room, Stevie undressed down to her bra and panties, stretched out on the bed, and, using the wall as a surrogate for Neil, cursed him for not being there.

Some habits die hard, if ever.

One of hers was turning to him for counsel and comfort whether she needed it or not. She didn't most of the time, but she valued his opinions—even when he handed them down like some pompous Solomon—whether she agreed with them or not.

He had taught her to think for herself and believe in herself, but helping her find her strengths had produced a weakness. It had tied her more strongly to him.

The husband thing, no.

Something richer and more rewarding than that.

One of their areas of recurring disagreement.

Neil needed her for a wife.

She needed, what?

Him to be around.

"Neil, honey, where the hell are you?!"

No answer from the wall.

Stevie closed her eyes to images from this morning's freeway horror that wouldn't go away, hoping to make more room in her mind for those final moments in Carl Houseman's office, when she—

Sleep closed in too fast for her to finish the thought, brought on by the psychological letdown and the oppressively dry desert heat easily withstanding the air conditioner unit droning away in the window.

"Hush little baby, don't you—"

The phone jolted her awake a little more than an hour later, in the middle of crooning a lullaby to a schoolgirl who had pushed aside her blanket and was screaming for her daddy.

It took her some seconds to realize she wasn't on the freeway.

"Neil?"

"Martin Halliwell, Ms. Marriner. Think y'all could make some time for me today? Me and Rick Savage? I'm on my way to Palm Springs to meet with him."

Something about the way Halliwell said it.

"Can I ask what about?" she said.

"I was hoping y'all could tell me."

She threw on a pair of black pants and a matching tunic top under a black cardigan shirt jacket, floral ballet mules to add some color to the outfit; pulled her hair into a ponytail, dabbed on some eyeliner and blush, grabbed her wide-brimmed straw hat and shoulder bag, and was downstairs ten minutes later.

Halliwell was seated across the room in one of the red felt armchairs with lace doilies on the armrests, long legs stretched and crossed at the ankles, staring out the arched picture window onto Delivery Street.

A noisy floorboard and, without turning to confirm who was approaching, he greeted her by name and invited her to take the chair opposite him. Ran a handkerchief across the top of his head, across his brow; dabbed at his lips before stuffing it in the breast pocket of his blue pinstripe, the only suit he seemed to own.

"This complexion of mine, deserts do me serious harm," he volunteered, loosening his bland blue tie another notch. "Used to sport a great tan, until the sun turned deadly on me. Also goes for other members my family. Y'all got pretty skin. Hope you take safe care of it. A thirty-sunscreen usually does the trick, and a good hat like you got there." His was on the side table, like the kind the "Duke" character wears in the comic strip "Doonesbury."

"A thirty. I'll remember . . ." Not interested in prolonging the small talk. "The meeting with Rick Savage, why should I be able to tell you about it?"

"Seems it was your idea?"

"My idea?"

"A guess . . . I heard from Mr. Gulliver this morning, to tell me about his first tête-à-tête with Mrs. Leigh Wilder. Next, he's reporting about an interesting exchange you had with the mayor."

Stevie's memory went into high gear, trying to remember how much she'd told Neil.

"Mostly personal. Neil told Richie I was with him. He phoned and invited me to dinner; sent a car. We had a great time talking the old days. He dropped me back. The end."

About as far as she'd got before quitting Neil's room in anger.

"Mr. Gulliver seemed to think y'all had more to tell him, but your discussion ended before that could happen."

"Reporters always think like that."

"Mr. Gulliver seemed to think y'all had occasion to meet Mr. Aaron Lodger."

"Oh, right." Like he had jolted her memory. "Shows you the impression the old guy made. Really old, Marty. Nothing like the dangerous criminal you painted."

"Can't tell a crook by his cover," Halliwell said.

Lame, she thought, but let him see she appreciated his humor.

"If they ever make a movie about his life, they should cast George Burns," Stevie said.

"Mr. Burns is dead."

"My point exactly."

Halliwell laughed out loud and made an invisible chalk mark in the air.

"Good one, too, Ms. Marriner." At once turned serious. "And

y'all learned how he became involved in the Imagine That! festival?"

"It was mentioned, but not really. Only that he helped get the funding, because he thought the festival could help make a strong statement against guns."

Halliwell blasted the window with a high-pitched *Hah*!

"Funnier than your last joke, Ms. Marriner. All's Mr. L usually has against guns is someone's head, getting ready to brain-paint a room."

"You asked."

"And that's all y'all heard in order to make you say to Mr. Gulliver that, if Mayor Savage was telling you true, I was feeding you and Mr. Gulliver a—How did you put it?—'a modest load of crap'?"

He adjusted his eyeglasses, scolded her with a look.

"Not all, Marty."

"The rest of it, then? You got to feeling so sorry for your old friend, you mentioned how the Treasury Department was busy connecting him to money laundering, other illegal goings-on with the San Gorgonios? He says no, not so, never, thereby making Martin Halliwell a lying shit hole?"

She noticed Halliwell's speech had taken another U-Haul turn somewhere, still the south, but not as soft-spoken.

"I didn't tell Neil that part, so how could he—"

"You denying?"

"Am I under oath?"

"I'd say under a cloud. Consorting with Mr. L, who you were instructed to steer away from. Revealing the root of an ongoing and confidential government investigation to a prime suspect; maybe making us abandon the investigation, thereby opening yourself up to possible criminal or civil charges."

Meeting Aaron Lodger, unexpected. An accident.

The other part, telling Richie: true. She did.

Certain Richie had reached a level of emotional honesty with her yesterday that made absolutely unnecessary the role playing and word games Halliwell wanted from her.

The way Richie had responded to the news, angrily, with urgent denial, only served to convince Stevie she was right in taking that approach, but—

"Neil didn't hear that from me, so how could you—?"

"From Mayor Savage himself. The mayor tracked me down this morning. Spelled it out. Demanded a face-to-face soon as possible, to resurrect his good name, he said; said how he wanted y'all there, too. Why I'm here. Why we're having this conversation. Why I'm ready to go, if you are."

Reached for his hat, started to unwind from the chair; spilling fresh sweat on his suit jacket.

She said, "He wouldn't have done that, called you, if he were guilty, would he?"

Feeling vindicated.

Halliwell smirked, again made a chalk mark in the air.

"Another good one, Ms. Marriner."

Halliwell drove, a T-Bird rented from the agency down the street, when he couldn't get the engine on his Honda to turn over, telling Stevie how growing up he had dreamed of owning one. "But not on my salary," he said. "Maybe one of these fine days, after the pension kicks in, and I'm doing my sunset years traveling around this great country of ours. The little woman and me on the road in a brand new Bird and tugging a little trailer behind us. Y'all can bet on it. I don't understand folks who want to see Europe and all, but can't find time for the beauties and wonders of the U.S. of A. All our national parks. The Grand Canyon. Mardi Gras time in New Orleans . . ."

Stevie was afraid, any moment, he'd break into a chorus of "God Bless America."

She'd thought about arguing for the Jeep, her driving, but changed her mind. This way she wasn't necessarily stuck with Halliwell for the return trip.

If the meeting went as well as she expected, she could stay, hang out with Richie, certain he'd have no objection to bringing her back or having Frank take her.

Define the message her vibes were sending her now about Richie. For sure, a way to take her mind off her miserable morning in LA.

"Ever been to St. Louis, Ms. Marriner? Where the Rams wound up to win their championship? The home of Stan Musial? Stan the Man? They have this fantastic arch hanging over the Mississippi River like some gigantic McDonald's that—"

Halliwell droning on and on.

She tuned him out, ignoring his conversational attempts at making peace. She wasn't buying it, not after the way he had come down on her.

She punched on the radio, found a station playing the hits, a disk jockey who sounded like a kid, working hard at barreling the resonance of his voice, giving it a Real Don Steele kind of urgency.

Punching up the volume whenever Halliwell raised his voice.

Eminem.

'N Sync.

The Back Street Boys.

Boogie Down Dirt.

Acts Richie said he was trying to line up for Imagine That!, to blend the new with rockers of the past he said he was close to signing: the Eagles, Tom Petty, Huey Lewis and the News. A Fleetwood Mac reunion, if Stevie Nicks could be talked into it again. Stevie Wonder. Aerosmith.

Hopefully, Ringo and the tour band of one-time heavies from other super groups that he'd put together. Sir Paul had passed, but George Harrison was thinking seriously of flying over and doing a walk-on, Richie said.

He was certain any direct link to Lennon would have the crowd of four or five hundred thousand, bigger than that, as boogie crazy as the Dead ever got a crowd.

Stevie wasn't so sure.

"Most of the people who come will come for the music, not the memories," she told him.

Richie said, "And to honor John Lennon."

She didn't say what she was thinking: "Especially if you have 'N Sync on stage." Instead, "I hope you're right, Richie."

Richie pushed an index finger into the tip of her nose and said, no less confident, "You'll see."

Halliwell, pork-sweating although the air had been on high the entire ride, saying something above the music about New England in the fall being too beautiful for words as he cruised the Movie Colony area, finally easing to a stop at the gate of a huge walled estate.

He identified them by name to the voice inside the talk box and the gate rolled back.

Richie welcomed them at the door.

Offered his hand to Halliwell, thanked him for coming.

No trace of anger.

A hug and kiss on the cheek for Stevie, his mouth half a breath away from hers.

In shorts and shirtless, exposing piles of toned muscle and acres of thick brown and gray body hair.

The Robin Williams gorilla look in a much better body, she thought.

Her vibes back, stronger than ever.

Sending her nasty thoughts with the good vibrations.

"Great news," he announced. "Are you sitting?"

"Not yet," Halliwell said as Richie guided them down a long hallway lined with dozens of his Gold Records and dozens more photos of Richie with a who's who of rock-and-roll and politics.

"Just before I left the office, phone calls," Richie said, his sandals on the inlaid tile slapping out echoes that bounced up to the exposed redwood ceiling beams. "The Boss himself wants to do the show."

"Wonderful, good for you," Stevie said.

He glanced over his shoulder and turned his smile into the sun. "Thanks; not all. We got Elton for sure and, catch this. Catch this. Barbra? Coming out of retirement one more time for a great cause?"

"Miss Streisand?" Halliwell said, perking up.

"Chances are great, if her people can figure a way to work around a conflict on her calendar. I think it's gonna happen, I really do. They said she's high into the idea of Wipe Out Weapons International."

"I'm thrilled for you, Richie."

"Thanks. I'm thrilled for me, too."

Gleefully, no artifice.

The large living room was decorated like pages ripped out of *Architectural Desert* magazine; nothing cheap, except the stack of newspapers on top of the coffee table, next to an empty bottle of Perrier. Ornately framed artwork to blend with the furnishings; except for a Warhol lithograph of Mick Jagger, nothing that would bring more than rolling eyes at a Sotheby's or Christie's auction.

"Either you guys hungry? I can have them fix something. Something to wet your whistle, maybe?"

Stevie shook her head.

So did Halliwell, who said, "Can we get to it, Mayor Savage? Why y'all needed me to make this drive up from Los Angeles."

"Give it five, okay? I'm expecting one more person."

Halliwell gave Richie an odd look. Removed his glasses and studied their thick lenses like they might show him who the person was.

Stevie was thinking: Aaron Lodger.

Richie took her by the hand, started for a sitting area facing a row of French doors that led out onto a courtyard and, beyond that, to the mountains and a painter's sky.

"C'mon, over there, Mr. Halliwell," he said, pointing. "Make yourself comfortable. Enjoy the view."

Halliwell got as far as the middle of the room when a shot rang out.

The sound of glass shattering, and—

Richie made an oomphing noise.

Did a half spin.

Fell to the floor.

More glass breaking.

The shot flew past Stevie.

Thudded into the wall behind her.

"Duck!" Halliwell called at her.

He was poised in a shooter's stance, two hands on an automatic, trying to find where in the courtyard the shots had come from.

Stevie sank in front of the next shot, almost landing on top of Richie.

Rolled onto her side as—

The next bullet sailed over Halliwell's head.

He crouched lower, giving higher rise to the hump on his back.

Outside, through the broken windows, Stevie heard the sound of receding footsteps; someone in a hurry.

Then, only the sound of her own heavy breathing, her heart attacking her chest the way the knot in her stomach had her on the verge of throwing up.

Footsteps growing louder up the hallway.

The shooter trying again?

No.

Frank Gordy.

An anxious look on his face.

Studying the scene.

Aiming a Glock.

Seeing his boss sprawled out on the floor as Halliwell turned in his direction, still holding the automatic, still in a shooter's stance.

"Rat bastard! The mayor is my friend!" Frank screamed.

Fired at Halliwell.

17

I've been whacked on the head before, coconut crackers that put me away for hours. This one was heavy, but off the mark, catching me more behind an ear; a blow that turned my eyes to pinwheels without delivering the knockout punch.

I saw my attacker, all three of him, making a beeline for the parking area; hopping into all three rented T-Birds.

I drew my Beretta and got up, intending to chase after him. My legs wouldn't cooperate. My knees wouldn't lock. I grabbed onto the hedge to keep from falling.

He sped past me and was halfway down the drive before I could try again; already through the open entrance gate by the time I took a step that worked and—

Heard another shot coming from inside the house.

Thought about it.

Ignored the rule that says the proper way to confront danger is to run in the opposite direction.

Dragged myself there and went inside not knowing what to expect. Kept shaking my head clear as I slowly worked up a long corridor with my back to a wall of Richie Savage's Gold Records and a pictorial memory lane; keeping a cop's grip on the Beretta.

Reached the end of the corridor.

Swallowed a ton of artificial courage.

Said a little dry-mouthed prayer.

Did a sharpshooter's turn, and—

Stevie shouted my name from across the room.

She was kneeling by a body on the floor. Contorted on its back. An expanding circle of blood for a pillow. Just enough red-masked face left to tell me it was Richie Savage.

"Stevie, are you okay?"

She did this funny thing with her hands that meant yes. Palms stained crimson, like she'd been finger painting.

"Richie, he's dead."

She moaned, touched his blood-matted chest again, as if it might make a difference.

My eyes shifted over to Frank Gordy, wearing a vacant stare, shaking his head in disbelief, ready to use the Glock on Halliwell, half sitting, half stretched out in the middle of the room, propped on an elbow, a hand trying to halt the blood trickling from his upper arm.

Halliwell sent me an urgent stare.

"Don't!" I commanded Frank.

Rage burned in his wet eyes.

"The mayor is my friend!"

Softer: "Don't, Frank."

Like an understanding parent.

"You gonna shoot me instead?"

"Shoot you?"

I suddenly realized I had the Beretta aimed point blank at his chest. I eased into an upright position and raised it at the ceiling.

"Better? Now, you do the same?"

"The mayor is my friend!"

"Mayor Savage was also my friend, Frank. Put the gun away."

"He was gonna shoot me, too," Frank said, using his chin to indicate a .38 automatic on the floor, just out of Halliwell's reach.

"Not so," Halliwell said calmly. "No more so than the idea I shot Mayor Savage."

Stevie, regaining emotional control, showing she agreed with Halliwell.

I said, "I'm your friend, too, Frank. Please listen to me. Are you listening, Frank?"

His eyes roved to me from the Glock, then to Stevie.

"Listen to Neil," she agreed, every word an effort.

"Listening," he said, finally.

I said, "Here's the deal, Frank. I'm going to call nine-one-one. That phone over there. You keep him covered until the police get here. He moves, kill him. You hear that, Halliwell?"

"Not a muscle," Halliwell said, sounding relieved.

"I was a better shot, he'd already be dead," Frank said, wiping at his eyes.

I put in the call, then—

Moved out of hearing range and phoned my paper.

Geller was running the desk.

Skipping our usual small talk, I said, "Think you can find a big fat hole for me on page one, Harv? I'm in Palm Springs, sitting with a goodie."

"Lot of dog fighting in today's editorial meeting, and we got hardly more than zilch. A clue would help before I go try and bump something, Gully."

"How's this? A gun battle in the last half hour at the home of Palm Springs mayor Rick Savage. The mayor murdered. A Treasury agent wounded. The *Daily*'s illustrious columnist attacked. The Sex Queen of the Soaps an eyeball witness and, even as we speak, yours truly with one of the shooters."

"Jesus! Exclusive?"

"Only if while I'm putting the pieces together you do something to destroy the wires, radio, TV, the Internet, and other forces of evil."

"I'm on it," Geller said.

I reached Leigh at the *Gazette* office and explained the situation.

"Cops on the way and then my story to file. It could be hours before I get the car back to you."

"But you're all right?" she asked, needing reassurance.

I checked my temple. Swollen. Tender to the touch.

"A little bump, but nothing to worry about. I've got a hard head."

A sigh of relief filled the receiver.

"Whenever you get the car back, it'll be fine. You can call from my place, that suits you."

"Maybe. If you haven't closed your next edition, I'll knock out something for you, how's that?"

"Daddy always predicted you'd be working for us one of these days."

"Leigh, you're sure you don't mind about Stevie?"

"Bring her along. What she's gone through, it wouldn't be the right time to leave her alone. Besides, I'd like to meet the woman who got the man who got away."

"Just so you know, I felt crappy yesterday, not telling you about Stevie when you—"

"That she was with you in Sunrise? Nathan at the hotel said something this morning, before you came downstairs, so not a surprise. It explained a lot to me about last night."

"You mean what happened at your place?"

"What didn't happen."

"I don't think one thing had anything to do with the other."

Like she hadn't heard me: "I'll have something warming in the oven, maybe order in a pizza, in the unlikely event either of you have any appetite left. Best I can promise is potluck."

"Leigh-Leigh, you're your mother's daughter," I said, grateful for her generosity.

"And my father's, Cookie Monster. Payback for the story you're going to write for me."

By the time the cops finished taking our statements, it was after seven and the story was already playing big on CNN and the networks. News vans were hogging the street outside the estate entrance, waiting expectantly to catch more than the sketchy details a police spokesman had released so far.

The evening temperature had cooled to somewhere in the dry mid-eighties, contributing to the growing crowd.

Movie Colony residents mingled on the sidewalks with dozens of the curious who'd heard about the murder and felt compelled to race over, snap souvenir photos or lay flowers along the wall, share dread and gossip among themselves and to the live TV feed reporters, in many ways like it was the Dakota and John Lennon all over again.

The circus noise drowning out the competing songs and sounds of the night birds and other desert creatures.

Detectives whisked Frank Gordy away in the back of an unmarked that drew a rumble of questioning sound, the "Who's that?" variety, but no one gave him significance, except one of the Movie Colony people who recognized him, waved and got a wave back, was instantly surrounded by crews from KCAL and KTTV, and told them, "I usually get my Lamborghini washed at one of his car washes. Great job at a fair price."

Frank was going to be booked on ADW, although Halliwell had advised the cops and a rep from the DA's office that he would not be signing a complaint.

"The man made an honest mistake," Halliwell said. "He believed I was the assassin who fired the shot that killed Mayor Savage. He was unaware the mayor and I were scheduled to meet here on business."

"What kind of business might that be?" asked the lead detective, fine-tuning his mustache.

"Government business. I'm not at liberty to say more to you at this precise time."

Halliwell flashed his badge.

His badge was bigger than the detective's.

The detective moved on to Stevie.

Richie's murder had pushed her into some private shell, but she managed to come out long enough to give a rambling account of the assault before imploring me with her eyes to get him to leave her alone.

He obliged, after getting her autograph in his spiral notepad, twice, once for his wife and on a second page for his lieutenant.

My turn next.

"And you didn't get a good look at the guy who slugged you?" the detective inquired, tamping down his mustache, so that the edges embraced the corners of his small upper lip.

"Not good enough to give you anything close to an ID."

"Miss Marriner says you two had come out here to talk about this John Lennon music festival thing that the mayor was putting together?"

"That's right."

"Think it'll still happen?"

Genuinely curious.

"I think so. I hope so. Mayor Savage had put enough of an organization together before today, so chances are good."

"Nice to hear. I was big, big about the Beatles when I was a kid, and then him, Lennon. I've been looking forward to taking the kids ever since it was announced. Rumors even the president could be showing up."

While I was rattling off my piece to the *Daily*, using an eyewitness to tragedy angle that put a little "exclusive" spin on the story, Halliwell left with the cops for police headquarters to file a stolen car report on the T-Bird he'd rented, leaving me with Stevie and questions I hadn't had a chance to toss at him:

If Halliwell needed a rental to drive to Palm Springs, how did he get to Sunrise City in the first place?

Why didn't he just go with Stevie, who told me she'd offered to drive?

Coincidence that Richie's killer picked the T-Bird for his getaway, and blind luck the keys were in the ignition?

More blind luck that the entrance gate was wide open when the killer tooled down the driveway?

Stevie was no help with any of the questions, or the ones I had for her while driving back to the hotel.

Sitting beside me in the Seville, but a million miles away, returning occasionally to share a memory about Richie Savage that kept telling me their romance those many years ago was more than a casual fling, maybe more than an intense fling.

No time for me to be jealous of a dead man.

"You're sure Armando followed you to Palm Springs?"

No reaction.

"Stevie?"

I reached over and stroked her hair.

She retreated from my touch, like it hurt, but after a second seemed to remember it was me and said, "What?"

"You're sure Armando followed you to Palm Springs?"

"Yes. Didn't I tell you that already?"

Like she wasn't sure herself.

"You said he pulled up outside the estate—"

"While we were turning up the drive and he stopped and got out to ID us in."

"In his Wrangler."

"In the T-Bird."

"Armando, not Halliwell."

Digesting what I said.

"Yes. In the Wrangler."

"But you didn't see him after that."

"Armando?"

"Armando."

"No. He was somewhere near, though. Always."

"You'd think Armando would have heard the shots when I did and come running."

She inched her head up and down a few times.

"So, where was he then?"

No response.

"No sign of him since. No sign of the Wrangler outside on the street."

"You say so."

The jazz station jock came out of a Cal Tjader cut and led into Ray Charles doing "Yesterday" with a dedication to the memory of Mayor Rick Savage, promising to follow it with some of Richie's greatest hits.

Stevie noisily swallowed some air.

Stopped me before I could punch in another station.

"It's okay, honey," she said. "It'll be fine. I'll be fine with it."

No Wrangler in the hotel parking lot.

The lobby empty and the registration desk untended, a little cardboard clock easel promising "Back at 9." It was already 9:20.

I slipped behind the counter to fish out our message slips.

Calls for Stevie from her agent and her lawyer. Twelve from *Entertainment Tonight*. Almost as many from *Extra* and *Access Hollywood*. One from Larry King, marked "Urgent" by the clerk; a request to call Larry at his private number no matter what the hour; the number and an advisory: "For Your Eyes Only."

For me, three messages from Leigh, spaced about forty minutes apart, two from the office, the last one from home, all reminding me she was on deadline and expecting a story.

Advising she'd opted for Subway sandwiches and their lower cholesterol count over pizza.

Reminding me to bring Stevie along.

Not likely.

What Stevie needed was a good night's sleep.

And, unless Armando was in his room with a reasonable explanation for his disappearance, I wasn't going to leave her alone.

I was playing a troublesome mind game with myself that began about an hour ago.

What if the shooter was our James Dean?

The target: Stevie, not Richie Savage, who stepped into a bullet meant for her.

If Richie had been the intended victim, the shooter got his top-shelf prize on the first shot and didn't have to try again with the second shot that barely missed her.

Except—

The third shot was at Halliwell, who was halfway across the living room.

That didn't make sense, did it?

Why Halliwell and not Stevie again?

Unless something had happened to disrupt the assassin's aim.

Forced him to flee.

Something like that?

Why not?

Happens all the time in the movies and, besides—

Logic is not the Monopoly money of a mind game.

When we reached Armando's door, I tugged Stevie to a stop while I rapped. Gave it a few seconds and tried again. Thought I heard shuffling inside and made a third try. Gave up and engineered Stevie into her room.

At once, she wriggled out of her jacket and tunic top, dropping both on the floor, kicked off her shoes, took out her pigtail band and shook her hair loose.

Raised her arms in surrender and, wheeling to face me, said, "That's all she wrote. Thank you, honey."

Stepped over and gave me a sister's kiss on the lips.

Turned away again and belly flopped onto the bed.

Seconds later was orchestrating the snore Stevie sends out whenever she's suffering extreme stress. Loud enough to get an answer from a bull elephant at the Griffith Park Zoo.

Before I could tell her I intended spending the night playing guardian angel.

I moved the armchair by the desk to a spot against the west wall, putting Stevie to my left and the door straight ahead. Found a limp pillow and lightweight blanket on the closet shelf. Was about to settle down with the Beretta in my lap when I remembered about Leigh.

I debated whether to call her from here or my room.

Decided here, rather than leave Stevie unguarded.

Besides, she was too zonked out to be awakened by the sound of conversation, but—

I was too hyped to sleep.

Maybe, use the time to pound out a new column?

Maybe, a personal remembrance about Rick Savage?

When he headlined Imagine That! in '85 and stole the show, and his only political messages were "Lennon Lives!" and "Rock-and-roll is here to stay!" delivered to a crowd of thousands in a city that rose overnight on the flatlands of the San Gorgonio Reservation.

No doubt Stevie would approve.

She answered my inquisitive stare with a snore the size of Texas.

Okay, then—

Yeah.

Jump across the hall.

Grab my laptop.

Nothing can possibly happen in the two minutes that'll take.

I crossed the hall and was putting the key in the lock when something hard pressed into my side and a voice I knew from somewhere, in a harsh tone that crossed a whisper with a hiss—a hissper?—said, "Door's open. Head in."

"Is there a reason that feels like a gun?"

"A .45. Want me to prove it?"

"Your word's good by me. Two thumbs up."

"Move it," he said, and made a point of digging the .45 in deep enough to score my painful grunt.

I turned the door handle, pushed open the door, and went inside. He was right behind me.

The toilet was flushing and a minute later, after some running sink water, Little Beaver stepped into sight wiping his hands.

Why the other voice was familiar.

It had to be Tonto.

In addition to working security at Captain Pabro's Gaming Casino, they apparently raided settlers as a team.

Little Beaver said, " 'Bout time," and tossed away the towel without looking. It caught the edge of the desk and dropped into the waste basket.

"Two points," I said.

"Huh?"

"Never mind."

What was I supposed to explain, where Stevie goes into snoring stress, my MO is amateur night at the Comedy Store? I know the type. They wouldn't have cared. If I told them it was my MO, they'd probably want to know, "Who's Mo?"

Leave bad enough alone, I rarely say.

Tonto shoved me and I stumbled into the room, almost tripping over my Nikes.

I wheeled around and said, "Was that nice? Would you like it if I did that to you?"

"Then I'd have an excuse to bust your face," he said, sounding like he meant it.

No question he could do it.

Besides having about fifteen years on me, he was built like one of the icebergs that nipped the Titanic. Broad and close to the ground. All rippling muscle inside a Gold's Gym T-shirt. Tight gunmetal gray shorts that showed off a pair of calves bigger than any ever delivered by Elsie the Borden Cow. Close-set ink black eyes squinting over high-rise cheekbones. A nose that couldn't make up its mind which direction it was heading.

Little Beaver was bigger, a near look-alike except for a classic Iron Eyes Cody–kind of Native American hawk nose. Maybe four or five years older than Tonto. Wearing his rich black hair in a pigtail reaching almost to his waist, where Tonto's mane hung loose to his shoulders. Hiding his muscles and most of a shoulder holster inside a summer-weight olive-colored suit.

Little Beaver said, "You were packing before. Where's it? The Beretta." Like his boss, Roy Bigelow, sounding like a candidate for *The Sopranos*.

Before I had a chance to answer, Tonto was on one knee and patting me down. Slapping the palms of ham-sized hands against the thousands of pockets in my fatigue blazer and cargo pants and grabbing a little too energetically around my crotch.

"Clean," he said, getting up.

"Where's it?" Little Beaver repeated.

I raised my right hand to take an oath and said, "I don't remember. Honest Injun."

They both scowled and split a glance.

"Remember, or—Dead Paleface," Little Beaver said, pulling a .38 revolver from the holster, Tonto's cue to point his .45 at me.

"Somebody will hear the noise," I said.

Tonto said, "You."

He had me there, too.

"I'm going to count to one," Little Beaver said.

I didn't want to tell them I'd left it on the chair in Stevie's room.

Tonto made it unnecessary. "He could of left it behind with the girl?"

"Absolutely not!" I blurted out.

"Sounds like you guessed right. Go over. Check it out."

"Over my dead body!"

Little Beaver cocked his pistol and wondered, "Anybody ever tell you you got a big mouth?"

Tonto stayed behind at the hotel, in Stevie's room with my Beretta, while Little Beaver took off with me driving the Seville, over my ranting objections, but his assurance, "My brother has no interest in the girl, except as an insurance policy that you don't try any funny business with me. We get there, I call and tell him. No call, then maybe a problem."

"Where's 'there'?"

"What? You go from being not funny to being not smart? Where do you think?"

"I think nothing better happen to her, pal, and that's no joke."

He wedged himself between the seat and the door, tilted back his head, and laughed into the roof.

"Now that's funny, pal. Like you got a vote, pal."

Fifteen or twenty minutes later, we arrived at Captain Pabro's.

About a quarter mile from the freeway entrance, Little Beaver had me swing onto a narrow service road that led to the back of the casino. He passed over his gate card to get us through a fifteen-foot chain-link fence topped with rolls of razor wire. The area lit up like Dodger Stadium. I could feel the surveillance cameras working us over as he told me to park near a door below the third teepee room roof, next to a late model four-door Chrysler.

"You don't need to lock it," Little Beaver said as we got out of the Seville. "Anybody unauthorized gets in here, they don't get out."

A light breeze had risen off the desert floor and blew warm air in my face.

"No thieves among the authorized?"

"Not for long."

The lock on the metal door clicked spontaneously.

Little Beaver pulled the door open and ushered me in ahead of him. The door snapped shut behind us to the clank of an automatic locking device.

The room was small, about the size of an average living room instead of the giant hall full of players I had toured earlier today. There was one felt-covered table with four sides instead of the eight player slots and chip wells you find on a poker table.

Roy Bigelow dealing across the table, pausing to check out the arrivals and acknowledge us with a nod.

The other man at the table barely giving us a glance, more interested in the cards he swept up one by one and hoarded from view.

"Mr. Neil Gulliver, come in, come in. Come over and sit here by me." Inclining his head to the left. His tone daring me to disobey. "Me and you, we got a shitload of meaningful things to talk over," Aaron Lodger said.

18

I slid into the seat next to him and he tossed his hand into the middle of the table, accompanied by a dry spitting noise of irritation. "This *momser* wouldn't know how to deal a good hand if his life depended on it." He studied me hard. "You know who I am?"

Roy Bigelow laughed like a junior executive. Turned it off when Lodger sent him a cold look.

I said, "I do, Mr. Lodger," and offered my hand.

He angled back like it was a weapon, dropped his hands in his lap. "Hands, greatest carrier of germs in the world. Not only in my opinion. Read up on it, you'll find out." He coughed to clear his throat and his Adam's apple did a jig. "The girl, how's she doing?"

"Sleeping deeper than the ocean when we left."

I threw a look at Little Beaver.

Lodger seemed to understand why without having to ask.

Calling to Little Beaver: "She okay?"

Little Beaver held out a circled thumb and forefinger.

"My brother's with her like you wanted, Mr. L. Waiting to hear from me."

He pulled a cell phone from his handkerchief pocket.

"Make the call from outside and stick around."

Little Beaver saluted, tipping an index finger to his forehead, and trooped out the back door.

"I know the look on your face," Lodger said. "Whatever they threatened, relax. Just to get you here. I told them not to mess harder than they needed with you and not a hair on her head out of place. Anyway, the brother's a *fageleh*." He rested his palms on the table. "It was the girl, Stevie, told you about me, why you know who I am?"

"Yes."

A look of incredulity.

"I never told her my name, so how did she know to tell you?"

Testing me.

"Richie Savage filled her in later, after you left."

"Richie, Richie, Richie." His voice struggling over the name, a sadness creeping in as his cold brown eyes moved off me and burned holes in the table's green felt surface. "Rest his soul . . . You knew him a long time."

"A long time *ago*, but not really well."

"He spoke highly of you anyway. Also about the girl." Emotions under control again.

"Richie knew her better."

Lodger waved off the remark.

"Nice girl," he said. "A real looker. She got balls, too. More than I would of suspected. Got her autographed picture framed nice, hanging in my den . . ." Drifting away, but back as fast. "Somebody else we both know speaks very highly of you." Gave it a beat. "Augie Fowler."

Surprising me with the name.

"Me and him go back I wouldn't want to start counting the years. I could always trust Augie when he was writing for the paper, before he went off and became this religious *mishugenah*, not that I'm one to put down anybody's beliefs, but—" Lodger pushed out a jet of noisy air. Shook his head and capped the thought there. "You think I can trust you the way I always trusted Augie?"

"How was that?"

"I tell Augie something—" Lodger ran a zipper finger across his slash of mouth. "He did what he had to after and he never mentioned me. Ever. I like my profile low. Kept me from problems like Bugsy had, like Mickey the C, in the old days."

"Try me."

"I got your word?"

Cunning written all over his face.

"My promise."

He suppressed a smile.

"You knew the answer I wanted."

"If you know Augie as well as you say you do."

"Don't take somebody's word, he always said. They give their word away. They got any honor, it's the promises they keep. He said you were always an honorable gent . . . Me, too."

He looked at Bigelow, who was absent-mindedly cutting the deck one-handed, filtering top cards into open slots or maneuvering them to the bottom.

Bigelow nodded vigorously.

"Good as gold," he said. "Better. Platinum."

"Let's get this thing about the casino here out of the way first," Lodger told Bigelow. Then to me: "We got wind by the grapevine you think there's funny business going on here and it involves me."

"Funny business?"

"Don't be coy, Neil Gulliver. It don't sit so well with me." He took a deep whiff of the vibrant miniature red rose in his lapel. "You seen the place today. Guided tour from my friend here." Bigelow nodded accord. "It already makes more money than the U.S. Mint. Only going to get better now that interested parties spent a few mil pushing through Prop 1A."

Getting Mickey Mouse animated.

"This place'll be big like a Staples Center soon, sixty or eighty mil going into it, and then see how the goose lays them golden eggs. It won't end with this casino, either, but that's a different story. One dream at a time."

"You're saying you're connected here."

Sternly, "Don't interrupt." His Adam's apple jumping up like the ball in some carnival game. "I never denied it, not that someone ever asked who liked to wake up in the morning. What I'm trying to get across is this—We'd have to be crazy nuts to do anything illegal that brought in the law and gave them the means for taking us down. Killing the goose."

"Such as?"

"There you go with the cutesy coy routine again . . . Such as involving this place or anything about the reservation in money laundering or other crooked schemes. The thinking that really brought you here, wasn't it?"

There were two ways Lodger could know that, from what I'd said to Leigh or what Stevie had said to Richie. Leigh could have said something to Bigelow, who'd passed it on to him. Or, Richie went straight to him with the conversation.

Because he'd shown a curious sensitivity about Richie's death, almost a father and son thing, I decided to try Leigh on him first.

"Your grapevine go by the name Leigh Wilder?"

"Yes." No hesitation. "My goddaughter."

"Your—"

"Goddaughter. As far back as I go with Augie Fowler, it was farther with our other mutual friend, her pop Ben, may his soul rest in peace. She called and told me, and I said not to worry, I would personally straighten this out with you."

"Leigh told me it was her husband, Michael Wilder, who was dirty. She has paperwork she's planning to show me."

"He was dirty, all right, but a different way. When he disappeared, good riddance to bad rubbish. I'm telling you so, so you don't have to bother seeing paperwork, whatever the hell that means. I told the same thing to Leigh."

"And you'd be upset if I did ask her to show me."

"Like you were calling me a liar. Someone does that, he lives to regret it. *Lives* in a manner of speaking, you know what I mean? Somebody spits on me, I don't call it rain."

Everything about Lodger, his voice, his body language, challenged me.

"What happened to Wilder?"

"He wasn't my husband. One day around, the next day—"

A shrug of his modest shoulders.

As good an answer as I was going to get from Lodger.

"The Imagine That! festival?"

"What about it?"

"Clean?"

"On federal land. Clean as a hound's tooth. Nothing to do with the casino. With the tribe only in that we needed to get tribal council approval."

Bigelow put his elbows on the table and pretended to be tugging at something horizontal between the clenched fingers of his hands.

"What strings are all about," he said, grinning.

Lodger frowned.

Bigelow stopped tugging, looked for something else to do with his hands.

"It's okay for you to go," Lodger said. "What else I want to talk about now with our guest does not concern you, Roy."

"I was thinking about leaving," Bigelow said, saving a little face. He pushed back from the table and rose. "I'll be out front. High sign if you need me."

"Yeah. Okay."

Bigelow crossed the room and exited through a secured door on the south wall. The sounds of a busy casino drifted our way in the few seconds the door was open.

Lodger said, "I see it in your eyes you still got some questions. Go ahead."

"Stevie and Richie talked about the festival." A pained look crossed his face at the mention of Richie. "He told her it was your idea to do it again."

"Lennon was a genius and his death a damn shame. It was time to remind people, a whole new generation that might not even know the name, for Christ's sake."

"He said you were underwriting the festival."

"The money from friends. Recoupable with interest. The charity a good one. Getting the guns out of the hands of the wrong people."

Spoken like he didn't see the irony of his words.

Aaron Lodger as one of the right people.

All I could do to keep a straight face, but laughing at the old man was definitely a bad career move.

No laughing matter.

"He told Stevie Martin Halliwell was with you when you proposed the idea. He said it was Halliwell who suggested I be invited to help get it off the ground."

"The T-man? Yeah? So what?"

"Stevie told Richie and I'm sure he ran to you with the news that it was Halliwell who got us involved; sent us here to dig out what he couldn't about the money laundering. Your part in it. Richie's part. Michael Wilder's. He's running an ongoing investigation designed to put you away."

Lodger's laugh reached the opposite wall.

"That'll be the day."

"I went down to Palm Springs today planning to put the question to Richie. I got there too late. I didn't get the chance to ask Halliwell, either, so tell me, Mr. Lodger—What's going on? What's really going on?"

"Why I sent them for you," Lodger said. "What I want to talk to you about. It's nothing like you think. Nothing."

"You got to go back a lot of years," Lodger said. "You were probably still in school. Halliwell's working his way up in the Treasury Department and he comes to pay respects. He's got a proposition to offer me, work he'll occasionally need done and in trade Treasury turns a blind eye on what I got going any time. *Quid pro quo* and, besides, you know the old saying about keeping your enemies closer'n friends?"

"What kind of work?"

"How many times I got to say 'don't interrupt' to you?"

He turned his face away, began telling the story to the chair Roy Bigelow had used.

"Work I already have people for when it's necessary, so it's no stretch. What it is is—There's people Halliwell and whoever else in Washington he's doing business with want out of the way sometimes. Whacked in a way there's no trail back to them. A congressman here, a senator there. Like Needman, the one who they wanted offed at the Lennon festival in '85. Made it look like some biker blitzed out on speed decided to get a trophy while Needman was yakking away up on stage. Political, but what did I care? Politics ain't my racket. I pay my taxes, even voted once. End of that story.

"Once in a while, though, not so political. Halliwell comes to me with the name of a troublemaker. Someone making the wrong kind of noise and needs the steam taken out of his tea kettle. Sometimes Halliwell has a blueprint, other times it's left to us. Either way it's good-bye, Charlie. You know what I mean? Not that we have a perfect score.

"We missed on Ford; twice on Ford. We missed on Reagan. Was not us on JFK or Bobby, I want to be real clear on that. Not either of them. I got tapped later, around Nixon's time, when Halliwell was new on Treasury's White House detail, he said, making heavy connections, looking to build a rep for himself."

Lodger's pause seemed to invite questions.

"How did you miss on Ford?"

A shrug. Turning a palm to the ceiling.

"I got sold a bill of goods about letting these crazies do the work. A Manson girl and an old lady who also belonged in a nut-house. Halliwell said let it go after that, so I let it go. Third time would of been the charm."

"Reagan?"

"The boys had to locate a substitute shooter at almost the last minute and that threw everything off. So Reagan got lucky, barely, and his people took the shots meant for him."

Shaking my head in disbelief. "Why did Halliwell make Ford and Reagan targets?"

"He didn't say. I didn't ask. None of my business."

I digested what I'd heard so far and said, "Who else?"

"You mean like Sonny Bono? Or you thinking he aimed for that tree on purpose?"

"Sonny was your friend. You hung out together. You—"

Flippantly, "Yeah, was. I got a whole lot of friends. Some of them more expendable than some others, but you want to hear something funny? Listen to this . . ."

He was back to giving orders.

"The name John Lennon mean anything to you?"

Thwap. He'd managed to stun me to silence.

Still addressing the empty chair, Lodger said, "Took the wind out of your sails, that one did. An absolute fact. Lennon."

Lodger reached for the deck of cards Bigelow had been using and dealt himself a hand of solitaire.

Immediately began cheating, like he was making up the rules as he went along.

I found my voice and said, "Mark David Chapman—"

"The trigger man, but it didn't start out that way," he said, laying a six of clubs on a seven of spades.

"How did it start out?"

"From me would be gossip. When you talk to Halliwell, if he wants to tell, you get it straight from the horse's patoot."

A thought had been building and now it spilled over.

I said, "You're out to get Halliwell, aren't you?"

"It took you this long to figure it out?" Lodger said, putting a black jack on a black queen. "I thought Augie had only smart friends. You want to know why?"

"I have an idea."

The deck froze in his hand and his head snapped around to show me a pair of venomous eyes.

"Tell me," he commanded.

"Richie."

"Yes, Richie, may he rest in peace."

"He made you kill Richie."

"Nobody makes me do anything," Lodger said.

Aaron Lodger said, "First things first. Understand I did not kill Richie. Richie came to be someone special to me." Still having difficulty speaking the name. "I shared that boy's dreams, more than I ever did with Sonny."

"You didn't kill him, but he's still dead."

"Making a joke?" Challenging me with his stare.

"Making a point. You have an idea who, don't you?"

"An idea? I know who. Halliwell and his people."

"How do you know that?"

"They come to me first is how I know. Halliwell, that fat fuck, who knows how I feel for Richie. He comes to me and he says, 'Mr. L, Richie has to go.' He says, 'Like it was with Sonny, too much ambition and he's already rubbing people the wrong way. As a mayor, so imagine what it could be like if he became a senator.' "

"When was this?"

"A month, maybe six, seven weeks ago. I hear him out and then I tell Halliwell, 'I don't have to hear any more. It's not going to happen, you understand?' He knows I mean it and he says, 'I'll pass on the word.' I tell him, 'Piss on the word, so long as you hear me clear. You go ahead and fuck with Richie, you're fucking with me.' Today, he fucked with me. Now it's my turn."

"What do you expect from me?"

"I give you enough here to go by. You put the rest in place to put him away for keeps, Halliwell. You put it all together and do your story and you keep me out of it, like you promised."

"All hearsay. I can't build a story on that, what I'm told by an unnamed source. Gossip. You said it yourself a minute ago."

"I know."

"Halliwell isn't the kind to break down and confess if I confront him, so—"

"He'd do to you what he did to Richie, if he ever got wind

what you heard just now from me. Also, the girl, just to stay on the safe side. The government doesn't need a war to kill people."

"Figuring neither Stevie nor I would like that, where does that leave us?"

"Still in the position of doing me this favor, but you didn't let me finish before you started interrupting again. I got more for you."

An impish grin growing on his face.

"Like?"

"Something to tie Halliwell to Richie's murder, may he rest in peace—The shooter."

"You know who the shooter is?"

"I know who the shooter is. I know where to find him."

Turning away from me and picking up the deck.

"I also know who Halliwell's got for his next target."

Playing a red deuce on a black four.

"Try this one on for size: the president of the United States."

My voice went away again.

I was still trying to remember how when the rear door clicked open.

I looked over expecting to see Little Beaver.

Instead, I saw Armando Soledad.

Lodger pointed Armando to the seat Bigelow had occupied and said, "Armando, tell him about the shooter."

I threw a palm between us.

"No! Tell me first where you were when you should have been protecting Stevie."

Lodger growled annoyance that I'd preempted his order.

Armando seemed amused by my agitation.

He lifted off his shades and placed them on the table in front of him, fiddling to make them sit horizontal to the table edge, then turned to Lodger with a look that asked for permission.

"Go on," Lodger said. "Same thing."

"With her all day," Armando said softly, shifting his eyes back to me, the accent at once exposing his European roots.

"Not when she was shot at and could have been killed."

The rebuke sailed past him.

"She drives in with the T-man. Anyone figures between him and security inside, she's okay. Next driving in are you and the guy who works for Savage. The gate should close, but instead it stays open. This is not right. I finish peeing in a Coke bottle and am hurrying to get out from my wheels when I hear them, the gunshots."

Pausing to check Lodger's sad, gaunt face.

Already more words than I've heard out of Armando's mouth since he came to work for us.

"A Bird races out from the drive in a big, big hurry. I've seen that enough times to know what it means. I can't do nothing about what's already happened inside. I gun up and take after the Bird."

"Okay, okay," Lodger said, impatiently. "For Christ's sake, cut to the chase." Realized that's what Armando had done. "You stay on the mother fucker. You run him off the road finally. Before he can draw, you put his lights out. You check his ID. Go on, tell him."

"In his billfold," Armando said, toying with the gold ring in his ear. "Shooter carries a badge. Identification that says he's a Fed. A T-man. Secret Service."

I said, "You put his lights out? Killed a T-man?"

Armando's face inched left and right.

"Only that I am quicker than him and get in control. I convince him to say to me what went on in the mayor's house. I give him a nap and get on my cell to Mr. L, because I know Mr. L will want to know."

Lodger said, "I've used Armando a few times on tricky business. He's a good boy. Knows his way around. Gets the job done. Show him."

Armando pulled a wallet from a jumpsuit pocket, pushed it across the table to me.

A Treasury Department badge.

ID that showed the shooter was a special agent working out of the Federal Building in downtown LA.

Paul Darren, the name on the driver's license.

Bad photo that makes him look older than his thirty-five years and about fifteen pounds heavier than the weight he claimed. Makes me wonder, Doesn't anybody ever tell the truth to the DMV?

I said, "Where's Darren now? You didn't give him over to the cops or I would have heard."

Armando turned to Lodger for direction.

Lodger said, "Sure, take him."

"It's not a good time now."

Lodger checked his watch, thin and expensive, some diamonds glittering on its face and the band.

"First thing in the morning," Lodger said.

I drove back to the hotel alone, Armando's Wrangler never more than two or three car lengths behind the Seville, Carlos Santana's spicy guitar, then some Herbie Hancock and McCoy Tyner riffing from the speakers, lots of bugs flying suicide missions into the windshield while I tried to make sense of everything I'd heard.

All the pieces seemed to fit, but—

Not quite.

I was dealing with what Augie Fowler characterized as "the *hole* truth."

He had often decreed: "Find the lies, fill the holes. Only then will the *whole* truth emerge."

Tonto was asleep in the chair, fingers laced on his lap, legs outstretched, a whistling snore overwhelmed by Stevie's sonic booms, together drowning out the TV sound. The picture popping in and out on a Jimmy Stewart movie I instantly recognized as Hitchcock's *The Man Who Knew Too Much*.

Like me, Jimmy.

I had developed a sense I knew so much I didn't know anything at all.

Armando startled Tonto awake with a hard kick to the instep. Tonto leaped from the chair into a fighting stance, his eyes vaguely searching the room until they settled on Armando. He untied the anger knots on his face and greeted him by name.

"Armando! How goes it, dude?"

Armando acknowledged the greeting with a nod and threw a hitchhiker's thumb over his shoulder.

Tonto let his smile lapse. Without comment, he reached for his .45. It was on the side table next to my Beretta. He holstered it inside the waistband of his shorts, underneath his T-shirt, and with a menacing scowl for me in passing, exited.

I retrieved the Beretta and followed him out a minute later, after Armando parked himself in the chair, promised me he'd still be there in the morning, and we settled on a time to go see Paul Darren, the Treasury Department agent.

In my room, I switched on the TV to catch the rest of *The Man Who Knew Too Much*. I'd long ago lost count of how many times I'd seen this version and still couldn't fathom why Hitch had bothered remaking his superior 1934 original with Leslie Banks, Edna Best, and a Peter Lorre years away from reaching his villainous heights.

Even bad Hitchcock is better than anyone else's idea of what a thriller should be. If I had to vote, Hitch's *The 39 Steps* and *The Lady Vanishes* probably top my list. Two other movies he made before coming to Hollywood and over the years became his own victim, inching away from greatness to a sad-to-behold ordinariness.

I finished the column about Richie and e-mailed it to the *Daily*. A nice piece, no prizewinner, but it might tear up some of his old fans. For Stevie, I replayed the time in '86, sometime after the Imagine That! festival, when Richie was headlining at the old Forum in Inglewood and invited us to hang out with him backstage.

Richie's opening act was competing with chants of "We want Rick!" that echoed all over the hall, outblasting the amps, while we trudged backstage corridors that reeked of Lakers sweat in the air and on the walls to a door marked "Do Not Enter."

Following Richie's instructions, Stevie and I entered without knocking.

Entering unannounced meant we belonged.

Knocking meant we were strangers and didn't belong.

The simple logic of rock-and-roll in a time when drugs collected a royalty on almost every band.

The space was about the size of a large banquet room, longer than it was wider, with grim green walls and a cold linoleum floor showing years of abuse underneath two banks of yellowed fluorescent lighting.

Scant furniture, some couches and chairs that could have been borrowed from a Goodwill Industries thrift shop, but stretching the length of one wall and half of another—

A buffet spread big enough to satisfy half the eighteen or twenty thousand fans out front. Hot plates and cold cuts. Dazzling platters of sushi. More varieties of salad than the irrepressible Carmen Miranda ever had on her sky-high tutti-frutti hats. Ice tubs filled with assorted wines and beers; about three dozen cracked bottles of Dom Perignon, the corks missing from all of them.

I heard later the food was exclusively for Richie and the band, whose smaller, shared dressing room was down the hall. The buffet was required contractually, itemized in the rider his agent routinely sent concert promoters and usually delivered after a show to some shelter for the homeless.

Except for the band and tour crew members, no one was permitted backstage or in Richie's dressing room. When he called me with the invitation, he said it had to do with building and keeping a mystique.

Stevie and I were exceptions to the rule, he said.

It would not be for years, until after he took up with her, that I remembered the night and understood why.

Richie was standing in the middle of the room, balanced on one foot like an ostrich and looking uncertain what to do with the other leg, a champagne glass in one hand and a gold coke spoon on a neck chain in the other.

He spotted us and called, "Hey, help yourselves," in a scratchy voice. Pointed to a glass-top table decorated with lines of coke. Licked at the trickle of blood descending to his upper lip from his left nostril. "Party is just getting started. You need a hundred to roll? Blondie, come on over and dig into Uncle Richie's pants pocket. You find anything else, you can have that, too."

Stevie punctured him with a look, squeezed my hand, and said, "I'm outta here."

Me, right behind her.

We never did see the show, except in the column I had just transmitted, where I forgot about the drugs and talked about the buffet as something Richie demanded not to prove his superstardom, but out of a deep-rooted passion to help the needy.

I suggested it was the same kind of need that drove him to politics.

Who knows?

Maybe deep down it was.

I talked about the contribution he might have made as a United States senator, if he'd lived to run and be elected, and—

I talked about his commitment to Imagine That! and drew on the lyrics to the tribute song he'd written and dedicated to John Lennon's memory, words as sad as a widow's wail and as strong as a child's love. As potently eternal as what the Boss would have to say years later about forty-one shots and a different death in Manhattan.

On second thought, maybe not so ordinary a column after all.

———

"Where'd Armando go?" I said.

"His room. While I showered and dressed."

I made a face.

"I wish you'd waited until I got here."

"From the look on his face, I think maybe Armando was wishing the same thing. I wanted to be ready."

"For what?"

"To go with you. He told me where you're going."

"I don't think so."

"You're out-voted, one to one."

Except for the dark pouches under her sad eyes and a mourner's mouth, rows of brow wrinkles that makeup had not covered, she looked and sounded like the night's sleep had carried her through the worst of her sorrow over Richie's death.

Changing the subject, Stevie said, "What kept you? You called to say you'd be over in a minute, five minutes ago. They widen the hall overnight?"

"The *Daily* called with some questions about tomorrow's column," I said.

True enough.

She didn't have to know I'd also used a minute to call Leigh and apologize to her machine about not getting there last night, report that the Seville was parked in the hotel lot and the key left with the desk clerk. Remembered to say I had her wedding photo and needed to get it back to her. Promised to call and set up something first chance.

Seeing Leigh no longer had to do with Halliwell and his scheming.

I was feeling genuinely contrite about the aggravation I'd clobbered her with unjustifiably and was hoping to make up for it.

Stevie said, "You wrote about Richie."

"You sound like it's a fact."

"I knew it. I could tell. What did you say?"

"You know so much, you tell me."

"Don't be cute. It doesn't always look good on you. Like now."

I described the column.

Stevie smiled and swallowed hard.

Moved in on me for a squeeze and a hug.

"You done did good, honey," she said.

A kiss on the cheek wound up on my lips, lingered there a moment or two before Stevie pulled away and crossed to the dresser to check herself in the mirror.

"I look like shit," she told my reflection.

"Only in your eyes," I lied, "but, on second thought, I don't think you want to go anywhere and be seen by strangers looking the way you look."

"The son of a bitch who shot Richie? I want to see him. Tell him what I think. This is one time I don't give a damn how I look."

She did a runway twirl to show off her v-necked white silk tunic over a pair of black cargo pants. Black leather boots. Small pearl earrings, a matching strand looped twice around her neck.

Piled her hair inside her sun-blocking straw and gave the hat a hearty tug. Reached for her outsized sunglasses and said, "What's keeping Armando? Let's get this show on the road."

19

Stevie drove, Armando beside her calling off directions that took us onto the San Gorgonio Reservation by way of Old Back Road, a narrow two-lane that served as a natural divide between the reservation and Sunrise City.

He guided us east about two miles across the foothills to Cattle Trail Lane, then up into the San Gorgonio range to an asphalted, two-lane speedway that cut across the flats at this higher elevation and was used by peat mining companies that had substituted the name Bog Boulevard for the original Indian name, Wet Lands Road. Crews working both sides of the boulevard ignored us as we raced by.

We headed higher again using an unmarked dirt road that wasn't much more than a horse trail and tribal members said was too sacred to give a name, although no one had ever been able or willing to explain to me what made it too sacred.

The trail was barely wide enough for the Cherokee, same with the next detour, a steeper incline cloaked by trees and overgrown scrub browned dry by heat that Stevie had to take in low, alternating cautiously between the brake and the gas pedals; the motor straining and grinding until we got to the next turnoff signaled by Armando, a flatlands trail bordered by slime-infested, mosquito-breeding peat bogs that all the companies had abandoned years ago because of their difficult location.

I remembered being here or somewhere around here once, during my first months at the *Sentinel* news bureau, when I was anxious to know all the territory I'd be responsible for covering. I never could find a reason to be here twice and limited my visits to the reservation tribal council meetings and an annual cattle roundup, when the small, scrawny herds were corralled and surviving newborns were branded with the tribe's intertwined SG logo.

I understood why Armando hadn't wanted to make the trip last night, but not why he needed to stash Darren the Treasury agent in so remote a location. I put the question to him when we were about halfway there.

"Wouldn't a Motel 6 have been more convenient?" I said. "Or the one where they leave the light on for you?"

Armando half turned, looking over his shoulder into the backseat, and gave me his "no answer" stare.

I didn't press him.

The only answer that came to my mind was not a pleasant one. Armando might be our bodyguard, but he was also working for Aaron Lodger.

The longer we drove the more I convinced myself I would find the T-man in no condition to talk to me.

Or to anyone.

"Here," Armando said finally.

He had Stevie pull over and park near an area shaded by towering, gold-leafed trees, where the trail bulged a little like it does at Kodak Moment scenic pullovers along the PCH. There were tire trails all over the place, some embedded in dried mud, others half-erased by a lazy breeze drifting over the landscape, still others that looked to be of more recent vintage.

Heat in the nineties slapped me in the face when I left the air-conditioned Cherokee, wondering out loud if this was a favorite gathering place of peat moss hobbyists.

Armando didn't get the joke.

His face remained immobile as he got out of the car and moved down the slight grassy incline to the bank of the bog, about ten yards away.

Stevie faked a laugh as she came around the front of the Cherokee to join us. She grasped my hand and, leaning closer, whispered out one side of her clenched mouth, "This is definitely no place for a meeting."

"You don't know the half of it."

"Do I want to?"

Armando called for us to join him. He was standing with his hands locked behind his back, studying the bog like some ship's captain searching for enemy vessels.

Stevie and I looked at each other.

I said, "Push comes to shove, when he pushes, both of us shove."

Stevie said, "I don't want to know."

We took our time heading over.

"You on one side of him, me on the other," I said. "For greater shoving power."

"You know that for a fact?"

"Something I remember from *Dateline NBC*."

"You made that up."

"Yes."

When we reached him, Armando said, "You have probably guessed by now, Mr. Gulliver."

"Paul Darren's in there pushing up the peat moss. The T-Bird? Also in there?"

"This place, not on any tourist map. We use it a lot of the time to dispose of our disposables."

"You couldn't just tell me that yesterday, that you had Darren fertilizing a swamp? Save us on gas, wear and tear on the tires?"

"Not why I had to bring you here."

Stevie said "Had to?" before I could.

"I don't make up the rules, Miss Marriner. I only play the game."

"You don't make it sound like a game I want to play."

He turned facing her and said, "Regrettably, you don't make up the rules either."

Stevie leaned back and gave me a look across Armando's shoulders that said she was ready to shove and run.

Armando noticed, read her right.

"Don't do anything foolish, Miss Marriner, and not you either, Mr. Gulliver."

"Like try to save my life?"

Armando said, "Let me try and do that for you."

Snapped a grip like a handcuff onto my wrist before I could get to the fatigue jacket pocket where my Beretta was nesting.

"Don't reach for your gun until I tell you," he said.

Squeezed a grunt and a nod out of me before releasing his hold.

Stevie said, "I'm going back to the car. I'm getting in and I'm leaving."

"To be brave is to be dead, Miss Marriner. People may be watching us now, so it's very important that you listen to me first; both of you."

"And if we don't?" I said.

"Then, I could be in the sad position of doing the same kind of work that you hired me to save Miss Marriner and you from in the first place."

"Okay, shoot."

"Honey!"

"I mean we're listening."

"I am going to turn toward Miss Marriner and take hold of her like I want to throw her into the bog. When this is happening, then you get your Beretta, Mr. Gulliver. Hit me over the head and make it look as real as you can. Then the two of you run to the car, go fast from here. When you are safely back in the city, reach Mr. Halliwell. Tell him what has gone on last night with Mr. L and now today. All right then, you understand?"

"Up to the part about Halliwell."

"There is no time to explain. Are you ready?"

"Halliwell first."

He thought about it a moment.

"Sometimes I also work for him," Armando said, and—

At once twisted and grabbed Stevie under her arms.

Lifted her off the ground.

Turned to face the peat bog, making swearing sounds as Stevie hammered his shoulders with her fists and slammed the metal tips of her boots into his shins.

I got the Beretta from my pocket, brought it down hard on the back of Armando's head, by the neck; harder than I'd intended and he probably wanted or expected.

The blow staggered him.

He lurched a few steps, releasing Stevie before he sank to his knees and fell face forward onto the sunburned grass.

Stevie hit the ground awkwardly, on one foot.

Fought to keep her balance.

Lost.

Fell.

Began rolling toward the bog.

I dove for her.

She was bare inches from sailing off the bank into the water.

I belly-flopped on the hard turf, and—

Made a groaning, one-handed clutch grab on her ankle.

A Willie Mays kind of grab.

Only different.

Neither of us moved for about a minute, catching our breath, then I got up and helped her to her feet and said, "Let's get the hell out of here."

We stepped around the motionless form of Armando and, hand in hand, started for the Jeep.

Halfway there—

Gunfire.

A cascade of gunshots spitting at us, turning the car to Swiss cheese; dogging our steps as I jerked Stevie away from open ground and swung her toward the pines.

Streaking in a zigzag pattern.

Pushing her ahead of me.

Using my body as her shield.

The shots following us.

Their sound receding, then disappearing entirely inside a cacophony of noises—irate birds and animals objecting to being disturbed—as we plunged ahead.

Made a path through the underbrush until, lungs on the edge of explosion, we stopped to catch our breath.

Bent over. Hands on knees. Bodies heaving.

Swallowing gallons of air.

"What now, honey?" Stevie said, palming the sweat from her face and neck.

"Nothing says they're not coming after us. We keep on going," I said, stashing the Beretta inside the waistband of my cargo pants, within easy grabbing range.

She said, "We can call for help if you remembered to bring your cell phone. Mine needs batteries."

"Who do we call? The California Mountainside Patrol? The St. Bernard and Brandy Keg Emergency Service Division of the Auto Club?" I made a thumb-and-pinky phone. "Hello, Auto Club? Come get us, please. We're at the intersection of Somewhere and Somewhere Else in the San Gorgonios."

"Hah. Hah. Hah."

"Besides—" Patting my pockets. "I think I left the damn thing sitting on the dresser."

"I would have guessed somewhere back in Los Angeles, next to your beeper."

"Wait. You may be right."

I lifted one foot by the ankle, then the other, did a fast set of knee bends and stretches, heard a few bones go "crack," and ignoring the muscle aches setting in from my recent rescue of my child bride, asked, "You ready, babe?"

Stevie finished her limbering up and said, "You have any idea which direction?"

"Rule of the hills. You head down. Eventually you have to exit."

"From here everything looks straight ahead."

"Straight ahead first, then down."

I started a slow trot forward, pushing the brush aside, Stevie right behind me, and behind us—

A voice demanding, "Hey, you! Stop!"

With visions of gun barrels pointed in our direction, I made a fast stop and threw my hands into the air.

It was too fast a stop for Stevie, who smacked into me and bounced to one side while I did my second nose dive of the day, picking up what felt like a full set of superficial cuts and scratches from the brushwood.

The voice, almost on top of me now, said, "You ain't got no business here!"

Deep-throated.

Coarse.

I thought I recognized it.

Rolled over and looked up.

Don't know who was more surprised—

Bobby San Gorgonio or me.

"You don't belong," Bobby said, pointing an accusatory finger. "Sacred ground. Captain Pabro don't allow strangers around here. People come don't belong—" He raised his chin to the clouds and made a clucking sound. "You get out from here fast."

No surprise, he was drunk.

I was relieved.

Bobby's finger moved and settled on Stevie. "Lady, you neither, so put that away and go on while the getting's good."

He meant the .32 she was aiming at him in a shooter's stance.

I moved into a half-sitting position, balancing on my elbows, and said quickly, "Ixnay, babe. Mr. San Gorgonio's an old friend of mine."

" 'Ixnay'? This is one hell of a time to show off your command of a second language."

She gave Bobby another once-over and shook her head in disbelief. Dipped down on her haunches and replaced the gun inside her boot.

Bobby growled at her.

"Was you making the noise back on sacred land? Waking up Captain Pabro. Bad. Waking up me, too."

I said, "People were shooting at us, Mr. San Gorgonio. We were running away from them. Our car's back at the bog."

He narrowed his eyes to the news, like he knew it meant something, only not certain what.

"Wait here, don't go no place," he said, and shambled off on unsteady legs in the direction we'd just fled.

When he was out of sight, Stevie said, "Once again you amaze me with your circle of friends."

"An enemy of the class system I am."

"A real no class kind of guy, huh?"

"No-classy enough to wonder how it is you neglected to tell me you were carrying."

"You thought these boots were made just for walking?"

"Just be careful you don't shoot yourself in the foot."

"Where you've squirreled your Beretta, you're the one to talk."

I got up slowly and brushed myself off; inspected the brushwood scratches on my hands and felt around my face for signs of damage.

A few serious bruises maybe.

No serious bleeding.

Band-Aid stuff.

Stevie said, "Tell me about the human distillery."

I was explaining Bobby to her when he charged through the

brush, hopping and skipping in that drunkard's kind of gait always favored by Frankenstein's monster.

"Nobody, nothing," he said. "Not a car or nothing."

"There was a man, unconscious near the bog, Mr. San Gorgonio."

Bobby shook his head vehemently.

"Nobody, nothing, not a car or nothing," he repeated. "You come on and get, before Captain Pabro is really angry at you for invading sacred land and Serrano sends the white eagle."

Stevie turned to me. "That's not good."

"Bad," I said, then to Bobby, "We don't know our way out, Mr. San Gorgonio. Maybe you can help?"

He weighed the question.

"Gonna cost," he said. "Ten dollars."

I pulled out my wallet.

"No!" Bobby said. "Not you. Only her."

He was as surefooted as he was loaded coming down the mountain, leading us along invisible trails in the thicket, and finally to the flatlands, daring us not to keep up when one of us faltered under the hot sun or in the sheer heat of exhaustion.

The pace seemed to invigorate Bobby and every once in a while he patted the half-torn hip pocket on his decomposing suit of rags, where he had hoarded the crumpled ten spot he demanded Stevie pony up before we started, rolled his tongue around his cracked and blistered lips, and cackled into the warm wind pushing at our backs, "Get there real soon to the promised land."

Sometimes he chanted, a language that could have been English or nothing at all, maybe only a collection of sounds that meant something to Bobby San Gorgonio, who appeared to understand himself perfectly, whether the words made him cry or laugh. He did a lot of both before Captain Pabro's casino became more than a dot on the horizon to our left and a road leading into Sunrise City became welcome reality.

Bobby stayed with us until we got to the Wyatt Earp Bar and Grill on First Street.

"Hallelujah!" he shouted at a sky still burning with sunlight, going orange and gold with the afternoon sun, and the word rang as true as a sailor's curse as he dug out the ten from his pocket, waved us on, and stumbled through the bar door.

Stevie said, "The promised land, huh?"

"One man's promise is another man's porridge."

"That doesn't make sense."

"Sunstroke," I said, tapping my forehead.

"Typical," she said, tapping my forehead.

We showered and changed clothes, taking turns guarding each other, and within the hour were heading for Los Angeles in Armando's Wrangler. It was still in the hotel parking lot where he'd left it and it took me only a few minutes to find the spare key in a hide-a-box under the left rear fender.

Leigh's Seville also was in the lot, her car keys still waiting for pickup at the front desk and nothing to indicate she'd received my earlier message.

I tried reaching her while Stevie was showering but, if she was home, she wasn't picking up. The office number also connected to an answering machine.

Martin Halliwell's confidential number only collected messages, same with the Treasury Department night number I got from a phone company mechanical voice.

I had better luck reaching Jimmy Steiger, my detective lieutenant pal with LAPD. Jimmy was home goaltending his six kids and three dogs while Margie, his wife, was off taking a night class in computer science at Cal State.

"She's in her third month," Jimmy said.

"Congratulations, but didn't you take an oath you were quitting after the sixth kid?"

"And after the fourth and fifth kids. I mean the third month of this class. Margie's thinking about starting up a business from the house. An Internet kind of thing. Like the world wide net couldn't possibly be wide enough without her. Buying and selling."

"Buying and selling what?"

"She doesn't know yet. I think they get to that in the fourth month, but tell me how you and Stevie are holding up. This Rick Savage shooting's been all over the news since it happened and Palm Springs PD didn't add much when I called over there to check on you guys."

"You should have called us at the hotel."

"I did. Nobody home either room, or Soledad, so I left a message with some guy on the switchboard."

"Never got it. Your mistake was dealing with a human being. Why answering machines and voicemail will rule the world one of these days."

"Good thought. I'll mention it to Margie when she gets home. Meanwhile, how goes?"

I brought him up to date, leaving out anything to do with Aaron Lodger because of the promise I'd made the old gangster, but enough remained to win a whistle of surprise in my ear.

"How much you buying into the idea Soledad was double-dipping, working for you and Halliwell at the same time?"

"Halliwell or somebody," I said, wishing I could tell Jimmy the rest of it, honor putting a sad crimp in honesty between friends. "Maybe I'll know better tomorrow, after I connect with Halliwell."

"Anything I can do?"

"Stevie and I are driving home tonight. Think you could arrange to resume patrol cruises for the duration, in case tonight's the night Dean decides to make another run at us?"

"What you've been through, wouldn't you guys be better off sacking out there tonight and getting a fresh start in the A.M.?"

"We're both more wired than tired and, besides, right now Dean's preferable to waiting for the bogey men from the peat bog to come crashing through the door here."

"Consider it done, pardner. I'll put in a call to Ned DeSantis after this and between us it should be working by the time you and the blonde bombshell arrive."

Even with two junk food stops to satisfy stress hunger that had been building since breakfast, we made great time to the Oaks, pulling through Stevie's security gate and up the driveway before ten-thirty.

The floods lit us and miniaturized TV cameras logged us on tape as we moved from the Wrangler through the door, and Stevie threw a few light switches and punched in the numbers that deactivated the Code Red silent alarm signaling news of an intruder to the Oaks' patrol service.

Take longer than ninety seconds and officers responded with guns drawn.

All things considered, a tough place to break into, but so was Richie Savage's place, and—

We froze simultaneously at the unambiguous sound of the

floorboards above us bending and moaning to footsteps moving north, seemingly to the hallway from Stevie's bedroom.

Unless it was Godzilla the Mouse, somebody had managed to circumvent the security system.

We stepped hurriedly out of the light, into the living room, taking protection from the arch while we drew our guns and I finger-signaled Stevie to stay put while I went up the staircase.

"No way, José," she whispered.

"Okay, you go up the staircase."

"No way, José."

"What's your better idea?"

"How do you know I have one?"

"Because, if you don't, we're back to me being brave and fool-hardy."

Stevie thought about it. "You get the door open, I go for the panic button on the door code panel. We are out of here until the cavalry arrives."

"Nothing brave and foolhardy about that."

"Right. Too exhausted for brave and foolhardy. It's use your brains time."

"I love a brainy woman. Will you marry me?"

"Not brave or foolhardy enough for that. Now, move your cute little ass. I've got you covered."

"I love it when you talk dirty."

"Hit it, Mel Gibson," she said. She nudged me with an elbow and settled her gun hand on her other arm, aiming the .32 about halfway up the staircase. "One-two-three-go."

I made my move to the door, threw it wide open, and—

Someone came thumping down the staircase at about five hundred miles an hour.

Stevie, startled, fired and missed.

The bullet thudded into a wall.

I jumped between Someone and the door.

Someone barreled into me, slamming me backwards and side-ways against the open door.

I lost my grip on the Beretta. It fell to the floor about the same time as Someone's back connected with the newel post of the staircase.

He cried out and pitched headfirst onto the Oriental rug.

Stevie yelled, "He's wearing one of my gowns!"

Someone spotted the Beretta and stretched for it.

It was about a finger-length away.

He tried for traction on the rug and got it, but not fast enough to reach my gun before Stevie reached him and rammed the barrel of her .32 against the back of his neck.

"Make my day," she said.

I retrieved the Beretta and said, "Tell me I didn't just hear you say what I heard you say."

"My Richard Tyler original. You know what that set me back?"

"I thought they came free, a trade for the publicity."

"Not if you keep them."

"If it's any consolation, it looked better on you than it does on him."

Someone made a fast swipe at Stevie's ankle and yanked her off her feet, reflexively firing the .32 as she fell.

The bullet zinged into the Oriental rug half a big toe from my right Nike and sent me dancing away from the door.

Someone had scrambled to his high-heeled feet.

He bolted through the door and down the driveway.

"And my goddamn Manolo Blahniks!"

"Do the panic button thing," I called at Stevie, and gave chase.

I saw him cutting left onto the garden path, toward a thick wooden fire door where the steel fence becomes an adobe wall, beyond a wishing well drained years ago and nowadays only good for an occasional bucket of dust.

Even in those three-inch heels, Someone was one swift drag queen and, after the day we'd had, there was nothing left in my legs. He was banging down the road by the time I got to the fire door; noticed the busted lock. The door his means of entry, too.

Behind me the house sounded like every car alarm in an eight-story garage had gone off at once. Stevie had pressed more than the panic button.

"What do you think?" she said when I got back there.

"You mean was it a garden variety stalker or our James Dean?"

"You think?"

I said, "A little too tall, a little too fast, and definitely not the gown our James Dean would have chosen."

Martin Halliwell called while we were monitoring the morning newscasts over coffee and toasted bagels, light on the butter substitute, heavy on the cream cheese and jelly, Stevie's idea of a diet breakfast; both of us too hungry to count calories; eyeing what was left of a frozen apple pie and a gallon of Ben & Jerry's rocky road from last night.

Two hours later we'd joined him in a miniscule private office in the Treasury Department's quarters at the Federal Building downtown; two guest chairs and a file cabinet; no pictures on the walls or signs of personal possession; for VIP visitors, he explained, seated uncomfortably on a chair that tilted more than he did, behind a scarred wooden desk, looking and sounding embarrassed to be there.

He took in the cramped space with a gesture and said, "Can y'all picture where they deposit confreres with less cachet or seniority than yours truly?"

The desk was empty except for a phone console. He went for it, buzzed someone, and said, "Halliwell here, Shirleen. Hold any calls, please." Turning to us: "Y'all been offered coffee yet?"

Stevie waved off the invitation.

"Tea? Soft drinks or bottled water? Got it all in what passes for a lounge. Might even be a Krispy Kreme left over from earlier, although they sure do go fast. Hit the stomach like the old Tyson one-two, before he started biting instead of fighting." A tired feeling to the line, like he'd used it before, and more than once.

I stopped holding up a wall and dropped onto the seat next to Stevie, planted my elbows on the desk, slapped my hands together, and too irritated with him for small talk, too edgy from lack of sleep to be polite, said, "Why didn't you return my calls until this morning? My messages said it was urgent."

Stevie reached over and squeezed my thigh, a signal for me to ease up.

"Owe y'all an apology for that, I do," Halliwell said. "The Palm Springs police were no sooner finished with me, I was flying to Washington on White House business, a command performance, and locked up tighter than old Uncle Zachary's liquor cabinet. Back only this morning, and yours the first call I returned." Sounding like he was trying to sell us a bridge. His smile ringing as true as the Liberty Bell. "So, 'Urgent,' you said?"

I said, "Armando Soledad."

"Your bodyguard fella, right?"

Stevie nodded.

"What about him that's urgent?" His eyes giant question marks behind his Coke bottle lenses.

"You don't know?"

"Not a clue, Mr. Gulliver."

Stevie said, "Yesterday, we thought he was going to kill us."

"Sounds to me then that y'all need to be more careful who you hire," Halliwell said, like he was auditioning for *The Tonight Show*.

"That's all it means to you? A goddamn joke?"

I clamped my hand on Stevie's thigh.

"Sorry, Miss Marriner. What jet lag does to me. Makes me giddy for hours afterward. Once more, my apologies." He pushed out a smile and turning to me said, "So, tell me, Mr. Gulliver, what's the urgency about this Armando Soledad that you seem to believe would involve me?"

I told him.

Halliwell grew increasingly intent as I moved the story from my casino meeting with Aaron Lodger to our escape from the peat bog.

He leaned forward, shoulders hunched, hands clasped so tightly his translucent milk-white skin began to glow with an undercurrent of red. Sometimes he nodded, other times he shook his head, and, when I was finished, he leaned back and whistled incredulously at the ceiling.

"Quite a tale, Mr. Gulliver. Quite a tale, indeed. Let me be sure I understand a few things correctly. He said he worked sometimes for Aaron Lodger and sometimes for me?"

"Yeah."

"Me," Halliwell said, tapping his chest. "You're sure about that?"

"Certain."

"He chased after the gunman who shot and killed Rick Savage, who also took bad aim at Miss Marriner and at me. Caught him and, you think, disposed of him and his rented car in a peat bog on the San Gorgonio Reservation."

"Correct."

"Who was a Treasury Department agent."

"Yes."

"Name of Paul Darren."

"Showed us Darren's wallet. His badge. His license."

"Uh-huh, and next morning, yesterday, he took you and Miss Marriner to this same peat bog to show y'all and then to pretend like he was trying to do away with y'all."

"Yes."

"In case anyone was watching."

"Yes."

"Armando Soledad said for y'all to come tell me this."

"Yes."

"Gone later—" Pulled his fingers away from his mouth and said, "Poof! Gone, like that, nowhere to be found when this Indian who rescued y'all went back to see."

"Yes."

Halliwell gave the ceiling another low whistle.

Eased back from the desk.

Locked his hands behind his head.

Said, "Quite a tale, indeed . . ." Thought about it more. "So tell me—Who do y'all think was responsible for all that shooting?"

Stevie said, "We were hoping you could tell us."

"The obvious answer? Aaron Lodger. Working a scheme to embarrass the department, get the department off his case. A phony attack to get y'all running. Soledad follows the gunman out in your car. Leaves the two of you to carry the message home to me, the agent in charge." He chuckled inwardly. "It wouldn't surprise me to learn the Indian was in on it, too. So convenient him being around. The shrewdness of Mr. Aaron Lodger has never been in dispute, my friends."

Before I could defend Bobby San Gorgonio, Stevie said, "Then Armando wasn't working for you?"

"No, Miss Marriner. He wasn't. Not now. Not ever. As sure as lilacs grow green, we put people like that on the payroll sometimes, but Armando Soledad wasn't one of them. Not to my knowledge; no ma'am. Besides, almost an insult to imagine one of our people as the stone killer of Rick Savage or anyone working for us would have leave to kill an agent. Man was lying, and—"

A smug smile.

Reaching for the phone again.

"Got a better way to show you than with conversation," he said. Tapped in some numbers. "Halliwell here. Think you could join me for a minute in the rat's nest? Some folks I want you to meet. Great. Thanks. Appreciate."

He hung up and broke out a Himalayan smile.

Propped an elbow on the desk, and rested his cheek on the palm of his hand.

Less than a minute later, a knock, and the office door opened.

Stevie and I turned to the sound.

Halliwell said, "Miss Marriner, Mr. Gulliver, I'd like y'all to meet the late Paul Darren."

20

The unmarked we had arrived in, piloted by one of Jimmy Steiger's off-duty detectives, was illegally parked in front of the Federal Building. Curly, the cop, was immersed in the *Daily*'s business section and a Starbuck's latté when Stevie slipped into the backseat ahead of me and said, "That pair talking top of the stairs, Curly, right outside the doors?"

The detective barely shifted his eyes. "One sporting a goatee? The other, crummy green blazer, no fashion sense at all?"

"Them. The guy in the blazer picked up on us the minute we left our meeting. The other, street level, in front of the elevators."

"Not your imagination, Stevie?"

She made a face and said, "What is it with all you male chauvinists?" Turned to me for support.

"No offense intended," Curly said. "Just that you had a rough night and all. Gets the old imagination running wild."

I said, "My gut reaction as well as Stevie's, Curly."

The detective nodded, now a believer.

Man talk can do that between men, make believers.

It's a macho thing; words like "gut reaction."

"Means there'll be a car lurking close by," Curly said, putting aside the latté and the newspaper. He turned the key and the Plymouth's engine kicked in with a vengeance; waited for a break in the traffic and glided into the slow lane. "A late model Olds from somewhere on our case now."

He caught a right turn on yellow and reported the Olds coming through on red. "Sloppy work, gentlemen," he said to the rearview, then to us, "You be ready to do your bunny hop the minute we get there."

When we reached Union Station, Curly did a fast brake directly outside the subway entrance.

"Go, go, go!" he ordered.

I pushed open the door and hit the pavement running.

Stevie was right behind me.

Past my shoulder as we dashed for the subway entrance, I saw Curly out of the Plymouth and racing to the Olds, which had skidded to a noisy, rubber-burning stop less than a car length behind us. He had his Glock out and was flashing his badge, shouting for the two men inside the Olds to stay put.

The Wrangler was parked by the station at Vermont and Sunset, about four miles from the house. From there it took us ten minutes to reach the 5 and two hours later we were in Palm Springs, waiting for Frank Gordy to meet us at the Old Blue Eyes Garage on Two Palms Drive, a short dead end street nine blocks north of the main drag lined with light industry and a run-down, low-end strip mall, where we grabbed a king-sized mushroom and sausage pizza with extra cheese at Nero's World Famous Pizza Pie Emporium.

Stevie was feeling pleased with herself.

We talked about it on the road and again now, between bites.

It had been her inspiration—Stevie's word—to deposit the Wrangler at the station and let Curly take us downtown, even though it would mean some backtracking later. The cop, reluctant at first, agreed to go along with the idea after talking to Jimmy Steiger, who saw no harm in humoring her.

No harm in humoring her.

> >
> >

Also man talk.

I saw no harm, either.

A dedicated ex-husband thing.

Besides, Stevie trusted Halliwell less than I did. He was hovering around zero on her one-to-ten scale going into the meeting, and nothing he'd said or done changed that, not even his pulling Paul Darren out-of-the-hat trick.

Stevie said, "You're absolutely certain the T-man was Darren?" and took another massive bite from her pizza slice.

"Matched the driver's license I saw right down to the wart by the side of his left nostril, and you shouldn't talk with your mouth full."

"Iyuswamtuhbesmore."

"My sentiment exactly."

She rinsed with Diet Coke. "I said I just wanted to be sure . . . And Halliwell acting like he didn't know either, not a clue."

"Acting. Good word for it."

"Good word. Bad actor."

Another mouthful. "SodemwasitthaArmamdochastngot?"

"Sodemwamamdochngot, that's your question? I want to be positive I have it right."

A backhand slap on my shoulder. More Diet Coke.

"I didn't realize I was still so starved . . . I asked who it was then you think Armando chased and caught and dropped in the peat bog."

I said, "Someone else."

"Who and why?"

"I don't know and I don't know."

"What was whoever he was doing with Paul Darren's badge and license?"

"Mdomobulthimwebubbafimow." My turn to chew and chat. I swished some Diet Coke. "I don't know, but I think we better find out fast. Get a handle on the holes in the whole truth and fill in the blanks, know who the bad guys are before we mistake them for the good guys and maybe wind up in the peat bog for real."

"Why we're seeing Frank Gordy."

"Why we're seeing Frank Gordy."

"What if he says no to us, honey?"

"Then Frank's not the loyal friend of Richie Savage he made himself out to be."

———

The Old Blue Eyes Garage was having a busy afternoon.

A dozen misshapen cars had been towed in before Frank got there forty minutes later than he'd said when I called from the freeway. At least two dozen others were stacked in the lot, in line for their turn in one of the six auto bays where mechanics in grease-stained purple coveralls were busy working on earlier casualties in the perennial battle of the road warriors.

Stevie was stretched out and sleeping noisily, a snore occasionally interrupted by a whimper, her ulcer forcefully reminding her it can take only so much sausage, garlic, and thickly peppered tomato sauce, even when it arrives on world-famous pizza.

I used the time to resume reading from a journal Augie Fowler had left with me before taking off for India, saying "It's special, so put it in a safe place for me until I get back, the He Who Would Be Me. If for some reason I don't get back, put it in a safe place anyway."

It was one in a series of diaries he'd been keeping for much of his adult life, for reference when he got around to writing what he called "The Great American Autobiography."

His "magnum opus," he said.

His "remembrance of things past, present, and future."

A thick scarlet-covered ledger Augie had filled on page after page with his precise, birdlike handwriting. One line pressed against the next. Barely any margins.

When I asked what made this journal special, he studied me for a dunce cap, intoned dramatically, "History is what," and pressed an upright finger to his pursed lips.

Used to his curious ways, I let it go at that and had Stevie put it in the wall safe in her den; forgot about the journal until this morning, in the shower, trying to decide who to trust least, Martin Halliwell or Aaron Lodger.

I remembered a common denominator: Augie Fowler.

Both claiming Augie as a close friend and confidant.

Remembered Augie's journal.

Thought it might contain a clue.

A stretch, but worth checking.

No other bright ideas wobbling around in my head.

Augie hadn't said anything about not reading it, so, before heading for our meeting with Halliwell, I took the journal from the safe and locked it in the Wrangler.

Later, surprised Stevie by suggesting she drive and, angling the ledger between my knees and the dash, flipped open the cover and began rifling pages.

> >
> >

The entries were mainly from 1980, late in the year, and the name that stopped me wasn't Halliwell or Lodger.

It was: Harry Nilsson.

The musical genius I'd met by accident when I raced to New York in 1980 to pay homage to the memory of the murdered John Lennon, the same trip that put me together with Augie, who like Harry had been in John's close circle of friends for years.

Harry Nilsson, inspiration and motor behind the first and second John Lennon Imagine That! memorial festivals.

Harry was dead now, a heart attack in January '94, the sad, predictable victim of his myriad vices, but he was very much alive in Augie's journal—

Augie reacting to news of John Lennon's murder with a rush of memories from 1973 and 1974—

When John, separated from Yoko, had taken up residence in LA, and seemed determined to destroy himself with booze, drugs, and a little help from his friends.

The Who's Keith Moon.

Bobby Keyes. Randy Dexter and Jerry Roach.

Sometimes, Alice Cooper.

Sometimes, John's Beatles-mate Ringo Starr.

Much of the time, Harry Nilsson, and—

Much more of the time, Augie.

FROM AUGIE FOWLER'S JOURNAL
December 8, 1980

Maybe the ninth?

Time standing still and moving in all directions at the same time as I wipe out the rotten news with thoughts of all the good moments we shared, John, the boys, and me.

How did we first meet up?

Music?

No, a bar.

A skuzzy little hole in the wall two blocks south of Hollywood Boulevard on Cahuenga that opened at six in the morning, meaning professional booze hounds didn't have to hold on longer than four hours after the 2 A.M. closing time before we could rev up again. There were others in LA but this one, the Answered Prayer, was my personal church.

Most of the alkies had to hole up in their car or hold up the wall waiting for the door to open, but I was one of the privileged few the owner, Laszlo, an easygoing Hungarian immigrant with an accent as thick as a prime filet down the street at Martoni's, let sneak in through the back door.

He was always good for a couple comp rounds when I got going with some of my crime beat war stories. Sad part is, he eventually became one of them, the victim of some speed freak who decided he was a med student and took a butcher knife to Lasz, turning him into a collection of body parts.

This particular morning, I wasn't the only early bird special in the gloomy cave, whose best light came from all the neon beer displays behind the bar counter. Two juicers at an isolated table across the room were making noise and smoke clouds and adding to a monumental migraine I'd brought in with me.

I shouted at them, "Will you two revelers shut the fuck up?"

The larger of the team made a megaphone of his hands and called back, "What?"

"Will you two revelers shut the fuck up?"

"You said that twice," he said, and began laughing like it was the joke of the century, a sound matched by the other juicer.

I stomped over to their table, meaning to do something about their insolence, not quite sober enough to know what, but I froze at the sight of the smaller, hawk-nosed guy in the beret, hiding behind a pair of granny shades and a two-day growth of beard.

Like a thunderstruck fan, I said, "You're John Lennon."

He said, "What about my John Lennon?"

The other one rose and said, "Me, I have to go to the john, Lennon."

"While you're bloody foogin' at it, go for me, too, mate. Don't know my legs can stand the traffic."

The other one headed off and Lennon said, "That was Harry Nilsson you just insulted, you know who that is?"

"Yeah. Not that I care, but how did I insult him?"

"You didn't laugh at his joke."

"I didn't hear one, unless you mean his face."

"Oh, quick that. Have a seat and stop your knees from quivering. Next round is on Laszlo. Laszlo!"

I sat down and John held out his hand across the table.

Repeated my name to make sure he had it right.

"Listen, then, A. K. Fowler, but your friends call you Augie," he said. "Harry gets back from taking his pee, make like you never heard of him in your life."

So that began it, my introduction to John and what became known as his eighteen-month "lost weekend." And, to Harry, who became my closer friend after John went home to New York and Yoko; Yoko, who came to blame Harry for John's LA peccadilloes and marked him *non grata*, when she might as easily have pointed the finger of lethal excommunication at Keith or Jerry Roach. Randy Dexter. Me.

After all, I was also there that infamous night at the Troub, along with John's first wife, Cynthia, and May Pang, his girlfriend—how's that for a pairing?—Jesse Ed Davis, Harry, and Jimmy Keltner, the session drummer, to see Annie Peebles.

In no time, John is loud and obnoxious.

Pretty soon he's coming back from the loo sporting a Kotex on his forehead.

The waitress edges down the tight aisle and wonders if he might quiet down. He gives her lip, orders another round. She says he's too drunk, so no more service.

John shouts, "Don't you know who I am?"

The waitress shouts back, "You're some asshole with a Kotex on your head."

Sweet Jesus, was that a night, one of many that John took to disavowing after Yoko let him come home again.

Another trapped in legend, the night at the Troubadour that got us tossed out onto the street, John and Harry and me.

Up on stage, the Smothers Brothers, making a comeback or something like that. Down front, the three of us making short work of Brandy Alexanders, one after another. It's a drink that tastes like a milkshake, has the kick of a mule; introduced to John by Harry, who treats them like mother's milkshakes; calls them "jug-o-nauts."

John, whose usual libation is Remy Martin, which he's capable of polishing off a fifth at a time, is gone quicker than Margaret Mitchell's wind.

John gets to heckling the Smothers, explaining to me later how he'd always sort of liked Tommy, but considered Dickie a prime asshole, so the mood just sort of fell upon him naturally.

John gets louder and louder, calling up to the stage, "Dickie, you're an asshole!" Ranting on about "pigs." Like that. And, Tommy trying to make light of it, but John only getting more and more vulgar.

Harry diabolically encouraging John.

The show sledding downhill and off the mountain.

People in the audience catcalling at John.

Troubadour people asking us to leave.

John refusing.

Resisting.

A scuffle.

Us, now the show.

Punches thrown.

John wrestled under control.

Us, dumped on the street.

John so angry he puts a period to the adventure by kicking the parking attendant.

The next morning, his name all over the news.

A waitress claiming she was hit by John and getting ready to sue him.

John sobering up and anxious to make amends.

He and Harry, sending flowers and a note of apology to the Smothers.

Out of Harry's hearing, complaining, "Harry doesn't get as much attention as me, the bum. God bless him, but—whose name do you see in the headlines, when it's him encouraging me all along?"

I remember saying, "John, why go along with it then?"

A shrug and a throwaway gesture.

"It's like Harry, Keith Moon, and them, they're on a suicide mission and I've become an elephant in a zoo. I'm trapped, but not able to get out."

Not long after, he made the attempt.

He turned to Harry one night, before the drinking had got too serious, and said, "Why don't we try doing some work instead of getting into trouble? My name gets in the paper, you never get mentioned and I get all the problems, and I'm the one with the immigration problems."

Soon after, John was producing Harry's *Pussycats* album for RCA, not one of Harry's best, his voice by '74 shot to galaxies far, far away on cigarettes and booze.

The work, being back in a recording studio, made some small difference to John.

Getting back with Yoko made all the difference in this blessed world, but—

〉
〉

Dear John, did you have to die to become immortal?
If you can hear me, John, answer me, God damn it!
In this life, John.
In this life.

Augie carried on like that for more pages, the stories at times funny, at times wistful, but always building to a relationship with John, another with Harry, that grew closer with the passage of time.

His handwriting growing smaller and tougher to read the more sentimental he became; his writing style close to what he once banged out on the *Daily* crime beat, reminding me how he'd influenced my own after I joined the paper, a move from the *Twin Counties Sentinel* Augie had made possible.

I could hear Augie telling me, "It's time you grew up some more, stopped confusing a byline with brilliance, and learned from the old master how to dig out truth the way an archeologist goes after another King Tut's tomb," and—

There it was, Halliwell's name.

I went back, scrutinizing earlier pages to see if there were references to him.

There were.

Augie in the air, on his way to New York, not because of John's murder.

Having to do with President Reagan.

Halliwell materializing less than accidentally in the next seat.

Aaron Lodger's name.

Augie waking up lost and confused in a New York hotel.

Shaken by the news of John's murder.

As much reading as I got through before Stevie and I reached Palm Springs and our pizza.

More reading now settled in the Wrangler, the windows up, the motor idling, air conditioning battling the midday heat to a draw while we waited for Frank Gordy to show up; thinking, at this rate we could be waiting for Frank Godot.

I learned about Augie joining up with Harry Nilsson and me, and Augie's initial anger over my beating him out of an exclusive interview with John's killer, Mark David Chapman.

Augie racing on foot down Central Park West, anguishing over John's death, desperate for a Brandy Alexander, unaware he's being tracked by Halliwell in a rented Chrysler until—

Halliwell stops and calls to him, "Need a lift? Climb on in, Augie. We got us a lot to talk about, you'n me."

Talk they do, enough of it set down by Augie for me to understand why he wanted the journal in a safe place.

Nothing as it had first seemed to Stevie and me.

Not the whole truth, but a bigger picture developing.

I was anxious to keep reading, but—

Loud, rhythmic honking emanating from a spit-shined hearse pulling into the Old Blue Eyes Garage.

Frank behind the wheel, his shoulder and half a head out the window, waving grandly at me.

I slipped the ledger under my seat, angled around to the backseat, and nudged Stevie.

She awoke with a snort and a start.

Bolted into a sitting position.

Waving her fists like she was warding off some demon.

Her groggy eyes shifting about, trying to make sense of her surroundings.

"Oh, yeah," she said, and gave me a questioning look.

I switched off the motor and said, "Showtime, babe."

We got out of the Wrangler and stretched out the kinks, Stevie ignoring several whistles from some of the mechanics and tow drivers.

Frank glided over and greeted us like we were his best friends in the world. He gripped my hand in both of his and gave it a generous pump, then did the same with Stevie and followed up with an impetuous hug, ringing her in his arms and squeezing tightly.

"I am so overjoyed to see you looking well after what we been through, sister," he said, and seemed ready to kiss her, but backed off wondering, "You miss him as much as me, the mayor? In time he would of made a great senator, do you know that?"

Pointing to the hearse, his smile competing with the sun, he said, "You see that, what I came in? For him, Mayor Savage, the funeral service coming up on us next week and I got to be sure there's nothing wrong under the hood and it keeps its shine, bright as new. He deserve the best. I say it now, like I always use to. I want everything to be sweet as custard for the man. And, you hear the news yet?"

He spotted the ignorance in our eyes.

"Thought not, that's how new it is. Don't even know if it's out.

Heard it from Mr. L himself, driving him to temple just now; why I'm a little late. Mr. L says he heard how the president himself is coming to Mayor Savage's service, going to speak a few words.

"They got to be friendly, the president and the mayor, when the president was spending time drumming up votes here in the Springs, do you know that?

"I was around when the president himself keep telling the mayor how he should run for senator and come help him out with his great plans for the country. Uh-huh. Uh-huh." His smile sank. "Now it won't happen." A simple declaration of fact. He gave a stray stone a hard kick, sent it sailing over the chain-link fence.

I said, "You sure, Frank? I'd heard the president was thinking about being here for the Imagine That! festival."

"Heard that, too, before, but Mr. L always knows best. He says it still could be, but the president want to speak some words about the mayor, so he's coming to the service. You going to be there, of course."

A command more than a question, sounding almost like Aaron Lodger.

"Of course," Stevie said, "but right now let me tell you why we're here, Frank."

He found something about the way she said it.

He took two steps back, folded his arms across a suit that must have set him back more than a few major body and fender jobs, cocked his head, and hoisted his eyebrows.

She told him what we had in mind.

Frank looked at me warily.

"The lady know what she talking about?"

"She took the words right out of my mouth."

"Mayor Savage's killer for sure?"

"As sure as I'm a candidate for sunstroke we stand here much longer, Frank."

He found another stone to kick.

It soared over the fence.

"Let's do it," Frank said. "When?"

Stevie said, "Tomorrow too soon for you?"

"Nothing too soon for me," he said, dry-washing his palms. "Mayor Savage was my friend."

Back at the Sunrise Hotel, surprises were waiting.

For Stevie, it was one of her *Bedrooms and Board Rooms* producers, Dar Armateaux, pacing the lobby nervously, hands jammed in his pockets, an anxious look smothering his young face and filling it with a jumble of worry lines.

For me, finally, a message from Leigh, whose Seville was still on the hotel lot.

Armateaux hesitated before moving on Stevie, sounding her name like a fan greeting a favorite outside a premiere, but his expression told another story. He didn't want to be here any more than she was interested in seeing him.

"What's the matter, Dar? They sent you because Benedict Arnold was busy?"

She tried stepping around him, but he kept shifting and blocking her way.

"We have to talk, Stevie."

"We don't. Read the rule book. How'd you know where to find me, anyway?"

"Your lawyer. He said to tell you that you haven't been returning any of his calls."

"I know that already."

"The same with your agent."

"Both exes—" Pointing at me. "Like Mr. Gulliver here."

"Don't let her fool you," I said. "She always returns my calls."

"Please, Stevie. It's a matter of life and death."

"My life or my death, I'm interested. Otherwise—"

"Houseman and Overman," he sputtered, verging on tears.

"I'll send flowers."

"Me, if I don't get you to listen."

"Is there room on the list? There are some names I'd like to add, like Mr. Smug, Ralph Bonner, and—" Snapping her fingers. "Buddy Sawhill. The name I couldn't remember!"

"Mr. Gulliver, can you get her to listen?"

"If it doesn't work out for you at the soap, you have a natural gift for comedy."

He started crying, the tears streaming down his cheeks and destroying his tube tan.

"Okay, okay," Stevie said, like she'd looked a minute too long at the puppy in the pet shop window.

Armateaux wiped his eyes, pulled himself together, and forced a weak smile. "Thank you," he said, sounding like he meant it. He looked around the lobby. "Somewhere private?"

Stevie thought about it.

"My room," she said, and started for the stairs.

When we reached her door, Armateaux glanced at me and asked her, "Just the two of us, would that be all right?"

I said, "I don't think so."

Stevie answered my look with one that said it was all right.

Patted her bag about where her .32 would be.

I waited for Stevie to turn the door lock before going to my room, planning to return Leigh Wilder's phone call as the first order of business.

Unnecessary.

I walked in to find Leigh lounging on the bed, talking newspaper talk into her cell phone.

As big a surprise as the last time I'd found a stranger in my room but, in her scarlet silk net mini-bra and matching panties, a more appealing Little Beaver.

"I have to go," she told the phone and snapped it shut.

Gave me a smile and a high sign.

Said, "Nothing to do with you, handsome. It's the damn heat in this room. Besides, you've seen more."

"And less," I said.

21

"In case you're wondering," Leigh said, "the clerk let me in. I told Forrest I wanted to surprise you. Surprise!"

I threw up my hands and feigned surprise.

"Adds to my secure feeling about this place," I said, closing and locking the door.

"Forrest's mommy and I go way back. She's divorced and moderately desperate. We play bridge and trade lies once or twice a month."

Her look as inviting as her body.

"So, where you been? I've been calling. Left you a lot of messages."

"I know. The car. The picture. Vegas, not that it's any of your business."

"Must be a pretty big advertiser for you to travel that far."

"Maybe a pretty big boyfriend," she said, raising her eyebrows a notch, a grin tickling the corners of her mouth, "and still none of your business."

She made a provocative roll off the bed and sashayed in my direction like a model working a fashion runway. Unhitched her bra en route. Stopped to make sure I got a good look at her breasts before she plunked the bra on top of my head and announced, "I'll be showering while you read."

"Read?"

She indicated the desk; a brown legal-size expandable file parked on its side next to the phone.

"More than anyone should ever want to know about that son of a bitch Michael Wilder." She understood the question my eyes were asking, and said, "I know Uncle Aaron told you you didn't have to see the paperwork. I want you to see for yourself, anyway."

She tapped the tip of my nose, added a kiss there, and said, "Of course, if you're still into showers *au deaux*, you are more than welcome to join me first."

Fluttered her eyes and pushed back her hair.

Added a pelvic thrust.

I shook my head. "Thanks, but feel free to lie about it to Forrest's mommy."

"At least say you like my tits."

I'd avoided looking, but now I stole a glance.

"I like your tits."

"Praise be, Lord," she said. "One less thing I'll have to lie to Forrest's mommy about."

She wriggled out of her panties and tossed them aside, turned, and moon-walked her way to the bathroom.

Halted in the doorway and turned to give me a frontal view.

"You don't know what you're missing," Leigh cooed.

"I think I do," I said. "Tell me, were you always this aggressive?"

"We grow into what we are, Cookie Monster."

Leigh retreated, not quite shutting the door.

Moments later, the sound of running water.

I retrieved her panties, removed the bra from my head, and placed them on top of the chartreuse and red peppermint-striped wrap dress she'd draped over the armchair backrest, then settled at the desk and opened her file.

It was crammed with manila folders, Michael Wilder's name hand-printed on all the index flaps, but otherwise no clue to content.

None was necessary after I'd sifted through the first half dozen folders.

Given bad investments in the stock market and several get-rich-quick land development schemes, a gambling habit reflected by five- and six-figure IOUs, Wilder had probably bankrupted the company store.

"Figure it out?" Leigh called across the room.

I looked up.

She was back in the doorway, toweling off.

"The only money Michael Wilder ever laundered was my family's, especially after Daddy was gone. The bastard came on board as our business manager and took Daddy's dream and spent it. Washed it right down the drain, never once letting on. I married for love and it turns out Michael married for survival.

"He'd built a shit mountain of debt by the time I took over the paper and, like a damn fool fucking moron, I left the business side to him so I could keep concentrating on the editorial side, the way Daddy always had. When the calls began coming to me because they couldn't get through to him and when the loan enforcers began dropping by to leave their threats, I confronted Michael. His answer was to disappear.

"I was desperate, so I went to Uncle Aaron and told him what was going on. He said don't worry about the threats, he would speak to the people, take care of that part, but I had to take responsibility for what was owed. It was a matter of honor, he said. I've been paying off the national debt ever since."

Her eyes flared with hurt and anger and something else.

I interpreted it as embarrassment over the realization I might start thinking less of her.

It also was a raw appeal for understanding, but—

Not sympathy.

Leigh was too strong to need sympathy.

It struck me that she and Stevie were worlds apart in most ways, yet so much the same in others. Or, was I simply reading Stevie into her? How much both their lives seemed to be built around father figures: one who was there in Leigh's case; in Stevie's, one who'd disappeared when she was just a kid.

Leigh finished making a turban of the bath towel.

Her shoulders sagged, and she held out her arms like a plaster cast saint, wondering, "Hold me, Neil?"

Okay, so maybe a little sympathy.

Just like Stevie sometimes needed.

I rose from the desk and crossed to her.

Took her in my arms and felt the press of warm flesh against my clothing.

Saw a new look in her eyes as she locked her hands at the nape of my neck.

"Let's do it," Leigh whispered in my ear, her tongue adding an exclamation point. "Now. Like the old days. Get naked and let's do it." Her voice crackling with passion, and—

Someone knocking at the door.

"Neil, honey? How long do I have to stand out here?"

We disengaged, me in a mild state of panic and Leigh unable to contain a look of amusement.

"Won't this be interesting," she said.

I dashed over to the desk, rammed the folders into the file, dashed back to Leigh, pushed the file at her, pushed Leigh and the file into the bathroom, gave her a look that said stay there, dashed to the armchair, grabbed up her bra, panties, and dress, darted back to the bathroom, tossed them at her, gave her another *stay there* warning look, pulled the bathroom door shut; tight. Paused to catch my breath, turned, and took a step toward the hall door, and—

Noticed Leigh's three-inch crimson strap sandals parked next to the bed.

Stevie's knocking more insistent.

"Honey? You there?"

A disturbed edge to her voice.

I stepped over and kicked the sandals under the bed.

Giant-stepped to the hall door.

In a moment was staring at a face full of irritation.

"You know I hate to be kept waiting," she said.

"Stretched out for five and must have dropped off," I said, manufacturing a yawn to hide the lie.

Stevie made a move to come in.

"Better your room," I said.

She examined me with her eyes, trying to make sense of my suggestion.

Shook her head.

"Dar hasn't gone yet. He's using the phone to call LA."

She squeezed past me and headed for the armchair.

Settled onto it with her legs crossed yoga fashion.

"I couldn't wait to tell you," Stevie said, instantly relaxed and more animated. "You are definitely not going to believe it."

"The show wants you back," I said, sitting across from her on the bed and stealing an anxious look at the bathroom door.

"That you better believe."

"Karen Walls. Off the show."

"Also yes, but it's the *why* part you're not going to believe. I almost didn't believe it myself."

"Maybe I should also hear it straight from the horse's mouth," I said, and started to rise.

"Sit!" Stevie said.

"Woof-woof-woof," I said, and sat.

She said, "It really is a matter of life and death."

"You have my attention," I said, prying my eyes away from the bathroom door.

"You remember that scene in *The Godfather*, where the studio boss finds a horse's head in his bed?"

"Jack Woltz. Played by the late John Marley. I don't know who played the horse."

Stevie frowned and said, "Aaron Lodger sent some guy over to talk to Houseman at the show, then Overman at the network. He told them Mr. Lodger was a fan of the show and would appreciate it if they would bring me back and get rid of Karen for good. They laughed at him, were ready to kick the guy out, until he reminded them who Lodger was and how they could either do what he asked or find time to pick out a nice plot at Forest Lawn. He gave them until this morning to come up with the right answer and wondered if Mr. Lodger should prove his seriousness by starting with someone else. He pulled out a list of names and began reciting them along with home addresses. The net result—They sent Dar Armateaux out to find me; told him his ass was grass if he didn't come back with the right answer."

"Which, of course, you gave him."

"I didn't, honey. I couldn't. Right now I don't know if I want to go back. I'd pretty much made up my mind to breach the damn contract instead of sitting still for the every-so-often, line-at-a-time crap they were talking."

"You tell Armateaux that?"

"Why do you think he's on the phone to LA? Still crying up a storm, I suppose."

"His name was on the list?"

"I told him to find a new address."

"You didn't."

"I told him I'd think about it and let him know. I'll call him tomorrow, after we finish up with Frank Gordy. He call yet?"

Before I could answer, the bathroom door opened.

Leigh emerged fully clothed.

Gave an airy nod to Stevie and, apologizing for the interruption, got down on her knees, eased my legs aside, and searched out her sandals from under the bed.

Got up, locked them under an arm, and said cheerfully, "You can drop off the photo later, Cookie Monster."

Waved good-bye over her shoulder and was out the door.

The room became as quiet as a mummy's tomb.

Stevie examined her nails while I examined Stevie.

Finally, she unwound onto the floor, aimed dagger eyes and me, and said sarcastically, "Cookie Monster?"

"I can explain," I said.

She said, "You always could, Cookie Monster. This time save it for someone who really cares."

Stevie slept with the chair angled under the doorknob, the .32 under her pillow, and not well, in her half-awake, half-alert state Neil more on her mind than any fear of an intruder or concerns about *Bedrooms and Board Rooms*.

She challenged herself, *Why the jealousy?*

How can I care and not care about Neil after all these years?

Where's the fairness in that?

Where's the fairness in exposing him to one boyfriend after the next, expecting Neil to understand my needs and accept them, yet unwilling to grant him the same privilege, the same courtesy, the same respect?

Not fair at all, and I don't like it at all, Stevie-girl, not at all.

Neil deserves better than that.

Better than me.

Better than me?

Better than me.

And what do I deserve?

No, wait!

Don't start putting yourself down, girl.

Too many people out there ready to do it for you.

Already doing it.

But not Neil.

Never Neil.

Neil, still loving me seven years after our divorce, against the reality that lightning doesn't strike twice.

Not for Neil and me.

Why, Stevie?

Because you say so?

Is that your final word on the subject?

Be honest now. Honest. Honest. Honest.

No, not the final word.

Just my final word.

For now.

Just for now?

Only for now.

Only for just for up to now.

Only I'd be lost without him.

Without Neil.

He's my best friend.

Till death do us part, but it doesn't take a marriage license for that.

It takes love.

All you need is love.

The rest is whatever happens next.

Stevie checked her watch.

Closing in on three.

She reached for the .32 and rolled out of bed, a minute later was knocking on Neil's door in her baby-dolls.

Almost at once the door opened the length of the chain latch. Closed and opened all the way. Neil standing there in his skivvies, bare-chested, hair a mess, eyes squinting into the hallway light; clearing his throat and opening his mouth to say something.

She stopped him with a kiss, threw her arms around him and kissed him again, longer and deeper, pressing tighter as he responded, surprising herself with the depth of her need to feel him close.

Pulled back to study Neil's face, to be certain she was still wanted.

"I accept your apology," he said, struggling to get out the words.

"That wasn't it," she said, having her own problem with speaking; breathing.

She took him by the hand and led him to bed.

Later, he said, "Your way of apologizing could get to be a habit."

"No it can't," she said.

She cushioned her head against his shoulder, and slept.

In the morning, Neil told her about Leigh.

This time she listened, happier than she let on as he explained how Leigh materialized in his room, but laughing with him when he described in exaggerated detail the comedy routine he'd gone through after hearing her calling to him at the hallway door.

"A shower *au deaux*, huh?" she said, and guided Neil to the bathroom, where they made noisy love again.

Afterward, they crawled back into bed and tried it one more time before Neil grew somber repeating what Leigh had told him.

"Bottom line, it doesn't add up," Neil said, looking uncomfortable with the realization, the way she'd seen him look dozens of times, whenever he felt deceived by someone he considered a friend.

Stevie could never get over the fact that Neil was so trusting for someone in a business as cruel as newspapers, where reporters held up a mirror to the worst about people, day after day using up page after page like it was so much toilet paper.

"Where does the two-plus-two fall short, honey?"

He rolled out of bed heading for the desk and was back in an instant holding three or four slender manila folders, which he handed over to Stevie.

"I missed these last night in my hurry to make Leigh disappear; noticed them after you disappeared. I couldn't sleep, so I studied them until this gorgeous creature came knocking at my door in the middle of the night."

"And where you hiding her now, this gorgeous creature? Under the bed?"

"Under me until a while ago."

Neil eased onto his side and found a place to kiss her where he knew he'd get a squeal and a giggle. Got it, then settled in a half-sitting position, propped up by a pillow and using his arms for a headrest.

Stevie angled on an elbow facing Neil and, using his lap for a desk, opened the top folder and began exploring the jumble of loose papers inside.

Gambling IOUs, some for hundreds of dollars, most of them in the thousands; four and five figures.

Most of them from Captain Pabro's Gaming Casino.

All of them signed by Michael Wilder.

More IOUs scattered in the other folders, some from the reservation, a smattering from casinos in Vegas, as well as promissory notes, letters of agreement, demand letters from lawyers, and dunning notices from collection agencies.

Everything signed by or directed at Michael Wilder.

"Man had a gambling jones," Stevie said. "Like you and the ponies before you reformed. Big, big. Ugly big."

"And, from the looks of it, he liked to draw to inside straights."

"What am I missing that I'm supposed to see, that the bulk of what he owed he owed to the reservation casino?"

"Anyone can see that. Try again."

"Is this a test?"

"Only if you pass."

Stevie inched up and settled next to Neil.

She roamed the files again, slower this time, aware he was watching her, but giving away nothing as she momentarily paused here and there to—

Of course!

What Neil meant, right in front of her, so obvious it had been invisible.

"The IOUs," she said.

"What about the IOUs?"

"They're here. If he hadn't paid them off, the casinos would still be holding them."

"And?" His hand gesture summoned more.

Stevie had to think about it, but not for long.

"If Wilder was looting the family piggy bank, he's not going to keep the IOUs around as souvenirs. A gambler gets back his IOUs, he gets rid of them, like you used to. Rips them up. Burns them. Flushes them down the toilet. So, it's more likely the paybacks came from someone who had nothing to hide, not someone who couldn't risk getting caught. Like Leigh, honey?"

"Not as much as before I came to the same conclusion," Neil said.

"She has that kind of money?"

"Not the way she was telling it. But thinking gets you thinking: she dresses like a million dollars. Can afford to drive around in a new Seville . . ."

"Then how? Where'd the money come from?"

"Why I'm having trouble with the two-plus-two, babe."

Between my memory and a map—and ignoring a few wrong turns—we arrived at Bobby San Gorgonio's sacred peat bog a good half hour ahead of schedule.

Frank Gordy and his crew had beaten us there and already were at work, under another one of those merciless middle of the day suns capable of melting steel.

Frank had brought up two standard tow rigs, a flat bed, and an ambulance from The Chairman of the Board Independent Emergency 24-Hour Ambulance Service, as well as a yellow Cad Eldorado Biarritz wearing dealer plates.

He and four beefy sweat factories in orange jumpsuits, bandanas around their thick necks and foreheads, had formed a semicircle in what was passing for a shaded area; Frank talking and jabbing an index finger in the direction of the bog; the guys nodding and grunting between swipes from cans of Bud.

Two men in deep-sea diving suits, oxygen tanks strapped to their backs, were padding in fins along the perimeter of the insect-infested bog, like they were trying to spot the Creature from the Black Lagoon.

Two other men were roaming the bog itself, cautiously, like it was a minefield; similarly attired except for "bog shoes," a cross between skis and snowshoes; pushing metal detectors over the deceptive surface; face masks in place.

Bogs take about ten thousand years to fully form.

They start as a relatively stagnant, shallow body of water, maybe twenty-five or thirty feet deep at the center, with a high concentration of tannic acid that tastes a lot like vinegar, say people who fell into bogs but managed to escape its sometimes quicksand grip.

Over the years, in the rain, snow, and wind conditions the Gorgonio range provides, especially at higher altitudes, dead grasses, shrubs, flowers, and trees fall into the water and begin to decompose—

But not entirely.

The process is inhibited by the cold weather seasons, so ultimately a covering of sphagnum moss is formed. Year after year, the process repeats itself, and with every new layer of decomposed vegetation there's a rise in thickness and in the acidity level.

The carpet covering that forms is strong enough to hold people in its thickest spots, but that varies from point to point and, one misstep, an unprepared stroller can drop out of sight permanently.

Stuff I remembered from a feature piece I did for the *Sentinel* in the period leading up to the first Imagine That! festival, one of dozens that either tried to make the San Gorgonio Reservation an appealing attraction for fans who'd be coming to honor John Lennon or told them what to steer away from once they arrived.

I was telling it to Frank after he greeted Stevie and me, offered us cold brews, and said, "How sure are you that Mayor Savage's killer is down in that nasty swamp thing?"

"A hundred percent," Stevie said, and wandered off to see if the ice chests by the trucks had any Perrier.

"If we find the T-Bird, we'll find him sitting behind the wheel," I said. Accepted the Bud greedily and repeated what I had told Frank yesterday.

"Not just some gooey awful remains not even a buzzard would want and no next of kin should waste good tears over. You still onboard with that observation, Mr. Gulliver?" I nodded. "Tell me again, please."

Frank's intelligent eyes fixed on me and I sensed his mind opening to lock in the explanation.

"Because of the acidity and the cold trapped under the surface, a bog is an almost-perfect preserving entity. Any body buried in a bog is quickly leached of its body fluids, so decomposition doesn't occur. In time, the body will turn dark, a dark brown color to black, but all the organs, the hair, the skin, everything, is preserved. A stab wound or a bullet hole would be as obvious as the day it happened, no matter how much time has passed."

He shook his head in apparent wonderment, and his mile-wide grin made laugh gullies on his face.

"I know from bagmen, but you the bog man," Frank said. "Can't be making all that stuff up, I know that already from some of my team I hand-picked for this job."

"Hey, Francis!" one of the bog walkers called to Frank. "I think we got something going here!"

"Say what, bro?"

Everyone turned to hear what the bog walker had to say.

The bog walker pointed downward.

"Be right back," he said.

Handed over his metal detector to the other bog walker.

Snapped on a light source growing out of the face mask.

Eased below the surface.

Stevie hurried over and seized my arm in anticipation.

Frank juggled himself on the balls of his feet, hands behind his back.

Maybe a minute later, up popped the bog walker.

Clutching vegetation with one hand, he used his free hand to raise his face mask, and shouted at us, "Is a car down there and— You was looking for a body? I found you a body."

22

F rank gave his crew a "go" signal.

They tossed their beers and got busy backing up both tow trucks to the lip of the bog, inching as close as they dared, the boom pulleys casting shadows over the sphagnum moss.

The divers were already somewhere under the surface, and both bog walkers also had disappeared, leaving their metal detectors to nest on a bulky rise of peat.

Frank Gordy paced like an expectant father, every few minutes checking his watch. Finger-snapping to four-letter rap blaring from one of the truck radios.

Stevie and I hung back out of the way, trading off on my second can of Bud while we waited for something to—

A diver materialized and hand-signaled for the pulley cable to be lowered. Down it came. He latched onto the hook and rode with it below the surface.

A minute or two passed before he popped up again and motioned the crane operator to raise the pulley.

Gears wheezed as it ascended, bringing a body with it, dangling from the hook on cross-straps, dancing to the wind as the tow truck moved inland before lowering its cargo to a level where it could be wrapped in a sheet of clear plastic and settled onto the ground by two of the orange clad sweat-hogs.

"What say?" Frank said, pondering over the corpse.

I didn't have to study the body to decide.

"Too black. This man was down there too long to be our killer."

I mentally wrote off the cadaver as somebody who would have celebrated more birthdays but for an Aaron Lodger or an Armando Soledad; nothing I needed to share with Frank.

"If at first you don't succeed . . ." I said.

Frank turned and instructed the diver to try again.

The diver dropped from view.

The other diver appeared and signaled for the pulley.

The rig angled about forty feet south of its previous location and inched back to the bog; set the cable pulley in motion.

The diver descended with the hook and was back shortly with another body. Another male. Again, the *corpus* too rich a cordovan brown to be of recent vintage.

Frank raised his sunglasses, gave me an odd look, and moved it over to Stevie, wondering, "You know any more about this bad-ass boggy place than you bothered telling me?"

Stevie and I traded blinks, turned back to Frank, and shook our lying heads in unison.

As two of the orange guys lugged the plastic shrouded body to the ambulance to join its mate—

The other rig honked out a musical signal.

It was straining by inches to move away from the bog, the Ortiz bar chains stretched taut.

"Looks like we caught us a big fish," Frank said.

"Or a bird?" Stevie said.

"Would suit me to a T," Frank said, flashing his smile at her.

Only the fish wouldn't cooperate.

Whether it was the weight of the catch or the angle of the ground, the tow truck stalled; the back wheels turning uselessly; a grinding noise blending with the radio rap; a driver shouting curses out the cabin window.

"Must be thicker here," I said. "Tougher cracking the surface."

Frank summoned the second rig.

It backed up to the bog and two divers dropped in with a set of heavier chains.

The driver waited for their signal, then moved parallel to the other rig and together they struggled forward.

This time it worked, and—

A T-Bird emerged slowly from the bog.

Badly in need of a wash and wax, the paint job where I could find it suffering from exposure to the tannic acid.

Frank closed in on the front bumper, stooped, and began rubbing at the license plate with a handkerchief he'd pulled from his hip pocket.

Cleared through to enough numbers to announce, "Uh-huh, uh-huh. This the right Bird."

It was impossible to see through the windows.

Frank told one of the orange men to open the door.

The fellow grimaced, rummaged for a pair of gloves in the utility chest on the truck bed, then tried the two handles. Both the driver and passenger side doors were locked.

He turned his hands palms up and looked at Frank for instructions.

"Bust a window," Frank said.

The orange man went to the truck bed, returned with a crowbar.

A two-handed swing, and—

Puke-colored water poured out of the T-Bird, like the orange man had cracked a water hydrant, soaking the orange man from the waist down.

"Son-a bitch!" he yelped, jumping aside. "Son-a bitch!"

He stepped up to the car, took an overhead swipe, and shattered the windshield.

"Son-a bitch!" he said.

"Chill, my friend," Frank said, approaching the Bird.

He motioned for us to stay back, leaned in cautiously, holding the base of his white seersucker sport jacket tight with both hands to prevent it from rubbing against the muck; too late to do anything about his embossed calfskin loafers.

"Uh-huh, uh-huh" he said and, turning to us, "Come have a look."

The T-Bird was empty.

"What's a hundred percent of nothing?" he asked Stevie with just enough sarcasm to put fire in her eyes.

I pressed my palm to her mouth to stop her from saying anything she'd regret later and reminded him, "It was me who predicted the mayor's killer would be in the car, Frank."

"Clear to me how two wrongs don't ever make a right," he said, easing out of his frustration. He cupped his mouth and announced, "Fellas, go toss the fishes back in the pond, get this here baby loaded onto the flatbed, and we're on our way."

They immediately set to work.

"You're quitting?" I said. "The shooter could be down there somewhere."

"Collecting dead people's not my idea of how to spend an afternoon profitably, Mr. Gulliver. I'm no grave robber and, for all I know, the entire U.S. Cavalry and Geronimo himself are down there. The police can figure how they want to deal with it and, meanwhile, the Bird might turn out to have some fingerprints or something to tell us some answers. Even not, got some repair and insurance value."

A fresh voice said, "The car also gets deep-sixed."

Paul Darren.

Joining us from the direction of the thicket Stevie and I had fled to the last time we were here.

"Miss Marriner, Mr. Gulliver, happy to see you again," he said, tipping the brim of his straw fedora, his face a beet red under a curtain of sweat clinging to his forehead. "We haven't met, Mr. Gordy."

The T-man held out his hand.

Frank let it hang there.

Raised his shades and studied Darren over his nose.

Said, "So who the fuck are you, telling me what to do?"

Darren's hand drifted into a pocket, like it had never been offered, but he kept the polite smile and said amiably, "I'm the fucker also telling you there are two old, reliable Uzis trained on us right now. You do what I suggest with the T-Bird so we won't need to add you and your boys to the body count in the bog."

"You threatening me?"

"No, I'm inviting you to be my prom date," Darren said, giving Stevie and me a "Can you believe this guy?" glance.

"Let me tell you what a threat is then, Mr. Whoever The Fuck You Are. You check out that beautiful, spanking new Cad that brought me? Something that looks like a long, lean dick poking out the tinted rear window just got lowered? Happens to be a brand new Carbon 15 Type 97 .223 gas-operated, semiautomatic rifle loaded up for bear and buttheads with thirty rounds. Pointed at your Chubby the Chipmunk ring-a-ding body and ready to turn it to cottage cheese I say the word."

"He means it, too," Stevie said, speculating.

Darren was uncertain. I saw the options crawling past his eyes one after the next.

He decided, "Be advised you're threatening an agent of the United States government, Mr. Gordy."

"Well, Mr. Agent of the United States Government, you were threatening a taxpaying citizen of the U.S. of A, so it makes us even."

Stevie said, "This is Paul Darren, Frank, the Secret Service agent we were telling you about yesterday, when we told you about Armando Soledad?"

Frank ingested the news.

A smile crept out slowly and reached both his ears.

He said, "So what's your story, baby? You going to lose your head over me, or you going to have the Uzis and whoever comes with them step on out and be counted?"

"Two of my finest," Darren said, and looked to us for help.

I put six inches between my palms and said, "Mr. Gordy came this close to killing your boss."

"I was there and saw it," Stevie said.

Darren pushed out a sigh, raised an arm above his head, and motioned to the thicket.

Out came the Uzis, racked and ready in the grip of the two T-Men, one sporting a goatee, the other wearing a crummy green blazer, the pair Stevie and I had last seen tracking us at the Federal Building in Los Angeles.

Darren saw our surprise and offered without prompting, "Agents Wald and Feeney were on you like fleas on Fido from even before you left home yesterday. Knew your game leaving your car at the subway, so they were back there before you were. The rest, elementary."

Bragging, like the three of them had won a war.

Stevie nudged my ribs. "How come you didn't notice?"

"Wasn't expecting, so wasn't looking," I said.

She said, "Wait! All of it's not so elementary. No way we could have missed them following us here from the hotel, honey. That's the only road in or out to this peat bog."

Indicating the road being used now by Frank's men.

All gone or on the way out, except for the two orange men loading the T-Bird onto the flatbed, one tow rig, the Wrangler, the Cad, and whoever was inside the Cad aiming the Carbon 15.

"We got here first, before any of you got here. Parked up about a quarter mile."

Stevie said, "How'd you know this was where to be?"

Darren realized he'd said too much and shut up.

Frank said, "Save that question for later, please, Miss Marriner," then to Darren, "Ask them to put the Uzis on the ground and step away, then we can all get more comfortable."

He said it loud enough for Wald and Feeney to hear.

They looked uncertain until Darren told them, "It'll be all right. We're all friends here."

They grounded the weapons, like parents putting their infant to sleep, and took three steps backward.

Waited for a new instruction.

Frank pulled his Glock out from under his jacket and made circles in the air with it. Aimed it at Darren's chest as the Carbon 15 retreated from view in the car window; told the other T-Men, "You just hold your places."

The rear door of the Cad opened.

Tonto got out unbending a muscle at a time and headed our way, gripping the semi like he was eager to use it.

Frank said, "Where's your brother?"

Tonto motioned upward with the semi.

Little Beaver had materialized on the road.

He also had a Carbon 15 trained for action.

As he moved to join us, Frank said, "Be Prepared is my motto. I didn't have to go to Boy Scout School to learn it."

Someone yelled, "Bad Indians! Bad, bad, bad! Fools all of you!"

It was Bobby San Gorgonio, who'd picked this moment to emerge from the brush. Screaming like a banshee. Weaving on unsteady legs. Waving his arms like windmills.

"Get out before it too late!" Bobby demanded, his words embalmed in booze. "I seen everything you done here and you shouldn't of. Sacred ground here. Captain Pabro don't allow bad Indians or strangers. Go, go, go!"

Almost the same speech Stevie and I had heard from him before, followed by the same clucking chant to the sky.

He stopped chanting suddenly and cupped a hand behind his ear. Closed his eyes and began nodding affirmation, as if acknowledging some voice only he could hear.

Answered with waves of senseless sounds before he made finger signs at us and said, "There must be punishment," in a voice
sober and crystal clear. "There will be punishment," Bobby said,
and stumbled back into the dense brush repeating the declaration.

Frank sent off a low whistle.

"Bobby San Gorgonio, just a crazy old drunk Indian who can't
even get pissing down his leg right," Tonto said, and turned to Little
Beaver for confirmation.

"Crazy old drunk," Little Beaver agreed. "Maybe time to shut
up his mouth?"

"What I'd call one righteous man on a mission," Frank said, "so
we'll respect his words and get us the go, go, go out of here. You
and your brother don't worry about him. You look after Mr. Feeney
and Mr. Wald there. Mr. Darren will be coming with us."

Aaron Lodger's home stood like a fortress on a flat of land carved
from a chunk of barren mountain at the eastern end of Palm
Springs, just shy of where the city meshes with Palm Desert. The
only approach was through a guarded gate at Gilbert Roland Road,
then past a series of kiosks manned by an armed guard or security
cameras all the way up a winding, paved road, almost a mile, to
the three-story, Italian-style villa inside a double-set of iron fencing
that doubled as a running track for Lodger's army of pet pit bulls.

There were at least a dozen by my rough count and their tur-
bulent growls smacked more of eating us than greeting us as we
passed the last inspection point.

Frank showed me where to park the Wrangler and said to stash
any weapons in the glove. In went my Beretta.

In a moment, we were met by a small man in elevator shoes
and a dab of mustache, whose loaded shoulder holster added another ten feet to his height.

He made sure I wasn't packing, then double-checked Paul Darren, but turned timid when it came to touching Stevie and took
Frank's word for her.

Stevie offered her shoulder bag, wondering in her put-on little
girl voice if he didn't want to be sure. He said no, how Frank's
word was good enough considering he probably would be the next
mayor of Palm Springs.

Frank saw the surprise registering on our faces, even Darren's,
and said contentedly, "Me, too. Was Mr. L's idea. He's my friend.
Same as he's your special friend, too, Miss Marriner. Why he fixed

it up so you got your job on TV back. He told me so yesterday, when I came here and told him what you had in mind for us to do today on the reservation.

"He said how much his boy, meaning the mayor, thought of you and me. He said, 'Go ahead, do it for them, Frankie, but be careful. I can't have anything happening to the next mayor of Palm Springs before he's elected.' Don't thank him or say I told you, though. You should wait to hear it from Mr. L."

Inside, the place was given over less to style than to safety, modestly furnished in early Sears, bars on all the windows and Rawling-Matts double-bolt door locks creating a quaint San Quentin effect.

Lodger greeted us in the den, more traditional in look: oak-paneled walls and parquet flooring; the obligatory bar a mile long in a room two miles square; giant Sony flat screen built into a wall and tuned on mute to MSNBC; a pool table and other adult toys; an antique Seeburg jukebox loaded with classical CDs, Brahms perfuming the air and much too pretty for me to be annoyed by pops and surface scratches caught to perfection on a state-of-the-art sound system; banks of book shelves filled with leather-bound classics and a smattering of current titles, some fiction, but mostly biographies and autobiographies of famous names from government and finance; available wall space covered with expensively framed photos of the famous and powerful; everywhere, Betty Boop dolls and figurines, the famous sex siren of the early animated movie cartoons staring back at me with her come-hither baby blues and insinuating bee-stung lips, perfectly formed calves and turned out ankles supporting a figure with more and better curves than the entire Dodger pitching staff.

Lodger saw me studying them as he arrived, and seemed pleased. I heard it in his voice as he picked up one of the smaller figurines, Betty Boop doing the hula, and said, "I grew up thinking how much she reminded me of every dame who wouldn't give me the time of day. Really something, these. Bronze, the lost wax process, or cold-cast porcelain, hand-painted. Only thing missing, her wiggle-walk, but look—"

He maneuvered the doll along the edge of the shelf.

"Not even that."

He replaced the doll, moving it around until he was satisfied with its position, adjusted a few others, then headed for the sitting area where Frank was goal-tending Darren; stopped to acknowledge Stevie, sitting at a chess board table a few feet away; then, took his time settling onto a hard chair across from them and fixed on Darren's anxious face.

As I crossed over to join Stevie, Lodger turned to me and said, "It is the same man we saw on the driver license? The man Armando supposedly caught up with and sent away for killing our precious Richie?"

There was no doubt in his voice, but for some reason he wanted to hear me say it.

"Yes."

"So, who was it then that you expected to find when you asked Frankie here to join your fishing expedition?"

"Armando, probably."

"And you got nobody instead, I understand, except for some old disposables nobody could recognize from Adam. The T-Bird, it was empty."

"Yes."

He nodded and, turning to Darren, said, "I want you to tell me what you know about Richie's murder. Tell me about Armando Soledad. Tell me why you're still alive or you won't be for very much longer."

Darren stiffened, grabbed his hands to stop them from shaking. Said, "Damn hot in here. Do you think I could have a glass of water first?"

Aaron Lodger said, "No."

"Whatever you heard from Armando Soledad wasn't true," Darren said.

Lodger leaned forward, arms resting on his embroidered silk dressing gown, and cocked his good left ear at the T-Man.

"In what way?" he said.

"Your boy popped the mayor for us. I was there to back him up."

"Explain."

Darren hesitated.

Stevie took a deep swallow of air and held it, afraid he would change his mind, delay their finally learning the truth about what happened that day.

She reached up, gripped the hand Neil had resting on her shoulder.

Nervously moved one of the gold plated chess pieces to an empty space; no idea of what the move meant.

Neil reached over and pulled the chess piece back.

He made a different move with it, diagonally across the board to the back row, and whispered, "Check," louder than he thought.

Lodger speared him with an ominous look.

Darren's foot tapped faster than his sweat was making rivers down his face and onto the bush of reddish brown and white hair growing out of his open-collared dress shirt.

Frank adjusted himself on the couch, moving away from Darren and closer to the armrest. He unbuttoned his jacket, revealing the Glock tucked under the belt at his hip.

The silent TV screen was showing pictures of starving families in some bleak region of Africa. The name captioned on the screen meant nothing to Stevie. The skeletal bodies, especially of the children, made her wince.

Whatever the music was ended and something else began. This time she recognized the composer, Mozart, but not what she was hearing.

"I don't like to be kept waiting," Lodger said. "Get on with it if you know what's good for you."

Darren swallowed hard and a gasping noise escaped from his throat before he said, "Rick Savage talked too much out of school and that got people saying he had to go before he got to the Senate, where he'd be a bigger threat. When you refused the job, Agent Halliwell turned to Armando Soledad."

Stevie said, "But Halliwell told us he'd never heard of Armando, and—"

"Stevie!" Lodger's voice stopped her cold. Turned into a grandfatherly smile. "Not even my favorite actress should interrupt . . . Go on, Darren."

"Soledad knows the work. He's always been reliable. We heard Miss Marriner and Mr. Gulliver needed protection, and we knew of their priors with Savage. We arranged for Soledad to get the job, and then we asked you to ask Savage—"

"Tell him! I tell people, I don't ask."

"To tell Savage to ask Gulliver to come on board with the new Imagine That! festival."

"Better."

"We knew it would be almost impossible for Gulliver to say no, especially when Agent Halliwell enticed him with the story about Gulliver helping to expose your money laundering at the San Gorgonio's gambling casino and how it'd spread to the festival.

How it also involved his one-time fiancée, the daughter of his old mentor in Sunrise City."

Neil squeezed Stevie's hand.

She patted his.

Lodger said, "Set me up at the same time you're getting rid of my Richie, that the idea?"

"We would never do that to you, Mr. Lodger."

Lodger leaned back in his seat and slammed down a fist on the table.

"Bullshit, you *momser*! What kind of *schlemiel* you and all them other damn Feds take me for anyway?"

His Adam's apple almost danced out of his mouth.

Darren threw out his hands defensively.

Raised his right arm and said, "The truth, Mr. Lodger, on my beloved mother's grave."

"Your own, you don't explain fast enough to suit me."

"Another reason to bring Gulliver in was to give us a head start on working it so he'd wind up spinning the story to suit us."

"The girl?"

"Entrée to Richie. It made sense and it looked innocent enough. We worked it so she and Mr. Gulliver would be there to tell the cops what happened as we desired it to be told. Some unknown assassin, a nut case, probably, who didn't like the mayor's politics."

"The shots at her, at Halliwell—window dressing."

"Exactly. Agent Halliwell arranged to see Savage, then dragged her along. You can figure out the rest."

"Except I want to hear it from you."

Darren bit down on his back molars; wheezed.

"I really could use some water."

"Frankie, spit in his mouth."

Frank looked like he was ready to oblige.

Darren shifted his face away from Frank and settled on a row of Betty Boops. Forced a cough to clear his throat and said, "I'd already cracked the compound with Soledad before Agent Halliwell and Miss Marriner arrived in the T-Bird. He popped the mayor and got off the cover shots while I headed for the T-Bird.

"I had to break a head to get there, Mr. Gulliver's as it turned out—" He threw an apologetic glance at Neil. "He also was supposed to be inside, but turns out he was running late, and Mr. Gordy with him. I tore out in the car and left it where Delgado knew to find it later. And that was that."

Lodger said, "Look at me and tell me about your wallet."

Darren's anxious eyes shifted to him.

"My wallet?"

"The one Armando brought to me. I look at you now, it was yours all right. A few pounds heavier."

Darren thought about it.

"In my rush, it must have fallen out of my pocket."

"Why'd you carry one at all? Boys doing a job for me, they never carry a wallet, any ID."

More thought.

"In case inside the compound I was stopped. It would explain what I was doing there."

He had developed a chronic blink, like Morse code.

"And you weren't concerned, maybe because you thought Armando would find it and get it back to you, when he came to collect the rest of his money?"

"Exactly," Darren said, sounding relieved. "That's it, exactly, sir." A face-lifting smile freezing in place.

"So, instead, Armando came right to me and gave me the wallet, said it was you on the trigger, that he had disposed of you and the T-Bird in one of our usual places. How do you explain that?"

Darren calculated the question. Said, almost defiantly, "Soledad was lying to you to protect his ass. He knew how you would probably react if you learned he was the trigger."

"No probably about it, not for you either."

Darren lost what little color was left in his face and his lower lip trembled. Enough sweat to water a garden.

Neil said, "That doesn't explain about the shooters at the bog when Armando took Stevie and me up there, or why he told us to get to Halliwell in LA and tell him about it."

Lodger said, "When you did, what did Halliwell say?"

"What Stevie was starting to explain before—Halliwell acted like none of it made sense. He denied ever hearing of Armando. He had no answer about the wallet except to summon Darren and show us he was alive. It didn't sound right. Why we decided to go back to the bog and try to find the T-Bird. If it was there, the truth would weigh in favor of Armando."

Stevie said, "We also thought whoever's bullets we were dodging may have had better luck with Armando."

"To shut him up, maybe?"

"Maybe," Stevie said. "Neil and I had to know."

"Now we're hearing something different, that Halliwell knew Armando well and put him on the trigger for the hit on our Richie."

"Yes."

"Darren, tell me why we're hearing different."

"I have no reason to lie to you, Mr. Lodger."

"Then Halliwell is the liar?"

"Agent Halliwell felt Miss Marriner and Mr. Gulliver already knew much too much. The story he told them suited his purpose."

"When you showed up today at the peat bog, was it his purpose to have you dispose of them?"

"No. Certainly not."

"And Frankie while you were at it?"

"No."

"The way you disposed of our Richie, God rest his soul?"

"No. I told you, it was Soledad on the trigger."

"But you helped set it up."

"Yes, but I was only doing my job."

Lodger said mockingly, "Only doing my duty. Where have I heard that one before?"

Stevie said to Darren, "So that was you shooting at us when we went up to the bog with Armando?"

Lodger said, "No, darling, those were my people."

The room grew quiet, except for Mozart.

He seemed amused by the reaction.

Lodger said, "I staged the whole business, using two of the casino boys, the same way later I allowed Frankie to go up and fish with you. I instructed Armando on what to do. I needed to find out how Halliwell would take it when you came running. What he would say. That would tell me where I stand with him . . . Not on solid ground, wouldn't you agree, Darren?"

Darren didn't answer.

"A fine how do you do for someone so available for his needs all these years," Lodger said. "He has my Richie done against my wishes and now what? You got thoughts, Darren?"

No answer.

Neil asked, "Did you know about Armando's part in the murder of Richie, whatever it was, before he took us to the bog? Did you have your casino boys take care of him after he sent us running?"

Lodger shrugged and said indifferently, "We'll ask him when and if we see him again."

"Mr. L, I need to say something?" Frank said, wagging his hand like a schoolboy in desperate need of a hallway pass. He'd sat quietly until now, fidgeting a lot, tapping a foot, finding new places to put his hands, but always giving the impression he was paying careful attention.

Lodger said, "Go ahead, Mayor Gordy."

Hearing himself referred to that way stopped Frank for a second, as if he weren't sure who Lodger meant. A sheepish grin melted back into a tightly determined face.

"He pull the trigger or not, this man here helped take out my friend Mayor Savage. I passed on my chance for that other one, that Halliwell, so I don't want to make the same mistake again, Mr. L."

There was no misunderstanding his meaning.

Lodger made a show of thinking about it.

Raised his watch close to his face.

Nodded and, turning to Stevie and Neil, said, "I think it's time for the two of you to be on your way."

"Darren?"

"Frank is letting his emotions run away with him, dear. Just a little more innocent conversation, then Mr. Darren'll also be sent on his way." Said gently, a smile in his voice, a grandfatherly upward turn to the corners of his mouth.

"We can wait," Stevie said.

"No, you can't wait," Lodger said, trying to shield his impatience with her.

Stevie had already seen the truth betrayed in his eyes.

Whatever the T-Man might be guilty of, to leave without Darren was tantamount to leaving him to die.

She looked up at Neil.

He sent back an invisible signal.

Neil also had seen it.

He seemed to be debating with himself, maybe a fraction less certain than she about what they had to do.

Could do.

She lifted her bag from the floor, pushed up from her seat, and said, "Not without Darren."

Immediately, Lodger's expression changed and judged her harshly.

"Just leave, darling. Save your dramatics for *Bedrooms and Board Rooms*."

Neil moved closer to Stevie and said, "You can't expect us to be party to a murder, Mr. Lodger."

Lodger said. "You stay, you risk it being more than a party, damn it."

Stevie pulled her .32 out of her handbag and, like a sprinter off her blocks, covered the distance to Lodger in seconds, had the gun pressed against his neck before Frank Gordy drew his Glock.

"Say the word, Mr. L."

"Frankie, Frankie, this is not a shooting gallery in here. Put the piece away. You, too, young lady, you really know what's up from down. You got inside because I let you. You get out the same way, or not at all."

Neil started to say something.

The sound of his voice drew Frank's nervous attention and the Glock swung in his direction, taking Darren out of the line of fire.

Darren lunged for the Glock.

Wrestled Frank for control.

The struggle sent them off the couch.

Rolling around on the floor.

The advantage shifting between them until the bigger, beefier Darren settled on top of Frank long enough to pry the Glock loose and smash it down twice on his cheek, both times to the sounds of shattering bone and Frank's cries.

The next blow, as Frank fought to get Darren off him, crashed on his forehead. He made a sharp noise and released his hold on Darren's arms. His arms hit the floor. He twitched a few times, then stopped moving altogether.

Darren jumped to his feet with more agility than Stevie figured for a man his size.

Neil was closing in on him.

Darren waved him off with the Glock and a warning hand, then half-turned to face Lodger and Stevie, fighting for air and wearing an expression of joyous anticipation as he moved forward aiming the weapon at Lodger.

"Now it's your turn, you Jew bastard!"

"You're finished, you won't get out from here," Lodger said calmly.

"Don't count on it!"

"You're a goner."

"So are you."

Stevie stepped in front of Lodger.

Darren screamed, "What the hell are you doing?"

"Saving your life, moron!"

"Too late for that. Move or I'll take you out, too, if I have to!"

"Over my dead body!" Neil bellowed, rushing the T-Man's blind side.

He brought a foot-high bronze cast of Betty Boop down on Darren's shoulder.

Darren bolted upright and lost his grip on the Glock.

Lodger had struggled to his feet.

Summoning a reservoir of strength that refuted an early impression of someone in his seventies starting to surrender to the physical intricacies of the aging process, he wrapped an arm tightly around Stevie's waist and, wearing her like a bullet-proof vest, worked his index finger over hers on the trigger of the .32.

Adjusted her aim to the right and up, surprising Stevie with his ease and speed in resisting her effort to stop him from getting a clear shot at Darren.

Lodger squeezed the trigger.

The shot caught Darren between the eyes and snapped him backward before he collapsed.

"You got it, you never lose it," Lodger gloated.

He let go of the gun and told Neil, "She's one of my very favorites, Betty as Miss Liberty. So prophetic, don't you think?"

Neil said, "I think we have a serious problem here, Mr. Lodger."

"No," Lodger said. "A clear case of self-defense any way you look at it, open and shut, and what better witness than the next mayor of Palm Springs? That right, Frankie?"

Frank was rousing, on his knees and crawling after any surface he might use to help lift himself. A battler on the ropes. Making inchoate noises. His fixed stare thicker than oatmeal.

Lodger advised Neil, "You ever need work, I got work for you."

He almost sounded grateful.

"That was a brave thing you did," he told Stevie.

She knew better than to tell him what was on her mind.

"I didn't have time to think about it," she said, and deposited the .32 back in her bag.

"Think about this on your way home, then. Worries you had over some James Dean? Stop worrying? When I was taking care of that little matter with *Bedrooms and Board Rooms*, I also took care of James Dean. It took some doing, a bigger favor, but I already knew the two of you would be good for it. Now, I'm certain."

23

The biggest hole of all in the whole truth:

We still didn't have the whole truth.

The notion played like a merry-go-round in my mind on the drive back to Los Angeles, prompted by a remark Stevie made once we were out of Palm Springs, packed and gone from Sunrise and cruising home untroubled for the first time in months about a revenge-minded killer tracking our shadow:

"It doesn't make sense, honey. Halliwell went to a lot of trouble. Too much trouble."

"Meaning?"

"If his idea was to kill Richie Savage, why not just go and do it? Why alienate Aaron Lodger by letting him know what he intended? Why go to the trouble of planning a new Imagine That! festival? Why get things more complicated by involving you and me in all that stuff about money laundering, whether it's true or not?"

"Anything else?"

"Probably, but it all adds up to the fact that Richie wasn't that important, was he? One time, a giant rock-and-roll star, but not yet in the Hall of Fame. The mayor of a hick town. Palm Springs, but still a hick town."

"On his way to becoming a senator, if a criminal like Aaron Lodger had his way, and he usually does. You think it had to do with a quota system? Keeping another criminal out of Washington?"

"Damn it, Neil. I'm being serious."

"Me, too," I said, and the second I did, what I meant as a joke became no laughing matter.

You know how it is sometimes, the most important things get misplaced in the back of your mind, only you don't know they're there?

Or how important?

Senator.

Washington.

I flashed on something Frank Gordy said to us after we met him at the garage:

"Mr. L says he heard how the president himself is coming to Mayor Savage's service, going to speak a few words. They got to be friendly, the president and the mayor, when the president was spending time drumming up votes here in the Springs, do you know that? I was around when the president himself keep telling the mayor how he should run for senator and come help him out with his great plans for the country. Uh-huh. Uh-huh."

He'd been told by Lodger, Frank said, and—

Another memory jog.

Something Aaron Lodger said to me earlier, that evening at the casino, right before Armando joined us and moved the conversation in a new direction:

". . . people Halliwell and whoever else in Washington he's doing business with want out of the way sometimes. Whacked in a way there's no trail back to them. A congressman here, a senator there. Like Needman, the one who they wanted offed at the Lennon festival in '85."

Telling me about assassination attempts on President Ford, President Reagan.

Telling me Martin Halliwell's next target would be the president of the United States.

Turning me momentarily speechless; not sure if Lodger was

being serious or making sure he kept my attention keyed to Halliwell as the real bad guy in everything going down.

"He meant it!"

"What, honey? Who meant what?"

I hadn't realized I'd given voice to the thought.

"This has been all about assassinating the president," I said. "Halliwell and his people murdered Richie as a means of getting the president to Palm Springs."

I reminded her about Frank, explained about Lodger.

Stevie reached across and patted my thigh.

"You need to get some sleep, honey. Talk about me being stressed out."

I crawled back into myself for a few miles, watching the night lights of cities come and go where the freeway once was bordered by vast stretches of grape vineyards or vacant lands begging to be developed; must have started dozing to the hum of the road, because Stevie was tapping my shoulder, telling me to wake up.

She said, "That doesn't make sense, either," like it was the final word on the subject.

"Meaning?"

"The president was going to be coming out here anyway, for the Imagine That! festival. Richie said it. Frank. It's been on the news. So, nobody needed a killing and a funeral to get at the president. All they had to do was wait a while longer . . . Not that I'm buying into your cockeyed theory."

"Next time don't wake me," I said.

Another memory jog.

This one in the middle of the night, pulling me out of a nightmare.

I was dreaming about the peat bog, Stevie shouting for me, an invisible voice in distress. I recognize that's her struggling in the middle of the bog, up to her neck in gunk; arms flailing, then reaching out for me; head disappearing, reemerging.

Oblivious to danger, I leap off the bank onto the peat. Some of it bears my weight well, some not so well as I step nearer to Stevie, who sinks out of sight again. I jump after her, seem to be falling through black time and space, where I recognize it's Leigh Wilder who's laughing at me and calling me a fool. Next I hear Bobby San Gorgonio, demanding we all leave at once or risk the wrath of Pakrakitat when the white eagle flies.

Stevie has found me.

She's driving the T-Bird.

She says, "Forget about Augie and let's get out of here. We don't belong here, honey."

She can't get the motor started.

Bodies are sailing by us.

Richie Savage.

Darren and his backstops, Wald and Feeney.

Tonto and Little Beaver.

The president of the United States, guided at the elbows by Halliwell and Lodger.

Other bodies too old to identify, but—

Not John Lennon.

Ageless.

I know him at once and greet him like an old friend.

He stops to remark, "They have a bloody foogin' concert in me honor to raise money to wipe out weapons, and it brings on one gun going off after the bleeding next."

"Imagine that," I say.

"Say it again," Harry says.

"It," John says, does a loop, and swims out of sight.

"He only said it once," Harry Nilsson says. "Where's Kalman? Kalman will say it twice."

"You mean Augie," I correct him. "Kalman is Augie."

I remember about Augie's journal.

Something I'd read.

Is it down here somewhere?

"I have to read it again," I tell Stevie.

"You read that twice," Nilsson says, and—

I'm awake.

I'm soaking in sweat.

I'm telling the darkness, "I have to read it again."

In the wake of what went on at Aaron Lodger's place with Paul Darren, I had forgotten about the journal. It was still under my seat in the Wrangler, where I'd shoved it when Frank Gordy showed up for our appointment at the garage.

I trooped downstairs, punched the house security system into neutral, and headed out to the Jeep, only—

The journal wasn't there.

Someone had removed it.

Possibly Stevie.

More likely one of Lodger's people after we were inside the villa.

Back upstairs, I stepped into Stevie's bedroom, tapped her out of a snore and into a shudder of disorientation that became a scowl as she shifted into a position with her knees elevated, a pillow stuffed between her thighs and her chest.

"Was it too much for you to see me in my own bed, into my first good sleep in months?" Her words a dry-mouth mumble.

"Did you do something with the journal?"

"Wha'?"

"Augie's journal. Remember, I was reading it in the car when Frank—?"

She cleared her throat and said, "Den. The safe. Found it in the car when we were unloading."

Readjusted the pillow.

Turned her back on me.

In a moment was snoring again.

I went downstairs and reclaimed the journal.

Went to the kitchen, made a pot of coffee, poured a cup, and settled at the service table. Rushed through most of the pages I'd already read, eager to resume reading where Martin Halliwell told Augie they had a lot to talk about.

FROM AUGIE FOWLER'S JOURNAL

Halliwell had his driver drop us off at the Essex House and followed me into the bar without comment. A few minutes later, he was picking out the giant cashews from the silver nut bowl and washing them down with sips of iced tea while I polished off my Brandy Alexander.

He signaled our waiter for another round and more nuts, inched closer to me in our high-backed corner booth, said in a conspiratorial whisper, "Y'all don't have to worry anymore about your friend Dutch Reagan."

"Huh?"

"The would-be assassin that your friend Aaron Lodger—"

"Dutch, but not Lodger. Lodger's no friend of mine."

"That's right, y'all told me. The shooter Lodger had in mind to take out your friend the president-elect is the same cracked pot who just murdered your friend John Lennon."

"Mark David Chapman?"

"Mark David Chapman," he said, and motioned me quiet.

The waiter brought the next round and replaced the nut bowl with a fresh one.

I ordered another round before he left. Finished my Brandy Alexander in a swallow and said to Halliwell, "You better be ready to explain that one."

"First, Augie, promise me we're off the record."

"I promise," I said, immediately wishing the booze had not made me answer so quickly.

Halliwell washed down a cashew and an almond and said, "The way the Department tracked it, Lodger had his eyes on Chapman for some time, recognizing the guy was kooky enough to go for that kind of deal. Maybe it was already in place.

"We have the president-elect in New York on his way to Washington—"

"Not what I was told when—"

"Course not, what with y'all flying east after talking with Lodger's gang lawyer Joe Conn? We're onto it fast, onto you, hoping you'll help get us where we don't know, where the hit is supposed to happen. We brought you to the Essex House, conditioned you, and found out you know less than we do."

"*Conditioned* me?"

"Nothing we have to talk about this time."

The waiter came and left. I pushed my second empty aside and settled the fresh Brandy Alexander in front of me. I knew I needed as clear a head as possible for what I was hearing.

"Cheers," Halliwell said, raising his iced tea.

What the hell. I gulped down half my drink.

Halliwell smiled, and set his iced tea aside.

He said, "So, we have Mr. Reagan in town and that basket case Chapman in town and, what do you know, Chapman was here to do John Lennon for himself, not President-elect Reagan for Aaron Lodger or anyone."

I leaned in and said, "But someone's still after Dutch?"

Halliwell pushed back and looked away, like he might be designing the answer he wanted me to have. His eyes seemed to fall on a plain-faced man under a shaggy-dog haircut who was hogging a nearby table for two, early to mid-forties, trying to read a newspaper in the soft light.

The man sensed he was being studied. He looked up and caught Halliwell's stare. Smiled at the T-Man.

"Damned faggots," Halliwell said, through locked lips out the side of his mouth. Turning back to me, he said, "The Department's official position is: Not very likely. We have made ourselves visible enough since Lennon was shot down to let the bad guys know we're on to them. Figure they're smart enough to back off, Augie."

"Back off permanently?"

He put his arms on the table and made a pyramid with his hands.

"Security around the president-elect was tight to begin with. Let's just say it's five hundred percent tighter now. Gives us maneuvering room to discover who else's in this with Lodger the Dodger and bring them all down before they can do harm to Mr. Reagan."

"I want the story, Marty."

"And I want y'all to have it, Augie, so here's the deal. Y'all keep your promise to me. Keep this under your hat. And stop chasing after your friend Dutch Reagan. He's not in the loop and has too much on his mind already to be burdened with this sort of fret. When we bring down the bad guys, y'all get the story absolutely first. A twenty-four hour head start, Augie. That is my own solemn promise to y'all."

He crossed his heart.

I took my time answering.

"Updates along the way?" I said.

"Updates along the way." Halliwell cracked a smile and offered me his hand. "We got ourselves a deal, Augie?"

"Deal," I said, but I was already convinced his hand was wet and clammy from more than the glass of iced tea.

Martin Halliwell was not a man to be trusted.

I know the type.

Sometimes I'm one of them.

Stevie said, "What is this, some new game?"

I settled on the bed, kissed her forehead, and said, "It's called *Wake Up, Sleeping Beauty*."

She slapped out blindly.

"You're no Prince Charming," she said.

Turned onto her stomach with the pillow over her head.

I pried the pillow loose, tossed it onto the floor, and read to her from Augie's journal.

She rolled over and pushed up next to me when I reached the part about Mark David Chapman and President-elect Reagan.

"But somebody did try and kill Reagan," she said.

"In 1981, less than four months after John Lennon was killed. About two months after Reagan was sworn into office. A different twisted shooter, John Hinckley, Jr. Paying some kind of crazy homage to his favorite actress, Jodie Foster."

"I remember some of it. I was eleven and Mama was always telling me how I'd grow up to be as fine an actress as Jodie was one day."

"Chapman went to prison. Hinckley got off by reason of insanity."

"And you see a connection somewhere?"

"Given the advantage of hindsight, yes. There's not a doubt in my mind that Halliwell and Lodger have been a team all these years. Believing that makes it easy to believe he told Augie the truth about Lodger having Chapman in mind as Reagan's designated hitter before Chapman went after Lennon.

He lied when he said that ended the threat to Reagan. He was only taking Augie off the scent until a new shooter could be lined up. Unfortunately for them, Hinckley turned out to be a lousy shot and Reagan survived."

"What does Augie write about that?"

"His journal only goes through the end of the year."

"So, you're still relying on what Aaron Lodger said to sell me on the idea that Halliwell likes to kill presidents. What is it, a hobby of his?"

"Not only presidents. Also people Lodger described to me as *troublemakers*. I don't know the reasoning, but I do know I'm calling the White House in the morning."

"Check the clock, honey. It is morning."

I gave it another hour and shortly after 9 A.M. D.C. time was connected to the White House press office; an intern on screening duty, dropping his voice two octaves and trying to sound important while taking down the requisite background information and the reason for my call.

I mentioned Rick Savage's funeral, my understanding that the president planned to attend, but otherwise was vague.

"Just a minute, Mr. Gallagher," he said, and was off the line before I could correct him.

I sat on hold for five minutes, presumably while someone ran a double-check.

The new voice was older, female, user-friendly.

"Patsy Breck here, Mr. Gulliver. How's it going in LA?"

"At this hour, even the asphalt is asleep."

She laughed.

I liked her already.

"I was based out there for a few years a few years ago and I remember how much I enjoyed reading your column in the *Daily*. It was right up there with that first cup of coffee in the morning . . . So. What do you have brewing for me?"

"Rick Savage's memorial service," I said, and repeated what I had told the intern and Patsy Breck already knew.

"I can confirm the president's intention of being there, but that's about all. We never reveal travel arrangements or other details in advance. You can understand that?"

"Of course," I said, "but there's something else I need to talk about, not with the press office, but—"

I locked onto something she'd said and cut myself off.

"You were based in LA a few years ago? I don't recall the White House establishing that kind of beachhead."

"Not exactly the White House, Mr. Gulliver. I'm with Treasury, the Secret Service. I was just breaking in then, learning the ropes."

"You know Martin Halliwell?"

"Of course. Why do you ask?"

"Me, too. Give him my regards, you see him."

I hung up quickly, cutting Patsy off in the middle of a sentence that sounded like it would end with a question mark, confident there was nothing I could tell her that the Secret Service didn't already know.

Wondering why the White House press office had been so swift to kick me over to the Service.

Wondering who I expected to be connected with to hear my warning, if not the Service. The president himself?

Wondering if Patsy was part of Halliwell's plot against the president.

Wondering if I was beginning to sound like a character in an Oliver Stone movie, spinning my own conspiracy theory.

What did Aaron Lodger say about JFK?

He wasn't in on that assassination.

I'd have to tell Oliver that if I ever bumped into him.

Stevie, roused by what wasn't the whisper I thought it was, rolled over and said, "The White House?"

"Yeah."

"What'd they say?"

"They said we're going to Richie's memorial service."

A week later, Stevie and I were sitting in the last row of the main chapel at Our Blessed Saints and Martyrs Church, rooting for the organist in her battle to discover the right key and tempo for the Richie Savage symphony of hits filling the air as invited guests dragged in from the afternoon heat and found places in one of the twenty or thirty benches that extended back from the flower-bedecked inlaid mahogany coffin resting on a flag-draped roller table in front of the pulpit.

On either side of the coffin was a mammoth photo blowup of Richie, nesting on easels whose legs were covered with two more mountains of floral wreaths. The smell of fresh flowers was everywhere, pushed around the hall by an air-conditioning system pumping at maximum strength. Frequent sneezes revealed a large assembly of allergies and sinus conditions.

One photo showed Richie on stage at the Hollywood Bowl the night he urged the audience to join him for the band's encore. Nine or ten thousand fans hit the aisles and almost made it up before a regiment of police pushed them back with enough force to launch a riot the *Daily*'s front page the next morning called "Hollywood Bowl-ed Over!"

The other photo was of an older, distinguished-looking Mayor Rick Savage embracing and being embraced by a beaming president of the United States.

Fifteen minutes away from starting and it was clear the memorial service would be playing to an SRO crowd, probably even if the president wasn't scheduled to be Richie's opening act.

No trick spotting the Secret Service types:

Bulky dark suits and glossy oxfords; lapel pins and ear plugs; a ramrod straight, tight-mouthed demeanor that I've always associated with people desperate for a bowel movement.

They were strategically positioned around the room, some sitting, most standing. Others were outside guarding exit and entry points or monitoring the metal detectors all the guests had to pass through in order to enter the church.

Stevie argued she could finesse her .32.

I insisted it get locked with my Beretta in the trunk of the Wrangler.

"What if someone does go after the president?"

"Check it out. More security than I figured."

"And if it's the security we have to worry about, like you've been preaching?"

"Too many witnesses. If any attempt is made at all, it won't be inside the church."

"Down Ramon Road, when Frank drives Richie to be buried near Sinatra's grave. He'll be more of a wide open target, is that what you're thinking?"

"Yes, unless the president is long gone by then."

"What if you're wrong?"

"I'll apologize."

Dozens of sagging rock faces were arriving fashionably late, most hidden behind dark glasses and disguise hats, as if they might otherwise be recognizable inside their double chins and thick bodies.

I debated with myself if any of the TV crews had spotted any but the most durable, the superstars who had defied time and held onto the spotlight, rich fat cats who would not fade away, playing life like the Buddy Holly anthem.

The crews would move inside in front of the president's appearance, to catch whatever sound bites he'd throw at them for the six o'clock news.

And, maybe, if the black curtain guarding the private mourners room to the left of the pulpit was parted, there might be a sobbing celebrity mourner or two, although so far as Stevie and I knew, besides Aaron Lodger and Frank Gordy and, maybe, some Secret Service, the only people in the room would be Richie's ex-wife and their three children.

Lodger had chartered a jet to fetch them from Arkansas.

"The least I could do," he said two days ago, when he called to make certain Stevie and I would be here.

"Richie, rest his soul, and her, they were getting along better at the end," Lodger said. "He didn't need her unhappy, saying all the wrong things in public when we got around to running for senator. Besides, my Richie really loved those kids, even if he never seen a lot of them."

Another six minutes before the scheduled eleven o'clock start. The organist began the Richie medley again, sounding no better than the first time.

Davey Plant, the one-time teen idol, caused a mild stir by tripping and falling as he wandered down the aisle looking for seats down front for himself and the green-haired, nose-ringed, groupie-garbed twenty-something clutching his forty-something arm.

He made me remember Rodney Muse pulling the same stunt one of the last times I saw Harry Nilsson.

The early nineties, under similar circumstances, after services at Blessed Sacrament Church on Sunset Boulevard for Sal Marino, the bartender who became owner of Martoni's, the music industry hangout that was our rendezvous point whenever Harry and I got together for a night on the town.

That had not happened for years.

We both seemed to get too busy at the same time.

The chapel was twice the size of Our Blessed Saints and Martyrs Church, room for five or six hundred. Richer and more ornate. Loaded today with dozens of the rock stars and other industry heavies who'd used Sal's place as their playground.

Harry and I didn't get a chance to talk until afterward.

He dropped me from a bear hug that had lifted me a foot off the ground and lost the eager smile to a glum expression.

Pushed his Ray-Bans onto his forehead and said, "I was supposed to go up there and talk about Sal, close as we were and all that saccharine shit, and the sons of bitches forgot to introduce me. I had good words to say, too."

"I'm sure Sal knows that," I said, trying to ease the obvious pain Harry was feeling.

"Don't you get it?" he said. "Sal's dead. The only thing he can hear is eternity. I wanted the pricks in the audience to know what a good man he was."

"Maybe they already do, or they wouldn't have come."

"Jesus, Neil! You losing your edge? I think you need a fresh dose of reality. They turn out to be *seen*. Sal is the excuse. Not the reason."

The assassination attempt came thirty minutes into the ceremony, only not on the president's life.

Father Geraldo-Geraldo had led the assembled mourners

through what I took to be some of the customary rituals and prayers of a funeral mass and then paused to tell them what they likely already knew about Richie, or could have gleaned from a hurried reading of his obit.

The priest, who looked to be in his mid-to-late fifties, probably knew Richie as well as he knew every name in the LA phone directory, but his mellifluous voice and gentle manner generated heavy weeping beyond the loud sobs tearing through the black-curtained private mourners room, while his slender body cruised with a ballet dancer's grace behind the chancel rail.

He duplicated his words in sign language, then repeated them in Spanish or an Indian dialect I figured for Cahuilla; the observations he deemed most significant in both Spanish and the Indian dialect.

Finished, he helped himself to a healthy swallow from the water glass on the podium, dried his lips with the back of his delicate brown hand, and waited to be certain he still had everyone's attention.

"As you are aware, we have been expecting to be joined by Richard's dear, close, personal friend, the president of the United States," the priest said in three languages and ten fingers. "And the president, good man that he is, fully intended to be here, but—" The corners of his mouth drooped. "A world crisis is keeping *el presidente* from us."

A rumble of disappointment moved through the crowd like a Dodger wave.

"The Arabs and Israel again, as you might suspect, as usual, but meaning no offense by that to either our Arab or Jewish brethren," Father Geraldo-Geraldo said, his fingers moving into a glide pattern.

A rumble of acknowledgment and contradictory whispers as he repeated his assurance again and again.

"But the good news," he said, addressing the mourners to the left, then the right, of the chancel rail. "The good news I have for you—" Back to the left. "Our president has sent a representative in his place, someone else who today will help us celebrate the wonderful life that was Richard John Arnold Xavier Savitch."

A dramatic pause, enough time built in to part the Red Sea.

Stevie rolled her eyes.

"Ladies and gentlemen, it is my humble honor—" Father Geraldo-Geraldo starting to sound like he was auditioning for the remake of *Going My Way*. "To welcome in our midst—" Cuing the organist. "The president-elect! Our vice president of the United States of our America!"

The organ began belting out what was either "God Bless America" or "Hail to the Chief."

The main double doors at the rear flew inward.

The vice president, wearing a conservative blue suit and black armband, stood statue-still for a moment, his left arm frozen in a greeting, then started down the aisle, trying to sustain a proper funereal demeanor while some of the mourners applauded vigorously and others began moving in on him, like they were anxious to press the flesh.

A cadre of Secret Service men accompanied him, one at each elbow, two in front of the vice president, two behind him and, behind those two—

Martin Halliwell.

Giving no indication he'd seen us.

Staring straight ahead, starting to sweat, and growing increasingly apprehensive as the mourners became more unruly trying to break through the protective curtain and get to the vice president. Chanting the vice president's name. Whistling their approval.

Stevie and I moved to spots behind the television crews from our back row seats, out of the traffic as the mob spread like pancake batter.

Father Geraldo-Geraldo, arms uplifted, implored order in urgent, frill-free English, Spanish, and Cahuilla.

The other Secret Service men moved in from their spots against the walls to help break up the crowd, but they were outnumbered and easily pushed back.

The TV cameras were capturing the kind of crowd frenzy Richie had not enjoyed since his glory days in rock and roll, and I saw from the look on Stevie's face that she'd had the same thought as me—

How much Richie had to be enjoying this final farewell.

Just then, somebody screamed.

Then, somebody else.

Followed by discordant words locking into one another, loud and indecipherable, as the mourners anxiously retreated from the vice president, aiming for the nearest exit, shoving aside reporters and cameramen on their uncontrollable way out the back doors.

On stage, Father Geraldo-Geraldo pleaded for order.

The organist was back on her untamed medley of Richie's hits, hard pressed to be heard over the uproar.

Stevie sprang toward the thundering herd, dodging and weaving to a sparrow-sized old woman in a beaded turquoise dress, who had been knocked down and was frozen in place on her hands and knees.

In a series of swift moves, she got the woman onto her feet and safely into a bench row before an hysterical Freddie Pitts of Pond Scum Alley toppled Stevie in a wild scramble to escape whatever it was that had caused the disturbance.

I started for her, saw she had done a serpentine roll and crawl to safety, and reversed myself.

Chased after Freddie.

Caught up with the bandy-legged bass player at a side portal that led out to the parking lot. Grabbed him by his bomber jacket and wheeled him around into my face.

Freddie looked like he was carrying a hundred pounds of coke in his eyes.

"I'm clean," he screamed, like it was a refrain from one of the band's hits. "Clean, dude, clean. Get what I mean?"

"I get what you mean," I said, and, ignoring the fifteen years and forty-five pounds he had on me, rammed my fist into his nose.

Blood spurted from Freddie's nostrils and spilled onto his crisp Pond Scum Alley T-shirt.

"Now you're dirty, dude," I said, leaving him dazed and confused as I headed back inside the church.

The mourners were pretty much dispersed and the gang in the aisle was made up of Secret Service suits, some battered more than others, all of them in various states of agitation.

Some agents talking into cell phones.

Others ordering what gawking civilians remained to keep out of their way. Wagging weapons for emphasis.

Stevie called to me. She was standing on tiptoes on a bench, staring down into whatever the agents were shielding from general view.

She sent over a disbelieving look.

Signaled me to join her.

The two agents blocking my way had another idea, even after I pulled out my press credential. They ordered me back. The honorary LAPD badge didn't impress them either.

The one with the wispy mustache and two-day growth of beard made a face that was meant to scare me off. The other one, also in need of a shave, had tightly set, piercing black eyes that gave him a threatening look naturally.

"What's the big deal? What am I missing?" I said, trying to maintain my cool.

302

"A kick in the ass, you don't move it," the one with the no-nonsense eyes said.

I pretended to be convinced, showed them my palms, threw out a conciliatory smile, and backed off three or four steps.

The agent with the mustache adjusted his tie and turned, opening a narrow space between them.

Close enough to what I'd hoped for.

I charged, catching them off-guard; pushed and squeezed through the space and climbed onto the bench behind Stevie.

Saw what she saw inside the tight wall of suits before the agents grabbed me and pulled me down and over to an outer aisle:

The vice president and Martin Halliwell were stretched out on the tile, close enough to be lovers.

The vice president's hands encircling some type of a dagger rising from his chest.

Halliwell's body slanted in such a way that I couldn't tell about him.

The agents jerked me to an outer aisle and slammed me against the wall. The one with the mustache, his voice not more than a hiss, commanded me to stay there until they got back.

No problem. I had just been rabbit-punched and could barely handle my legs. My right shoulder felt like it had been yanked from its socket.

Stevie recognized the physical misery registering on my face.

I answered her look of concern with a smile and a gesture that said I'd be okay.

She pointed to the inner circle and mouthed the word "Dead."

I held up two fingers.

She held up one.

Aaron Lodger was being led up the aisle by Frank Gordy.

He stopped when he reached me.

"An eye for an eye," Lodger said, inclining his head toward the pool of Secret Service agents, and continued on his way, measuring one slow step after the next, shaking off Frank's efforts to hold onto his elbow.

I gritted my teeth against the pain and hobbled after him.

Whispered in his good ear, "What happened here—You did this, didn't you?"

Lodger looked at me the way a king looks at a commoner, made a mocking noise, and without missing a step said, "We'll finish the memorial service for Richie, may he rest in peace, I'll call and let you know when it's going to be, like maybe in a week, maybe two weeks; when all this *misheghas* is over."

"That wasn't my question."

"It should of been," Aaron Lodger said. "Come on, Mayor Gordy, let's get the hell out of here. We got things to do."

2001

24

On January 6, not quite four hours after the Electoral College votes cast on the Monday after the second Wednesday of December were unsealed and read by the president to both houses of Congress, as established in federal law, the vice president—now formally the president-elect—was pronounced dead at Bethesda Naval Hospital in Maryland. An assassin or assassins unknown at Our Blessed Saints and Martyrs Church in Palm Springs had claimed a second victim.

As the process of government moved swiftly to elevate the late president-elect's vice presidential running mate into the White House, Stevie and I were working to get our lives back to their old running order, believing the John Lennon Imagine That! Memorial Rock Festival was behind us, although I knew deep down it wasn't over for me.

I knew I wouldn't be satisfied until I had answers to questions still bothering me and could tidy up loose ends that got in the way of tagging -30- onto the story.

If the festival was only Martin Halliwell's apparatus for setting up the murder of Rick Savage—Paul Darren had confessed as much—why the business about money laundering?

Why the need to involve Stevie and me?

Were we a pair of bit players along as window dressing, the reluctant "Sex Queen of the Soaps" for her glamour, the newspaperman to ultimately help spin the facts, whenever and however unwittingly?

Did Halliwell foresee the body count rising the way it did? Darren and two other agents. Armando Soledad. The vice president of the United States. Halliwell himself.

Unlikely.

More likely, he underestimated the emotional attachment someone like Aaron Lodger could develop for a Richie Savage, and the error cost Halliwell his life.

With Halliwell dead, maybe I'd never get any answers.

I was wrong.

Thanks to Aaron Lodger.

Aaron Lodger called me on my new unlisted number on top of the Presidential Inauguration. Presuming I recognized his voice, skipping any preliminary small talk, he said, "Hello. We still got you, right." Presented as a statement of fact.

"For what, Mr. Lodger?"

"The Lennon thing. Imagine That!"

"It's on again?"

"Never off. I got Frank in charge since Richie left us, God rest his soul, it being something meant a lot to Richie, so it means a lot to me.

"Same *macher* acts like before, and better, like they all want to be part of our thing, Frank reports. The old and the new, people I never even heard of. Garth Brooks? Faith Hall? Like John Lennon is bigger now than he was alive. What twenty years dead can do, you know what I mean? No different from my old line of work. Same goes for monsters and *momsers* like the Bug, Bugsy, and old Mickey Cohen. Like Charlie Lucky, Lansky, and Costello." A memory grunt. "Paul Simon, who I have heard of. Stevie Wonder. John Elton and the other piano player with two first names, Joel Billy."

"Elton John and Billy Joel."

"Someone from The Who? Wait, I'm pulling out the list. John Entwistle? Also a Johnny Mitchell. James Brown. Him I know. Three Dog Night, you know them? Someone called Sting? Fleetwood Max? Four pages long already, and the phones never stop ringing. Oh, and the president of the United States.

"Not this new one, the same one we were expecting from before, who's going to come out and dedicate a piece of land to Richie's memory, like Lennon has his Strawberry Fields in New York in Central Park. We don't got a name for it yet, so you can also help there, dreaming up a name, besides writing stories about it. So—I can count on you."

Lodger wasn't asking a question.

"I said, I can count on you."

I heard his irritation at being made to wait and could visualize his Adam's apple starting to throb while I thought about risking the consequences with someone who took poorly to being disobeyed.

I said, "Mr. Lodger, do you remember what I asked you at Richie's first memorial service?"

"I look to you like I got Alzheimer's? We didn't do any talking the second one."

"I'd still like an answer to my question, Mr. Lodger."

The phone seemed to go dead in my ear until, finally, "I heard that about you from our mutual friend Augie Fowler, how once you sink your pearlies into something . . ."

Lodger spent another moment or two quietly weighing the matter.

"Come out and see me, we got to talk about the festival anyway," he said. "I'll tell you what you want to know when I see you, but understand—I'll deny it faster than you can say Jackie Robinson, anyone ever gets wind, right after I arrange dealing you away for keeps."

"Sure, that was me done it," Lodger said. "I paid back Halliwell good, the bastard."

"And the president-elect?"

His eyes burned into mine.

"You remember I still got your promise from before?"

I zipped my lips.

We were at Richie's gravesite, sitting on a polished black marble bench Lodger explained he'd ordered installed, because, "I'm visiting enough with Richie, God rest his soul, I don't have to be uncomfortable in the bargain every time I come here."

Today was a beautiful day for it, the sky an azure blue, barely the essence of a warm breeze floating past the desert landscape; in the distance familiar sounds of animals trading secrets we'd never learn.

Nobody was within a hundred yards of us, but Lodger kept looking over his shoulders, surveying the landscape while he spoke, quietly, sounding like a man proud of his craft.

"Halliwell calls me up and he says we got a problem on our hands that's bigger'n any differences between us," Lodger said. "Seems the president-elect is not a fan of our disposal program and has put out the word it's over and done with once he takes office. The people behind the program, they want him out of the way and what do I think.

"He's gotta go then, I say, and we cook up this idea of the vice president showing up instead of the president at the service for Richie, God bless his soul, but first I make sure Halliwell's also going to be there.

"The cocksucker says yeah, to be absolutely sure there are no foul-ups—like I'm new at this game?—and so it comes off looking legit to the media from his end.

"Halliwell takes care of business from the angle of the president, who has been behind the disposal program forever, a hundred and one percent, while I work the setup here at this end.

"No trick to it.

"I get Roy Bigelow to pack the church with people from the casino and the reservation we can trust, who don't mind making a small bundle rioting on cue.

"I get my acer there dressed to fit in with the crowd.

"He knows he can't walk in with a piece, because of the security that'll be tighter than my late Uncle Manny, may he rest in peace, so instead he sharpens a pair of ivory letter openers and wears them in his hair, part of the whole Indian get-up *shmear*.

"Day of reckoning, that's all she wrote, and like I said to you then, an eye for an eye."

"If it was about you getting your revenge on Halliwell, why bother with the vice president?"

"Same reason the bastard Halliwell said, to make it look good to the media. A vice president or a president gets it—par for the course. A Secret Service *macher*—they never stop looking, worse than the cops or the FBI. Besides, business is business and the vice president wasn't good for the program."

"A program even with Halliwell gone?"

He looked at me disdainfully and said, "The Halliwells of this world are never gone."

Heading back home, I made a one-stop.

"I'm surprised to see you," Leigh Wilder said.

"I would have called first, but I wanted to catch you dressed."

"Lucky you," she said. "Unlucky me. Come in anyway."

She stepped aside and I passed into the house, heading for the fireplace mantle in the living room, where I set the silver-framed wedding photo of Leigh, Michael Wilder, and the bogus Elvis in approximately its old spot.

"There, finally." Turning around, I said, "I can't tell you how guilty I've felt not getting the picture back to you before now."

"Does that mean I won't have anything to look forward to after this?" Leigh said from across the room, trying to sound forlorn.

She batted her eyes demurely and added a pout.

On the front porch, dusk and backlighting had obscured how delicious she looked in the scarlet cashmere turtleneck hugging her body the way I once did, worn over a dark brown skirt cut on the bias that showed off those wondrously long legs, their curves barely diminished though she was barefoot.

She joined me at the mantle and leaned in to study the photo in a way that pushed her hard against me.

"I would have been better off marrying Elvis," Leigh said, and grazed my ass with her hand. "Or you in a pinch, Cookie Monster." She pinched me and invited me to pinch her back. "Or, anything else you think you can muster up, be my guest," she said.

I was tempted, but I hadn't come here after my meeting with Aaron Lodger to rekindle the flame. I stepped away from her. "Just conversation, Leigh-Leigh."

"What's to talk about? Your ball and chain? Where is she anyway? Don't tell me Stevie let you stray this far without a leash."

"Stevie doesn't know I'm here."

Leigh moved around the coffee table and flopped onto the couch, struck a pose that reminded me of the erotic paintings by

Balthus. Her hands underneath her head; one leg raised and the other dangling over the side; her skirt hiked just enough to reveal she wasn't wearing panties.

"Now you're talking," Leigh said, breaking into a smile.

"Stevie's in Paris, meeting with Roman Polanski about a possible remake of *Repulsion*, Stevie in the Catherine Deneuve role."

"Even better," Leigh said.

I wandered across to the piano and settled on the bench, began picking out a meaningless tune with one hand.

"Let's talk about him," I said, drawing her attention to the family portrait above the fireplace.

"Daddy? What about Daddy? He were here, he'd approve. He always said, if anybody was going to fuck his little girl, he hoped it was you. Not exactly in those words, of course."

"Never, I'm sure, in words that called for you to fuck me in more ways than one, like you've been trying to do all along."

"I've been trying—?" She inched up and pushed herself into the corner, fixed her skirt. Stared hard at me looking for the joke. "You mean it, don't you?"

"I know the whole story, Leigh-Leigh, or most of it; why you've been playing the nympho with me."

Leigh compressed her face into a "You're talking crazy" look that dissolved into an overconfident challenge, as if she were calling my bluff.

I said, "What I heard from the Treasury Department about Ben, about your father, being tied in with the mob. Tied in with the San Gorgonio casino. Raking in hundreds of thousands of dollars. Hiding it from the government. Facing arrest and prosecution. It was all true."

"Lies!"

"All true, Leigh-Leigh. You denied it to me when I told you and I believed you because it's what I wanted to believe about Ben. For all that sweet man's goodness, he cheated the government on his taxes, but he had his reasons.

"The newspapers weren't doing well and Ben was not about to let them go under any more than he was prepared to see his family suffer. He'd already hocked everything up to his eyes, so dishonesty became the best policy, and your dear old Uncle Aaron was there to guide him. Everything went along smoothly, until Michael Wilder entered the picture."

Leigh slammed a fist on the coffee table.

"He stole from us. He raped the business."

"Yes, also true, and your father couldn't do anything about it, because Wilder somehow learned how Ben was stepping over the line himself. It probably wasn't difficult. Ben was lousy when it came to bookkeeping, he was the first to admit it, so his illegal numbers must have been there for anyone to find who came looking, right?"

Past denial, Leigh lowered her eyes and her head, played her chin in and out against her neck.

She said, "The bastard found where Daddy kept his second set of books, the ones Daddy had Mommy take care of. He stole them and held them over Daddy's head, but I didn't learn that until a long time after Daddy's heart attack."

"From the Treasury Department. Martin Halliwell."

I waited for her answer.

She glared at me and said, "You're telling the story."

I said, "Halliwell must have told you he'd take care of your problem with your husband, let you keep the newspapers, even let you stay in business with dear old Uncle Aaron and the San Gorgonio casino, but you had to help him in exchange. He turned you into a snitch. Worse."

Leigh's eyes moved back to the family portrait and began spilling tears.

"What did Halliwell tell you before I got to Sunrise? I don't think it was, 'Your old fiancé is working for me, too.' Halliwell was not in the business of trust. I can hear him telling you, 'Keep your eye on him, do whatever you have to, so I know at all times what he's about. *Whatever you have to.*' Before me, did Halliwell have you doing a lot of whatever you had to, Leigh-Leigh?"

She withered me with her look.

"Go to Hell!"

"When you disappeared to Vegas, was it taking care of business for Halliwell? Maybe, with Halliwell? He was gone the same time. He said to Washington, but why not to Vegas? Maybe, you two developed a little something for one another?"

"I said go to Hell."

"Will Los Angeles do?" I said, and headed for the door.

Leigh blocked my way.

Slapped my face.

"That was for Daddy," she said.

She locked her fingers behind my head and pulled me to her

mouth. Burned my lips with hers. Captured my tongue and used it for a straw. Let go, and said with the same kind of intangible regret Billie Holiday brought to the blues, "You could have had it all, Cookie Monster. Instead, you have it all wrong."

"All of it?"

I knew that couldn't be right.

Too much of what else I had heard from Lodger before we parted today meshed too well with what I'd been told earlier by Halliwell, and Leigh had just confirmed Ben's involvement.

"Enough of it," she said, reluctantly. "What I did for Halliwell, I also did for Uncle Aaron."

Contempt crept into her eyes.

I had no way of knowing if she meant it for Aaron Lodger or for herself.

"Who's worse, Neil, your enemy or your friend, when you can't really tell one from the other?"

I had no answer for her.

"You and me, I was doing that for myself. Maybe it was ego at first, evening the score with the man that got away, or just jealousy over your snake queen of the soaps, but it got more real than that. Too real. It really did. For me. No matter what you choose to believe."

Leigh shrugged, arched her back and strode to the door, opened it wide, and said, "Good-bye, Cookie Monster. Whatever you're about to say—please don't."

The next time I saw her, almost three months later on April 20, Leigh was hanging out backstage at the third John Lennon Imagine That! Memorial Rock Festival, chatting up a punk rocker with spiked rainbow hair and enough tattoos and body piercing to interest P. T. Barnum's heirs.

She spotted me and turned away, squeezed the rocker's grapefruit-sized bicep, and pulled him in the direction of "Superstar City," or so read the elaborately hand-painted canvas banner strung across the entrance to the performers' compound, a collection of luxury trailers and motor homes inside impenetrable telephone pole and cast-iron fencing, guarded by a battle-ready detachment of marines from Camp Pendleton armed with cameras and autograph books.

According to the show rundown and what I'd seen so far, there were dozens of names to harvest, from rock-and-roll's golden days to nowadays, which belonged mainly to rappers of various stripes, some of them jailhouse criminal.

There was something or someone for everyone.

The list Aaron Lodger had recited to me months ago was mostly accurate and the additions since showed more magical major league names.

Hall of Fame entries like the Eagles and Aerosmith. Al Green. The Allman Brothers Band. Bowie. The Bee Gees. Martha Reeves. Led Zeppelin, reunited one more time. John Fogerty, late of Creedence Clearwater Revival. Crosby, Stills & Nash. Neil Young, who'd do a solo spot and then, maybe, join the other three; Neil hadn't made up his mind yet.

Chuck Berry.

Little Richard.

Joni Mitchell.

Linda Ronstadt.

Randy Newman.

Nine Inch Nails.

Ian Anderson of Jethro Tull.

Stevie Nicks of Fleetwood Mac.

Willie and Waylon.

Paul Williams.

Mickey Dolenz.

U2's Bono.

Brian Wilson, composing genius behind the Beach Boys, whose response to the musical challenges created by Lennon and McCartney was the memorable and still constantly amazing landmark "Good Vibrations."

Jimmy Webb, who'd secured his own place in the pantheon of contemporary music with "MacArthur Park," other standards such as "Wichita Lineman," "Galveston," "By the Time I Get to Phoenix," and "Up, Up and Away."

On and on and on.

Eminem.

Radiohead.

No wonder the excitement and anticipation had grown to international proportions by the time tickets went on sale and original crowd estimates leaped higher by the tens of thousands, and scalpers massed outside the festival grounds entrances, further feeding the frenzy with rumors that the three surviving Beatles had been spotted inside, that Yoko, keeper of the flame, would come out at some point to greet the celebrants, escorted by Paul.

A crowd thrives as much on rumor as reality.

Here, both were as big as their biggest dreams, their greatest hopes for an unbelievable, once-in-a-lifetime, lot larger than Woodstock or any of 'em rock-and-roll spectacle that would spill over into a second day and—

Make them part of a history-making occasion they could tell their grandchildren about.

By which time memory would have made it bigger, better, more of a mind-boggler, the bill filled with acts that never were there, on stage or in the crowd, where acts of personal experience blended with mythic passion would hold the kiddies in thrall as grandma and grandpa told all.

Such is the wonder of rock-and-roll.

Anytime, for all times, anywhere in the world.

The marines also were there to help the Secret Service protect the former president of the United States, who had his own secured compound on the San Gorgonio Reservation, a mile and a half away from the festival site.

He was keeping the commitment he made last year to Palm Springs Mayor Rick Savage, the former president explained to Larry King and, two nights later, to Ted Koppel, when they asked about concern for his personal safety in light of the wanton murder of Senator Needman at the 1985 Imagine That! festival and, more recently, the senseless killings of the president-elect and Mayor Savage.

"My word has always been my bond," he told King and Koppel. "Besides, we cannot live out our lives in fear. I will be attending in their honor and of course to honor the memory of John Winston Lennon."

A marine chopper was set to land the former president on the pad directly behind the stage fourteen minutes after the festival got underway with the singing of the National Anthem by Aretha Franklin and Whitney Houston, accompanied by Stevie Wonder on a Mighty Wurlitzer—

About twenty minutes from now.

Next up would be Joe Cocker, doing "With a Bullet," the song Harry Nilsson wrote and recorded in John's memory, as a fundraiser for the National Coalition to Ban Handguns.

Harry's song was adopted afterward by Wipe Out Weapons International and it became the official theme song of the first Imagine That! festival, performed by Harry in his only stage appearance apart from an impromptu New York appearance with the Monty Pythons, when he tripped, stumbled, and did a swan dive into the orchestra pit, giving new meaning (Harry often declared later) to the venerable show biz expression "Break a leg."

Harry.

My mind couldn't let go of him and how much I wished he could be here today, to see what he'd begun.

Harry.

We'd shared an occasional adventure now and then, after I returned to Los Angeles and started working for the *Daily*, and my memory flashed me back to sometime in early '93. It had been a long while since Harry and I had spoken or seen one another, maybe since Sal Marino's funeral.

I called to check in after one of our mutual friends, director Stanley Dorfman, who'd filmed the first two Lennon festivals that never got released and were now hot items on the bootleg markets, told me Harry was experiencing serious financial problems.

Serious enough to have given Harry a heart attack on Valentine's Day.

I hadn't known.

Harry sounded too glad to see me, a racing enthusiasm I sensed was covering up some form of depression.

He wondered what I was doing now—yes, right now—and insisted we meet somewhere for lunch.

Yeah. No question.

Harry needed company.

I had a column deadline to meet and my managing editor, Ronnie Langtry, the Spider Woman herself, had ordered me in for a command performance that was bound to turn into one of our usual war of words.

The Spider Woman could wait.

Harry mattered more.

What friendships are all about.

I caught up with Harry at the old Trumps at Melrose and Robertson, what would later become Morton's. He was sitting at the bar, sending up smoke signals over a Brandy Alexander while he contemplated the mysteries of a Jasper Johns litho hanging on the wall.

I almost didn't recognize him.

Behind the Ray-Bans and the neatly trimmed goatee, he was a bloated caricature of the old Harry and had taken on an unhealthy pallor.

But his smile was as genuine as a lover's touch and so the bear hug before we adjourned to a table for two in the back of the cramped dining room dressed with more Johns art and tables full of familiar Hollywood faces engaged in loud conversations.

"True," he said, when I put the question to him. There had never been any artifice between us. "It got some play in the news, but not like it might have been ten years ago when I was still almost as hot as Madonna's saliva."

"Missed it."

"Good. Glad. All-seeing, all-knowing Harry got shafted by his shifty business manager, who's currently on vacation at the state's expense. A four-year hitch on three counts of grand theft, while I had to file for bankruptcy . . .

"I never believed this could happen. It was my greatest fear growing up and it's still my greatest fear, the worst thing that could happen to me, to not have money again and to someday have to live back on Alvarado Street . . .

"I went to bed one night a financially secure family of eight and woke up the next morning with three hundred dollars in our checking account . . . I thought I was worth five million only to find out I was virtually penniless . . .

"Things are improving now, but I'll admit there was a time I was scared . . . I went through my Rolodex till the corners were all bent. Called friends and spread the word that I needed work. Some of them came through, like Ringo, who loaned me twenty-five thou, and—"

"You should have called me, Harry."

"On your salary? Getting loaded together is one thing, Neil. Sharing a load like that, something else."

Harry put down his empty Brandy Alexander and tested the one the waiter had just delivered, along with one for me.

"Nice. Cheers."

"Cheers," I said, trying not to be angry at having to find out this way, this late.

It must have shown.

"If it's any consolation, you're not the only mate I didn't call. Even misery can be choosey about the company it loves."

"I could have called Stevie. She's been raking it in on her soap and wouldn't have thought twice about it before—"

"Why I'm talking about. Or, she'd know someone who knew someone . . . You have to build the wall somewhere and Berlin is out of the question . . . Didn't even tell Kalman, if that's any consolation to you."

"It's not."

"How's Stevie otherwise? Still too bright and beautiful to reunite with her most ardent admirer besides me? I have a song I've written and demo'd, for an album I'm trying to get some interest on . . . It's called 'What's a Two-Hundred-Forty-Five-Pound Man Like Me Doin' on a Woman Like You?' Should dedicate it to Stevie. What do you think? You think she'd like that?"

A big Nilsson grin.

"You're not funny."

"You say something funny then, Neil, how's that? I need things to make me laugh these days."

I cupped an ear. "What?"

"I said I need things to make me laugh these days."

"You said that twice, Harry."

Harry laughed.

And less than a year later, on January 15, 1994, Harry was dead of a heart attack.

So, then—Joe Cocker . . .

After Cocker performed Harry's "With a Bullet" in his trademark epileptic fashion, Mayor Gordy would bring on the former president to "Hail to the Chief," performed by Rap Master PT-109 and the Mummy Freaks.

The former president would say a few words about John before asking Aaron Lodger to step onstage and join him in dedicating "Savage Fields"—Lodger's own inspiration—while noting that the April 20 date coincided with the opening of "Strawberry Fields" in Central Park in 1982.

Lodger would be trailed out by a cortege of fifty or so San Gorgonio tribal members, driving a gaily decorated dump truck brimming with rich soil removed from "Savage Fields."

They would recite the traditional prayer and blessing while

spilling and spreading the soil on stage, then dance the traditional dance that pays homage to Pakrakitat, led in all this by the newly elected tribal council leader, Captain Felix X. Penn, identified in Imagine That! press releases as an indirect descendant of the legendary Captain Henry Pabro.

(The Indians might be legit, but the traditional stuff was invented by Vern Twace, whom Lodger had brought in from Las Vegas, where he'd choreographed "Jumpin' Jubilee," "Hot Rod Rumble," "Viva! Viva!" "Liberace, Eternally Yours," and other flashy, fleshy stage reviews for all the leading Strip hotels.)

Then, as the Blue Angels flew overhead, and the Flying Elvises parachuted onto the concourse in front of the giant stage that eclipsed anything any Woodstock ever constructed, and the Budweiser blimp's electronic signboard sent messages of peace and love filtering down through the sweet-smelling pot clouds—

Show time.

Everyone would do at least one song and an encore, the pace of the show guaranteed by revolving stages that made it possible to set up one act while another was out front.

Leading off in the crisp, dry air and waning light of late afternoon with the Rick Savage Better Late Than Never Memorial All-Stars jamming through a medley of John Lennon hits.

It never got that far.

By April 20, the crowd had been building for over a week on the reservation and was turning ugly and anxious, riled by tent city living conditions designed for twenty thousand, not the more than two hundred thousand celebrants who were being pushed to the breaking point by overpriced food and bottled water, overgrown garbage dumps, overflowing toilets, and an overanxious security force that made a game of clubbing and pepper-spraying.

Hundreds of injuries were being reported, especially in the evening, during spontaneous mosh pit sets that competed for attention throughout the expansive festival grounds.

Rapes and sexual assaults.

Widespread muggings.

Souvenir and concession booths looted.

Cars overturned; trailers burned.

The desert heat, oppressive by day and barely tolerable at night, seemed to inspire the problems, added to a growing sense of impending disaster, and the Bureau of Indian Affairs issued a call to put an end to the show before it began.

At a hastily arranged press briefing in his "Superstar City" Quonset hut, Aaron Lodger scoffed and suggested putting an end to the Bureau instead.

"They don't like it, they can tell it to the marines," he said, bringing a fist up by pounding his other fist into the inside of his elbow. "They got enough other affairs to worry about without worrying about mine."

By show time, the sale of stolen admission bracelets had added ten thousand more bodies to the tension-stained grounds and there was a growing dread in everyone but Lodger that the crowd would rise up and try to capture the stage.

It was a rumor spreading as fast and wide as the barfing epidemic allegedly caused by sun-spoiled meat used to create the "Sitting Bull Burgers" at the Wee Willy Wampum's Food Bar locations, and—

Rumor became truth while the San Gorgonios were dancing their choreographed homage to Pakrakitat.

It began with Bobby San Gorgonio, who stumbled out from the side of the stage opposite where I was standing.

He raged at the dancers, pounding and kicking them with blind fury.

Pulled Captain Felix X. Penn from their ranks screaming, "You blaspheme! You and all of you. You bring down the wrath of Pakrakitat and Captain Pabro, demon man. Beware the white eagle. He is coming to show you the bottom of the well, the darkness that destroys the light."

Captain Felix X. Penn seemed truly frightened by Bobby San Gorgonio's admonition.

He crossed his forearms in front of his face as Bobby rained blows upon him like an overwrought drummer, backed away and disrupted the scraggily row of dancers doing what seemed to be a variation on a conga line.

One-two-three kick, and—

A kick propelled Captain Felix X. Penn into Bobby San Gorgonio.

Bobby tottered backward on his heels, trying to regain balance, arms turning like windmills, still shouting warnings at the captain, until—

He tripped over a coil of heavy lighting cable, and fell backward off the stage.

Silently disappeared from my sightline, just before my attention was drawn to a graceful white eagle that seemed to have flown in from nowhere.

The eagle circled the stage twice, then soared above the crowd, and quickly became a speck in the distance.

At once, as if reacting to a signal, the crowd made its move.

By sheer mass broke through the barriers meant to keep them thirty yards from the stage.

Created human lifts and ladders that boosted them up the twenty feet to stage level.

Swamped the ground and spilled around to the backstage areas, staring down the marines who had rifles and handguns pointed at them, challenging the marines to fire.

Chanting, "Shoot! Shoot! Shoot! Shoot!"

The sound growing louder as more and more rioters joined in, drowning out the demands of Aaron Lodger, who was giving his Adams apple a workout screaming into the mike, "Stop it! Stop it immediately! Get back! Go back! God damn it to hell, show respect!"

Clutching the mike stand for support with both hands, legs quivering under the weight of his body.

The old gangster's voice dictatorial, but unimportant to the mob.

Those who bothered to hear him responded with jeers and catcalls.

Musicians who had climbed onstage packing guitars and mouth organs, some with banjos, staked out areas and began a jam. It grew bigger and noisier, and no one seemed to notice how bad it sounded, a bunch of soloists mainlining like this was their audition of a lifetime.

Lodger turned and ordered them to leave.

Everyone.

Everyone!

Everyone, God damn it!

A bare-breasted woman in khaki cutoffs and a green and gold dragon tattoo that circled her back and used her nipples as the dragon's eyes, whose one thigh was almost the equal of two Aaron Lodgers, joined him at the microphone.

She said something out of mike range and impossible to hear at this distance, pointed to the blond-haired infant sucking on a teat, picked Lodger up with her free hand, and steered him to the lip of the stage.

Said something else lost in the uproar, lifted him one-handed off the flooring, and sent Lodger into the crowd on an underhand pitch before Frank Gordy could get there to rescue him.

The mob swallowed Lodger as quickly as I had once seen a bog walker disappear.

Meanwhile, the Secret Service had formed a defensive box around the former president and rushed him from the stage.

They were screaming for everyone to clear a path as they charged past me and down the stairway to the helicopter pad.

A few rioters stepped out to block them.

They were gun-whipped out of the way.

The rotor blades were kicking into high gear as agents shielded the former president from hurled beer bottles and cans while he scrambled into the chopper.

The door pulled shut

The chopper lifted.

Headed off in the direction of the former president's compound.

Exploded into a million pieces.

Lit up the sky in a fusion of color and smoke.

Rained debris in all directions.

Wounding hundreds on the festival grounds.

Causing shrieks of pain and panic, then—

Quiet.

Like someone had flipped off the sound switch on life.

I felt something warming my cheek.

Blood.

Escaping from where a sliver of metal had lodged like a nasty splinter.

A protester sprinting past me from the direction of the chopper pad paused mid-step to say, "Some cortisone will take care of that."

Gave me a thumbs up over his shoulder.

It had happened too fast for me to swear it was him, but I was certain anyway that behind the shades and new beard was Armando Soledad.

I called out his name and started after him, but he had already melted into the crowd.

Onstage, Frank Gordy finished tapping the mike head for sound.

Satisfied it was there, he launched a capella into the John Lennon anthem, "Give Peace a Chance."

Frank was no Sinatra, but he didn't have to be.

The anarchistic musicians drifted into the melody, one instrument after another.

The crowd revived and joined Frank on the vocals.

A choir of two hundred thousand or more people were finally in harmony with what the Imagine That! festival was always meant to signify:

Give peace a chance.

Imagine that.

25

oney, tell me again you're okay."

"I'm okay, babe."

"I mean, the truth. Are you okay?"

"It was a scratch. A Band-Aid took care of it."

"Will you have a scar?"

"Probably."

"A big scar or a little scar?"

"Will it make a difference?"

"Size always makes a difference," she told Neil, adding a little groan of delight.

"You have a new boyfriend, don't you?"

"You didn't answer my question."

"Answer mine."

Silence. Waiting him out.

He said, "Smaller than the scar you left on my heart when you left me, babe."

"I didn't leave you, honey. I divorced you. When I get home, I'll kiss your teensy widdle scar and make it better."

"A start," Neil said. "Who's it this time? One of your costars? No, wait. The director. It's this thing you have for directors."

"He happens to be a fine director. Wait until you read the notices I got."

"For your acting, or just the usual notices?"

"Neil, I'm a big hit over here in London. The critics all loved me. Why they exercised their option and I'm still doing the play and couldn't get back for the festival."

"Yeah, the director . . . I got a call yesterday from your dear friends at *Bedrooms and Board Rooms*, begging me to put in a good word with you about going back on the show."

"What did you say?"

"I said, 'If I can't get your sex queen to go back with me, what would ever make you think I can get her to go back on the show?' "

"Be serious."

"That was me being serious."

"I'm never going back, honey. They did not want to keep me around before Aaron Lodger made those threatening noises, I was not about to go back on that basis. I have far far too much self-respect for something like that."

"Also far far too much talent."

"You mean it?"

"Of course, but the veddy English accent you're doing on me now could stand more work. I blame the director."

"Thank you, honey."

"I'm proud of you, babe."

"I love you, honey."

"I'll catch the next plane."

"Great, just so long as it's not to London."

Stevie hung up the phone and said, "Sorry about that, Albert. Where were we?"

"Act two, page forty-seven."

She and her costar had been running lines when Neil called, a play the National had offered them for later in the year, impressed by their chemistry onstage as well as the box office heat they were generating.

"Yes, thank you." She found the page, ran her finger down.

"Here . . . You truly think it was fate that brought us together, Guy, darling?"

"Certainly, fate, if that's another word for fortune."

"My inheritance, you mean, don't you?"

"My good fortune in being this near to you, Diana, a bloke like me, who will bed you, you allow him, and after bless the skies for the stars."

Stevie looked up, to the other end of the sofa, where Albert lounged with his legs stretched out onto the coffee table, shoeless feet and thighs spread wide, giving her one of his overdrawn come hither looks again.

"That line's not in the script, Albert."

"As ever, in my mind, pet."

"Not in the cards, either, Mr. Marshall."

"Even if I run out and get myself—" parodying her—"a teensy widdle scar?" Flashing her with his heavy-lidded blue eyes. "Then, maybe, you'll allow me to show you how we Brits define a proper size?"

Stevie pushed herself tighter into her corner and threw one leg over the other, locked at the ankles.

Said, "My inheritance, you mean, don't you?"

"You drive me insane, Stevie."

"My inheritance, you mean, don't you?"

"I suppose it's the same with your Neil Gulliver from all I keep reading in the papers. A wonder he's not in some Bedlam years ago."

She put down the script.

"There is a difference, Albert."

"What's that?"

"That's none of your business."

"You still love him."

"That's none of your business either."

"I could hear it, Stevie, past the act you were putting on with him just now the phone, except where you told your Neil Gulliver you loved him. No act there. Nobody that good an actor in the world, except maybe me, of course."

"Of course."

Albert gave her his impish look, smoothed out his razor-thin mustache.

He said, "With all due deference to your Mr. Gulliver, I'll try you once more tomorrow, darling, and as often as it takes, you do understand?"

Searched her face for a glimmer of hope she knew better than to let him find.

"Better than you, darling," she said.

Thinking, *I don't. Don't understand. Another time, we would have been in bed long before now.*

Albert was as close to her type as they come, but—

Something, some need, some yearning, some desperation, seemed to have gone out of her over the past year.

Men. The flirtations. The flings. The one-night stands and longer-term romances that withered on the vines of sour grapes, as if she had willed their failure even before they began.

Lately, they had stopped mattering the way they once did.

Something to do with Richie Savage and his death?

Maybe.

Something to do with Neil?

Maybe.

More probable.

But bigger than that.

More growing up, could that be it, Stevie?

A better understanding of what she couldn't see or say, but somehow understood anyway?

Maybe.

Where had she read that life, at best, was a catalog of unanswered questions?

"It's more than that. Much, much more," Albert said.

"What?"

"My line, precious, in this compost pit of a play the National is looking to us to rescue."

Later, after Albert was gone, luxuriating in a tub full of soothing pink bubbles, Stevie found her thoughts drifting back to Neil; wondering if she should call, to hear him tell her again he was okay—a scar, that was all—once he had put her mind at ease about her decision not to fly back home for the festival and miss any performances.

She also needed to hear that again from him.

"It's not as easy as Shaq missing a game to collect his bachelor's at LSU," Neil had said, trying to be as comforting as the bath was now. "Six thousand miles away, flights back-to-back, jet lag. The show must go on and all that. Besides, Stanley got it all on tape.

You'll be able to see it later, unedited and unexpurgated, the good, the bad, and the ugly."

"You said before there were problems with clearances."

"Still with some of the acts, the music publishing, so they taped on spec. Now, it's also the Feds. They impounded the footage to do a Zabruder. They're looking for anything that might show who planted the explosive device that blew the chopper into the history books."

"What do you think?"

Neil hesitated.

"No opinion to speak of, babe."

Stevie could tell at once he was holding something back from her. She didn't press. It could wait until she saw him.

Besides, Albert was eavesdropping.

Trying to be discreet about it, eyes scanning her big, overpriced flat on Curzon Place in fashionable Mayfair when they weren't undressing her.

What a cock hound, that one.

With her, though, he was barking up the wrong bitch.

She used both hands to bring a tide of bubbles to her breasts, studied the effect on her nips as they rose again and stiffened to her gentle massage; shut her eyes to better make it Neil's hands working so conscientiously to create the tingling sensation.

She began to wonder if, maybe, she should have invited him to London, as quickly dismissed the thought.

Forced her mind someplace else.

The wheel of memory spinning.

It came up Neil again.

When they couldn't keep their hands off each other even if they wanted.

Didn't want.

Couldn't get enough.

Either of them—

Too much in love to believe there would ever be a final chapter written to their marriage.

The wheel—

Spinning again.

Stopping a couple years after the second Imagine That! festival, in '87, a dinner party at the elegant Hancock Park home of Howard Hobart, who had gone from being the rock jock powerhouse known as "Humble Howie" to a program director who could make

〉
〉
〉

or break a hit by putting it on the air at K-POW! in LA and eighteen stations he controlled around the country.

Neil, trying to help get her a break as an actress.

Trading an invitation for a story after he heard that his friend Harry Nilsson was going to be there with Terry Southern, the screenwriter whose credits included classics like Stanley Kubrick's *Dr. Strangelove*, the revolutionary *Easy Rider* that made Jack Nicholson a star, *The Loved One*, and even a Steve McQueen hit, *The Cincinnati Kid*.

"Humble Howie," who turned out not to be that humble, was only too glad to oblige. He liked the power he wielded. It was on display all over his Cape Cod–style farmhouse. A wall of gold and platinum records given him by grateful acts and record companies. Another wall with framed, autographed photos, Howie hugging or being embraced by some record star, a lot who needed no help to get a hit, like Barbra herself. Another wall of framed thank-you letters and postcards, an entire section given over to John and Yoko, friendly, chatty handwritten notes that were signed *Johnyoko* or *Yokojohn*, as if they were one and the same person, many of them decorated with casual sketches by John.

"I still hear from Yoko every once in a while," Howie said when he saw how entranced she was. "Just last Christmas the phone rang and it was her, calling out of the blue, just to wish my lady and me a merry Christmas. Yoko is the keeper of the flame, you know? Quite a wonderful woman. Y'know, you should do a feature about her one of these times, Neil."

Neil agreeing for the sake of agreeing while he shifted anxiously on his sneakers, on the lookout for Harry Nilsson and Terry Southern, who were nowhere in sight and now almost an hour overdue.

Besides being drinking and whatever else buddies, they had co-written and were getting ready to do a movie called *The Telephone* for Hawkeye Entertainment, their production company.

When Neil heard that from Harry, he thought maybe there could be a part in *The Telephone* for her.

The starring role sounded right.

Neil's dreams for her after two years of marriage were as big as her own, almost as big as Mama's, but he thought it would be best to plant the idea with Terry Southern, not put his friend Harry on the spot.

If Terry Southern saw her and was impressed enough, he could present it to Harry as his own idea.

Why not?

The movie version of his novel *Candy* had starred some unknown, some girl who won a Miss Teen International crown or something and found herself in the title role, acting scenes with Richard Burton, Charles Aznavour, Walter Matthau, James Coburn, and Brando, no less. Even Ringo.

A plan, Neil said.

Neil was full of plans for her in those days, when he wasn't working or at the track or on the phone to a bookie, trying to outguess the handicappers and the odds-makers in the *Daily Racing Form*.

Even Mama had to agree when Stevie told her.

"Why not?" Mama said. "Maybe Neil has better luck with people than he does with the ponies?"

It didn't work out that way.

Not that night with Harry and Terry Southern.

Neil was doing his amateur best at the baby grand in the parlor when they finally showed up, urged on by Humble Howie and some of the other guests feeding on diminishing trays of sumptuous southern-style hors d'oeuvres, a lot of deep-fried this and that homemade by Humble Howie's wife, who was called "Missy Humble" by everyone.

An attractive, soft-spoken brunette a good head taller and at least ten years younger than her fiftyish and cueball-headed husband, Missy Humble had been going around the last half hour fretting about her overcooked chicken and ribs and various sauces that might be drying out beyond salvage.

Neil had replaced Lamont Dozier at the keyboard, after Lamont whipped through a medley of hits he'd cowritten over the years with the Holland brothers, songs that helped make Motown the great Motown and created stars like the Supremes, the Four Tops, the Miracles, and Martha and the Vandellas.

Everyone knew the lyrics and was singing along, even Persis Khambatta, the stunning, liquid-eyed Indian actress who had shaved her magnificent black tresses for the first *Star Trek* movie, but nobody louder than Tony King, who was running a record label for the Rolling Stones.

Neil took over at the piano on a dare from Tony, after he said something about being a Bill Evans fan and they got into a disagreement over how Bill Evans might have been as responsible as Miles Davis for the clearly melancholy aspect of Miles' historic "Kind of Blue" album.

Neil saying you didn't have to go any farther than Bill Evans' liner notes to know that, and that even Miles' ex-old lady, Francie, had told him something like that one night at the Hamburger Hamlet on Beverly and Robertson, where she was working as a hostess, suggesting Bill Evans may have written "Flamenco Sketches" and "Blue in Green" with Miles, who got the only credit.

Tony King saying he didn't read, so Neil would have to prove it.

Neil already one and a half scotches over his limit, so high enough to sit down and give it a try.

His fumbling fingers finally rescued by Harry and Terry Southern making a loud entrance, like Stevie had seen Steve Martin and Dan Ackroyd make on *Saturday Night Live*, playing those two wild and crazy guys.

High on apologies and whatever else for being late.

Harry the Bear, hugging Missy Humble off her feet, then the same with Humble Howie and Tony King, who squealed with delight and gave Harry a hard kiss on the forehead before he pointed an accusatory finger at Terry Southern and said, "You old bugger!"

"You must have me confused with some other old bugger," Terry Southern said, delivered in a slow slosh of humor. He pushed his black horn rims against the bridge of his hawkish nose and ran a hand through his unruly hair while he checked the room for appreciation, like he'd just invented the punch line.

"I know, I know, I know," Tony King said, squeezing his lean and stylishly handsome face into mock dismay. Upgrading his English accent to confess, "Gets to a point you know so many buggers, you can't tell one from the other."

Harry said, "Maybe if you'd take more time looking them in the face?"

"Harry, Harry, Harry. It doesn't work that way," Terry Southern said. Stroked his beard. Wondered, "Any way a gent can order a drink around here?"

Humble Howie said, "Name your poison, Terry."

Terry Southern gave Humble Howie a hard stare and said, "Life."

Harry gave Terry Southern a thumbs up before noticing Neil

and said, "Knew it! Nobody else plays Bill Evans like my mate Neil."

"I thought it was someone doing Elton," Terry Southern said.

Tony King said, "Not him. I know everyone doing Elton and that chap's not one of them."

Harry said, "Move over, Neil," and squeezed onto the piano bench.

Started jamming on "Goodbye, Yellow Brick Road" and declared, "I'm doing Elton!"

Began pounding out his version of Bill Evans, then did a fast shift to George Shearing, then Ray Charles, then Dave Brubeck, then Stevie Wonder, then an evil Barry Manilow and a wonderful Billy Joel.

Calling out the names like a carnival barker as he moved effortlessly from one to the next before proclaiming, "Ladies and gentlemen, anyone here who goes both ways—"

A grandiose hammering of the keyboard—

"A little touch of Schmilsson in the night!"

Playing and singing "As Time Goes By" from *Casablanca*, his fingers steadier than his voice, nowhere near as fine as he'd sounded on his album; breaking into the lyrics after he announced, "This one's dedicated to the lovebirds Stevie and Neil Gulliver from yours truly, coming to you from the staid Warren G. Harding Room high atop the turgid Throckmorton P. Gildersleeve Hotel in moderately beautiful downtown uptown Saturday night."

In all, there were fourteen guests at the dinner table and platters of food for at least twice that many.

To go with the chicken and spareribs, Missy Humble had cooked fried okra, garlic mashed potatoes, fresh green beans in a butter and lemon sauce, and small ears of corn drooling in salt-and-peppered butter, along with basketloads of hot-from-the-oven baking powder biscuits. Save room for dessert, she kept advising, listing homemade apple, fresh peach, and mixed berry pies served under mountains of whipped cream.

By Neil's prearrangement with Howard Hobart, Missy had seated her directly across the table from Terry Southern and next to Harry Nilsson. Neil was at Humble Howie's end of the table, between Barbara Dozier and music marketing executive Macey Lipman's wife, Ruthie.

"Just keep on your best face for Terry and otherwise be your-self," he reminded her on the drive in from their place in Arcadia and again as they pulled up to the Hobart's.

"I'm scared, honey. My stomach's already in my throat."

"A little stage freight never hurt anyone. If you were calm I'd be worried you didn't care enough. You'll be fine. Great. You'll see."

"What if Terry Southern doesn't like me?"

"Then he's a fool. Think positive. The worst that can happen is nothing will happen. When he was running Columbia Pictures, Harry Cohn didn't like Marilyn Monroe and let her go. Darryl F. Zanuck at Twentieth Century–Fox was smarter."

"I'm not Marilyn Monroe, honey."

"Of course not. You're Stephanie Marriner, babe. One of a kind."

Terry Southern seemed to ignore her.

He seemed more interested in his wine and trading shots down the table with Tony King and Harry—

Until he caught her staring hard at him.

He looked to her like a poorly weathered version of the Terry Southern Neil had spotted for her on the crowded cover of the Beatles' *Sergeant Pepper* album, over with Lenny Bruce and Oscar Wilde, Marlon Brando and Tom Mix; the only one on the album cover wearing sunglasses.

"Yes, spouse of Harry's mate?"

"I didn't say anything," Stevie said.

"Almost as rare a quality to find in a woman nowadays as a pearl in an oyster," Terry Southern said. "Are you a pearl in an oyster?"

Without stopping to think, Stevie snapped back, "I'm a par-tridge in a pear tree."

He registered surprise, raised his black horn-rims, and leaned in for a better look at her across the table.

"Who are you on the other three hundred and fifty-three days of the year?"

"Bond," she said. "Jane Bond."

Harry decided, "The two of you must be related then. He's bottled in bond."

"Pickled in brine would be more like it," Stevie said.

Everyone at the table laughed.

Even Terry Southern appeared amused.

"I don't suppose you're an actress," he said.

"Someday," she said, trying not to sound too anxious.

He gave her another once over before calling across to Harry, "What a shame."

Harry said, "What's a shame?"

"Twenty years ago, she would have been ideal for the role they gave to Tuesday in *The Cincinnati Kid*. I can even see her in *Barbarella*, instead of Jane. In *Candy* instead of the Ewa girl . . ."

It was hard to know if Terry Southern meant it or had found an excuse to mush-mouth off his credits.

Neil knew an opening when he heard one. "Why not the new movie Harry says you guys are writing and producing?"

"Yes! The new movie."

"The Telephone."

"Yes! Yes! *The Telephone*."

Terry Southern smiled.

"Only role that would work is the lead," he said. "The lead, Harry."

"The lead," Harry Nilsson repeated.

His head jerked up and down.

He lifted himself from his chair on unsteady legs and raised the bottle of red wine he'd commandeered for himself and was drinking straight out of.

"Rabies and gentlemen. Mr. and Mrs. North and South America and all the ships at sea. Flash, you heard it here first," Harry said.

Stevie felt her heart start to dig its way out of her chest. She laced her hands under the table and gripped them until they hurt.

Harry said, "My Southern-fried mate and I have signed Whoopi Goldberg for the lead role in our forthcoming epic, *The Telephone*." Then, like he was Groucho Marx: "Let's hear it for Whoopi or make whoopee!" And chugalugged from the wine bottle.

Stevie tried not to let her face betray her emotions.

She stared down the table at Neil.

Neil answered her with that McQueen grin of his that almost but not quite masked the disappointment in his eyes.

He got up and raised his wineglass.

"To Whoopi," Neil said. "And to Darryl F. Zanuck."

Stevie opened her eyes.

Poked at some bubbles.

Thought, *Yeah, give Neil a call*, before she closed her eyes again

and gave the memory wheel another spin.

26

Augie returned to Los Angeles in June.

He called me his first morning back and I joined him for lunch at the Order of the Spiritual Brothers of the Rhyming Heart, anxious to see what changes if any living the Hindu mystics existence for eight or nine months had wrought in my quixotic friend and mentor.

We settled in Augie's office at his mission-style *casa grande* above Los Feliz Boulevard, at a handcrafted table set up by the bay window, enjoying the beauties of Griffith Park across the way. Trees and foliage in colors beyond the basic browns and golds. Sneaky blues and violets. Subdued reds and obstinate yellows. Hundreds of chameleon tones without names that change as often as Mother Nature chooses to show off her independence.

"When you lose the world, you find yourself," he said to my question. He picked up another of the Big Macs ordered in by

Brother Saul, bit off its juicy head, followed with a grab of French fries. "I found that who I am is what I am, amigo."

"And who are you, Augie?"

He shook his head.

"Telling you would not be me," he said, sounding more subdued than I'd ever heard him.

"You never had that problem before."

"It's not a problem now. Now, it's a solution."

He turned his good eye on me like a microscope, anxious to see some depth of understanding.

I must have passed inspection.

"I see hope for you yet, kiddo," he said. "Finish your fruit and yogurt. A lot more where that came from. The tree of life is never bare."

The rest of Augie's Big Mac disappeared. He washed it down with iced coffee and devoured another handful of fries.

"Living alone in a cave and depending on the kindness of strangers for food hasn't diminished your appetite."

"In India, the people consider the cow sacred and so do I, amigo, but for an entirely different reason." He unwrapped his third burger, good indication that the extreme gauntness he'd brought back with him wouldn't last long. "Now, talk to me. Tell me what I missed."

He absorbed everything I had to say without interrupting me, unusual for Augie, and when I'd finished, got up from the table and crossed the room to his bank of filing cabinets. He checked labels for the one he wanted and unlocked it with one of the dozens of keys he had on a ring clipped to the belt of his paisley cassock.

He did a little rummaging and made a happy noise.

Pulled out and displayed a ledger that was a twin to the one I had brought back with me.

Did some page turning and silent reading punctuated by memory grunts.

Understood the question mark on my face.

"Just a lot of names," he said.

Augie returned the ledger to the file drawer, pushed the drawer shut, and double-checked the lock.

Padded back to the table.

"People in government who were running Halliwell and the disposal program twenty years ago," he said. "High up, a lot of them. High, high. Some still around twenty years later. More have come along since. I don't know who they are yet."

"Yet?"

"You read it in my journal. My deal with Marty. I keep my mouth shut. Marty keeps me posted. I get the story first, a twenty-four-hour jump, after he catches all the bad guys."

"Halliwell isn't catching anyone anymore."

"Then the story will have to wait, won't it?" Augie was serious. "Marty kept his end of the deal, and I have to keep mine, kiddo, same as you have to keep the promise you made to Aaron Lodger. That's the way our world works, yours and mine. Always has and always will."

"Going public with the story, we can be saving lives."

"We are, amigo. Starting with us. To thine own self be true. To thine own self be smart. I never needed a cave to learn that."

Captain Pabro's Gaming Mecca burned to the ground at the end of the month.

The fire had started somewhere in the highlands of the San Gorgonio mountain range, run the ridge like a flaming tornado, then rolled down to the flats, jumped fire walls, and leaped across the freeway, shutting down lanes in both directions for a week.

Called the worst blaze in county history since "The Big One" of 1876, it took ground and air crews from four counties almost three weeks to bring it under control.

No lives were lost, but area hospitals were filled with victims of smoke inhalation among San Gorgonio tribe members and patrons of the evacuated gambling casino, whose manager, Roy Bigelow, shoulders sagging and eyes red-rimmed, but in a voice crackling with bravado, assured the TV cameras that "a bigger, better casino will rise from the ashes of this tragic tragedy. You can bet on it."

The fire passed over the homes of the San Gorgonios, who managed to save most of their livestock, and Captain Felix X. Penn, head bowed, his calloused hands mangling his trucker's cap, looked at America through television lenses and promised to never again insult "the great and good god Pakrakitat, who sent us a fiery warning mixed with charity and mercy to never again embarrass him, defile and disgrace his image, as we did at the music festival that ended so tragically."

He claimed to have seen the tribe's sacred white eagle glide down from the mountaintop and briefly settle onto the ceramic nest on the middle teepee of Captain Pabro's casino scarcely moments before smoke and flames began licking at the clouds and darkening the summer sky.

Fire authorities saw it differently, asserting that "The Bigger One" was set, as was his yearly custom, by Bobby San Gorgonio.

Bobby had the boneless bounce of the scarecrow in *The Wizard of Oz* and the fall from the Imagine That! stage had only injured his drunkard's dignity. Immediately afterward, he had disappeared into the San Gorgonios and not been seen since, so at least for the moment there was no way the cops could haul Bobby in for his yearly denial.

I got a call from Frank Gordy in early July.

His performance calming the crowd at Imagine That! had brought Frank a slew of national commendations, a visit to the White House, a shot on *60 Minutes*, singing appearances on Regis, Oprah, Letterman, and Leno, and an offer to be on a future *Survivor* series.

It also gave Frank a landslide victory in the special election called to fill the vacancy left by Richie Savage's death, where his supporters hailed him as the "The Swinging Champion of Peace."

One of his first acts had been to excavate the peat bog where we'd once gone searching for a T-Bird, Paul Darren, and Armando Soledad. The city crews had since produced a mess of bodies, dozens, many beyond recognition, with more to come now that the fire was out and it was safe to go back.

Dental records had helped make some identifications.

The slow and expensive process of DNA testing was being used on the others.

Some hits, some misses.

Frank was on the phone to me about the latest hit.

"Thought to call as soon as I learned he worked at your old newspaper, out of Sunrise City same as you, 'til the day he up and disappeared. Small world we got ourselves."

I said, "Charlie Stemple."

"Charles Stemple. He's the one, all right. He was there a long time ago, when you couldn't of been much more'n a kid. How'd you know?"

I said, "I was a kid, Frank," and told him how.

Frank said, "What do you suppose he was doing up there at the bog?"

I didn't have to think about it.

"Looking for a story," I said.

The same month, Stevie's play moved from London's West End to Broadway.

She invited me back for the opening, leaving word on my machine that a ticket for a center seat in the fifth row was waiting for me at the box office.

Her performance was exceptional.

All the laughs where they belonged, and a speech at the end that had everyone choked up or in tears, me included, and won her a standing ovation, solo curtain calls that I stopped counting after twelve, and bushels of bouquets from her fans and well-wishers.

Mine was the three dozen long-stemmed red roses.

I saw them in a tall crystal vase on her make-up table, the only flowers there, after the crowd of well-wishers had thinned out enough for me to slip inside her dressing room.

She was shaking hands, signing autographs on *Playbills*, graciously accepting compliments, glowing with the knowledge she had achieved one of her lifetime goals:

Success on Broadway.

I made myself invisible in a corner until everyone else was gone and we were the only ones left, and I had her to go with the victory smile she'd flashed me the moment she saw me there.

We embraced, a kiss long enough to be special, and she asked, "How was I, honey?"

Her body tensed with anticipation.

"You know how you were. You heard it out front, then in here. You'll hear the same thing tomorrow from the critics."

That wasn't enough for Stevie.

She'd been a child of insecurity too long to settle for the verdict of strangers.

"I need to hear it from you," she said.

The next day, we met for lunch at the Inn on the Park and afterward, indifferent to the merciless summer sun that had pushed the temperature into the high nineties, strolled over to Strawberry Fields.

The triangle of land directly across Central Park West from the Dakota was full of people finishing their meals on the sunburned lawn or nearby benches, passing through with a nod to memory, or pausing to consider the centerpiece of the Lennon memorial, a circular mosaic of inlaid stones delivered from countries throughout the world.

The mosaic was barely visible under several layers of flowers and potted plants, handmade signs, handwritten love notes, artwork, incense candles, other trinkets, and tributes meant to establish a bond with John.

Nearby, street vendors were hawking Lennon T-shirts and albums.

A man in his forties sat cross-legged at a spot about twenty feet away, where the pathway fed into the park, and was performing Lennon's "(Just Like) Starting Over" on a guitar with a busted string, pausing often to thank people who tossed coins into his soda-can bank. A woman about his age, leading a black, white, and chestnut-colored Cavalier King Charles Spaniel almost as well groomed as she was and looking every inch like it had just stepped from a sixteenth-century British painting, joined the street troubadour for a chorus before stuffing a bill inside the can.

Other Lennon songs competed for attention from portable cassette and CD players, drowning out parents who were trying to educate their kids to exactly who John Lennon was and why they had come here instead of going straight to the zoo, the Empire State Building, the Statue of Liberty, Radio City Music Hall.

Stevie eased onto her haunches and rearranged some of the mosaic topping to expose the single word in the middle:

IMAGINE.

She had one of the roses from my bouquet pinned onto her V-necked tee. She undid it and placed it alongside the word, fussing a bit until it was positioned exactly to her liking.

A little girl on roller blades, maybe eight, her face all blue eyes and freckles, struggling to keep her balance, made an awkward stop, using Stevie's shoulder as a cushion, and inquired in a breathless voice, her tone just this side of recrimination, "Did you remember to make a wish?"

"Yes, I did," Stevie said, adjusting the ribbons on the girl's pigtails.

"What did you wish for?"

"If I tell you, my wish can't possibly come true. Didn't you know, that's one of the wishing rules."

"It won't come true anyways," the girl said, defiantly. "Mr. John Lennon, he's dead, so he can't come back."

"How do you know that's what I wished for?"

"That's what everyone comes here wishes for."

Her head made long trips up and down.

"You hear the music the people are playing, baby doll?"

"So?"

"So, Mr. John Lennon is not dead and won't be as long as you can hear the music."

The little girl made a face.

"You're one crazy lady," she decided, and skated away.

I called after her, "Yes, but she's my crazy lady."

Turned and stared through the trees to the Dakota.

Imagined I could hear John working out a new song on the piano in Yoko's office.

Tried to imagine what songs Mark David Chapman had been hearing for the last twenty years, serving his life sentence inside an isolated cell at Attica Prison.

I prayed it was nothing by John Lennon.

In my mind, better than a life sentence.

Author's Note

At once, to put curious minds to rest, yes, I knew John Lennon. We weren't mates, at best nodding acquaintances over the years, when we might encounter one another at some rock-and-roll event or haunt, especially during the period John was living his "lost weekend" in Los Angeles.

Harry Nilsson.

Yes, well.

Better than well.

Better than that, too.

John came first, with Paul, George, and Ringo, at a time in late 1965 I was thinking seriously about trying to build an independent public relations company that would test the concept of PR support for record labels and their acts.

Rock and roll was still in its infancy, something most adults anticipated was out to corrupt the world, and public relations for recording artists was mainly handled inside a company by somebody's secretary, whose work day was bothered every so often by a journalist looking for a freebie jazz or middle-of-the-road album.

The void led me to freelance what became recognized as the country's first regularly scheduled pop music column in a major newspaper, on Sundays in the old *LA Examiner*, where I sat down with record artists as diverse as Paul Anka, Judy Collins, the emerging Frank Zappa, whose musical genius far outstripped the notorious image Frank projected through his Mothers of Invention, and the ultrabrilliant Brian Wilson of the Beach Boys, whom I joined in his legendary living room sandbox one bright Bel Air afternoon as Brian pounded out on the keyboard chunks of what was yet to become "Good Vibrations."

The weekly column opened doors for me.

The column became my springboard to creating the PR firm that in time became the largest company in the world specializing in music, represented at least seven hundred record labels and acts, made *Esquire Magazine*'s first "Hot 100" list of rock music heavyweights, and walked off with the first *Billboard* magazine "Publicist of the Year" honor.

And, man—

What a time to be around.

One group after another, English and American, hitting the charts, changing the face of music beyond the dangers first threatened by Bill Haley and the Comets, with "Rock Around the Clock," and, of course, the hip-shaking villain of villains, Mr. Elvis the Pelvis.

So many of them are now enshrined in the Rock and Roll Hall of Fame.

Some are no less deserving, but mostly forgotten. They are footnotes to a time that's never coming back, when the music business was run by people who truly loved music and joined the revolution, not corporate suits mostly taken with bank notes and the bottom line.

Some are living out their lives in relative comfort and growing old watching their kids grow up and goaltending the grandchildren, spinning LPs and truths that may have become taller tales with the passage of thirty or thirty-five years and memory lapses turning Top One Hundred chart-makers into Number One smashes.

Some, less lucky, are trying to figure out why they got a bum rap from rock and roll while rapper bums collect the millions of bucks and all the good gigs where they're maybe lucky to grab nostalgia tours and motel lounge dates; where they're reduced to selling albums in the lobby after a show, produced at their own expense on their own labels, because major record companies nowadays are only interested in The Next Best Thing.

Some are wishing they were dead and still working on it while the beat goes on.

Some are already dead, like Joplin, Hendrix, Morrison.

Like Brian Jones.

Like Keith Moon and Cass Elliott.

Like Harry Nilsson, with time his own assassin.

Or—

Like John Lennon, a mourned victim of a madman's need to be famous.

I initially met John during the time the Beatles were further captivating and capturing America on a concert tour that began at New York's Shea Stadium with about fifty-six thousand fans, mostly young girls, screaming hysterically, shedding tears, and wetting their undies.

They had flown to Los Angeles for a brief intermission at the Bel Air mansion of Alan Livingston, president of the mop tops' label, Capitol, and his wife, actress Nancy Olson, that capped with a garden reception for the town's biggest movie stars, ultra-elite movers and shakers, and, of course, their privileged children.

I was there as one of the media guests of Ron Tepper, the inventive PR strategist who'd soon be running Capitol's publicity machine, watching a lot of faces as famous as the ones on Mount Rushmore cutting in line ahead of kids to get to the Beatles, who sat on a row of bar stools and greeted the passing crowd like unassuming kings enduring a command performance.

A year later, in August of 1966, I was starting to do some independent PR work for Capitol and part of the scene in Studio A when the Beatles arrived in an armored truck and were trooped inside through the equipment door, under heavy guard—like the treasure the group had become for Capitol—to charm a press conference crowd made to feel that getting on the list was as significant an accomplishment as getting tickets to their upcoming concert at Dodger Stadium.

The Beatles arrived and departed the baseball field via chopper, a stunt subsequently borrowed by hundreds of major-league acts after rock went big time and began playing more and more outdoor stadiums.

And, a memory borrowed for the Imagine That! festival in *The John Lennon Affair*, albeit for a different kind of passenger and a decidedly different purpose (just as in real life, years later, I recycled the armored car arrival in having Three Dog Night deliver an album to ABC-Dunhill Records within minutes of a deadline that otherwise could have cost the group a six-figure penalty).

Jump cut.

Years later: Sometime in 1978.

I'm breaking fresh, hot bread over lunch at the Palm in West Hollywood, a major address of the see-and-be-seen music scenemakers, with Mike Maitland, the beleaguered president of MCA Records. Host Gigi Delmaestro has seated us on display at a key up-front wall booth for four, under my caricature, so anyone who matters can see the smile on Mike's face that gives the lie to his problem.

Talk in a business that historically turns out Top Ten rumors as fast as the Top Ten hits has the classy, low-key, veteran in trouble and on his way out for the usual reason: profits are down. Or, because the label isn't breaking its share of new acts. Or, because some of the big names whose contracts are up will be moving to hotter labels for bigger bucks.

Take your pick.

Given enough time to mature, rumors become truth.

I'd been consulting MCA and I'm still consorting with Mike, who's been a hero of mine since I got into music PR, when he was running the overachieving Warner Bros. label. He's confided the truth to me—the truth being, of course, that the rumors are true.

He needs something to offset them and provide him with staying power and is seeking my thoughts.

Often, coming up with the best thought takes no thought at all.

"Lennon," I said.

Mike looked at me blankly.

I said, "Lennon has no record deal. I hear he and Yoko are in Japan, doing nothing. Supposedly, he's quit recording for good. Get on a plane. Fly over there and do a deal with him. Whatever it takes. It'll shut down the rumors. Instant prestige for MCA. For you. The kind of magic Lennon brings to any situation."

Perhaps selfishly, I relished the idea of getting the opportunity to work with John at close range.

Mike seemed to absorb the suggestion and be turning it over in his mind. "Not a bad idea," he said, finally. "Let me think on it."

Nothing happened.

I raised John's name with him two or three times after that.

Each time, Mike would look at me like he was hearing it for the first time.

He would nod with interest, break into an appreciative smile, and tell me, "Not bad. Let me think on it."

Maybe it was Mike being polite, maybe his response had something to do with the slow onset of the Alzheimer's that eventually overtook him, but he was soon gone from MCA.

And, in September of 1980, the remarkable David Geffen met with John and Yoko and agreed to release their album in progress, *Double Fantasy*, on his fledgling Geffen Records, without having heard any of it.

Less than three months later, on December 8, John was dead, but his legacy and legend continued to grow with the single that would be at Number One on *Billboard* magazine's chart by the end of the month, "(Just Like) Starting Over."

My beginnings with Harry Nilsson were far more personal and closer, certainly far more enduring, than with John and over the decades led to a lot of crisscrossing of paths with John.

He was still working his day job, the night shift as a computer clerk at a bank's clearing house, and sleeping on the couch at a girlfriend's cramped apartment while cutting his first LP for RCA Records and trying to peddle his songs to other recording acts when we were introduced at Martoni's restaurant in Hollywood.

I was kibitzing with the bartender, Sal Marino, who'd wind up years later owning the place, when he arrived with Grelun Landon.

Grelun was Elvis and the Colonel's man for RCA, a role he'd play for twenty-six years, and the earliest advocate of Harry's genius. As an adjunct to my fledgling PR firm, I was managing a group called Don and the Goodtimes that I'd made a recording deal for with Epic Records and landed a role as performing regulars on Dick Clark's *Where the Action Is* TV series.

Grelun thought some of Harry's songs might be right for them.

"Gre's your biggest fan," I said, taking Harry's hand.

"What?" Harry said, raising his voice high above the barroom noise.

"Gre's your biggest fan," I said.

"You said that twice," Harry said.

It was a gag easy to laugh at, especially when I fell for it time and again that night and many times afterward, and it led to a camaraderie that persisted over the years, until the day the phone rang and I got the news Harry was dead.

A premature tragedy neither unforeseen nor unexpected

Not in the least surprising.

A couple, three years earlier, Harry and I had had one of our occasional catch-up lunches at Le Dome on the Sunset Strip, parked at table seven by owner Eddie Kerkhofs, where we could see and be seen among the rock and rollers and film and TV dragons who'd also made it a personal choice hangout.

Over a Brandy Alexander for Harry and an iced tea for me, he almost absent-mindedly pulled a Ziploc sandwich bag packed with snow from a windbreaker pocket, dug into it with a teaspoon and offered me a snort—declined—before loading up one nostril, then the other.

He redeposited the bag while I looked around anxiously, dreading that somebody might have noticed, half-expecting a ton of DEA agents to come busting in after us, and casually told me what his doctor had told him, on reflection maybe a bit too nonchalantly.

Harry said, "The pills, the coke, the booze, he says I have to give up two out of the three or I'm going to die."

I said, "Why only two out of three?"

"Quit all three at once, my system wouldn't be able to stand the shock and I'd go like that, the doctor said."

However Harry handled it, he'd bought some time and, I heard later, was pretty much in the process of climbing out of the financial bind he'd been pushed into by his trusting nature with people who'd abused his trust as badly or worse than any of the crap he routinely invited into his system.

Memory can be a natural cleanser, and the news of his death carried me back to some of my happy times with Harry.

One of the earliest:

Hanging out at sessions while he finished the debut LP, *Pandemonium Shadow Show*, with producer Rick Jarrard nursing him through George Tipton's arrangements; Dick Bogert on the sixteen-track board. There were highly personal songs, like "1941," "Without Her," and "She's Leaving Home," along with outrageously clever cuts like "Cuddly Toy," the one covered by The Monkees not so long after it had been rejected by my band, Don and the Goodtimes, as not matching the quality of their own originals.

Later:

The shared joy on the advisory an advance copy of the album had reached the Beatles, prompting a surprise call to Harry from John Lennon. Harry stunned from the moment John introduced himself, reeling even before John told him, "Man, your record is fucking fantastic. I just wanted to call and say you're great."

(I still have on a record shelf gathering gray layers of dust the promotional box of goodies put together by RCA to introduce Nilsson—one name now—and that album, intact, including the copy he'd inscribed "To my dear friend what's his name. Luv, Harry.")

Another time:

A wakeup call at three in the morning, a familiar voice on the other end of the line singing in double-time, "Happy birthday to you, happy birthday to you, happy birthday, dear shithead, happy birthday to you."

My wife, Sandra, nudging me and passing over the phone, announcing, "For you. Harry Nilsson."

The last time we had lunch at Le Dome:

Admiring Harry's Ray-Bans while we waited outside for our cars.

Harry whipping them off his head, pushing them at me, and refusing to take them back.

Demanding I keep them.

Insisting they were now mine and that was that.

My sense of some underlying need, so I honored it, much as I chose to try and honor my generous friend's memory even before I settled at the PC to begin writing *The John Lennon Affair*—

By making Harry a leading character in the novel, even though here as in real life he would be moving in the larger shadow of John.

Someone like Harry Nilsson, anyway.

Readers may think they found truths encapsulated in the fiction, shards of reality that screamed out *roman á clef* at them, but it isn't so, of course.

Maybe recollections worth borrowing and building upon, a little bit here, a little bit there, a collage of events and people from the past—including my time running a news bureau in a desert town next to an Indian reservation, near a gambling casino—pasted into the marvelous world of invention and imagination.